I0760740

FOR THE RECORD

Love In Vancouver
Book Two

JEN-LEA MERCY

FOR THE RECORD
Copyright © 2025 by Jen-Lea Mercy,
Love Hard Publishing

Human Authored™, Reg #: 8781676
https://authorsguild.org/human

For permission requests, write to: jen@jenleamercy.com

Cover Design: Miblart

Interior Design: Love Hard Publishing

Editing: CKnightWrites and Lisa Caro

Proofreading: Amber Justice

Beta Readers: Amber, Sarah, Lisa, Lindsay, Debbie, Myra, Charlie, Greylin, Michelle, Dianna, Shannon

Québécois French Translations: Sabrina Araujo

1 2 3 4 5 6 7 8 9 10

https://linktr.ee/jenleamercyauthor

Foreword

The sex scenes in *For The Record* include light, on page kink, such as restraints, blindfolds, and brief mentions of the St. Andrews Cross, spanking, and gagging.

For The Record **also touches on some sensitive, off-page topics. If this concerns you, please check the trigger warnings before continuing. These can be found on my website @** https://jenleamercy.com/

******ALSO, the French/English glossary is located inside the back-matter.***

Dedication

For my Beta Team,
Thank you for helping to shape this story, and for your endless confidence boosters when my self-doubt took over.
This one is for you.

Chapter 1

Sawyer

Eleven months, eight days, ten hours.

If she thought long and hard about it, Sawyer could likely pinpoint the night of her husband's death down to the final second. Eleven months, eight days, ten hours, and thirty-eight minutes ago, Olivier was killed while taking a scenic route to the mountains with one of his many lovers. And eleven months, eight days, *twelve* hours ago, his hands had wrapped—

No. Sawyer picked up her plastic cup of on-tap hard cider and took a calculated sip, just enough to be seen drinking; there was no way she would let half of Vancouver witness her lose control tonight. She was sitting in a warehouse of all places, the flashing strobe lights streaking across the dance floor making her flinch and the blaring music inside the LGBTQ+ event competing with her friends for Sawyer's attention. Even if her mind wasn't already elsewhere, Sawyer doubted she could think clearly.

"Hey, Chef." Cindy nudged Sawyer's shoulder, and Sawyer caught her friend's concerned smile. "Everything alright?"

Such a loaded question to ask, and for a lingering moment, Sawyer considered the half-truths and lies that came to mind. "Why wouldn't it be?" she finally scoffed over the music, lowering her gaze once more to the flimsy cup in her hand. She usually preferred indulging in one of the finer shelved reds when she went out, such as the decadent 2007 Sassicaia from Italy or one of the reliable brands her husband had carried at the restaurant. Locally procured from the Okanagan Valley, Mission Hill's 2018 Oculus was a thousand flavors superior to tonight's forgettable cider. In fact, this entire evening out was proving to be one big blip in Sawyer's tightly-wound, predictable life.

"Well, for one, you've been scowling into your drink for the past ten minutes or more," Lori unhelpfully pointed out, smothering a grin as she lifted her cup to her lips.

An arm went around Sawyer's shoulder, and seconds later Cindy was pulling Sawyer closer to call out, "It's been close to a year, Sawyer. You deserve to be happy. You owe it to yourself to get back out there. Let's dance and have fun."

"I'm too old for this scene," Sawyer admitted, briefly meeting her friend's eyes before frowning at the makeshift dance floor. It was a miracle they had even snatched one of the handful of tables toward the back of the warehouse. Hordes of people in their early twenties danced to the thumping electro music drilling into Sawyer's ears. The only good thing to come of the last two hours were the occasional Indigo Girls songs she'd heard, but then again, they were so heavily remixed they were barely reminiscent of the originals.

"You're no older than me, and I'm here. C'mon Sawyer, let loose for once," Cindy laughed, nudging her again, only grating more on Sawyer's nerves. It'd been so long since she'd felt free enough to be out with the girls, let alone what it felt like to "let loose."

How does one even achieve that?

"Mrs. Desmarais, is that you?"

Sawyer cringed at the overtly loud, alcohol-sweet-smelling slur entirely too close to her ear. Ugh, the drunk girl's voice sounded like nails on a chalkboard, causing the hairs on the back of Sawyer's neck to stand up. She swiveled in her seat, one of her infamous scowls appearing as she took in an all too familiar face.

You have got to be fucking kidding me.

An old school friend of Sawyer's twenty-year-old daughter, Bree, stood behind them, her scantily clad dress burning a nightmarish image deep into Sawyer's mind.

Talk about awkward.

"It's Sawyer Lavoie now, Madison," she confirmed, unable to mask the bite in her tone, but her statement fell on drunk, empty ears.

"Nice to see you, Mrs. Desmarais!" The younger woman's parting smile was rife with desire and intent, and Sawyer sat in muted shock as Madison turned to her trio of friends and shouted, "Bree's mom is a total fucking MILF!"

Sawyer inwardly groaned, wishing to all get out that the music had been loud enough to drown out *that* remark. Clearly, Gen Z lacked the manners and finesse of sexual repression that had been so firmly instilled in Sawyer years ago.

She arched one finely sculpted brow at her friends, not bothering to speak. Her expression said it all. *See what I mean?*

"Honey, I don't think that girl has an issue with your age," Lori shouted, looking past Sawyer to where the group of friends had disappeared into the crowd. Her dark brown eyes held a hint of mischief to them.

"And she's not the only one. Look for yourself," Cindy remarked, a certain gleam in her eyes that told Sawyer she was just getting started. Her longtime friend pointed to the dance floor, directing Sawyer's attention to a woman dressed in an androgynous style. Not counting the blinding effects of the strobe beams, the lighting was low in the warehouse, yet it was blatantly obvious to Sawyer she was being watched. She swallowed, narrowing her eyes at the same time Cindy clapped her back in excitement. "What about that one, huh? Ruggedly promising for a night of fun."

Sawyer shot her friend an annoyed look. "I didn't come here to pick up anyone." She wouldn't have come at all, except that she hadn't wanted tonight to be yet another occasion where she let her friend down. But why did Cindy need to make a hobby of trying to match-make? Her love life had been Cindy's focus for longer than her cheating husband had been in the ground, and that was only with the minuscule contact they'd still had while Olivier was alive.

"You didn't come here to dance and celebrate my birthday either, apparently, even after I practically had to get on my knees and beg. Really makes me regret surprising you with a ticket," Cindy decided, getting to her feet and tugging Lori's hand to follow. "Too bad; we were hoping to enjoy a rare night out with our workaholic friend."

"I am *not* a workaholic."

"Come again?" Cindy leaned closer in disbelief. "Must be all the noise, because I'm sure I heard you wrong. Sawyer, honey, you clock in twelve to fourteen hour shifts day in and day out at the restaurant! I had to book you three weeks in advance to even try to show up tonight!"

The truth of Cindy's words had a pang of guilt niggling in the shadows of Sawyer's chest, but she pushed the feeling back down. If she got sentimental over every little thing her friend had said over the years, then she'd not have the backbone she did.

Cindy pressed a kiss to Sawyer's hair. "I know you love to cook, and I also know running the kitchen saved you in so many ways over the years. But Olivier is gone now, and you're here. Revel in your newfound freedom."

Sawyer's jaw locked, and she forced herself not to engage further. Not only was it the wrong time and place, but frankly, young Madison wasn't the only one crossing boundaries with Sawyer tonight. Cindy desperately needed to learn how to leave things be. Sawyer glared at her friend's back as Cindy guided her wife out to the dance floor.

Cindy would never truly understand, and that had always been the problem in their friendship. She and Lori were childless, and both had wonderful parents. Besides Bree, cooking in the restaurant she co-owned with Olivier had been the sole thing in Sawyer's life she could always count on to nourish her emotional well-being. It was because of Sawyer's dedication that Desmarais was currently sitting at number one for the best French/French Canadian Fusion restaurant in all of Vancouver. Desmarais had recently earned one of the few coveted Michelin stars in the province, evidence of many years of hard work. Now that she knew a Michelin star for her restaurant was possible, keeping it and earning a second one was all Sawyer could think about.

Cindy was right about one thing though. Now that Olivier was gone, Sawyer was adamant about taking back her life. The way *she* wanted to. *If only Cindy—and everyone else—could stop getting in my way.*

An intoxicating whiff of smoke, pine, and rosewood was Sawyer's only warning before Cindy's chair was nudged to the side, and the woman she'd seen eyeing her a few minutes ago was squeezing into the now empty space. "Hey there, beautiful. Care for some company?" A cocky grin appeared as the younger woman looked down at Sawyer, her chiseled jawline and fresh, disconnected undercut up close and personal. Perspiration dotted her flushed cheeks and upper lip, bringing undue attention to the silver septum piercing above that perfectly curved mouth.

Sawyer opened her mouth, ready to tell the stranger to fuck off, and accidentally inhaled their cologne again. The scent was engulfing. It was dizzying, sexy even. Not sexy enough to sway Sawyer's definitive plans to go home alone, but enough that it had her chancing a second look. Her gaze landed directly on the nametag pinned to the left side of the stranger's floral dress shirt. *McCoy* was written on the top, along with *she/her* pronouns directly below it.

"You are ... mmmm," McCoy began, an exaggerated gust of air leaving her lungs. "Nice outfit. I wish I could pull that off." Sawyer scrunched up her face as McCoy continued to grin. The appraising once-over was so disgustingly obvious Sawyer considered throwing her drink.

Her gaze narrowed to slits. She glanced at the forgotten cider on the table, noting there wasn't enough *to* throw at the obvious womanizer. Maybe she could suffer through flirting long enough for McCoy to buy her a drink, and *then* she could toss it? But that would be a waste of her precious time and a perfectly mediocre drink. What kind of name was McCoy, anyway? Was it a last name? Had she been given the wrong name at birth and chose McCoy after watching one too many Westerns?

"How does it feel to be the most gorgeous person here tonight?" McCoy continued, and Sawyer grimaced. She wasn't a fan of the rehearsed bullshit some people used to get into another's bed. She believed in stating intentions in the beginning. *Say as you do and do as you say.*

"I'm bored," Sawyer said flatly because *she* practiced what she preached. It wouldn't be fair to either of them if she pretended otherwise. She turned back to her near-empty drink, raising the cup to her mouth only to have the melting ice cubes knock against her teeth.

Instead of leaving, however, McCoy pulled Cindy's chair closer and took a seat. "I'm McCoy. And you are?" she tried again, peering up at Sawyer with a pair of captivating meadow-green eyes framed by a thin layer of eyeliner.

Sawyer swallowed. She should be turned off at the fact McCoy was like a dog with a bone, not silently cursing her half-starved libido for the pulsing response. "You're still here?" she forced out, harsher than she meant to, but come on. Even playgirls got the hint eventually, right? "If you can think with your brain rather than your adolescent hormones for five seconds, then you'll figure out exactly how uninterested I am."

McCoy looked stunned for half a second before a chuckle rose from the fine column of her throat. "Noted, ma'am. My apologies. Enjoy the rest of your night."

Sawyer watched her leave, allowing herself to briefly linger on McCoy's backside and strong thighs as she disappeared into the crowd once again. She might not want sex with a stranger, but she wasn't dead. Her eyes worked just fine, and McCoy was ... well, she was something alright.

Sighing now, she checked her watch; almost 1 a.m. Late nights and early mornings were an everyday occurrence for Sawyer, but that didn't mean she wanted, at forty-three years old, to be sitting alone at a club. *One more drink, and then I'm leaving,* she thought, glancing around their table for anything that might get stolen if she left it. She swiped Lori's purse for safekeeping, acknowledging that there was also the risk of someone stealing their table, but she couldn't sit there for a minute longer.

At the bar, Sawyer gripped her purse and Lori's to her chest, scowling at quite a few people who bumped into her, one who smelled faintly like vomit. She had to yell her order three times before the bartender heard it, and she was contemplating slipping behind the counter to pour the cider herself when, through a swarm of sweaty bodies, a couple off to the side of the dance floor caught her eye. The first thing Sawyer noticed was the floral dress shirt, as not too many there tonight were dressed like they were on a Hawaiian cruise. And then she saw that smooth undercut that Sawyer's fingers had itched to feel only thirty minutes before. She narrowed her gaze on the scene, a sour taste in her mouth now as she watched McCoy make out with someone else. Sawyer must have been one in a long lineup of potential lovers for the night. Disgusting. But what did Sawyer expect from a twenty-something womanizer?

As she turned her attention back to the bar, she was supremely glad she'd dodged *that* bullet.

Mornings were not what they used to be for Sawyer.

She remembered getting up at 5 a.m., five days out of the week, to go running before Olivier woke. On the rare nights Sawyer got home at a decent hour with Bree in tow or to relieve the sitter, she'd still have to wait up for Olivier to come home. She'd found she couldn't sleep until he was safely in bed, passed out from too much drink or sex. The thought of Olivier waking the neighbors if he forgot his key or him roaming the house in the middle of the night with Bree unaware had always given Sawyer anxiety. So, she'd waited. God, she'd resented him for that. Every morning, she would go for her run and then, like a good little housewife, still have breakfast laid out by the time Olivier woke for work.

Now, on Sundays, Sawyer ran without the pressure of rushing home after. It was the perfect start to her day, and after so many years, she had a trail she liked. She'd leave her house located in the gorgeous Dunbar-Southlands, a neighboring suburban community that rested just outside Vancouver, and head further west until she reached Musqueam Park. She'd run the two-and-a-half-kilometer loop before heading home again.

"Not fucking now, body," Sawyer gasped as a wave of dizziness came upon her just as she was clearing the end of the trail. She bent over, rested her hands on her thighs to support some of her weight, and waited for the nausea to pass. Her breathing was ragged, and as Sawyer struggled to draw air into her lungs, she cursed her chronic high blood pressure. From undue stress and overworking herself, her doctor liked to remind her when she squeezed an appointment into her hectic week. "Relaxation is key", he'd say.

Sawyer scoffed. It was difficult for her to relax, even while running. Relaxing was the *last* thing her brain needed. No, all that would do is get her lost in memories, and who needed to be stuck inside that fucked up carousel ride?

"Not today," she repeated, straightening to her full height. She tilted her face toward the sky, her eyes shutting of their own accord as the early morning rain cooled her heated cheeks. There was nothing like running in the rain. On mornings like this, she forwent her usual Spotify playlist in exchange for the soothing raindrops splattering against her windbreaker. The *slap slap* of her sneakers against wet pavement, the air's moisture creating visible puffs each time she exhaled, was the calming conclusion to Sawyer's long week.

Sawyer continued jogging rather than running the five blocks to her house. She slowed to a walk once she reached her street, dropping her hands on her hips as she fought for another lungful of much-needed air.

Her smartwatch chirped with an incoming notification as Sawyer trudged up her laneway a few minutes later. She enjoyed the burn in her thighs and calves with each step, and a satisfied smirk left her as she checked her watch.

Bree: Good morning, Maman! I'm just up for a pee break but will look forward to you sending pictures of everything you're doing today. Absolutely no work!

"Good grief, they're conspiring against me," Sawyer dropped her arm away and let it slap against her thigh as she reached her doorstep. Per the urging from her family doctor during her last checkup, Sawyer tried like hell now to take Sundays off. Dr. Cooper claimed she needed a rest day, and apparently, Bree agreed. Unfortunately, avoiding work when the restaurant was such an integral part of her life was harder than it looked for someone who thrived on structure.

"Good morning, Chef Lavoie!"

Sawyer looked up from where she had the key in the front door to see her elderly neighbor waving. It wasn't the first time, nor would it be the last, that she rolled her eyes at Dr. Chen's refusal to call Sawyer by her first name. "What brings you out so early, Dr. Chen? Making house calls?"

The old woman laughed, taking Sawyer's question as a friendly jab. "You know I'm retired. Came out here because I'd forgotten to put up the car window last night. The front seat was soaked through."

"I'm surprised they still let you drive."

Even pushing eighty, Dr. Chen had excellent hearing, and she scoffed good-naturedly. "Enjoy your Sunday, Cranky! Don't call me if you cut yourself later."

"I won't since you're a retired gynecologist!" Sawyer hollered back, sniggering as she pushed into the house.

She was in the shower when a frustrating, albeit intriguing, image of the rugged woman from the night before came to mind. Turning McCoy away had clearly been for the best. Games were for children, not grown women. No matter how lonely she got in her big house with just Patches to keep her company, she'd never trade in her self-respect.

"Speak of the devil, and she appears," Sawyer muttered when the long-haired calico rubbed her whiskers against Sawyer's leg as she toweled off. "Hey, cutie."

"Meow." Patches stared up at Sawyer with an expectant look on her adorable bicolored face. One side was completely black, and the other orange, with thin strips of black above the eyebrow.

"This one, Maman. This is the one I want," Bree had proclaimed years ago as they'd stood in front of the litter of kittens.

"And then she went off to college and left you here with me," Sawyer murmured, bending down to stroke the soft, thick fur on the feline's chest. She tsked. "You poor thing."

Drying down her torso, Sawyer pulled the material gently over the long scar a few inches from her belly button. Staring into the bathroom mirror, her gaze fell to where her fingertips were lightly tracing the thin red mark.

"Stop. It wasn't meant to be."

Sawyer inhaled, straightening her spine so her breasts jutted out. Her scars were there as a reminder, not for self-pity.

Chapter 2

McCoy

Lately, every single time she made a bet with Sloane, she came to regret it. Coy liked to believe her sister enjoyed living vicariously through her since, between the two of them, Coy was more suave with the pickup lines. Sometimes, though, it really felt like Sloane loved watching her crash and burn. Coy stared up at her bedroom ceiling, a disheartened sigh escaping her lips. To say the night before hadn't gone as planned was an understatement. The bet had been simple. Decide on a possible one-night lover, inform Sloane, and go make eye contact with said stranger. There, Coy would obtain a name and/or number, whisper a few sweet nothings into the femme's ear, and for one night have them forget every other lover before McCoy Miller. It should have been an easy bet, one Coy could have done blindfolded or sweaty and dirty after a hard day at the shop. Winning beautiful femmes over was practically a personal goal of hers—one she'd achieved more times than she cared to think about.

But, as she was staring into a pair of incredible smoky gray eyes the night before, all Coy's training and smooth pickup lines had gone awry. She'd been nervous, which *never* happened, and instead of playing it casual and easing the femme into conversation, she'd become a babbling idiot who missed all the nonverbals until it was too late.

But hell, the woman at the warehouse had been *stunning*. Older than Coy's twenty-seven years, perhaps late thirties or early forties, with a tanned complexion. Silky smooth waves of black hair had covered one cheek, the rest cascading down her back. A few age lines bracketed her sensual mouth, but in no way had it taken away from her natural beauty. And the way her off-the-shoulder red top had fallen had exposed the finest throat and collar bones Coy had ever seen.

Coy rubbed a calloused hand over her face—to wipe the sleep from her eyes and also to hopefully snap herself out of the slump of rejection. The action caused Ash's hand to dip lower onto Coy's stomach but thankfully didn't wake them. She didn't want anyone to see her this bothered over a woman, especially one of her one-night stands. There was a likely possibility the woman from the night before was straight, but Coy's gaydar rarely failed her. There had been enough suppressed lady-loving vibes emanating from that dominating personality and sexily accented voice to have Coy picking her tongue up off the floor.

She was mystified. She couldn't remember the last time she was turned down flat. Elementary school, maybe? She groaned, knowing that was a bit of a stretch, but fuck, charming her way into a woman's bed was part of her identity. McCoy Miller—daddy's girl, twin sister of Sloane, car-obsessed mechanic, mountain bike enthusiast, and playgirl extraordinaire.

Ash snuggled closer to McCoy, their sleepy voice breaking the silence in the room. "You're up early."

Coy peered down at her friend and occasional lover, pressing a kiss into their hair before pulling back the blankets. "Sorry if I woke you. Go back to sleep." She slid out from under Ash, scooting to the edge of her king-sized bed. One glance over her shoulder witnessed Ash doing as instructed, their enticing ass wiggling a little as they got comfortable under the covers once more. Coy got to her feet, lumbering down the apartment hallway to the bathroom.

She was washing her hands when the unmistakable sound of glass breaking made her slap the sink faucet closed mid-clean. Muffled crying commenced, and Coy's heart leapt in her throat. She'd know upset Sloane anywhere. Dashing from the bathroom, she landed directly in Sloane's firing range, barely dodging a picture frame flying over her head to hit the man behind her.

"Fuck!"

"Get out, Lucas," Sloane sobbed from her bedroom doorway. She wore just a thin tank top and hipster briefs, too distraught to notice they now had an audience.

"That's what I've been trying to do, you crazy bitch!" Lucas growled. Coy's eyes flared at the venom in his tone, and instant rage boiled in the pit of her stomach and set her teeth on edge. No one spoke to her sister like that.

"Clearly not fast enough, Lukey," she drawled, bending to scoop his bundle of clothes up that Sloane must have thrown out of her room. Coy shoved them into his naked torso, probably a little more forcibly than necessary she realized when he stumbled into the wall. *Fuck, cool it, She-Hulk*. Sometimes, she forgot her own strength.

"Well, if Sloane would stop—"

"Nope," Coy cut him off. "Fuck off." She grabbed his arm, guiding him through the apartment to the front entrance. "I don't give a shit what Sloane did. You don't speak to her like that."

Lucas did the honors of opening the door, huffing in frustration. "She can't handle a breakup. Not my problem, Coy."

Coy snatched Lucas's shoes from the boot rack, handed them to him and said, "I'd say it's been a pleasure, but the truth is," she gave him a little push past the threshold, into the hallway of the apartment and smirked, "I never liked you, Lukey. B-bye now."

Coy closed and locked the door, rolling her eyes at Lucas's several choice words out in the hallway. It took about a minute, but she finally heard his footsteps retreating. Sloane was curled up in a fetal position atop her messy bed when Coy walked in. Her face was buried in the pillow she was hugging to her chest, but Coy could still make out her hushed words. "D-Did he say why?"

Sighing inwardly, Coy climbed on the bed behind Sloane. It always took her some time to think of the right things to say to placate her sister, especially when all she wanted to do was rejoice. Sloane had only dated Lucas for the last three months, but they were three months too long in Coy's opinion. "C'mere," she murmured, pulling her sister into her arms. "I'm sorry, Sloane. I know how much you liked him."

"I loved him, Coy."

Coy fought the desire to roll her eyes. *She literally says that for every relationship. Like what the actual fuck?*

Sloane's unrequited instalove crash and burns were one solid reason Coy didn't do relationships. No way in hell would she let someone in deep enough to break her heart. Not after seeing what Sloane went through, or witnessing their father mourn their mother for most of their childhood. Nope, a quick hit it and quit it was more Coy's style.

"I know you did, honey. Let it all out, okay? I've got you. Shhhhh, I've got you," Coy soothed as she wrapped her arms tighter around her sister. She kissed Sloane's forehead, one hand making slow, comforting circles over her back.

Sloane sobbed into the crook of Coy's neck, a gross mix of snot and tears leaving a sticky trail along her skin. "Why does this always happen? Things start out so well, you know? I become everything they need, and it's still not enough."

Becoming everything they need was part of the problem, but Sloane was in no shape to hear it. When she wasn't being a smartass, Coy's sister had one of the biggest hearts around. That she fell too hard too fast was the thing, and despite stereotypes, Coy figured the general population wanting a relationship wasn't necessarily looking for an immediate "lesbian" U-Haul. "I think," she began, reaching for the extra pillows on the bed. She tucked them behind her so they propped her against the wall more, "you just haven't met the right one yet. It's not you, Sloane. It's the situation, the timing, the person. It's not you, okay? You're perfect."

Coy used her thumbs to wipe away her sister's tears, watching as Sloane's green gaze met her own. "You might not believe it, babe, but eventually, you'll realize Lucas did you a favor. You deserve way more than he can give."

A humorless laugh escaped Sloane, and she glanced away. "You're just hoping I'll end up with a woman. The only person you've ever approved of was Alice."

Coy furrowed her brows. When had she given Sloane that impression? "I just want you to be happy, Sloane. No matter who it is, so long as they're good to you."

"Yeah? And what about you? You deserve to be happy."

"What makes you think I'm not?" Coy tapped her on the nose, giving her a wan smile. "Now, what'll it be? I'll send Ash home, and we can do one of two things with our Sunday: drink our sorrows away and binge *Bridgerton*, or hit the trails."

"Whoop!"

"Gonna beat you there!" Coy maneuvered her bike's handlebars over the rough mountainside terrain, the thick tires sliding easily over the rocks and exposed tree roots on the trail.

"Cockiness will get you nothing but dust in your face out here," Sloane shot back, already acting as if Lucas was forgotten. Sure enough, her purple high-end mountain bike started inching past Coy as they grew closer to the sloped bend. Their cousin J.D. was well behind them, already choking on the dust left in their wake.

With a vigorous push forward, Coy was once again head-to-head with her sister. She'd drunk too much the night before; the typical bloat the day after made her feel like a deadweight on top of her bike. That was the only reason her sister was squeezing past her right now. Well, that and perhaps a teensy part of her felt bad for Sloane. "C'mon!" Coy exclaimed as her twin reached the bend first, her gloved hands firmly on the handlebars as she shifted her body and expertly guided the mountain bike over the slope. Coy could hear Sloane laughing, basking in the small win, knowing they were equally competitive. Her quads burned from exertion, the plantar fasciitis that had plagued her since high school already stabbing the heel of her left foot, but she pushed on. There was no way she was losing to Sloane without a struggle.

"Hold up, hold up!" Coy called once they'd made it into a clearing once more. She watched as Sloane reduced her pace and followed suit, eventually coming to a halt off the trail in the wooded area.

"What's up?"

Coy held up her hand, out of breath as she reached for her water fastened to the bike's holder. She chugged a quarter of the bottle before panting out, "Let's wait for J.D. He probably passed out between the ten and twelve-kilometer mark."

Sloane sniggered, reaching to undo the strap on her full-face helmet. She lifted her bottle of Gatorade to her lips, saying between swallows, "How come you're quieter than me today? Still hung up on the good ol' crash and burn from last night?"

Coy rolled her eyes, letting her sister's ribbing slide for the time being. Honestly, it was just good to hear her laughing again so soon after Lucas. There was a high possibility Sloane wasn't as into him as she'd thought. "How'd you know, anyway?"

Sloane shrugged. "She wasn't there to take anyone home. Her posture was stiff and closed off, and she hardly glanced at the crowd the entire time you were checking her out. Not even a legend like yourself could land a mark if she was a million miles away."

"Too bad, huh? She was something else."

"You and your age gap attraction," Sloane chuckled, teasing Coy about the sapphic books she read. What could she say? Older women were more experienced and weren't afraid to go after what they wanted in the bedroom. "After all these years, you still trying to make Frankie jealous?" They could hear the fast-paced crunch of tires a good stretch away, and Coy figured they had about twenty seconds before J.D. caught up.

She adjusted her goggles and got ready to go again. If her sister only knew how unattached Frankie was to Coy. Her sex life with Sloane's boss, the edgy lone wolf who ran one of the more popular gay-friendly pubs in Vancouver, was strictly casual. She doubted Frankie could love *anyone,* let alone feel true jealousy. With the older woman, Coy was able to give in to her submissive desires without falling in love. There was no compromising with Frankie, and that emotional barrier was the key reason their non-relationship worked. There *was* no jealousy.

Frankie would just as soon hogtie Coy to the bed and use the paddle on her than bask in anything Coy could do for her. *To* her. And that was fine. Hell, sometimes that was exactly what Coy needed at the end of a long day. But sometimes, she wanted to be the top calling the shots. Frankie understood her in a way no one else did.

J.D. came flying around the bend, his clothes full of drying mud and gravel like he'd fallen a time or two. He noticed them too late and zipped past, having to backtrack once he'd gotten safely off the trail. "Hey, you know, I'm thinking this trail is beyond my experience level."

Coy grinned. "You insisted on this trail if I recall. 'I can do it, Coy. I'll even bet you I can!' Aren't you glad I didn't take that bet?"

"You bet on literally everything."

"Well, that's an exaggera—"

"J.D., you're bleeding!"

Coy abruptly shut up, pulling down her goggles to follow Sloane's anxious gaze. "Fuck, you're not lying. Cuz, did you land on something sharp in one of your falls?"

"I-I did, I think, once," J.D. admitted. He frowned down at his ribs, where his shirt was torn. Blood oozed from an exposed wound, staining his Granny Smith apple green T-shirt.

"Let's pull our bikes more out of the way so I can look at it," Coy decided, her tone leaving zero room for debate. Already regretting how far away they were from a hospital, she hoped to all hell J.D. just had a messy scratch.

In less than a minute, Coy had her cousin sitting shirtless on a fallen log while she rummaged through her emergency pack. "Tell me again, Sloane, how carrying all this stuff is overkill?"

"Yeah, yeah, Mom," Sloane groused, her face inches away from J.D.'s armpit. "That's quite a gash."

Coy got closer and whistled, observing the road rash and deep laceration, and then examined the rest of him for any further signs of injury. "Anything else hurt? I'm sorry we didn't slow down sooner."

J.D. shook his gorgeous head of sandy blond hair. "Nope, and I can hardly feel this one. I'm sure it'll be fine, but I know what you're like, Coy."

"Oh?" Coy grunted, slipping on a pair of medical gloves. She tore open a couple packets of alcohol swabs, arching a brow up at him. He looked younger than his twenty-three years, his face still bearing all the perks of youth.

"Yeah, you know. Like you'll nag me the entire way home if I don't let you patch me up."

"McCoy *is* trained in First Aid," Sloane reminded him, handing Coy the tweezers.

"The only one here, I might add. So shut it, cuz." McCoy smirked, enjoying the hiss of pain as she poured disinfectant solution over his ribs. "Hold still." Using the tweezers, she carefully dug out bits of dirt and splinters from the wound before applying ointment and gauze.

It was a basic clean and patch job for the most part. J.D. had been lucky, but that didn't extinguish the guilt gnawing at Coy as they got back on their bikes. She was responsible for them when they were this far out. She was the most experienced, and yet her head had been everywhere but on the task at hand. Racing against Sloane hadn't been the best idea, but Coy had been preoccupied all day. Thoughts of a beautiful stranger had taken up more than enough rent in her mind, and to what end? It's not like Coy would ever settle down with one woman. So, what about *this* one had her so bent out of shape?

CHAPTER 3

Sawyer

THUMP, THUMP, THUMP.

Sawyer rubbed the persistent ache at her temples, pulling away from her open laptop to fish a bottle of Tylenol from her desk drawer. Not that pain meds had helped the last three times she'd dropped two into her palm. The pounding in her temples might as well be another heartbeat, it was so loud. She popped the capsules into her mouth, washing it down with the half-finished vitamin water she'd brought from home. The wall clock above the door laughed at her, each chime of the second hand reminding Sawyer there were still two more hours before she was homebound.

"One hour to go, people! We can do this!" she heard Barb yell from the front line, ever optimistic. Her sous-chef preferred to look at how long it was before closing rather than how long it'd also take to clean and go home. A loud whoop from the rest of Sawyer's staff followed Barb's encouragement in the kitchen.

Sawyer's gaze returned to the screen in front of her. She'd received a reply email from yet another mechanic she'd sought out in hopes of a possible car rebuild. She quickly scanned the unedited response from someone named Darryl, glossing over the spelling errors until her gaze landed on "*... would require taking the car to my shop.*"

"Like hell it will," Sawyer huffed aloud, scowling so hard at her computer that it was a wonder the sheer force of it didn't shatter the screen. Her headache flared in response. What part of her carefully laid out stipulations for hiring someone to rebuild the hunk of steel in her garage did Darryl not understand? The car stayed put, and that was her final offer. Sawyer wanted to keep watch on the progress via her garage surveillance, and she couldn't do that if the car was sitting unsupervised across town.

"Idiots."

It was challenging to find adequate people these days.

"Dustin, where's my *pouding chômeur*?"

Barb's voice rang out once more from the kitchen, another reminder that her workday wasn't finished. Sawyer sighed, knowing she needed to head back out there. Sneaking into her office for a quick reprieve was just that. Shane was expecting her, likely still looking forward to learning the next step in making gravy for the meat pies.

Not bothering to spend the minute it would take to reply to the email, Sawyer stood, chugging the remaining water before tossing the empty bottle in the recycling. Her stomach felt empty since she'd eaten toast and avocado hours ago at breakfast, but when she ate, it burned like the worst indigestion imaginable. The discomfort didn't seem worth it until she couldn't bear the hunger any longer.

She returned to the line, checking on Micah on meats and her second station chef, Leon, before sidling up to where Shane was removing the giblets out of the gravy pot. "Yeah, just like that," Sawyer greeted him, ignoring the pang in her belly. She swallowed, pointing to the flour already measured out on the counter. "Now add a little of the drippings to your bowl, and slowly mix in the flour. Yes, just like that."

While Shane did as she instructed, Sawyer kept a watchful eye on the rest of her staff. Barb was busy belting out orders while Leon removed a casserole from the oven. Micah had just plated a fine-looking beef filet, and Dustin was adding final touches to the desserts going out.

"Make sure there isn't a detail missing on those plates!" Sawyer reminded her team, glancing between Micah and Dustin. "Earning our first Michelin star was only the first step. Now, we need to put in the hard work to keep it."

"Understood, Chef."

"Heard that, Chef, thank you."

Sawyer nodded, turning back to Shane, and frowned at how he just stood there staring blankly into the pot. "You should be stirring every half minute and chopping the garnish in between. You need to be able to multitask if you want to make a career of this."

Sawyer had always been a firm believer that being a great chef didn't necessarily mean going to a culinary school. Preparing a Michelin star-rated dish was more than just memory or learning different cuts of meat in a classroom. The knowledge came from deep within, like all the senses coming alive to feel out if the bouillabaisse had the right amount of saffron or if the crème brûlée was cooked at the right temperature. Some of Sawyer's signature dishes were created purely on instinct. Bree often joked that Sawyer's sixth sense was knowing if a recipe was perfect or not. She wasn't sure if such a thing existed, but if it did, Sawyer owed it to kids like Shane to find out. But that didn't mean she made things easy.

Shane ducked his head, the tops of his cheeks coloring as he mumbled, "Sorry, Chef."

"I don't need an apology; I need you to learn the proper way. I promoted you to commis chef because I thought you had potential to be more than just my dishwasher," Sawyer explained, registering the bite in her tone a little too late. She rubbed the back of her neck and swallowed, her mouth exceedingly dry. She was tired and short-fused, and her nausea was back with a vengeance, but taking her issues out on her staff was never a good idea. As she opened her mouth to apologize, Shane waved her off.

"I'm okay. Thank you, Chef. For the opportunity to learn from you."

Sawyer frowned, unsure if he was being genuine or not. She decided it was too late in the evening to care either way and nodded. "Don't forget to stir. I'll check on you in a few minutes." She left him to his task, checking with Micah and Leon once more before heading for her sous-chef. "Looks like things are winding down. I'll be in my office until close, but call if we suddenly get a rush, okay?"

Barb nodded, accepting a salad for inspection. "Sure thing. Feeling alright?" Sawyer had asked her to expo earlier in the evening since she was busy with Shane. She could have gotten one of her other chefs to train him but preferred to be present when bringing green chefs into the fold. That way, they learned to do things her way.

"Yes, just have loads of paperwork waiting for me." The lie came easily to Sawyer. She'd been lying for years, desperate to remain in control even when she felt anything but.

"Kelly should be doing that for you." Barb gave her a knowing look as Sawyer turned away.

Sawyer checked on Shane one last time before making her way into the back office. As she fell into her swivel chair, she had just enough time to grab the garbage can under her desk before she threw up. "Ugh," she muttered, swiping the back of her hand over her mouth.

For a moment, she just sat there, gazing at her closed door, exhausted beyond measure. She'd been living and breathing Desmarais since the moment she'd been handed the keys. She'd raised Bree while pouring her heart and soul into the restaurant. Hell, she'd lost count of how many times Bree had gone to work with her if the sitter couldn't make it. Sawyer had changed diapers in her office, and had propped Bree up in her bouncy chair on the pastry table while she'd rolled out dough. Besides a three-week recovery period fifteen years ago, Sawyer had worked twelve or fourteen-hour shifts practically every day for more than twenty years.

How was it only now she was feeling the repercussions?

I must be burning myself out, just like Bree is always telling me.

Sighing, she pulled out the small bottle of mouthwash she kept in her bottom drawer, gurgling and spitting that into the garbage as well. Her stomach felt slightly better, so she chanced her luck on the container of saltines beside the phone. Maybe they would stay down longer this time.

Bach filled the speakers of Sawyer's Range Rover as she drove home, the classical music soothing the weariness inside her as the SUV glided through the serene suburbs of Vancouver's west side. At half past midnight on a Monday in the Dunbar-Southlands there weren't many other vehicles out save for the taxis and Uber drivers.

The drive home wasn't long enough to mentally rehash the day she'd had, but that could come later once she was neck-deep in a soothing bubble bath with a glass of red close by. The thought sparked a rare smile. She slowed the Range Rover down as she approached her house, the luxury two-story looming over her as she pulled into the drive. Solar lights lit up the driveway as she drove past, pausing at the two-door garage long enough to jab the opener button.

She sidled up beside her late husband's covered sports car, shifted into park, and shut off the ignition. Stepping from the Rover, Sawyer scowled at what was left of the McLaren. Olivier had been obsessed with the fucking thing, no doubt loving the one ton of yellow carbon fiber more than Sawyer and Bree combined. Or at least it felt as if he did. Sawyer holding on to the broken vehicle made no sense to her friends and daughter, but they couldn't possibly understand.

Olivier had taken and taken from her, often leaving her physically spent and emotionally bankrupt. Then he'd died before she could break free, so in the end, it was as if he'd won.

Sawyer needed to reclaim the control she'd lost by Olivier dying, and, come hell or high water, the ridiculous car that had made her a widow would be part of the process. Therein lay the agenda, one that would seem extreme to anyone else, but having the McLaren rebuilt could be exactly what she needed. She just had to persuade someone who was capable enough to not only rebuild the engine, if necessary, but the exterior of the car as well. The day after Olivier's funeral, Sawyer impulsively gathered up all his belongings and threw them in the trash. Everything, even his toothbrush. It hadn't been one of her finer moments, to say the least.

Had she been thinking clearly, Sawyer would have savored the act of destroying Olivier's possessions like she'd done with their wedding photos years before. Throwing them out wasn't enough for Sawyer. Even though Olivier was dead, defiling his once precious belongings would have given Sawyer immense satisfaction. Now, all she could do was hope restoring the McLaren would give her the closure she needed.

Chapter 4

McCoy

"Are you seeing it? Abs?" McCoy asked, pointing the camera on her phone to the mechanic shop she stood in front of. High above the entrance doors, a brand spanking new business sign rested. What was once Miller's Mechanics was now Miller's Mechanics & Restoration. With the new, specialized garage her pops had built in the last year behind the original shop, McCoy could officially offer her services in auto body repair as a licensed technician.

Abi, one of her dearest friends, let out a happy squeal, "Coy, it looks amazing! You must be so freaking proud of yourself right now. I can't wait to see it in person."

Coy rocked back on her heels, her barely restrained excitement causing the phone to almost slip from her hands as she turned it to face Abi again. "Not gonna lie, this face?" she gestured to the megawatt grin permanently on display, "hasn't changed since Pops texted me the news last night."

"It's no wonder. I love this for you, babe." Abi smiled at her affectionately. Downtown Vancouver was set as a backdrop as she bustled down the street toward the office. Her cheeks were rosy from exertion, and the bag slung over one shoulder looked to be on the heavy side.

"Thanks for letting me brag," Coy said with a laugh. "We still meeting for lunch?"

"Absolutely. I've had you penciled in since last week," Abi joked, blowing Coy a kiss through the phone. "Can't wait to see you."

"You too, Abs. See you later." McCoy ended the video call, pocketing the phone and taking a moment to examine the sign again. Pride swelled in her chest. Everything she had was thanks to her father and the love of cars he'd passed on to her. Now, as an auto body technician *and* a mechanic, Coy could bring something else to the family business.

Bending to pick up the takeout breakfast she'd placed on the pavement, both arms were full as she headed into the shop and went through to the back office. "Knock, knock," McCoy said, ducking her head through the half-open door in her father's cramped shop office.

"Coy! Come in, come in," Greg Miller greeted warmly, lowering the newspaper in his hands long enough to wave her inside.

"Sooo, you didn't see last night's score yet, I take it?" Coy drawled, pushing the door all the way open with her steel-toed boot. She set the tray of coffee and box of Tim Horton's donuts on the desk before handing her father his breakfast sandwich.

"Don't tell me they lost again, Coy," Greg groaned, tossed the paper to his desk, and unwrapped his breakfast sandwich. Almost as an afterthought, he grumpily added, "Thanks for breakfast."

Coy smothered her laugh, taking long breaths in through her nose to try to appear somber. Razzing her dad was one of her life's greatest perks. "They fought hard, Pops, but those last few plays were ..." Coy shuddered. "Nobody was coming back from that."

"Goddamn, and I missed it! I should have given Ma a firm no when she asked me to come over. Surely, the front door repair could have waited another day."

"When have you ever been able to say no to my nana?" Coy pulled the chair out, the metal frame scraping against the tiled floor. She plopped down, leaned back in the seat, and rested her dirty boots on the edge of his desk. Cracking open her coffee, she took a drink and smiled as she watched her father. Greg was still muttering under his breath, angrily chowing down on his sandwich as he rifled through the paper to the sports section. "Besides, live life each day like it's your last, right? No regrets—that's what you taught us. Nana's not getting any younger."

Their eyes met briefly before Greg nodded once and went back to the paper, "Oh, I know it, kiddo. And she's slowed right down since your papa passed."

Coy nodded, hating to hear the truth out loud. "I'm hoping to pick up a few more odd jobs this summer to help with the updates on her house. She'll have the stairlift in no time, Pops, then she can move her bedroom back upstairs." She had scored a few shifts at the bar over the winter, and although it wasn't her thing, she would work every night if it helped her nana out. The problem was that Frankie often didn't need more staff, and it didn't bring in money fast enough for Coy's liking.

"Well, you know I appreciate the help with Ma's medical bills and the renovations Coy, but please don't work yourself to death, okay?" He gave her a pointed look. "Try to enjoy the summer."

Coy smiled but said nothing. Helping her father get a stairlift for Nana and a ramp to her front door was the least she could do. Family stuck together. "Has Nana given any more thought to moving into community care?"

"You know she can't bear to give up the farm. She'll likely drop dead one morning feeding the chickens."

An unpleasant image of her nana's hens plucking at her corpse came to mind, and Coy let out a shudder. "Jesus, Pops. Next time, give me a ring, yeah? If I'm not busy, I don't mind driving out to help."

"At least Ma gives you notice when she wants you for something," Greg grumbled good-naturedly, raising his face again but this time to give Coy a wink. "You end up with a cooler worth of freezer meals."

"And pie. Don't forget the pie. Oh! And ice cream."

"See? Spoiled rotten." Greg stilled for a moment, his face scrunched up in confusion at whatever he was reading. When it finally registered, Coy sniggered as her dad's surprised gaze flew to hers across the desk. "Are you fucking serious right now? The Jays didn't lose! Talk about giving your old man a heart attack!" Then he laughed his big barrel laugh, the one where he held his gut at the same time and threw his head back.

Coy loved watching him like this, so happy and without a care in the world. He'd been dealt a tough hand after their mother died, having to raise rambunctious twins while still mourning the loss of his wife. Besides Sloane and her nana, he was Coy's favorite person in the world.

"It was intense. I watched it at the bar with Sloane while she was working. She said to tell you that 'Bo played a rockin' game,' whatever that means."

Greg chuckled again, his hazel eyes lighting up. "That girl and her bets, I swear to God. I guess I should be grateful neither of you got involved in some shady gambling ventures growing up."

"Nope, our family bets keep us pretty busy," Coy joked, biting into her own sandwich. She ate her sausage, egg, and cheese on an everything bagel because she loved how the onion seasoning on the bagel blended nicely with all the other flavors. Not to say she'd turn down a different sandwich if she was handed one. Eating was one of her top five pastimes. Working on cars, biking, hanging with friends, eating food, eating pussy …

Coy smirked, unable to help herself. When would she ever *not* love doing that?

"Well," Greg said, finishing the last of his coffee and tossing it in the garbage. He stood up and slipped into his coveralls. "We best get to it, kiddo."

Nodding, Coy stuffed the last of her breakfast in her mouth before grabbing the box of donuts she'd picked up for the guys. She followed her dad out of the office.

"Morning!" Chip, her dad's oldest friend and employee, just about barreled into her as he made a beeline directly to the donuts. "Oh, kiddo, you're too good to us old fellas!" Chip boomed jovially, clapping Coy on the back as he stuffed half a Boston cream into his mouth.

"Yeah yeah. Watch the wet clothes around the food." She smirked, eyeing his sopping jacket. It had been raining steadily since late the night before. When Coy had checked the weather online, she'd been disappointed to discover it wasn't supposed to clear until the following day.

By 7:55 a.m. J.D.,—Coy's cousin and Greg's part-time technician and receptionist—showed up ready for the workday. By eight, the first two customers were pulling into the parking lot. Coy lived for the hustle of a busy day but learned long ago to treasure the lulls, too. It was there she tinkered with different engines in the back of the shop or read up on new makes and models. She was always learning, always looking for a problem to solve. It was the one thing she loved most about being a mechanic—putting her tireless curiosity and logic to good use. And of course, ladies loved a handy soft butch who knew their way around an undercarriage.

"Oh, erm, sorry there, girlie, but when I booked the appointment, I'd asked for McCoy specifically," a lanky, middle-aged man named Troy informed Coy. She had been about to drive his Mercedes-Benz into the service bay when he'd bolted out of the reception area, hot on her heels.

Coy looked at him blankly, raindrops pelting down over the bridge of her worn out *Miller Mechanics* cap and waited for him to notice her name tag. It was stitched into her coveralls in big red letters. Maybe it was time she spoke to her father about new, flashier uniforms. Troy, with one massive hand on the driver's door, continued in a firmer voice, "Nothing against you, honey, but the guys down at the office said he's the best mechanic in Richmond."

There weren't many things that could set Coy's teeth on edge. She believed she had a fun-loving personality and looked at life as a glass half full, but she fucking hated it when men called her pet names. Whether they acknowledged it, the expression was condescending, and it pissed her off.

"I *am* McCoy." She pointed to her name written as proof, and scowled when his gaze dropped to her chest. Yup, new uniforms were in order. She was seriously tired of the same old shit. Maybe a new cap with their names printed on the front would work. "Now can we get on with it?"

"You're McCoy? The *best* mechanic in Richmond?" A disbelieving laugh escaped Troy. He stood taller and straightened his suit. "I'm sorry, I'm just surprised is all. Honestly, I thought you were ..."

"A man? Nope, sorry to disappoint. Now, it says here you're scheduled for an oil change and a ..." Coy paused, glancing at the clipboard in her hands before adding, "a second opinion."

"Erm, yeah, my usual mechanic said I needed new rotors and a caliper, but you know what? I can probably just wait around until someone else is available."

Yeahhh. Coy was done. She nodded once, before leaving him in the parking lot. She headed straight for her father, who presently had a Nissan hooked up to diagnostics, and dumped the clipboard onto his lap. "Here, he wants someone else. I'm going for lunch." Not bothering to wait for a reply, Coy grabbed her keys and jacket from the office and headed back out into the rain.

Coy decided to take the scenic route to Denny's since she was earlier than planned, texting Abi before leaving that she was still good to meet her. She should have anticipated the lagging traffic on the No. 2 bridge, but the frustration of her last customer plagued her. As a queer woman, working in a male-dominated field had its ups and downs. Thankfully, working for her father curbed most of what Coy imagined others dealt with daily, but not all. The backward thinking of the occasional cis man made her want to throw a fit and shake them down from their holier-than-thou pedestal. And Troy was *nothing* compared to some that showed up at the shop. Some guys, even the younger generation, were downright ignorant towards her.

"Ah, damn," Coy muttered, taking in the traffic accident cleanup ahead of her on the Sea Island Way bridge. Vehicles were lined up at least one football field length in front of Tegan, her Jeep Wrangler, waiting for the flagger to give the okay. "Damnit," she repeated, annoyed with her luck so far that morning. When it rained on her parade, it sure as hell poured. Coy squinted at the fat raindrops rapidly hitting her windshield as her wipers tried hard to keep up. At this rate, she'd be lucky if she arrived for lunch on time, let alone early. She tapped her fingers impatiently against Tegan's steering wheel, trying to lose herself in G Flip's vocals blaring through her headphones. Tegan was an older model Wrangler, complete with a CD player and not much else on the interior, but she had taken Coy on some of the best rides of her life.

With Sloane riding shotgun, they'd been all over B.C. with Tegan, taking narrow back roads and muddy off-road trails. Coy had fine-tuned Tegan's exterior in so many ways, starting with a hard/soft top conversion kit years ago. Since then, she'd upgraded to larger tires with better traction and a bull bar and skid plate for off-roading adventures. Coy and Sloane had driven up the hardest trails in the province through the summer and again in the winter just to see what Tegan could do.

The traffic was moving at a snail's pace, and Coy debated if she should call Abi and cancel. But she was likely already on her way to Denny's, taking an extended "work lunch" from her job at Cairns Corp. Coy was three blocks away from the Denny's when she spotted a black Range Rover Sport pulled over on the side of the road. The tire on the left rear was flat and looked like it had been driven around for several blocks before stopping. The driver was getting back into the vehicle.

"Seriously? She's probably gonna drive on the rims again." Making a split decision to help, Coy flicked on her blinker and eased Tegan onto the street's shoulder, parking in front of the Rover. Pocketing her keys, she sent Abi a quick update before hopping out. "Hey there," she called out, waving at the blurry figure now sitting behind the wheel of the Rover. The rain wasn't letting up, so it was probably a good thing she was back inside the dry vehicle. Coy reached the SUV, tapping lightly on the windowpane. "Looks like you could maybe use some help?"

The only part of the woman she could make out through the foggy window was the long black strands of wet hair. Coy took a step back, suddenly very aware of her grease-stained coveralls and the rain washing away her eyeliner. As the driver's door began to open, she raised her hands in a non-threatening way and added, "I'm a mechanic. I don't mind getting you fixed for takeoff again. If you want."

One long, tantalizingly tanned leg played peek-a-boo with Coy seconds before the door was shoved open. Coy's jaw went slack as a familiar scowling face moved dutifully from the vehicle. And just like the night at the warehouse, all Coy could do was stare.

"You're a mechanic, you say? No kidding." If the tone in the woman's faint accent was any dryer, she'd sound almost robotic. She gave Coy an unimpressed once over, her sensual lips setting in a hard line. "I've already called roadside assistance; someone should be with me shortly."

French. It was definitely a French accent, Coy decided, but not from France. Québec, perhaps? Coy's body hummed in response, leaning forward of its own accord. A mixture of water and makeup trickled into her mouth as she replied, "There was an accident over on Sea Island Way. I saw two tow trucks loading the vehicles on, so it might be longer than you think."

"How convenient for you, running to my rescue ... *McCoy*."

Ah, she remembers my name!

Coy's morning was getting better already. And she would gladly listen to that delectable lilt all day and night if she could. The way the woman's r's rolled off her tongue had her wanting to taste them. Taste her. Fuck, and the way she pronounced Coy's name had her fantasizing about doing a lot more than just tasting that sassy mouth. Coy tried like hell to tamp down the strange pinch of anxiety in her stomach, but a nervous laugh bubbled out, and then she was rambling, "That's me, ma'am. Helpful McCoy. Super helpful, just like everyone's friendly neighborhood—"

"Do not finish that."

"Yes, ma'am." *Dude! What. Are. You. Doing?*

"Quit it with the ma'am. My name is Sawyer," she bit out, crossing her arms over her chest again. And then she tapped the toe of her high heel on the wet pavement, pulling the sleeve of her cardigan back to check her watch. "Well? Are you changing the tire or not? I'm late for a meeting."

Coy held back her grin, enjoying Sawyer's bossiness and little click of her heel. There was nothing she loved more than a dominant woman.

"Excuse me," she husked, brushing past Sawyer to the driver's door. A static tingle shot through Coy at their brief touch, and something between a sigh and a gasp left her lips. "Whoa, did you—" Catching the impatient roll of Sawyer's magnetic eyes, Coy clamped her mouth shut again.

Okay then. She's gonna reject that, too.

Gritting her teeth, Coy leaned into the Rover, turning the key over long enough to activate the tire suspension button. Once the light went off, she turned the car back off and checked that the brake was secure.

"Changing a tire is something everyone should learn," Coy explained, meeting Sawyer's gaze on her way to the vehicle's trunk. She lifted the hatch, gesturing to the traffic whizzing past them. "It can be dangerous on the side of the road. It would have been better to pull into a parking lot first."

"Think we can skip the lesson and just get on with it?"

Coy raised her eyebrow, slightly taken aback by the surliness in her tone. "I am 'getting on with it.' I can teach as I go."

"I'd much rather you didn't."

Sawyer looked like a drowned rat standing there, her clothes inappropriate for the weather, but she had enough fire in her stormy gaze to make Coy feel like she was sitting before a blazing wood stove. She fished out her keys, offering them to Sawyer and trying to ignore how ridiculously breathless she was. "Why don't you go sit in my rig? Beats standing in the rain."

"I happen to *like* the rain." Sawyer stiffened, turning her nose up at Coy's offer.

Coy shook her head, not knowing what her problem was, but pocketed her keys again. If Sawyer wanted to show up to her meeting looking like she'd showered in her clothes, then who was Coy to stop her? The stubborn woman should wear a raincoat or use an umbrella.

Aware of her beautiful, speculative audience, Coy uncovered the blocks and lug wrench from underneath the trunk floor. The spare tire was below the Rover, but the bolt keeping it in place was accessible through the trunk. Coy used the wrench to loosen it, feeling it give way after several rotations with the wrench. Next, she stuck a wedge block behind one of the front and rear tires to keep the SUV in place. She'd only worked on a couple Rovers before, so it took a minute to establish where it was safe to place the jack, but it was smooth sailing from there.

"So, what type of work do you do?" Coy wondered when the silence became unbearable. She was unusually nervous with Sawyer's gaze on her, and for the first time in her life, she truly wanted to know the answer. She was suddenly dying to know everything.

"Why do you deem it necessary to constantly fill the silence with useless chatter?"

Coy huffed a laugh, ignoring the immediate throbbing between her thighs at Sawyer's harsh demand. She shook her head, loosening the last lug nut on the flat tire and trying to rid herself of the hot image of the older woman shackling Coy to a spreader bar. She seemed the type to know her way around kink and dominance. If she didn't, Coy bet Sawyer was a fast learner.

"What can I say? It's my lucky day running into you, and I don't want to waste a second of it. I was on my way to lunch with a friend, but it must have been serendipity that brought me here to you." The sound of Sawyer's scoff drew Coy away from the spare tire she was fitting on.

"Do you actually believe the bullshit you spew? Or is everything just a game? Women are not shiny prizes to be discarded when boredom strikes or when you find a new toy. Everything comes so easily to your generation. You don't know what it's like to be forced to conform."

Coy didn't reply right away, not knowing what to say and smart enough to know she'd pushed some buttons. Her brain stumbled over the last thing Sawyer said about being forced to conform and repeated it over and over until she thought she'd go crazy without knowing.

"So, I'm right, then? About you? You do like women."

"You're unbelievable."

Coy hoped her grin looked natural as she reached for the last lug nut to fasten into place. She tried not to let Sawyer's words bother her. After all, the woman knew nothing about her. Coy offered no empty promises when she picked up a partner to spend the night with. She explained from the beginning that she wasn't looking for anything longer than one night. How did that make them "toys" in Sawyer's eyes? She furrowed her brow in thought.

"There. You're good to go." Coy loaded the flat tire and tools into the trunk and wiped her greasy hands on her coveralls. She'd wash them better when she was back in Tegan. Once she had disengaged the Rover's suspension, her eyes met Sawyer's.

"Here, for payment. I don't want to owe you any favors." The purse Sawyer fished two embossed certificates out of was bigger than Coy's first aid kit, the cardboard clutched in her fist already going limp in the rain.

"Desmarais," Coy read, scanning the contents of the card. It looked to be an upscale fusion restaurant of some sort. It was the first she'd heard of it, but that was no surprise. She'd never had a reason to go fine dining. "'The bearer is entitled to two complimentary meals.'" She glanced up at Sawyer, thoroughly lost.

"For payment," Sawyer repeated, impatience making her hands jerky as she opened her car door again. "I don't have cash on me. I don't suppose you carry an Interac machine on you?"

"No payment was necessary but thank you, Sawyer. I appreciate the gift."

"Not a gift, McCoy." Sawyer was already climbing into her Rover. "A repayment of a debt." With a flick of her hand, she closed her door, effectively ending the conversation. Seconds later, there was a low purr as the engine came to life.

Coy waved goodbye before heading back to Tegan. She was drenched as she started the Jeep, and an unsettling feeling burrowed deeply in her gut as she watched Sawyer drive away. Sawyer had repeatedly thwarted her attempts to flirt, so shouldn't her rejection lift whatever chokehold she had on Coy?

As she examined the coupons still in her hand, Coy wondered if she'd ever see the older woman again.

CHAPTER 5

Sawyer

THE FOLLOWING MORNING, SAWYER was still fuming over yesterday's fiasco. She couldn't understand how someone she'd had the misfortune of meeting twice could get under her skin so detrimentally. McCoy—*whatever-her-name-was*—had slithered under her skin and plagued her thoughts. Thankfully, however, she'd never warmed Sawyer's bed.

"If only she didn't have that stupid, cocky smile," Sawyer griped, slowing down at a red light as she made the daily commute to work. The problem was that she couldn't figure out how to remove said smile from her cerebrum. It should have been illegal to smile that wide and with not one dimple but two. Yes, something about McCoy set her blood thrashing, and not in a good way.

Her phone rang through the Rover's speakers as she drove through the intersection. Glancing at the display on her dash, a smile that only her daughter could pull out of her stretched Sawyer's lips from ear to ear. McCoy was forgotten as she pressed the steering wheel to accept the call. "Hey, love! Don't tell me you're just getting up?"

Bree's soft laughter from the Range Rover's speakers was the missing warmth in Sawyer's frigid heart. Her emotions were waking with the melody, sparking to life, and she was beyond grateful for their close relationship. "Good morning, *Maman*. You know habits are tough to break."

Ugh. You can say that again. Case in point, she'd dumped a full carafe of coffee into the sink that morning after remembering it was just her and Patches in the house. As much as she'd grown to resent Olivier, for years she'd had a purpose around the home. No, more than that. She'd had an obligation to fulfill, and now that it was no more, Sawyer felt unsettled. She didn't know who she was anymore outside of work.

"Indeed. How late were you up last night?"

"Ohhh, 'til about two. I watched the entire season three of *The 100* with Scott. We baked *pouding chômeur* between breaks, but it never turns out as well as when you and I make it."

"I miss bringing you with me to work."

Sawyer winced as the truth spilled out, not wanting Bree to feel sorry for her. Their after-school routine may have ended a couple years ago, but they were still some of Sawyer's fondest memories.

"Me too. I miss cooking and baking in the backhouse with Barb and everyone. I always felt safest at the restaurant with you. I ... I hope you know that."

Sawyer's throat and sinuses burned as she forced herself to remain calm. Walking into work with tear-stained cheeks just wouldn't do. Neither would sobbing into the phone to her daughter. Bree witnessing her come apart was the last thing Sawyer needed. It hadn't happened in years, but Sawyer knew her daughter would rush back to Vancouver if she thought her mom wasn't coping. Sawyer couldn't let that happen. *We've both sacrificed too much to just throw it all away.* She would do anything to make sure Bree's future wasn't in jeopardy. Just as she had for the past twenty years.

Despite her best efforts, Sawyer's vision blurred. Fuck, she was crying. Silently, but there was no way Bree couldn't hear it in her traitorous voice. She wiped a lone tear from her cheek, and said in a tight voice, "I

... Thank you for the call. I've gotta go now, Bree. Talk tomorrow, love, okay?"

"Sure, take care, *Maman*. I love you. *Je m'ennuie de toi.*" *I miss you.*

Sawyer swallowed, the thickness in her throat making it difficult to speak. "You too, baby," she rasped, dropping the call lightning fast. "Pull it together," Sawyer scolded, her voice rough in the vehicle's silence. "There's not a damn thing to cry over anymore."

"Where's my beef filet! That Michelin star isn't working for itself, people." Sawyer checked the timestamp on the chit hanging on the line. She hated when orders were late going out to the dining room. It was unprofessional and usually resulted in Sawyer or her manager kissing someone's ass and giving them a percentage off their meal. An utterly avoidable compromise if she had a competent team working with her.

"Hot behind!"

"Here you go, Chef." Two plates of steaming beef filet with a Rossini-style sauce slid in front of Sawyer, waiting for her final inspection. Micah looked up at her expectantly, wisps of blue hair tumbling from their cap. Unshed tears brimmed past their long eyelashes. "Sorry, Chef. I-I had a little mishap with the seasoning."

Sawyer gritted her teeth, exhausted from all the excuses this shift. All it took was firing Dustin to throw her team out of sync the entire supper rush, but it couldn't be helped. Kelly, her front house manager, had caught him in a compromising position with a server mid-shift. There wasn't enough time for fraternization on the best of days, let alone using a fleeting "bathroom break" to screw a coworker in a storage closet.

"Hold on a minute, Micah," she replied when the young cook turned to leave. Sawyer focused on the plates, giving any smudges of sauce an efficient wipe before sprinkling garnish over the top. She handed them off to the waiting server. "Give table twenty-seven our sincerest apologies and discount both meals."

"Certainly, Chef." Connor thanked her and took off out front.

"Barb and Shane, cover the line, okay?" Sawyer held up her hand, indicating they'd be gone for five minutes or less.

"Come with me," Sawyer instructed the young employee, not waiting to see if Micah followed. She walked swiftly through the kitchen, heading into her back office, where she leaned against the desk. Micah entered, dragging their footsteps. Their head hung low, and every few seconds, Sawyer caught the quick squeeze and release of their fists against their pant leg. Hell, Micah looked as if they were headed toward their own execution. Which was ridiculous, considering Sawyer couldn't afford to let more staff go during service. Despite what everyone on shift might have thought, Sawyer didn't make a habit of firing the help so close to rush hour.

"Problem-solve with me, Micah. How can we ensure I don't have to apologize to any further customers tonight? Do you need to take your break and regroup?"

"I'm ... wait, you're not firing me?" Micah blurted, their flushed cheeks and wide eyes the epitome of confusion. Sawyer silently shook her head, and after more sniffling and tear wiping, Micah continued in a low voice, "I'm good, Chef."

"Are you certain? Because I need you at your best out there, and I'm not just talking about the recent dish. Accidents happen when your mind isn't in the game." Sawyer shot a pointed glance down at the fresh burn mark on Micah's wrist. Gauze covered it now, but the wound was a not-so-subtle reminder of how dangerous a busy kitchen was.

"I didn't know Dustin was cheating on me," Micah sobbed, stepping closer, and Sawyer stiffened when it looked as if the young person might try to hug her.

"Excuse me?"

Sawyer breathed in, trying to find the sympathy required in her role as head chef. Some days it was harder than others, sympathizing over trivial bullshit when the personal lives of her staff had no business there in the first place. “Micah,” she said, aware of the hardness still in her voice. Ah, fuck it. Sawyer was who she was, and sympathetic wasn't it. “I’m sorry about Dustin, but workplace romances are overrated, not to mention the distraction can lead to accidents in the kitchen. I hope you’re able to learn something from this incident.”

Cis men are not to be trusted.

No, that wasn’t right. Not all men were like Dustin and Olivier. Some out there surely treated their partners with the respect they deserved.

Micah nodded, accepting the tissue Sawyer handed them off her desk. They gestured to their face with one hand, looking demurely up at Sawyer. “Did that happen when you weren’t paying attention?”

Sawyer scowled, her own hand reaching up to touch her left cheek. The thick layer of foundation hiding the jagged, rough edges usually dissuaded questions from her staff. She gave Micah a small nod, just enough of a reply to satiate their curiosity. Swallowing down a lump of unease from the reminder, Sawyer marched past to the door. “Let’s get back out there.”

“Tonight went well despite everything, don’t you think?” Barb said two hours later as she waited for Sawyer to lock up Desmarais. “Shane seems to be catching on, and the customers left happy.”

“It was a good day,” Sawyer agreed, shouldering her duffel bag. They started out to the parking lot. The rest of her staff had left about ten minutes before, but Sawyer liked to do one last check throughout the restaurant before leaving for the night. Barb always waited for her, even though Sawyer had told her before how unnecessary it was. She loathed small talk even more than watching people squirm during awkward conversations with her.

Her SUV came into view, the shiny black of the brand-new back tire stealing her focus. Just like that, the irritating mechanic who had helped came to mind. McCoy, with her endless flirtations and annoying, know-it-all grins. Sawyer had been so thrown off by the day before, she'd forced herself to stay put in the rain to prove a point. There was no way she would have let that arrogant womanizer get the upper hand and see how flustered she'd been. Sawyer could have reached for her umbrella in the back seat, but when her retort of loving the rain slipped out, she didn't have the gumption to go back on it.

Now, Sawyer couldn't help but revel in the irony of her predicament. It was true she was searching for someone knowledgeable to rebuild the McLaren, but McCoy could be the last mechanic on the face of the earth, and Sawyer *still* wouldn't call on her.

"Good night, Barb. Thanks for today," Sawyer told her, unlocking her car. She gave her sous-chef a small wave before climbing into the Rover. She watched Barb do the same and waited for her to leave before following her out of the parking lot.

CHAPTER 6

McCoy

FUCK, I THINK I'M dead. I think she finally killed me.

Coy sagged against the restraints fastened to the St. Andrew's Cross, unable to hold herself up for another second. There wasn't a single part of her body left untouched by Frankie, but as Coy floated on a wave of peaceful subspace, the earlier pain had long since ceased to exist. Purple dots danced behind her closed eyes as a mist of fog enveloped her mind and body. She couldn't muster up enough energy to flutter her lids open and see what Frankie was doing. The clang of buckles on the leather straps as they came off from around her ankles was just white noise, and yet, she was vaguely aware of her legs giving out, boneless from the time spent in such a rigid position.

"You did so well, my pet. So very well." Frankie's voice sounded far away, like she was in another room. Strong arms scooped Coy up, and seconds later, the restraints around her wrists came free as well. Then, she was being carried across Frankie's playroom toward the bed. Coy's smile was sleepy, almost dreamlike, and she nuzzled into Frankie's embrace.

She came aware again to a warm washcloth passing over her abs and then lower, between her legs. Her eyes flickered open, Frankie's curvy form coming into view above her. Her legs were folded underneath her on the mattress, and she was still wearing a pair of lacey underwear and an unbuttoned blouse sans bra. The curve of one heavy breast teased

McCoy as Frankie bent lower, and she stared lazily at the tantalizing hint of flesh.

"Here, drink this."

Coy blinked, unaware she'd dozed off again. She gave Frankie a grateful smile as she held a glass of water to her lips. "Thank you, Mistress," she whispered once she'd swallowed. The water was cold and refreshing against the rawness in her throat. *From too much screaming,* she silently mused.

"Of course." Frankie set the glass down on the nightstand, before leaning back against the headboard and opening her arms to McCoy. "Come, my pet."

Coy nodded. Of course. Of course she'd go to Frankie. She allowed her head to rest in Frankie's lap, sighing in contentment at the feel of Frankie's fingers carding through her hair. Sleep claimed her again, and when she woke next, soft classical music and faint light had basked the playroom in a serene ambience. Coy was still snuggled into Frankie, her face nuzzled directly below a plump breast, and her hand curved around Frankie's hip. The subspace had mostly faded, and for the most part, Coy's emotions had leveled out. Her favorite part of doing a scene was the act of letting go. Sure, she could be a brat when she wanted to, but it only made the eventual reward after her "punishment" that much sweeter.

Coy lifted her gaze to where Frankie had her head resting against the headboard. Her eyes were closed, but she was slowly stroking Coy's back. "How do you feel, pet?" she cracked one eye open.

"How come you never let me touch you?" The words were out before Coy could stop them. She grimaced, silently cursing her post-orgasm-addled brain. She knew the response she'd get, but it still stung when Frankie's hand stilled on her back.

"Pet." Frankie's chuckle was low, but there was a slight edge to it, a silent warning. In the years since she became Coy's part-time Domme, she'd never taken her clothes all the way off. Coy had been so caught up in appreciation of what Frankie represented sexually that she'd not truly cared how one-sided it all was. The truth niggled at her. Why was Frankie's emotional distance bothering her now, after all the time that had passed?

Alarms went off in Coy's head as she felt her throat swell with emotion. She studied the older woman's guarded eyes. Sawyer's equally distrustful gaze flashed in her mind, and Coy swallowed as another idea occurred, one that cut even deeper.

Is a playgirl all they see of me? Coy mentally scolded herself at the silent question. Please, when had she given anyone a chance to see more?

"Pet," Frankie crooned again. She slipped out from under Coy, sliding her lithe body over hers. She cupped Coy's heat in her palm. "I can't be fucking you well enough if you still have the energy to worry about my needs."

Coy chewed the inside of her cheek. Staring into those eyes didn't create butterflies like they used to. Instead, it left her hollowed out and confused. Frankie was as captivating as she'd always been, but something was different. It was hard to describe. Coy just knew that when Frankie closed her mouth around Coy's nipple, and she squeezed her eyes shut, Sawyer's eyes stared back at her.

Coy double-checked the scrawled handwriting on the paper her dad had given her at closing the day before. He hadn't left a name on the note, just an address on Vancouver's west side, to "see about a car".

"Not much to go on," she reflected, staring out at the expansive house beyond Tegan's mud-covered windshield. Surely this wasn't the right address? Coy rubbed the sleep from her eyes, fatigue from her night with Frankie bearing down on her as she checked the paper in her hand for the fifth time. Why would someone clearly this wealthy have any interest in a small, family-owned business in Richmond? Okay, so one guy deemed her the best in the business several months ago and started tossing her name around in conversations, but it wasn't as if the general public knew of her or Miller's Mechanics. Correction: Miller's Mechanics & Restoration.

Damn, that had a nice ring to it.

"You've got to be kidding me."

Coy's head snapped toward the arctic voice outside her window, and her mouth fell open as she came face to face with none other than Sawyer. The woman who, lately, was never far from Coy's thoughts.

McCoy couldn't stop her cringe. If Sawyer had a window into her brain, she could just imagine the beautiful woman's glower.

"Sawyer?" was the only thought she could put into words. Sawyer, goddess Sawyer, Sawyer who came across as someone who could spank McCoy and she would welcome it. *That* Sawyer, who was now notably fuming outside.

"Why are you here? How did you get my address, McCoy?"

Unable to stop staring, Coy lifted the paper still in her hands. "M-Miller's Mechanics?" *And Restoration.* "You called for a quote."

"Not from you. I spoke to the owner, Greg." Tanned hands flew to Sawyer's hips, and she frowned, her nose scrunching up adorably.

"My father." Coy nodded, reaching for the door handle to climb out of the Jeep, but Sawyer held up a hand to stop her.

"Well, you can tell your father I'll be speaking with him tomorrow. You aren't exactly what I had in mind for this project."

With that, Sawyer swiveled on her feet and walked away, leaving Coy to stare after her in mounting confusion.

"'You aren't what I had in mind,'" Coy reiterated later as she sat slumped down on her best friend's sofa. She was in a weird mood since being so abruptly dismissed by Sawyer. Ugh! The gall of that woman!

"She really didn't let you look at the car?" Abi set a steaming mug of coffee down on the table in front of Coy, sounding as perplexed as she was.

Coy shook her head, thanking her for the drink. "The worst of it is Sawyer knows I'm a mechanic! Like, what did I ever do to her, Abs?" Coy whined, promptly pouting her lip in Abi's direction, a put-out expression on her face. "She's so cold. Frigid really. A perfect ice queen in my very lackluster life."

"Lackluster. Uh-huh. I think you've been listening to too many audiobooks." Abi attempted and failed to hide a smile behind her coffee mug, the print on the ceramic screaming, "Kiss me, I'm important!" in bold letters. Her long caramel-brown hair fell over one shoulder as she reached for a cookie. The glacier blue of her eyes sparked with amusement. "Sounds to me like your ego got the brunt of it. Sawyer's the same one who turned you down at the warehouse and then again when you changed her tire, right? You didn't somehow meet another Sawyer in the last week?"

"Yes," Coy groused, finally lifting the mug to her lips for a drink. Dark, robust flavors hit her tongue, and she groaned in appreciation. "Damn, was this made out of your Cairns Corp new employee welcome gift?"

"It is, but who gifts each new employee a top-of-the-line specialty coffee maker and free gas for the year?" Abi shook her head, clearly still amazed at how giving her new boss was.

Coy thought of the fiery red-haired beauty behind the gift and grinned. Courtney Cairns was certainly one of a kind.

"You've been there a few months now. Think you'll stay?"

"Absolutely. I mean, at least for now. Full benefits and pension." She gestured to her latte. "Generous boss. Besides, the salary is decent, and I don't plan to live in this shoebox forever."

They both chuckled, and Coy glanced around at the limited space and furnishings in Tess's annex. It was a small suite on the same property as Tess's parents. Coy was sure it had been meant for a mancave at some point and was renovated to suit Tess. It was entirely too small for them both, especially since Abi moved back to Vancouver with, as Tess put it, a "half dozen bins of shoes". Upgrading to something bigger would serve them both well.

Sawyer and her too-big house came to mind, because of course it did. Despite the chip on the older woman's shoulder the size of the Grand Canyon, and the fact she didn't like Coy, an hour didn't go by without Coy thinking of her.

The bathroom door opening pulled Coy's attention from where she absently tugged at a loose piece of thread on her jeans. Tess appeared before them, fresh from a shower and wearing loose-fitting drawstring pants and a blue tank top. Her blond hair still looked damp as she bent down to kiss Abi.

"Mmm, you smell delicious," Abi gushed against Tess's mouth. She pulled away to nuzzle her nose in the column of Tess's throat.

A slight pang started in Coy's chest from watching them. Their max-level cuteness often gave her the ick. At the pub, for instance, Coy had zero patience for the heart eyes Abi and Tess cast across the table at each other. However, right now, while she sat in their home—because it *was* their home now—a curious pang fluttered in Coy's chest. Her friends looked so happy together, and questions she'd never thought before popped into her brain.

Would she one day want that? And what would she do to keep a relationship like that? What would she give up? Most importantly, would there ever be someone for Coy who was worth risking heartbreak for?

Out of nowhere, Sawyer came to mind.

"Your undercut grew in fast," Tess remarked, surprising Coy a little when she ran her fingers over the new growth. Coy loved her top knot, disconnected undercut hairstyle, but Tess was right. The bottom required a buzz every two weeks. Her hair took more maintenance than Tegan did to look good.

"I won't object if you wanna trim it," Coy said and tossed Tess her best cheeky grin.

Tess considered her offer for a moment before shrugging. "Sure, why not? I don't have anywhere else to be. Let me grab the clippers."

"Appreciate you, barber!" Coy called as Tess disappeared into the bathroom again.

"Yeah, yeah."

Chapter 7

Sawyer

She'd never tell a soul, but sometimes Sawyer still had nightmares about boiling hot cooking oil. The way the water from the potatoes had caused the oil to explode on the larger burner of her gas stovetop. The scalding, immediate blistering effect, and the pain ... it was the kind of excruciating damage one never forgot. No matter how deep into the nightmare she was, something in her subconscious continually snapped Sawyer out of it. She'd often wake with a scream trapped in her throat as if a piece of her was still as in shock as she'd been in the moment.

When the nightmares first began, she'd started going to therapy, but it hadn't lasted long. The third time she heard the appalling labels of *trauma* and *victim* spew from the doctor's mouth, Sawyer had decided she'd had enough. A victim, she was not.

She was a fucking *survivor*.

"... Still there?"

Sawyer blinked, dazed, aware she'd spaced out while on the phone. She was still leaning her back against her kitchen island, the pot of boiling pasta safely cooking on the stove before her. Boiling anything made her uneasy these days. She cleared her throat, cutting her friend off. "Yeah, I'm still here, Cindy," she croaked, pushing herself off the island.

"Lori and I wanted to know if you'd come for dinner next weekend. We could have a few drinks and throw on a movie after or something."

Patches jumped up onto the kitchen island, her whiskers twitching as she sniffed out the Parmesan cheese. Sawyer shooed her off as she replied. "If I recall, we tried that for your birthday a few weeks ago, remember? We ended up booking an Uber to take us downtown."

Cindy laughed, not at all trying to deny it. "In my defense, I didn't want the warehouse tickets to go to waste. Luckily for me, there is only so much begging you can stand before you cave."

"It was rather humiliating on your part," Sawyer scoffed, retrieving an opened bottle of Cabernet Sauvignon. She poured half a wine glass worth, leaving the rest corked on the countertop. She wasn't going out tonight. It was Sunday, her only evening off, and Sawyer had a date planned for one. It would involve a lot more wine, a bubble bath, and an episode or two of *Master Chef*. Alone. Just the way she preferred it.

Liar.

"Well, I promise dinner will be adventure-free. Just the three of us."

"I'll think about it," Sawyer said.

"You better."

"*But*, I make no promise," she added, grateful she'd thought to answer the phone on her Bluetooth. She turned off the burner and grabbed her oven mitts. "You know I have my eye on the prize. I should be living and breathing Desmarais."

"You always do. Have you given any more thought to me coming to cook now that Olivier isn't in the picture? I'm bored to tears every day I go to work."

"Hold on, Cin, I need my full concentration."

"Mm-hmm, go ahead. What are you making, anyway?"

Sawyer carried the steaming pot to the sink, almost tripping over Patches, who had wrapped around her feet, and carefully poured the pasta into the waiting strainer. "Seafood linguine," she replied once her breathing could relax. Using her tongs, she dished out a serving from the colander into a waiting glass bowl.

"Great choice. I brought home a plate of pad thai for us from work. I was too tired to cook, and Lori was working late too."

"Sounds exquisite. I haven't had pad thai in ages. Perhaps since Bree moved out," Sawyer acknowledged, tossing the seafood sauce gently into her linguine. She twisted it all onto a large serving fork, carefully lifting it out and onto her dinner plate.

"With the long hours you put in at work? I believe it. So, Lori and I were thinking," Cindy's voice softened, and alarm bells immediately went off around Sawyer. The only time her friend used that tone on her was when she was seconds away from stirring the pot.

"Go on." *If you dare,* she almost added.

"Well, we know about your visits to the doctor. I mean, you told us your doctor thinks you're under too much stress," Cindy quickly added, and Sawyer's mouth thinned from growing impatience.

"Just spit it out already, Cindy."

"We think you're working too much," Cindy blurted over the line. Sawyer rolled her eyes, but her friend wasn't finished. "And when you get home, you park beside a decimated hunk of steel that your shit husband died in before you head into a house you live in alone. Something's gotta give, Sawyer. It's as if you're purposefully trying to hold onto as much stress as possible. Hire me to take over some of the workload, sell the house, scrap the car. *Something.*"

"Are you done? I think you're done." Sawyer's tone left zero room for debate, but there was something to be said for stating the obvious. Cindy was crossing the line, friend or not. *No one* dictated how much weight Sawyer's shoulders could bear, not anymore.

"It's not as if you'll find a team willing to fix the McLaren in your garage. C'mon Sawyer, be reasonable. The space isn't *that* big, and besides, who wants to be spied on while they work?"

"For your information, I already found someone," Sawyer seethed and then froze at the implication of her words. "Finding someone" would imply she'd given reasonable thought to any of the correspondence she'd had so far. Which she hadn't. Why bother wasting precious time when she knew the interested mechanics and auto body technicians wouldn't work out? When had she taken to blatantly lying to her friends? Was getting the upper hand really that important to her?

Sawyer raised her eyes to the ceiling as the truth dawned on her. There *was* one allegedly skilled individual she hadn't given the time of day to. A person who made Sawyer curse her sexuality on one hand and made her yearn for something she'd never experienced on the other.

Picking up the cheese grater for her block of fresh Parmesan, Sawyer griped out with slightly less edge in her voice, "Not that it's any of you and Lori's concern, but I found a mechanic in Richmond who is willing to rebuild the car." If she was going to lie her way through this conversation, she may as well commit to details.

Tabarnak, McCoy!

Heaven help her. The flirtatious womanizer was like a wildfire, determined to burn a path into Sawyer's life no matter how many times her flame was extinguished.

At ten the following morning, Sawyer stepped inside the small front shop of Miller's Mechanics & Restoration, wrinkling her nose as the pungent odor of spilled engine oil and coolant gave her a temporary sensory overload. The three waiting room chairs—if you could call them that—were occupied, with one bowing greatly under the weight of a snoring heavyset man. Sawyer checked the gold-plated watch strapped to her wrist, sucking her teeth at how late in the morning it already was. Her GPS had given her the runaround in finding this place, having to bypass multiple construction areas. If McCoy knew how to check Facebook messages, then Sawyer wouldn't have had to take time out of her hectic schedule to drive to Richmond.

"Does no one work here or ...?" Sawyer tapped her foot impatiently, peering over the counter to see if the receptionist had passed out on the floor. Did a hole-in-the-wall place like this not even come with customer service? Absurd. The entire situation for why Sawyer was there in the first place was fucking absurd.

"He does," a woman spoke, nudging the sleeping man with her elbow. "Wake up, Chip. You've got a customer."

Sawyer balked. "I'm not a ... I'm here to speak with McCoy. Never mind, I'll find her myself."

"Whoa, whoa, now hold on a minute." Chip slowly got to his feet, eyeing Sawyer with her hand resting on the door leading out to the shop. "This is Coy's place of work. Greg put a stop to all the suitors months ago. It was getting out of hand."

Sawyer quirked a brow, silently assessing this new information. *So, the playgirl has a fanbase. Surprising but not impossible.* She made a tsking sound, opening the door regardless. "If you think I'm here to bat my eyelashes at her less-than-suave pickup lines, you're sorely mistaken." With that, Sawyer swung open the door, ignoring Chip's uproarious laughter as she closed it behind her.

The shop was loud, with machines whirring and objects clanging, and much larger than Sawyer first thought. A man who didn't look much older than her was standing under a Ford F-150 with an oil pan. His lips parted in surprise when he noticed her, but Sawyer walked straight past to where McCoy was. She was also working on a vehicle secured onto the lift, but it looked like she was replacing something behind one of the wheels. She was talking to someone and flashing that irritating grin that seemed to spark Sawyer's temper as much as it unnerved her. She spotted a younger man a few feet from McCoy, holding a phone up as the mechanic spoke. Was he recording her?

"Switching out the rotors on your car is easier than you think," McCoy explained into the camera, and Sawyer watched, dumbfounded, as the young blond-haired man shifted the camera's focus to the rotor, or whatever it was McCoy was working on. "If you follow these simple steps, then this is something you can save on by doing it yourself at home. Or, if all else fails, come on down to the shop! I don't mind fixing you up. Thanks for tuning in! Until next time, my Queens."

Sawyer rolled her eyes so dramatically the movement hurt before turning to leave. She'd driven across town to … reconsider the possibility of McCoy working for her, but the mechanic was so clearly full of herself that nothing positive could come from Sawyer hiring her. She didn't do TikTok, and no one she hired would be plastering their face all over social media when they were supposed to be working.

"Sawyer, hey!"

Sawyer sighed and checked her watch again. She had wanted to look over the schedule at work before Kelly posted them, but unless she called in a request, it wouldn't be happening. They went up each Tuesday by two.

McCoy appeared in front of her, taking a long swig out of a steel canister. A thin sheen of perspiration coated her soft features, and where there wasn't sweat, there were grease marks. A black bandana was tied around her neck, further adding to Sawyer's assumption of her cowboy obsession. She had industrial piercings in both ears, and small spacers occupied her lobes. The disconnected undercut was freshly shaven, and the top half of her chestnut brown hair was plaited down the back of her head today. McCoy wasn't so much pretty as she was handsome, Sawyer decided, with rounded cheekbones and black eyeliner that purposely drew attention to her striking green gaze. Hints of a tattoo flashed under her coveralls as she placed a hand on Sawyer's shoulder.

"I was hoping I'd see you again."

Sawyer stepped back, brushing McCoy's touch off. She didn't know a lot about cars but could safely assume engine oil came out of clothes about as well as cooking oil did. And she was wearing one of her favorite Veronica Beard blazers today. She straightened, temporarily glancing at her shoulder where the mechanic's touch still lingered, before refocusing on McCoy. She got straight to the point. "Have you ever worked on a McLaren P1?"

Sawyer waited, watching the wheels turn in McCoy's brain until her exquisite gaze lit up. The expression on her face was priceless. "Worked on ... no."

That was good to know. Sawyer needed to consider that McCoy may be too inexperienced for a car like the McLaren.

McCoy's devilish smile was back, alerting Sawyer of an incoming word vomit of playgirl bullshit. "Does this mean you want me, after all?" she gushed, looking every bit like an all too eager puppy starving for her attention. How the younger woman could somehow come across as a confident flirt and desperate at the same time was a mystery. And she wore everything she felt clear as day on her face. Sawyer found it rather fascinating if she were being honest.

Her gaze was scrutinizing as she waited for McCoy to realize her slipup. When she did, her eyes widened to impossible depths as she spluttered, "T-to give a quote, I mean. Not like *want* want me. Unless—"

Sawyer held up her hand, halting McCoy mid-ramble. A niggle of amusement threatened to rise to the surface. "Be at my house tomorrow morning by eight and we'll talk. Not a second later. Oh, and McCoy?"

McCoy blinked up at her, her cheeks flushed. "Yes, Mistre ... S-Sawyer?"

Sawyer's eyes widened for a fraction of a second before she got herself under control. Her nostrils flared as she gestured to McCoy's septum ring. "You have a glob of grease headed up your nose."

Chapter 8

McCoy

"And then I said—" Coy paused mid-story to swig back a mouthful of beer. All eyes were on her at the table, each one of her friends in varying degrees of absorption into her recap with Sawyer that morning. She thumped the table with her palm for added effect. "I said, 'You want *me* to work for you after you all but kicked me to the curb last week? Dream on, you cold, unfeeling, un ... beautiful bitch.'"

An odd mix of a choke and snort of laughter came from Abi, and Coy turned to look just as beer shot from her nose.

"Gross," Coy complained with a laugh. "What, you don't believe me?"

"Not for a second," Krystal said, laughing too.

"I can't speak for everyone, but you lost me somewhere between dream and unfeeling." Taunya gave Coy a dubious shake of her head, but a broad grin was plastered on her face. She reached across the table to squeeze Coy's arm. "Babe, you're way too sweet to ever say that to a woman or anyone else with tits and a vulva."

"I could have said it," insisted Coy, although it lacked fervor. The truth of her interaction with Sawyer was ten times more embarrassing. How she'd eagerly welcomed Sawyer to the shop after being dismissed was humiliating. Coy prided herself on giving and receiving the same amount of respect, and yet, when Sawyer spoke of the car like she hadn't been a complete bitch just the week before, Coy had lapped it up like the golden retriever Abi joked she was. There was just something about Sawyer that made Coy lose all sense.

One, she smells amazing. Like blackberries, spring rain, and ... pastries? Coy wondered if that was an official perfume. If it wasn't, it should be.

She sipped her beer, one arm casually draped over Abi's shoulders, and listened to her friends discuss their partners. For once, Tess hadn't joined Abi, and Coy was secretly grateful to have the fab five reunited for the evening. She glanced toward the bar where Sloane was busy behind the counter and did a double take as Naz's tall frame came into view. Her second closest friend, and the only one who enjoyed the strip clubs like she did, was perched on a bar stool chatting to Sloane. Sloane appeared to be at least half listening as she made drinks, and that alone piqued Coy's interest. From the day they'd met, Sloane had thought Naz was an obnoxious flake. What could they be talking about?

Abi squeezed Coy's arm, drawing her attention back to the table rather than whatever game Naz was trying out on her sister. "You okay?"

Their eyes met, and Abi must have read something in Coy's because she slipped her hand in hers and tugged. "Come pee with me."

"Abs, that's not exactly a group activity," Coy protested but followed her out of the booth, regardless. Abi still held her hand, and the pair got more than a few looks from customers as they crossed the pub. One person, who Coy had seen quite a few times talking to Frankie, narrowed her gaze on Coy as they passed. They would no doubt run to Frankie, claiming Coy was having sex in the bathroom. Coy rolled her eyes at the thought. She'd had about all she could take today of dominant women.

Thankfully, the restroom wasn't busy, likely because everyone was getting ready for Monday night's slam poetry. Abi turned to face Coy the moment they were alone by the vanity. "Okay, now talk to me, playgirl."

Coy winced at the nickname her friends had dubbed her for as long as she remembered. It wasn't meant to be a dig, but tonight, it sort of felt like one. Was her playgirl label the reason Frankie had never trusted her enough to let down her many protective walls? Hell, Sawyer had practically called her that herself. To be fair, Coy had approached Sawyer in a club with the intention of giving her one night she'd never forget. In the past, it was all Coy had ever promised her lovers. It had suited her fine, but now?

A gush of air left Coy's lungs. "I dunno. I guess I'm noticing things I never have before," she admitted, peering into the mirror at Abi's reflection. It was easier to discuss heavier things when she wasn't actively looking someone dead on. She studied Abi's outfit, appreciating how the dress accentuated her curves.

Abi gave Coy a slight shove, joking, "Hate to break it to you, but you've been noticing me for years."

Coy smirked. "But can you really blame me?"

"Not at all, I'm hot." Abi fanned herself, and Coy snorted in amusement.

They were silent for some time, Coy gathering her thoughts and deciding what her issue was of late at the core. It all seemed to tie in with Sawyer somehow, and she said as much to Abi. "It bothers me that she doesn't like me. Especially since she's all I can think about." A sardonic laugh escaped, and she shook her head helplessly. "I don't even know if she's married, Abs. This woman is twisting me up, and I barely know anything about her. Just that she's loaded, and she owns a French fusion restaurant not far from where you live."

"Desmarais?" Abi wondered, excitement now in her eyes.

"Yeah, you know it? She gave me this after I changed her tire." McCoy pulled her wallet from her denims, fishing the coupon out for Abi to examine.

As Abi scanned the contents, her smile widened. Their gazes met. "Coy, we're gonna have fun with this."

"Are you getting out sometime today, or ...?" Sawyer asked the following morning, standing outside McCoy's Jeep with her arms crossed. One eyebrow went up in a *"Well, are you?"* notion before she turned and headed for the garage. Coy stared at the captivating sway of Sawyer's hips as she walked. This morning, she had dressed in a black hoodie and a sexy pair of matching running shorts that once again showed off enough leg to seriously question Coy's choices. What was she doing here after Sawyer had all but tossed her to the curb the week before? Was she that much of a masochist?

No, it was all about earning extra money to help her nana out. Well, that and the exotic beauty of a supercar sitting in Sawyer's garage. Coy was a mechanic and car lover; slipping hints of Coy possibly getting the chance to not only see one of the rare McLaren P1s up close but that she might actually get to rebuild one was practically catnip to car enthusiasts everywhere.

"Well, Tegan girl, wish me luck," Coy whispered, giving her first love an affectionate rub on the dash as she hopped out. As she noticed Sawyer standing inside the spacious garage with her arms crossed, the heady rush of anticipation that coiled Coy's stomach was new.

"Is this her?" Coy blurted out as she approached Sawyer. She was rocking back on her heels, brimming with excitement as she eyed the car hidden underneath a black covering. She grinned sheepishly, sending a quick prayer above to keep her cool this time around. For some reason, she couldn't stop becoming a bumbling idiot when she was within touching distance of the older woman.

"*Her*?" Sawyer deadpanned, casting Coy a speculative glance. She gestured to the car hidden underneath the covering. "Undress *her* gently, or you'll get hurt."

An awkward laugh escaped Coy. Maybe she had a sense of humor after all? "Sure thing," she agreed, giddily closing in on the McLaren. She glanced at Sawyer over her shoulder, and for a moment, she was thrown off by the brief look of pain on her face. Coy reached for the car's covering, pulling out the stretch elastic along the edges and filling the silence as she went. "Did you know there were only three hundred seventy-five P1ss ever made? In 2013, the advanced technology that went into this type of supercar was ahead of its time. Of course, now, other companies have followed suit and have been more than successful recreating the best parts of the P1 and making them their own."

"You sound like my husband."

Coy froze, canting her head Sawyer's way. Disappointment settled over her. "Husband?"

Of course, a beautiful, driven woman like Sawyer would have a husband. She probably had kids, too. *Maybe that's why she's in the closet.*

Sawyer turned away, rubbing her arms as if she were cold, and Coy would have stopped what she was doing if she thought Sawyer would be accepting of a hug. She didn't, and as she began pulling off the cover, she heard bitterness in Sawyer's husky voice. "Yes, except he would never believe there was a better car out there than his precious McLaren. He was an *esti d'cave.*"

"What the actual fuck?"

Coy's eyes bugged out as she revealed the supercar. The rapid tic in her throat felt like she was uncovering a corpse, not a car, and she hadn't quite reached the midway point when she stumbled backwards. "Is that blood?"

"Olivier's, yes."

Coy jumped at the sound of Sawyer's voice so close behind her. The hairs on the back of her neck prickled, and she couldn't look away from the caved in windshield and driver's seat for the life of her.

"I-I don't understand. Y-you want me to rebuild *this*?"

Sawyer clasped her hands together, watching Coy. She took a step closer, and Coy took an exaggerated step back until she was pressed against the tool chest. Sawyer's chuckle was dry, humorless. "I didn't kill him, if that's what you're thinking. What I really want to know is, are you capable of rebuilding a car like this?"

"I ... I am, yes, but ..." Coy trailed off, trying to understand what the hell was going on. "Why would you want to ... Wait, is your husband still alive?"

"No, I'm afraid not."

The disassociation in Sawyer's voice gave Coy chills. She darted her gaze back and forth between the car and the woman staring back at her. Sawyer seemed a lot less shaken than she should have been, considering. That was Coy's unprofessional opinion, of course. *She* felt like she might lose the breakfast sandwich she'd eaten before her arrival.

"Y-yet you want me to rebuild it? Sawyer, did he die in this car?"

Sawyer waved her hand as if the question was inconsequential. "Yes. I've been wanting it rebuilt for some time but haven't found anyone worth hiring. Until you."

"Worth" hiring? Coy didn't believe that for a second. It felt an awful lot like Sawyer had a vendetta against Coy, and setting her in front of her poor husband's deathmobile was a payback of sorts. For what, she didn't know. Surely a little harmless flirting wasn't the equivalent of scaring the bejeezus out of someone?

Coy's head was spinning. She chanced another look at the car again. One entire side of the car would need to be rebuilt. Two of the tires were twisted off, the engine likely a goner. And she wasn't entirely convinced of Sawyer's sanity. Coy had gotten involved before with a lesbian that hadn't been a hundred percent, and let's just say it wasn't something she was eager to have a repeat of. "Um, like, my mind is blown right now. Can we maybe talk about this outside?"

Coy all but ran outside, taking long pulls of fresh air into her lungs. She wasn't being blasé at all, which was embarrassing, but she couldn't help it. Something about this whole thing seemed off.

"You seem troubled, McCoy."

Coy stopped pacing and turned to look at Sawyer, at her calm features. Coy's hands rubbed the back of her neck as she stood there, not knowing what to think. "Sawyer, I've rebuilt cars before, even ones from accidents, but none where a person died in it. They send those cars to the junkyard."

"And I want this one rebuilt to its former glory. I won't stand here and rehash all the reasons with you, McCoy," Sawyer bit out, setting her cold eyes on McCoy. "I have money, lots of it. If you're up to the task, you'll be paid handsomely for it."

Handsomely? Who spoke like that? Coy shook her head in confusion. "So buy a new one. Do you know how expensive it'll be to repair a car like this? We're talking almost a complete restoration, Sawyer."

"Do you question all your customers until they decide to go elsewhere?"

"What you're asking me to do is ..."

"Crazy? It's only crazy when you're not seeing the full picture."

Coy nodded, agreeing with her there. She clasped her hands together. "Okay, so give it to me. Explain why this needs to happen."

"No." The hardness in Sawyer's voice made Coy's head snap up to look at her. She was glaring again, her angular jaw clenched so hard it was a wonder her teeth didn't break under the pressure. "I'm offering your father's company a lucrative job. If you take it, this will be the last conversation we'll have about the McLaren. You'll either accept my conditions or walk away."

Coy swallowed, confused by her body's reaction to Sawyer's. Even when she was downright hateful, Coy couldn't stop the intense attraction she felt for the older woman. "What conditions?"

Sawyer stepped closer to Coy until they were almost touching. Then she reached into her purse and pulled out another slip of paper. Coy's eyes widened. "Is that a … contract?"

Sawyer nodded once, just a jerk of her pretty head. The side part in her hair hardly swayed with the movement. Their eyes met, and as usual, Coy felt as if she was caught up in the turbulence of storms. "Take some time to read it over. My number is on the bottom. You can text me if you have questions or when you've made a decision. I work a lot of hours, so most of the time that you're here, you'll be alone. I'll be letting you into the garage only via a smart app."

"Excuse me, what? Pops won't go for that. The business isn't insured for off-site projects." Coy's cheeks heated at going toe to toe with Sawyer.

Sawyer only shrugged. "Then work for me on your own time. I don't care, but the car stays in my garage. Like I said, I won't be here for most of the time but will still be able to keep an eye on things with my surveillance from time to time."

Coy scanned the contract. It was basic, to the point. No stealing, no recording of the process, commit to six days a week, be punctual, but contact Sawyer if she can't make it for some reason. Coy fought the urge to roll her eyes when she noticed that Sawyer had written in three different areas—and underlined them—that Coy was not to flirt with her.

Like we'd even see each other much.

"I'd have to work early mornings. Like, early early." Coy glanced up at Sawyer, explaining, "I work at the shop at nine, and in the evenings—"

Sawyer held up her hand, silencing Coy just as she'd done in the shop. It should be an infuriating trait Coy hated, but she didn't. At all. In fact, a flush of warmth spread over her each time Sawyer's assertiveness sprung forth.

"That's not an issue. I'm awake by five and leave for work by eight."

Coy nodded. *Am I actually considering this?*

Not having her breathing down Coy's neck could be a positive thing, and she needed the money for her nana. She licked her lips, aware of the subtle drop of Sawyer's eyes as she did so. Was this contract for Coy's benefit or Sawyer's? Whichever it was, Coy had a feeling she was already in way over her head.

Wait 'til Abs finds out about this.

Chapter 9

Sawyer

"Sawyer, it's good to see you," her doctor rushed to say as he closed the door to the exam room. Dr. Cooper was a tall, lean, middle-aged man with an early onset of fine white hairs that he kept cut low to his scalp. He'd been Sawyer's family doctor for almost as long as she'd lived in B.C., and she trusted him.

"Yes, well ..." Sawyer pointedly checked her wristwatch for the time before clasping her hands together. She leveled her gaze at him. "We're both busy people, George, so I'd appreciate it if you didn't waste both our time by beating around the bush."

"Straight to the point as always. You're not even going to let me ask how Bree is? Alia says they've been keeping in touch." Dr. Cooper smiled, but not unkindly. He pulled up a chair and sat down, a yellow folder already in his hands.

Sawyer laced her fingers together over her knee, proud of herself when only the faintest sigh left her lips. This was the issue with knowing your doctor outside of the exam room. *And our daughters meeting at the same private school.* "She's well, thank you. And Alia?"

"She's great. She actually just flew home for the summer break last week."

"Fantastic." Sawyer squeezed her fingers together, needing something to distract her other than the time ticking by on the wall clock.

"I know you're anxious to get going," Dr. Cooper chuckled, "so tell me. What have you been doing to reduce your stress since the last time we spoke?"

Sawyer could have groaned. *Not this again.* "What you suggested I do. Take Sundays off, relax in a bath, and do yoga."

Okay, so technically, her bath typically involved wine, and her yoga consisted of stretching before her daily morning run, but who had time for an involved yoga session? Running *was* her relaxation.

"What about changes to your diet?"

"Sure. I'm limiting the sugar." Truth was, there wasn't much Sawyer *wasn't* limiting these days. Nausea was an ever-present dragon to be bested.

Dr. Cooper jotted notes down in Sawyer's file. "And how much sleep would you say you're getting each night?"

Sawyer huffed, not liking where this conversation was leading. George should know her well enough to respect that some conversations were off-limits. She checked her watch again, not having time for this. "I get enough, George. Now please, don't we have something other than my day-to-day to cross-examine?"

Dr. Cooper studied her, wariness clouding his features. Sawyer tracked his movements, watching as he raised his hand to pinch the bridge of his nose between his fingers. He seemed pretty stressed himself, but Sawyer didn't comment on it. Silence stretched out in the small space as the doctor looked over Sawyer's file, and as the seconds ticked by, the pulse in Sawyer's throat began a steadily increasing *thump-thump*.

"Well?" she prodded, gesturing to the file with a flick of her wrist.

"Your blood test came back showing elevated levels in your cholesterol. On account of this, I'd like to begin treating it with statin meds." Dr. Cooper glanced up from his notes to look at her. "And if it's alright with you, I'd like to arrange for you to have a stress test done."

"A stress test," Sawyer repeated, trying the words out. What would that entail? "Would it be in the office here? I can't miss more work because I have to travel across the city."

"It would be with a specialist. I'll refer you. And Sawyer, this is the kind of thing you'll want to miss work for. It's important. Work isn't the only thing in life, you know?" The sympathy in Dr. Cooper's eyes was too much. Sawyer couldn't take it, and she ripped her gaze from his, but still, he continued. What was with everyone in her life overstepping? "Alia told me Bree often posts beach pictures on Instagram. Have you thought of going on vacation at some point? You could go and see her. After losing Olivier, and before that, losing—"

"That's enough." Sawyer jumped to her feet, shooting him a glare before she hastily shoved her arms into her raincoat. Her hands shook slightly as she snatched her purse from the floor. "Refer me wherever you need to, but I have to go now."

"Sawyer, wait—"

"Bye for now," Sawyer interrupted, a forced smile gracing her lips as she walked past him and left the exam room. She kept her head held high as she passed the reception desk, and it wasn't until she'd enclosed herself inside the elevator that she let herself truly breathe again.

"Merde," she whispered into the silence. Her back pressed against the elevator wall, and she leaned into it, letting the added support hold her up.

A good routine was a must for someone like Sawyer. It was predictable, safe. She liked knowing where she and everyone else were supposed to be and when. Predictability and structure had given her a semblance of power in a life where she had so often felt helpless. Living with Olivier, she'd learned over time what made him tick, what caused him to explode, and her rigid routine each day helped thwart most of the impending aftermath.

Unfortunately, her desperate need for control eventually became so extreme that the simplest wrench in her schedule could sometimes throw her entire day off.

"And how much sleep would you say you're getting each night?"

What a joke. Two or three hours if she was lucky, five on Saturday nights if she took a sleeping aid before going to bed. For years, she'd been haunted by *that* night, and frankly, some things were better remembered in the dead silence of an empty house.

Some people.

"... You could go and see her. After losing Olivier, and before that losing—"

"God, pull it together," Sawyer brokenly whispered, squeezing her eyes shut as the hot shower water pelted over her face. A sob escaped from the crushing weight in her heart. She pressed her hand over the spot, trying to lessen the agony threatening to capsize her.

She turned away from the water, leaning her forehead against the slick tiled wall as she cried. Fucking days like today. Sawyer loathed them with a passion, hated how off-balance and hormonal they made her. It was times like now when she struggled the most to keep the past where it belonged.

Her other hand rested against her stomach as if wishing for her pregnancy would suddenly bring back what she'd lost. Turbulent images of her life fifteen years ago mocked her, cutting her so deeply it was like it was happening all over again. Sawyer moaned, sinking to the shower floor. She pulled her knees against her chest and cried her heart out.

Snot and tears mixed with the water raining down on her, but she didn't notice. She was a prisoner of a different time, lost, just like all her could-have-beens.

"Chef, you wanna check this before it goes out?"

Sawyer blinked, slowly peering down at the *blanquette de veau* and *tarte pine aux pommes* in front of her. Heading to table eight and thirteen. Right. She cleared her throat, reaching for her towel to tidy up the caramel sauce. "Good." She nodded to Amber, one of her part-time servers, and flicked her wrist to send the young woman out front.

Sawyer was off her game tonight. Not enough to be noticeable, she hoped, but the lack of her usual precision to detail was nagging at her. Fatigue had her shoulders drooping and her brain cells sizzling like a steak left on the grill too long. Between her episode that morning and her inability to think of little else than Dr. Cooper's planned stress test, she was ready to throw in the towel. Sawyer pulled at her collar, the heat in the kitchen too much tonight.

She snatched the incoming chit from the machine, always a few seconds late this shift, and hollered, "Four orders of *fèves au lard* all day with mustard pickles OTS!"

"Heard that, Chef!" Barb returned.

"How's the *bouillabaisse* coming for twenty-six?"

"Less than a minute, Chef. I've got about five more servings, and then we'll have to stretch it," Leon said behind the seafood line.

"Stretch it out now. No sense waiting."

"Copy that, Chef."

Tristan, a new hire for the floor, appeared by Sawyer's side. "Chef, a customer is asking about what's included in these coupons. It's the first time I've seen them, but it looks like your signature on the bottom."

Sawyer examined the two vouchers, paying special attention to the grease smudge on one corner. McCoy's face instantly came to mind, and she bet if she sniffed the slips in Tristan's hand, they'd carry a hint of her cologne.

She wrinkled her nose. Why would she think of *that*?

McCoy hadn't given Sawyer an answer yet regarding the McLaren, and Sawyer was curious to see who would accompany her to an upscale French fusion restaurant like Desmarais. Honestly, she had expected McCoy to give the vouchers away. She didn't strike Sawyer as the fine dining type.

"Barb, cover the line!" she called to her sous-chef, removing her apron. To Tristan, she took the vouchers from him and said, "Which table?"

"Um, thirty-four, Chef."

"Thank you. I can take their order, Tristan. Check back when their meal is ready to go out. In the meantime, go change your shirt. You've spilled sauce down the front. Any one of those customers out there could be a food critic."

Tristan examined his black dress shirt like he was seeing the stain for the first time before his gaze darted up to Sawyer's again. "U-understood, Chef," he stammered and scurried from the kitchen.

Sawyer paused just inside the front house and took a breath. She always had to screw her head on a little tighter and focus when she greeted customers. Heads often turned, as if people in the dining area had never seen a chef approach a table before. And, well, interpersonal skills weren't Sawyer's strong suit. She held her chin up proudly and forced her feet to move, but in reality, her knees quaked, and her entire posture felt unbalanced.

McCoy had a deuce seater corner table, not too far from the bar, so Sawyer was able to use that to her advantage. Instead of flouncing right out in the middle of the restaurant where everyone could see her, she got within earshot first.

"You look happy, Abs. Settled."

McCoy's smooth voice rushed over Sawyer, doing wonders to excite and annoy her at the same time. She didn't know why, but there was something about McCoy that made Sawyer's pulse work harder when she was around.

"I am. Life is falling into place, Coy. Tess's ..."

Sawyer drowned out the other woman's voice, focusing only on the nickname she had for McCoy. So, the mechanic didn't go by her full name all the time? *Interesting*. Sawyer wondered who had the privilege of calling her Coy. Friends, or was it a pet name reserved for lovers?

What is wrong with you? Get your head in the game! Two stars, remember? Sawyer took a deep breath, exhaling as she stepped past the plant and came into view.

"Cheers to that, babe," McCoy was saying, and Sawyer watched as she raised her wine glass to toast the other woman. "Abs", as McCoy called her, was a gorgeous woman with stunning glacier-blue eyes and caramel-highlighted light brown hair. She looked closer to Bree's age than McCoy's and light years younger than Sawyer felt on the best of days. She didn't know why but seeing her smiling and giggling with McCoy made Sawyer's stomach clench.

She approached their table, standing tall with her hands folded behind her back, and cleared her throat. "Good evening."

McCoy's mouth dropped open when she noticed her. "Sawyer!" She was handsomely dressed in a black buttoned short-sleeved dress shirt with red suspenders. If there was one thing Sawyer could say about the younger woman, it was that she certainly had an eye-catching, eccentric style. Her body art covered one whole arm, and on the other, it looked like just an upper half sleeve. Sawyer's gaze lowered, observing McCoy's black cargo shorts and the large tattoo covering most of her muscular calf. Decorative socks were pulled up as far as they could go. Handmade bracelets adorned both wrists. Quite a different look from her usual work attire.

Sawyer glanced back and forth between McCoy and her mysterious friend, finally narrowing her eyes on the mechanic. "You had a question for me?"

McCoy visibly gulped, like she was trying to draw in all the air in the room. "Ah, um ... uh-huh," she stammered, staring up at Sawyer with a pair of widened, pretty green eyes. Her chiseled jaw was slack as if merely looking at Sawyer made speech impossible. An intriguing dusting of blush stained her cheeks. The striking red bowtie fastened around her neck obscured any rosy skin underneath, but Sawyer imagined it was as arousing as the display before her now. She could admit this—she very much enjoyed a frazzled McCoy. There was nothing like putting cockiness in its place.

"Coy and I were wondering what you recommend at Desmarais," Abs smoothly cut in, making Sawyer bristle. Abs shot McCoy an amused smirk before giving Sawyer a wide smile and tilting the menu closer. Pointing to the one dish most customers inexperienced with a French menu ordered, she said, "I was thinking of trying *ratatouille* since it was always a childhood curiosity of mine, but what do you recommend, Chef Lavoie?"

Oof, she was a smooth talker; Sawyer could tell already. It was hard to hate a woman who came off so friendly. Not to mention, she memorized Sawyer's last name just to use it later in conversation.

Sawyer relaxed a little, admitting, "*Ratatouille* is excellent. Rich and flavorful, but I suppose it depends on what you're in the mood for." Her gaze returned to the second woman at the table, watching the moment McCoy realized she had an audience. Perverse enjoyment filtered through Sawyer when McCoy almost knocked her wine glass over. She sniggered, turning back to her enchanting guest. Scanning the menu momentarily, Sawyer pointed out a few of the more popular options.

"Desmarais's *bouillabaisse* soup is our most popular right now, as most of our fish come fresh from the market each day. Or if you're craving stew, then Barb makes the best *blanquette de veau* this side of the Pacific." She paused, adding, "If simple and wholesome is on the menu tonight, my version of the *Québécois tourtière* should hit the spot."

"Tor-tortei what?" McCoy sputtered, perking up in her chair like Sawyer had offered her the keys to her house. It was hard to concentrate on anything except the exhilarating way McCoy was watching her. She looked willing to do anything, even get on her knees for Sawyer right in the middle of the restaurant.

Where did that come from? she thought, clearing her throat. Sawyer repeated in a thick voice, "*Tourtière*. It's a meat pie. Savory, double-crusted—"

"Sold," McCoy cut in, a silly grin on her face now. Somehow, she managed to be both annoying and endearing.

"I'll have Barb's specialty," Abs added, smiling up at Sawyer. "Thanks for coming out here. Coy hasn't stopped talking about the project she'll be helping you with."

This was news to Sawyer. McCoy hadn't bothered to contact her after their meeting the day before. She hated being the last to know things and couldn't stop the scowl from appearing as she eyed the handsome butch. "Is that right? So, you've decided you can follow the stipulations I've laid out?"

McCoy visibly swallowed, and Sawyer silently acknowledged the thrill she got from the submissive action. That was good. If they were going to be spending time together, there could only be one boss. It sure as hell wouldn't be a young player with a *look at me* bow tie around her neck.

"Erm, well, I mean. I've been told I flirt with my nana, sooo ..." A gust of air left McCoy, and she blushed for the second time in five minutes. That had to be a record. "I might not know the difference. But I promise not to hit on you. Intentionally, I mean. Unless you want me to." She clamped a hand over her mouth, glaring at her friend's fit of laughter from across the table.

Sawyer scoffed at the ridiculous reply. Even nervous, McCoy couldn't seem to help the crap that came out of her mouth. "To be clear, McCoy, I *never* want you to hit on me. If you're going to be working for me, that's all that'll be happening between us. *Comprendre*?" With McCoy's nod of agreement, Sawyer glanced between them once more. "Good then. Enjoy your meal."

As she walked away from their table, she heard the roar of Abs' laughter as she reprimanded her friend. "You told her you hit on your nana?"

Sawyer smirked. She'd thoroughly enjoyed that part as well.

Chapter 10

McCoy

"Hey, hey, sorry I'm late. Did I miss much?" Coy wondered, slowly lowering herself into the armchair beside her father's old recliner. Her muscles protested with the effort, but she sighed the moment her ass molded into the plush seat.

"Bo just got hit while up at bat," Sloane supplied from her place on the sofa. Watching the Sunday baseball game with their dad had been a tradition of theirs for years, and one Coy made happen no matter what else she had going on.

"The Jays are playing strong, but the Yankees are always one step faster today," Greg added excitedly. He reached into the cooler beside his chair, pulling out a beer for Coy. "'K, it's back on."

Coy turned her attention to the sixty-five-inch flat screen on the wall. She'd bought it for his fiftieth birthday the year before. Sloane had bought him a new recliner, but he'd loved his old one too much to give it up. The new one was currently sitting in their apartment, and there was a constant battle between their friends about who would sit there.

"Whoa, Vladdy baby is on fire!" Sloane commented to no one in particular, one hand digging into her bowl of popcorn. Vladimir Guerrero Jr had been her favorite player since he'd joined the roster in 2019.

Coy sipped her beer, her attention to the game taking a back seat as the McLaren, and by proxy, Sawyer came to mind. She couldn't imagine keeping something her loved one had died in. It didn't matter if it was an exotic car or a thousand-dollar bed she'd bought at Sleep Country. If death touched it, that shit was gone. Goosebumps broke out on her arms just thinking about the McLaren. Sawyer had acted so aloof about the whole thing. Was it because the accident happened a long time ago, or was there something Coy was missing?

"So did you sign the paperwork for the car job?" Greg asked during the next commercial break. He shifted in the recliner, giving Coy his full attention.

"No, not until I see her tomorrow. Why—do you not think I should? She won't hire me otherwise, Pops." *Not with that level of obsession with contracts,* Coy snickered to herself.

"Who is this?"

Coy glanced at her sister again. "Her name is Sawyer—the woman from the warehouse, remember? I told you about the flat tire."

"Pause, game's back on," Greg told them, all business. Coy sighed, reining in her impatience. Her father was as hardcore as fans got. He had his Blue Jays jersey and cap on, and it wasn't unheard of for him to occasionally jump from his seat and yell at the TV. "It's not a bad idea. I just wanna make sure you're able to commit to that contract. It'd take up way more time than you're used to, Coy," he said a bit later. "But man, luck must have been on your side when you said you were looking for extra work this summer."

Coy agreed, and then her father wanted a refresher rundown of the kind of work the McLaren needed. It took the entire commercial break, so she had to wait until the following one to reel in her dad's attention again. "Since I have to rebuild it there, do you think an industrial lift would fit in? I haven't measured the ceiling height or door clearance, but it looks like a standard two-car garage."

Greg considered that for a moment, stroking his short goatee like he did when he was in deep thought. He had the same hair color and similar eyes as she and Sloane. "What about a scissor lift, just to be sure? It's small, and you can move it back and forth with a dolly. They usually hold three tons or more. And then you can buy car dollies to roll the McLaren over to the lift. Just buy an attachment that supports the caliper where the rims are missing. She's paying for it all, right?"

"That's what she said." Coy nodded. She hadn't thought of a scissor lift, which was just one of many reasons she loved talking things out with her dad; he was always a fountain of information. "Great idea. Think you could help me get it on the lift when the time comes?"

"I was hoping you'd ask." Greg laughed his big belly laugh. Talking shop was the only thing that excited him more than sports. "If this Sawyer woman gives the okay, I'd love to get a good look under the hood. We could take J.D. along."

"Okay, game's back on, *boys*," Sloane drawled. She didn't share the same love of engines. If it wasn't for Coy, her sister's red T-top Trans Am wouldn't even have a name. Coy shuddered at the thought. "Sara" had been named the same day she'd named Tegan.

They watched the final inning with minor interruptions. Coy still had Sawyer on her mind, but now it was back at Desmarais and how gorgeous she'd looked in her chef's uniform. Coy had been shocked stupid when Sawyer approached their table, looking sexy and confident and truly boss-like. Conversing over menu options had gone well until Abi let it slip that Coy planned to take the job. Sawyer had clearly been thrown with that tidbit. Her eyes had widened seconds before narrowing to slits on Coy. She wasn't someone who enjoyed surprises, and a part of Coy had felt guilty.

For once, she wanted to do something Sawyer was okay with, and it wasn't merely the insane attraction she felt making her feel this way. She wanted to know things, details she'd never wondered about before. What made Sawyer smile? Did she love being a chef? Was she as passionate about her job as Coy was with hers? What kind of food did she like? Coy could learn a lot about a person by knowing those answers.

Setting her empty beer bottle on the coffee table, Coy dug her phone out and pulled up Sawyer's number, which she'd already added to her contacts. It felt strange to soon be working alone on Sawyer's property when they'd barely said a civil word to each other. Or rather, Sawyer hadn't said as much to *her*. Coy's thumb hovered over the SMS box as she hesitated, wondering what was on Sawyer's "safe list" of questions to ask. But Sawyer had said to text if she had some, so there was that. If Coy could think of some that didn't include the *whys* or *WTFs* concerning the supercar, she should be golden.

Coy pulled up a new SMS under Sawyer's name, deep in thought. She had a feeling she could ask the simplest of questions, such as the color of the sky, and Sawyer would tell her to lose her number. But what if Coy supplied facts rather than asked them?

Only one way to find out.

Coy: Hi, it's me, McCoy. You never requested a background check or anything so I thought I'd fill you in on a few things about me. In case you have nosey neighbors or something LOL. 1. I was arrested once at a protest but the charges never stuck. 2. I listen to a lot of gay music and audiobooks while I work, sometimes without headphones in. 3. Dogs love me. You've been forewarned! If your neighbor has one, chances are I'll get acquainted with them or their human. And 4. You make the best food I've ever tasted.

Coy chewed her thumbnail, her stomach in knots as she waited for Sawyer to reply. After five minutes, her attention waned, and she was sucked back into the game. It wasn't for another hour before she heard the ping of her phone.

Sassy Sawyer: Random, and nothing to do with the job. Typical Gen Z.

The corner of Coy's mouth quirked up. Such a Sawyer thing to say.

"I think we've got it, kiddo." Greg grunted as they gave the McLaren one final push onto the lift.

"Ah, it's looking gooood, Pops," Coy exclaimed, dashing to shove the gearshift into park as soon as the car was in place. She let out an excited laugh, rushing back to her father's side. They bumped fists before Coy clapped him on the back. "Let's get the blocks on."

"It's too bad J.D. couldn't make it," Greg commented, tossing her a tire block. While he'd been at the shop that morning, Coy had to come early to Sawyer's to accept the lift delivery. As soon as Miller's Mechanics & Restoration closed at noon, her dad had found his way here. The only hiccup so far was forgetting to give Sawyer a heads-up that the delivery was coming earlier than planned. It ... hadn't gone over well.

"J.D. took off with Sloane to Squamish," Coy muttered, squatting to slip the protective mats in place under the McLaren. "Sloane's a little put out that I took a side job when biking is picking up now. The trails are getting nicer every weekend."

"Well, I've always said, twin or not, you can't do everything together. You always go out on the trails with Sloane," Greg reminded her. Once the car was secured, they walked over to the hydraulic controls.

"I know. I'm not doing it to piss her off. I just think this job could be a great opportunity." Not to mention she'd get to see a lot more of Sawyer. Nothing wrong with that. Nothing at all. "It doesn't help that we usually work opposite shifts."

"Might be good to schedule time next week, though. Sloane's cut from a different cloth than you, McCoy. She doesn't do well alone." It wasn't anything Coy hadn't heard before, but the reminder dulled her grand mood anyway.

"Did you read the instructions?"

Coy nodded, glancing down at the plate fastened to the top of the control system. For a few grand, the lift was remarkably handy. While it'd been bought on Sawyer's dime, McCoy wondered if, by the end of this, she could sweet talk her into having it. Based on the fact she was paying to have the McLaren rebuilt rather than scrapped, Sawyer likely threw away money like it was nothing. "Watch and learn, Pops." She heard him chuckle as she pressed the locking mechanism. Then she pressed up. It took a moment for the gears to shift into place before the machine began to lift.

"So, this is what's got you two cackling like fools out here," Sawyer said from the doorway. Coy glanced over her shoulder with a grin, but Sawyer looked unimpressed. "I could hear you from the kitchen. Thought Tim the Tool Man was in the house."

Coy furrowed her brow. "Tim the Tool Man?" But her father gave Sawyer a good-natured laugh.

"I loved that show!"

"I'm so excited," Sawyer drolly replied, sounding anything but, "to have *two* McCoy's in my house."

"Puh-lease, he wishes he was as cool as me." Coy snorted a laugh when her dad popped her on the shoulder. He was so easy to razz. Once Sawyer had gone back into the house, Greg nudged her.

"She's pretty, Coy."

Coy wrinkled her nose. "You're being gross. And we're not an item."

"You think she's gross?"

Groaning, Coy covered her face with one hand, trying to block out him *and* his embarrassing questions. "What? No. Sawyer's gorgeous. You're gross for bringing it up."

Greg scratched his goatee, humor shining in his hazel eyes. "I think she likes you."

Coy started the lift again, shaking her head. "God, please don't tell her I think she's attractive. I know when a woman likes me, and that's not it."

"We'll see."

She shook her head at his need to always have the last word. Their banter could go for hours if she didn't cave now. She tilted her head toward the McLaren and moved her hand to the release button on the control panel. "Lift is working well." They watched the car lower back to the floor. Coy was eager to get started on the disassembling process. It was only then she'd know what she needed for parts.

"Want to stay and help?"

"I'd love to, kiddo, but Miranda is coming over tonight. I'm cooking."

"Ahh, nice. I really like her dad." Coy smiled.

"Yeah, she's pretty amazing, isn't she?" Greg agreed. Coy walked him out to the driveway, watching as he climbed into his truck. It rumbled to life before Greg glanced at her out the window, "Hey, want me to bring you some supper later?"

Coy waved him off. "Not unless you're taking your honey out for a drive. I won't be blamed for getting between you and Miranda." Greg let out a sly chuckle, raising his arm on a wave and driving off.

Coy headed back into the garage, still smiling a little as she set up her Bluetooth headphones. A moment later, her current sapphic audiobook came on. She'd read the ebook version of *The Stepmother* by Melissa Tereze a while ago, but listening to the sexy British narrator just hit differently. Melissa was one of Coy's favorite indie authors. She wrote sex scenes so steamy Coy had no choice but to reenact a few of them. To make sure they were realistic, of course.

Earlier, Coy had done a thorough walk around the McLaren, taking notice of the extensive exterior damage. The roof and windshield were semi-caved in, the former likely due to the car rolling. Without removing anything that hadn't already broken off on impact, she could tell two rotors were cracked, one rim twisted right off its axle. The suspension or control arm behind it was likely damaged. The spoiler hadn't been engaged at the time, so it might have survived the accident. The firefighters must have had to cut off the door, and the frame rail had taken the brunt of the damage. Both front fenders would need replacing, but there was the possibility of having to order a new tub that would be costly.

Today, Coy wanted to at least get started on removing what was left of the windshield and vacuuming the car out before she left. But first came the wipers. Using her ratchet attachment, she removed the wiper arms and cowl panel. The panel was still in good condition, but the wiper arms had been bent.

As Coy moved on to cutting out the frame of the windshield, it was hard not to think of Sawyer's husband. She'd never been so personally involved in salvaging a car before. It felt intimate, knowing the few details she did. The aged blood stains on the microsuede steering wheel and dash were distracting, and she kept wondering just how the accident had happened.

When that was done and she'd set the remnants off to the side, Coy plugged in the Shop Vac she had brought and got started on cleaning out the interior. She was halfway done when she nicked her thumb on a piece of broken door jamb.

"Fuck," Coy shut the vacuum off and squeezed her thumb, looking for glass inside the seeping wound. There likely wasn't any, given how modern windshields were made, but Coy grabbed the First Aid kit she always kept inside Tegan's glove compartment. She was applying a Band-Aid when Sawyer entered, dressed like she was heading out the door again. Unfortunately, the audiobook she was listening to was about five minutes into her favorite sex scene. Sawyer's eyes widened just a fraction, no doubt catching the way the narrator's husky voice pronounced the word pussy. She came to an abrupt stop at the foot of the stairs, one hand clenching the railing like her life depended on it. A hint of a blush darkened her beautiful cheeks.

Then Sawyer noticed the drying blood on Coy's hand. "Cut yourself already?" she demanded, her voice at a higher octave than normal. "Are you even up to this task? Tell me now so I can put my money elsewhere."

"Believe me, I'm up to the task." The reply wasn't supposed to sound seductive, but unfortunately, it was how Coy's brain took the assignment. She inwardly groaned, watching as Sawyer's back went rigid.

One, two, thr—

"Do I need to post copies of the contract around my property?" Sawyer gritted through clenched teeth. Wow, the woman really didn't appreciate come-ons, even unintentional ones. "Here's an idea, Casanova. How about instead of practicing your ridiculous one-liners, you memorize this look of disinterest on my face? And turn that noise off. I don't need my neighbors thinking I'm watching porn."

Disinterested my ass, Coy thought, her mouth tilting up in one corner as she went to switch off the audiobook. She'd seen the gleam in Sawyer's eyes at the restaurant. There was *something* she liked about Coy, whether she knew it yet or not. She opened her mouth with every intention of correcting Sawyer's use of the name Casanova, considering it was a term reserved for a man, but that wasn't what came out.

"You hold an awful lot of judgment for someone you don't really know. If you want, I could change that for you."

Unbridled surprise flooded Sawyer for about two seconds before her features went blank once again. "Haven't you been spamming me with unsolicited info about you for six days now?" One eyebrow raised with the question, and Coy thought she saw a hint of a smirk on Sawyer's face as she held up her phone in reference. "You like dogs, have terrible taste in music, and would rather spend your savings on your car than go to Europe. Really, McCoy, I know more about you than I ever needed or wanted to."

Coy's whole body flushed with heat, and she shifted uncomfortably on her feet. She'd been called out, and damn, Sawyer was hot when she challenged her. Coy responded to Sawyer like she used to with her grade ten math teacher, only the allure was a hundred times more powerful.

"I like you. I don't know why, considering you don't give me the time of day." Coy cracked a grin, darting a quick glance at Sawyer before looking away again. Her heart thudded in her chest so loud she was almost certain Sawyer could hear it. She swallowed. "I like the way I feel when I'm around you."

Silence permeated the garage. The air felt charged now, and it crackled with unseen tension after Coy's admission. She slowly lifted her gaze to where Sawyer remained on the garage steps, an inscrutable expression staring back at her.

"Well," Sawyer stated after a moment. She cleared her throat, and Coy watched as she marched to her Range Rover. "Lock up when you're done."

"Have a great day, Sawyer," Coy told her, raising a hand in an awkward side-to-side wave.

"Ahem, yes. You as well, McCoy."

And then Sawyer was in her SUV, driving out of the open garage and away from Coy.

"Smooth, Coy. Real smooth," she muttered to the empty room.

Chapter 11

Sawyer

Sawyer: *Comment ça va, mon amour?* I'm about to bake your favorite dish this morning.

Sawyer smiled softly, rereading the SMS before pressing Send. Her hand fluttered to her chest as she thought of her daughter so far away. She'd been in San Francisco for over a year, and Sawyer hadn't made the time to visit.

I need to change that. There had to be a way to have the restaurant succeed and still take a week off to fly to California.

Without sacrificing those stars you want so much? Doubtful, a voice niggled at her.

Sighing, Sawyer set her phone down and picked up her cooling mug of coffee instead. As she took a sip, she glanced around the empty kitchen. It was peaceful here this early at Desmarais. It would be another hour until Kelly arrived, and Sawyer enjoyed the solitude. Now that she was short a pastry chef, there was an extra workload, but it was nothing Sawyer hadn't dealt with before. After twenty-three years, she'd seen more than enough Dustins of the world that firing one didn't faze her one bit. Running a respectable restaurant was crucial, not just for the restaurant's long-term success, but to her personally. It had always been a sign that, over the years, no matter what awful thing was happening in Sawyer's life, hearing how wonderful Desmarais was always made her feel better.

Sawyer washed her hands and set about baking Bree's beloved *pouding chômeur*, a simple, maple-based cake anyone could make. It was all about the quality of the ingredients that went into it and the delicate balance of slowly combining and alternating the dry mix and the milk with the rest of the wet ingredients. As biased as it might be, Sawyer refused to use anything other than real Québec maple syrup in her recipe. Come to think of it, perhaps that was why Bree had so much trouble making it. *She was missing a touch of home.*

Once the batter was well mixed, Sawyer used a heavy ladle to pour it all into waiting pans. When most of it was out, she picked up the oversized mixing bowl and scraped the remaining batter into the pans as well, smoothing everything out before putting each one in the oven.

Sawyer heaved a sigh, blowing a strand of her dark hair free from her vision. Her chest rose and fell harder than it usually did after carrying the trays and lugging the flour bin around.

"Certainly not in your twenties anymore, are you?" she muttered, taking a long drink from her stainless-steel water bottle. Her eyes drifted closed as the cool liquid trickled down her throat. She sighed again, this time in contentment. She wasn't in her thirties anymore either, she mused. What was a young thing like McCoy Miller doing chasing her? Sawyer shook her head, her gaze landing on the edge of the island where she'd left her phone. It didn't make a lick of sense.

Their strange interaction Saturday before Sawyer had gone to work had been at the forefront of her mind. The things McCoy had said, the odd tingle of anticipation and longing Sawyer felt at hearing them. It was ... peculiar. What's more, when she'd finally fallen asleep the last two nights, it hadn't been her usual nightmares. It had been of McCoy—or more specifically, McCoy's mouth on Sawyer's, her strong hands parting Sawyer's thighs ... Sawyer had woken that morning slick with arousal, the memory of McCoy's lustful green gaze staring up at her while her lips and tongue were buried in her sex.

Sawyer flushed with the reminder. Oral pleasure wasn't something she had a lot of experience with. And she'd never once climaxed from it. Sex with her husband had been an uncomfortable experience at the best of times, and earlier in their marriage, Olivier had made it abundantly clear he had never enjoyed giving oral.

How do I know my next partner won't think the same? Or that I won't feel just as uncomfortable?

It was one of many worries Sawyer had. Not dating took care of the issue easily enough.

Curious about how McCoy was doing alone in her garage, Sawyer pulled up the surveillance feed on her phone. It was closing in on eight thirty, so it was possible the younger woman had already left for her day job. To Sawyer's surprise, McCoy was leaning against Olivier's old workbench with the phone pressed close to her ear. Sawyer glanced at the McLaren. McCoy had got several parts off in just the six or so hours she'd been there over the last two days. The work area appeared clean now, as if McCoy was getting ready to leave her house.

"Who is so important that she'd risk being late for work?" Sawyer mused aloud. Glancing around her spacious kitchen at Desmarais to make sure she was still alone, curiosity got the best of her, and she unmuted the video.

McCoy's smooth lilt immediately floated over Sawyer, doing weird things to her insides. "Stop that," she scolded her traitorous body and scowled into her phone.

"Aww, you know I'm never too busy to talk to my favorite woman," McCoy practically cooed into her phone.

Sawyer's hackles rose with the obvious affection in McCoy's voice, and she had to release the tight grip she had on her cell. *Who* was McCoy talking to? Just how many women did she have?

"I'm sorry I haven't been over. How about I come Friday after work? I could stay the night," McCoy continued into the phone, now toying with her car keys as she talked. Not an ounce of stress or impatience emanated from her body.

"She works for her father. No wonder she's not worried about being late," Sawyer huffed, unsure if she was more annoyed at that fact or watching—and hearing—McCoy sweet talk some naive woman right in front of her.

Sawyer's throat flushed as realization kicked in. *She* was the one invading McCoy's privacy. *God, I'm spying on a private conversation. What is wrong with me?*

Clarity snapped her out of it, and Sawyer set the phone down on the counter to stretch. She was about to close the surveillance feed when McCoy said the last thing Sawyer expected.

"I love you too, Nana. I'll see you Friday."

Nana?

A surprised bout of laughter bubbled up from Sawyer's throat. McCoy was speaking to her *nana*?

"You are just full of surprises, aren't you?" Sawyer said softly, closing out the app. As she returned to the sink to rewash her hands, try as she might, she couldn't fully erase the smile from her face.

This is precisely why I don't bother making big breakfasts, Sawyer thought two days later as she juggled a bowl of beaten eggs under one arm. With her free hand, she grabbed the tongs to flip the bacon sizzling in the pan, cursing in both French and English when the fat spit out at her.

"Should have stuck to my usual," she grumped aloud, setting the tongs down again before whisking the last of the eggs. Bach played on the Bluetooth speaker attached to the wall beside the kitchen's entrance, and she hummed the low notes as she tossed freshly chopped chives into the eggs.

After her early morning run, Sawyer had felt better than she had in a long while. The nausea had been almost non-existent, and the idea of a home-cooked breakfast—*with bacon*—sounded too good to pass up. Unfortunately, having to defrost the package first was a time waste in her already carefully constructed routine. Now she was running behind, and her island was in a state of disarray with loaves of bread rising and fresh cinnamon rolls taking up residence.

Clang! Clang! Clang!

The faint sound of McCoy's hammer had Sawyer pausing mid-stir. She'd let the younger woman in shortly after five, and every so often, she could hear the racket.

A shrill ring echoed in the kitchen, and it took Sawyer a minute to realize it was her landline jangling on the wall behind her. Huh, random. No one ever called her on that old thing. She let it ring, stirring her eggs around in the frying pan before she turned off the bacon.

Apprehension tickled the back of her neck as an image of a hurt and scared Bree flashed through her mind, and she snatched the phone from its cradle. "Hello, Bree?"

Melodic laughter floated through the line. "Not Bree, I'm afraid."

Sawyer frowned at the familiar sound. "Cin? Why are you calling me on here?"

"Well, good morning to you too, crank. I wouldn't have rung this number if you could stay attached to your mobile. Where is it this time? In the bathroom?"

"In my purse, ready to go to work," Sawyer said in exasperation. Fetching her favorite aged cheddar from the fridge, she placed that and the grater on the counter. Then she stirred her eggs one last time before turning off the stove. She spied the time on the wall clock resting between the kitchen and living room. "I'm running late, Cin. What can I help you with?"

The drill went off in the garage this time, and Sawyer's thoughts raced to the woman wielding it. McCoy had shown up in the same overalls and work boots she wore every day while working, but a teensy part of Sawyer was dying to see what was underneath. A T-shirt or a sports bra? Was her skin slick with sweat?

Mm-hmm. Sawyer's teeth sunk into her lower lip at the tantalizing image of how McCoy had looked the first time she'd worked on the McLaren. She had stripped her overalls down to her waist, and the black sleeveless shirt she'd worn had shown off defined muscles and tattoos.

"Yoo-hoo. Sawyer, are you listening?"

Not even a little.

"Sorry, can you repeat that?" Sawyer gave her head a shake, focusing on Cindy and her food once again.

"I was wondering if you'd given any more thought to dinner this Sunday?"

"Oh ..." Sawyer hesitated.

"You completely forgot about it, didn't you? C'mon, how long has it been since you went anywhere other than Desmarais? Not including the warehouse a month ago or a doctor's appointment."

"A while, I suppose," Sawyer reluctantly admitted. It'd been a year or more since she'd even stepped foot in a grocery store. That was what DoorDash and curb pickup were for.

"I suppose it could work. Unless I get bogged down planning the new menu."

Cindy chuckled. "Finding reasons to bail already, I see."

"Excuse me? I'm too fucking busy to 'find' reasons, Cindy," Sawyer said tightly. She turned the burners off, her movements jerky. She should *definitely* hang up now.

"I'm just playing with you, Sawyer. No need to bite my head off. Honestly," Cindy grumbled, "No sense of humor."

Sawyer bit down on her tongue, hating how defensive she was. She sighed. "I'm ... sorry. I've got a lot going on right now. I'll just ... Call me tomorrow, will you?" She clicked off before Cindy could reply, tossing the phone onto the island. Closing her eyes, Sawyer took several long breaths to loosen the tightness in her chest. The pulse in her temple was throbbing with a vengeance.

"Why do I bother?" she groused, feeling her appetite evaporate as she looked at her breakfast on the stove. She'd been ravenous only a few moments ago, but Cindy had a special way of getting under her skin in the simplest of ways.

"*Tabarnak*, Cindy." She carried the frying pan to the garbage and was about to toss the eggs when the sound of a saw coming from the garage slowly registered. McCoy. Rather than waste the food, Sawyer could ask the mechanic if she was hungry. But what message would that send? Sawyer certainly wouldn't be offering breakfast each time McCoy was here to work.

It had been almost a week since McCoy had admitted she liked Sawyer. A week of unspoken tension between them and too much of saying one thing and meaning another. At least on her part, and that wasn't like Sawyer at all. Her body responded differently when she argued with McCoy than when she would argue with Olivier. Her heart raced with excitement, not her usual fight or flight response. She felt desirable, not at all like the woman she'd been for the last fifteen years.

Sawyer could admit her dislike of McCoy might not be as authentic as she'd initially thought. Their banter felt explosive and sexual and completely out of control. The annoying throbbing between her legs and hardened nipples when she thought of the other woman attested to that fact.

Sawyer eyed the frying pan with a sigh. *It* would *be a shame to waste.*

Deciding, she plated the bacon and scrambled eggs she'd intended for herself, along with a fresh cinnamon roll she'd baked earlier, grabbed utensils, and carried the plate down the long hallway to the garage. Through the window of the door, she spotted McCoy immediately. She was once again dressed down to a ribbed men's tank top, her coveralls bunched and tied around her strong waist. Everything about her was strong, Sawyer was reluctantly coming to realize. It was always warm inside the garage, and as Sawyer entered, she tried not to focus on the trickle of sweat drizzling down the younger woman's temple. Her powerful, tattooed biceps flexed as McCoy cut off pieces of the McLaren's front frame. What was left of the fender sat a few feet away on a pallet.

"Sawyer, hey," McCoy greeted her, abruptly shutting off the grinder. She grinned—which, much to Sawyer's dismay, she was able to do with her eyes as well as her lips. Every time she did *that* to Sawyer, the pit of Sawyer's stomach dropped out a little more.

With indignation, to be sure.

"Here," she announced, thrusting the breakfast plate into McCoy's hands. Staring at the oil creasing her fingertips, Sawyer instantly regretted not putting it on a disposable dish.

"Wow, thank you. I'm starving, thanks," McCoy sputtered, her cheeks flushing almost immediately.

Perhaps McCoy isn't much of a Casanova after all.

Sawyer nodded in response, her gaze wandering over McCoy's stocky form as she took a seat on the nearest rolling stool. She didn't like the awareness she had of McCoy. She didn't like McCoy, period. Not really. The younger woman was obnoxious, arrogant, grinned way more than was healthy, and—

And speaks sweetly to her nana. And has impeccable manners. And likes you.

"Is that for me, too?"

Sawyer's eyes narrowed, irritated that her brain once again went on a tangent. It was one thing to do so when she was alone but another entirely if the object of her fascination was in touching distance. Embarrassed, she glared at McCoy, who was now moaning over the cinnamon roll Sawyer had made, then down at the coffee she hadn't realized she'd carried out to the garage with her. "No."

"Erm, okay."

"I'm going inside. Make sure the garage door is secured shut before you leave."

"No problem. Oh, I meant to tell you I can't make it here this weekend," McCoy called after her.

"Oh?" Much to her dismay, Sawyer's interest was piqued. Goddamn McCoy. And goddamn her jealousy. "Plans with, what was her name? Abs?" The words were out before she could stop them. Sawyer had been dying to know more about Abs since they'd come into her restaurant the Monday before.

"Abs?" McCoy looked confused at first, but then she wagged her head from side to side, her green eyes glittering with amusement. "Abi's just a friend, I promise. I mean, there was one time I wanted more, but she didn't, and anyway. I'm single and ready to mingle." Her nervous chuckle was like a footnote in her drawn-out flurry of nonsense. The moment she realized she'd unintentionally flirted was almost comical.

"You're like one of those cheap greeting cards at the dollar store," Sawyer deadpanned, disguising her sudden desire to laugh with a cough instead. She refused to give McCoy the satisfaction.

"Sorry," Coy blushed, which was a remarkable feat to witness under the grime and drying sweat on her face. She bowed her head. "And um, no. To your question," she jumped to add. "My nana needs help around her place, so I'll be there most of the time."

A teensy part deep in Sawyer's frozen heart softened with the easy admittance. When they'd first met, she'd have never in a million years pegged McCoy as the family type. She didn't mind being wrong on this one ... not that Sawyer planned to tell McCoy as much. She stood up straighter. "You said most of the time. What are you doing with the rest of it? Clubbing with friends? Working your charm again, perhaps? You agreed to commit six days a week on the McLaren if I recall correctly."

McCoy's lips parted, her jaw slack and her eyes filled with surprise as she looked up at Sawyer. The column of her throat bobbed up and down as she swallowed. Her nostrils flared. "I ... are you serious? I literally just said I'd be helping my nana." A frustrated laugh slipped out, and McCoy glanced from Sawyer to the McLaren before a scowl appeared. "Can you not make an exception? I didn't realize there was a timeframe on the fucking blob of death sitting before us."

"Clearly," Sawyer agreed, lifting her coffee mug to her lips to hide her grin. Her stomach fluttered, but not from indigestion. Grumpy McCoy was pleasing to look at. And to tease. She turned away. "I'll expect you Sunday evening and then Monday morning, per our original agreement. *Bonne journée,* McCoy."

CHAPTER 12

McCoy

IT TOOK A LOT to ruffle Coy's feathers. Like, a *lot*, a lot. And yet, Sawyer Lavoie managed to do what few could. She ruffled the feathers. The fricking peacock, oh-so-confident hypothetical McCoy feathers. And *laughed* as she did so. Never in Coy's life had she been so equally frustrated and turned on. The gall of that maddening woman! Did Sawyer expect Coy to be at her place every moment she wasn't at her day job? And the way she'd asked for specifics, like she deserved to know what Coy was doing or with whom. Which she definitely didn't. It wasn't Sawyer's business if Coy planned to take someone new home for the night. She'd seemed almost jealous at the prospect, but that wasn't possible. Right?

"You're miles away tonight," Abi said, sneaking one of Coy's fries. Coy and her friends were at O'Rourke's to see the latest live band. They came almost every week, but for the first time in probably ever, Coy had considered backing out.

She sipped one of her favorite on-tap dark ales, loving the smoky taste as it slid down her throat, and shrugged. "Just not feeling it tonight, I guess." Then, knowing Abi wouldn't simply leave it at that, Coy added, "All the extra hours this week has me wiped."

And I'm still salty as hell over the shit with Sawyer.

Thankfully, Abi didn't press any further. Coy was content to be left alone, only half listening to Taunya's latest work ordeal at the hospital.

She sipped her ale, perusing the crowd in the pub that night. It wasn't overly loud yet, as the band hadn't started, but Coy found herself rubbing at the tension forming at the base of her neck. There was too much going on around her, and it took a minute before she spotted Naz and Ash cozying up against the wall near the restrooms. Naz caught Coy's eye across the pub, a wicked grin appearing before she captured Ash's lips with her own. When they came up for air, Naz held her hand out in Coy's direction. Coy shook her head, waving them off before returning to her beer.

A hand landed on Coy's arm, and Coy glanced over to see Abi staring at her, eyes widened in surprise. "Did I just witness a three-way proposition?"

"Er ... I mean, yeah, I guess." Coy smirked, trying to shake off her weird mood. Hooking up with Naz and Ash would certainly help with that, right? She needed to go back to her roots and keep things superficial and casual with possible lovers. Not get hung up on mixed messages and stolen glances from Sawyer.

Fuck, why can't I go five minutes without thinking about her?

Coy sighed, lifting the glass to her lips again. It didn't help that every time she thought of the time and energy it'd taken to try and bond with Sawyer, an uncomfortable blush appeared, and her pulse began to race. *Shame.* That's what it was. She was embarrassing herself trying to get Sawyer's attention, and to what end, exactly? She should never have sent those random facts via text message. *So stupid.* Sawyer was probably incapable of bonding with anyone, and surely not with someone as opposite in personality as Coy happened to be. Sawyer just demanded and made ludicrous assumptions about people. Well, enough of that. Coy wasn't putting herself on the line anymore.

"Well, tell them you're mine tonight. I know how you like it when a femme gives you an order." Abi booped Coy on the nose with one long finger, affection warming the icy blue of her eyes.

Coy huffed a laugh, and a warmth as inviting as a gentle breeze blossomed in her chest. Somehow, Abi always knew what she needed to lighten the mood. "Touché, Abs. So what? Is the barber's company lacking this evening?" She dodged a swat from Taunya.

"Quit picking on my sister, or I'm gonna start in on yours, playgirl."

"Ooh, protective, are we? Good on you, Tauni." Coy clinked her mug of beer against Taunya's glass before switching into her best British accent, "We in the sibling sisterhood need to stick together. After all, we are the guardians of many sibling secrets and, of course, broken hearts."

"Ugh, that accent, though." Abi snorted a laugh, feigning a long shudder.

"Long-winded, but I'll take it as an agreement of no future douchery." Taunya pointed her finger at Coy in mock warning.

"What are you ..." Tess's stare was quizzical as she tried to piece together the current conversation. When her head looked like it could explode, she gave up, slumping in her seat and picking up her beer. "Know what? Never mind."

Krystal looked amused. "You're not used to Coy's eccentricity, Tess? She's special, but we adore her anyway."

"H-hey. I take offense," Coy protested with a surprised chuckle. She'd have thought Taunya would use that line, not Krystal. "Aren't you supposed to be the quiet, shy one?"

Abi booped Coy on the nose again. "Didn't you get the memo? Krystal's evolving now that Tess is in the group." Everyone laughed at that, even Tess.

Sloane approached their booth carrying a tray of appetizers, sliding in beside Krystal as she placed the tray down. "Whew, I'm zonked, and it's not even eight."

"Did you go on the trails today?" Coy frowned when her sister snatched the lager from her hands to take a drink.

"Yeah, me and J.D. Trying to get as much time on the trails as possible so I can win the rally this year. J.D. bet me in a race—and lost, of course.

Kind of stupid to bet against me, but I'd never turn down an extra twenty bucks." Sloane snatched a chicken wing from the basket Taunya was lifting from the tray.

Coy's brows knitted together as she considered Sloane's words. *Why would she bet on that?* Of course J.D. wasn't ready to go up against her on the trail. Instead of starting an argument, however, she just gritted her teeth and said, "Well, don't overdo it. And I hope you're drinking plenty and eating. I made a batch of energy balls last night."

"I saw them, Mom, and thanks." Sloane rolled her eyes but thankfully never truly got offended by Coy's smothering. She couldn't help it. Most assumed Coy was the wild one out of the duo, but Sloane was the one who took most of the risks, on and off the trails.

"Oh, and here." Sloane fished a folded-up note from her jeans pocket, handing it across the table to Coy. Slipping from the booth, she blew everyone kisses before picking up the serving tray once more. "Later, bitches. And Coy, make it snappy. She's in a mood."

"What if I'm in a mood? Does no one care?" Coy whined when her sister left, peeking at the note in her hands with one eye closed. She swallowed.

Come to me.

F

"Secret admirer?" Krystal asked, sparking with interest.

"Ooh, is it from *la très belle Madame*, along with her diabolical issues?" Abi eagerly asked, reaching across the table to try to grab the note.

Coy outmaneuvered her easily, tucking the note into the back of her jeans and muttering, "I shouldn't have told you about Sawyer."

"Told me?" Abi laughed. "I met her."

"Sawyer who?" Taunya threw in, already munching her nachos and appearing entirely too invested in Coy's story.

"And I can see the appeal," Abi continued with a wink. "Sassy Sawyer's definitely a hottie."

"And I definitely shouldn't have let you see my messages." Draining the contents of her beer, Coy wiped her lips with the back of her hand. A kind of nervous excitement brewed in her stomach as she got to her feet. "I have to go."

"Coy, wait," Abi called, running after her in the nearly empty bar. She grabbed Coy's arm, drawing her to a halt.

"Easy with the grip, Abs."

"Are you still fooling around with Frankie?" Abi's voice was soft, almost concerned for Coy, as she peered down at her from four-inch heels.

"Not really your business, but yes."

"But didn't you just tell me all about Sawyer the other day and how confused you were?"

Coy cleared her throat, thinking of her stare-down with Sawyer earlier. Even if Sawyer was attracted to Coy, she was too uptight to ever act on it. Coy had about as much chance with the ice queen as she did winning the lottery. She pulled the contract out that she'd been carrying around in her back pocket since that morning—rereading it for the fifth time to see if it indeed stated six days a week—and flicked it with her middle finger. "Look at this. Besides laying it out that I'm not allowed to snoop in her house, record the process of the rebuild, and that I have to be on time, she typed in bold letters how I'm not allowed to flirt. Not once, but *three* times. She doesn't want me, Abs. I'm pretty sure she hates me, judging by this and the comments she made this morning. Besides, I'm not like you, okay? I'm not cut out for just one person."

"Frankie isn't good for you, and you know it."

"I've gotta go," Coy repeated, not wanting to have this discussion right now. She gave Abi a quick hug and left her standing there, heading toward the back of the bar. She checked behind the counter to make sure Frankie wasn't there before continuing on to her office.

"I was beginning to think you weren't coming," a low voice greeted Coy as she closed the door to Frankie's office.

Coy took a deep breath and squared her shoulders. "Of course, I'm here ... *Mistress.*"

CHAPTER 13

Sawyer

WHAT HAD CHANGED BETWEEN them? McCoy hadn't so much as batted her eyelashes Sawyer's way in the last week and a half. Why? And, more importantly, why was the lack of attention so disconcerting?

As Sawyer glanced around the front house dining room, observing the faces she'd come to know over the years, those questions circled her thoughts like vultures to prey. Had McCoy met someone and quickly gotten bored with Sawyer? She couldn't imagine jumping into bed with a stranger. Passion hadn't stolen her common sense since she was sixteen, so she couldn't see any logic behind a one-night stand. To each their own, she supposed. Still, the thought of McCoy sleeping around unsettled Sawyer.

Sawyer massaged the tension in the back of her neck, spotting Barb in her peripheral vision. Her sous-chef watched her, likely waiting for Sawyer to commence the pre-shift meeting. Picking up her glass of ice water, Sawyer took a long drink before saying, "Let's get started, shall we? Mikey, what have you got?"

"Thank you, Chef." Mikey, Sawyer's front house supervisor, glanced at the notes he'd written down. "We've been getting a lot of compliments on this season's added menu dishes, namely the fresh take on our *bouillabaisse*. And I've heard quite a few customers commenting how nicely the new light fixtures suit the dining room."

"Very good," Sawyer acknowledged. "By the way, let Kelly know by shift's end what inventory needs to be ordered."

"Certainly, Chef."

"What else do you have for me? Kelly, what about you? Any potential hires coming my way?" Sawyer asked, sparing a glance at her phone resting on the table before her. She toyed with it absently, her gaze trained on her manager, but her mind wandered. McCoy had showed up that morning sporting a fresh undercut, the fine hairs trimmed low to her scalp, and the urge to slide her fingers over it had come on so strong that Sawyer had dug her nails into her palms. Hours later, she still bore the indents. Since when did she fantasize about burying a piece of herself into someone's hair of all places? She was off-kilter, thinking and almost doing things she'd never considered pre-McCoy.

Kelly filled her in on the handful of résumés passed in, but only two seemed promising for an interview. Sawyer gave her the go-ahead to set them up, preferring to stay out of it as much as possible. Cindy's offer of coming to work for her circled back more often than not, but it was more of a last resort for Sawyer. She liked things done her way, and Cindy, well, she wasn't one to easily fall in line. Truly, Sawyer would be doing her friend a favor by not hiring her.

"I have news," Sawyer informed everyone once Kelly was finished. "Last night, while Desmarais was closed, I had video surveillance installed in all the storage rooms."

Murmurs broke out over the dining room, loud enough to drown out Sawyer's next words, so she paused and took a sip of her water. When she held her hand up, the voices abruptly died off as all eyes focused on her once more. Sawyer curled her lip, disgust slipping past her collected features. "In light of recent ... events going on behind closed doors, higher security is a must. Furthermore, the surveillance company replaced the cameras near the washrooms and walk-in fridges with newer models."

It was truly a shame. Having an outstanding ability to float in the kitchen had allowed Dustin so many liberties in the three years he'd worked for Desmarais. She'd spent a long time waiting for her husband to install cameras in the storage rooms, especially after a significant theft years prior, but he always gaslighted her when the topic came up. She later found out why. Dustin wasn't the first she'd stumbled upon with his pants down. As rumor had it, Olivier had been with at least two of the servers while Sawyer was on shift. He'd always found some way to humiliate her. Needless to say, surveillance was long overdue.

"It should go without saying, but I feel like I need to remind everyone to keep Desmarais as drama-free as possible. That includes sneaking alone time with any of the staff."

"Olivier used to," someone in the back murmured, probably hoping Sawyer couldn't hear.

Fury mottled her cheeks, and her fingers gripped the edge of the table hard. "*Esti*!" she said through gritted teeth. "Olivier is dead, and quite honestly, I could do with never hearing his name spoken in Desmarais again. Now that he's gone, I not only run my kitchen, but I'm also the sole owner of the entire restaurant. You'd do well to remember that. I'm paying you to work when you're here, not slip away from food prep when it suits you. Do I make myself clear?"

Sawyer's gaze swept the room, landing on each one of her staff to make certain they were all on the same page. Kelly sat across from her, pride evident in her warm eyes. "Yes, Chef." A chorus of replies rang through the room.

"Good." Sawyer took a deep breath, letting it out slowly before she spoke again. Taking another drink, she said in a much calmer voice, "Just so everyone understands, I'll have Kelly draw up new contracts for everyone to sign at the next meeting. That'll be all, then. Thank you all for the hard work."

"I thought you handled them well," Kelly said, picking up her notepad and mug of coffee. Her office was just off the dining area. She used to share it with Olivier, when he seldomly made an appearance, and hated every minute of it.

"Oh yeah, the staff love when I lay down the law," Sawyer wryly replied. She picked up her phone, swiping the passcode in to see that her daughter had replied to Sawyer's latest text. They'd been trying to schedule a video call, but so far, their schedules weren't lining up.

Bree: I can try to stay awake if you want to call when you get off work? Xoxo

"Bree," Sawyer explained to Barb, who stood waiting for her. She gestured to her phone, "We've been playing phone tag."

"Good to see Bree is still a mama's girl," Barb said with a fond smile. "I'm lucky if my kids call me once a week, let alone FaceTime. Kylie has the new baby, and Trent is so caught up with getting his Masters."

"That's life, unfortunately." Sawyer sighed, following Barb into the kitchen. "I'll be in my office for a bit if you need me."

"Got it, Chef."

Sawyer sunk into her office chair the moment the door was closed. Tension radiated through her shoulders, neck, and up behind her eyes. Lately, it had been taking less and less to get her to this point physically. How would she get through the next eight hours if stress was taking its toll so soon?

She took two Advil before opening her text thread with Bree again.

Sawyer: Okay, I'll let it ring twice and then hang up so I don't wake you or Scott. *Je t'aime*, darling.

Sawyer pressed Send before returning to her home SMS screen. At once, she saw the thread she'd kept of her and McCoy's conversation. She'd found herself slipping into the thread repeatedly over the past week, rereading McCoy's daily facts she had previously deemed annoying and attention-seeking. Now, she was shocked to find she missed the consistent interaction with the younger woman.

Is this somehow a punishment in McCoy's eyes?

It was the only thing that made sense. McCoy had been acting off since Sawyer had instructed her to show up that Sunday evening, almost two weeks before.

"She's certainly sensitive," Sawyer commented, opening the thread yet again. McCoy never complained about the one-sided conversation, and Sawyer secretly enjoyed learning about her this way. It was informal and much less daunting than trying to connect with someone face-to-face. Interpersonal connection had never been Sawyer's forte. But this ... this was doable. If McCoy had continued, Sawyer might have relented with a few facts of her own. Now, they'd never know.

She settled more comfortably into her chair, scrolling mid-way up to McCoy Miller's fact number six she'd sent weeks before.

McCoy: 6. I want to backpack through Europe. It's always been a dream of mine but I've never been able to save for a trip just for the sake of it. Something always delayed it.

McCoy: 7. I've had the same password since highschool. *Ilu-vb0Obies96* lol. I've tried to change it a bunch of times but can never remember the new one.

McCoy: 8. I probably shouldn't have told you that. Just in case you're into cybercrime, ya know?

McCoy: 9. You have the most beautiful eye color I've ever seen.

She watched from the living room as her friends spoke in hushed tones in the kitchen. They were washing up the dishes together after a delicious meal of chicken cordon bleu and herb and garlic rice. Occasionally, one of them would giggle, and then a minute or two of silence would follow as they kissed. And each time, Sawyer looked away, uncomfortable. It wasn't sex itself that bothered her; she and Olivier had quite a regular sex life at one time. No, it was the unbridled passion emitting from both Cindy and Lori. Twenty-three years later, they still wanted to be together. Was it lust, or love, or both? Olivier had never looked at Sawyer like that, but maybe it was because he'd known. He'd *known* she'd never look at him the way Lori looked at Cindy.

"Admit it, you're glad you came over."

Sawyer looked up from where she was perusing the extensive vinyl record collection. Cindy was standing a foot or two away, two glasses of wine in her hands.

"What's not to enjoy? The meal was superb, the company lively." Sawyer accepted one of the glasses Cindy offered.

Cindy clinked Sawyer's glass of wine lightly with her own. "Cheers. It's good to see you too, old friend. Don't tell her I told you, but Lori was beside herself last night when I confirmed you were coming. I woke up to her baking fresh sourdough bread."

Sawyer's answering grin was small, but the confession left a comical image of Lori racing frantically around the kitchen before she had to leave for work. Lori wasn't a chef by any means, so the effort made it all the more special to Sawyer.

"Ugh, I'm stuffed." Cindy patted her stomach and led the way to the sofa. She flung herself down, some of the wine tipping out onto the sofa and floor in the process. Sawyer's eyes widened as she tried not to think of the stain it would leave in the microsuede. "How's Bree doing? She'd mentioned something about social work not being what she'd had in mind the last time she FaceTimed Lori and I."

"Really?" Sawyer was genuinely confused. And *disappointed*. It was the first she'd heard of it, and she usually spoke to Bree at least once a week. Why was she the last to know about the goings on with her daughter? She opened her mouth to say so when Lori strolled into the living room.

"What'll it be? Scrabble, Pictionary, or Ticket to Ride?"

"*Master Chef*?"

Cindy and Lori groaned at Sawyer's innocent question. "What? I haven't watched the latest season yet."

"You can watch that at home. C'mon, when was the last time you stayed for a board game?" Cindy asked, tossing the throw pillow in Sawyer's direction.

"Fine, then. Scrabble."

"Scrabble it is, then," Lori announced, setting the game down on the coffee table.

"You're nothing if not predictable," Cindy added with a chuckle.

Sawyer narrowed her gaze on Cindy between sips of her wine, but it was true. At least with Scrabble, she could surmise the best way to accumulate the greatest number of points. She was a little tipsy, so she wasn't thinking when she said, "Will there be snacks with this game?"

Lori laughed, climbing to her feet again. "I'm on it, Chef Lavoie."

A gush of air left Sawyer as she blew a raspberry. "What an awful nickname."

"Oh, you love it. Don't even pretend otherwise."

Sawyer rolled her eyes but found herself smiling. She stared after Lori as she disappeared into the kitchen, her long, flowing dreadlocks bobbing back and forth as she walked. Sawyer sighed.

Cindy nudged Sawyer's hand, which was draped over the back of the sofa, her gaze trailing after Lori as well. A soft smile breached the edges of her mouth. "You could have what we do, Sawyer."

Sawyer frowned, her good mood quickly fading. She was sick and tired of Cindy constantly in her ear about romance. It was highly overrated, short-lasting, and quite often fiction. "I *had* that, if you recall. All it proved was how resilient I was. That, and someone actually being home when you got there wasn't set in stone."

"You had Olivier." Cindy shook her head sadly. "He wasn't your first, second, or third choice. Do *you* remember? You told me that shortly after we met, how akin you felt to me right away. That seeing how I lived gave you the realization you'd needed."

"Cindy, please."

"The acceptance to be yourself."

"I knew who I was. And so did Olivier," Sawyer hissed, not wanting Lori to hear them. She looked away, lifting the wine glass to her lips. "Knowing and living your authentic self are two very different things, but you've never had to figure that out. Be glad for it."

"It wasn't always easy for me either, Sawyer."

"Oh? Were you forced into conversion therapy, too?" Sawyer's voice dripped with sarcasm. She pressed her fingers to her throbbing temples. Four glasses of wine were probably her limit. "I didn't think so. It fucks you up, Cin. To grow up believing you have an illness, terrified to even look at a girl, let alone befriend one. To *love* one."

"Well, this conversation changed drastically in the few minutes I was gone," Lori commented, letting out a strained chuckle. She placed two bowls down, one of chips and one of M&M's.

"I'm just explaining to Cindy how we can't all find happily-ever-afters. Some of us are better off alone."

"And I'm politely disagreeing with you. You'll never know unless you try. You have a lot to give, Sawyer. Someone out there deserves to know the real you."

For some ungodly reason, McCoy's lazy smile the first time Sawyer had seen her came to mind. It was like a sucker punch to the already crater-sized hole in her gut. If she had been standing, her legs probably would have buckled.

"I have Bree," she replied, softer than she'd thought possible. She thought of the babies she'd lost, especially Brian. Olivier used to say Sawyer's miscarriages were God's way of making certain she atoned for her sins. As if marrying him in the first place hadn't been enough penance. She'd buried who she was out of fear that everything her father and the church had stuffed down her throat was the truth. She'd endured a loveless marriage, and for what? Even her parents had turned their back on her after Brian's death, choosing to side with Olivier rather than offer her and Bree emotional support. It was then she realized how much of a monster her father truly was. He'd excused years of abuse against her for the sake of his church, and Sawyer had refused to live a second more of it. She turned her back on that faith and vowed to herself never to speak to her parents or Olivier's family again. Fifteen years later, they were all as good as dead to her.

No, life had dealt her too much pain to start over, even if it meant finally coming out of the closet. Bree was all Sawyer needed to remind her of the goodness still left in the world. Her throat was raw as she added, "I've done my time. Why would I voluntarily submit to another sentence?"

This time, Lori reached out to comfort Sawyer, her soft brown skin on Sawyer's a stark contrast. All the hand-touching and sympathy had her cringing. "I'll say this, and then I think we should move on to our game. Falling in love with the right person is the opposite of a jail sentence. It feels like you could have all the time in the world with them, and it still wouldn't be enough. They see you, heal the brokenness inside. They become the other half of you, the best half."

Sawyer swallowed, aware of her pulse slowly picking up at Lori's words. All Olivier had ever done was bring on more misery than he was worth. She'd never once felt that kind of love for someone. How was it she was in her forties and still felt so monumentally inexperienced?

Chapter 14

McCoy

After five weeks of working part-time and dodging Sawyer's hot and cold moods, the McLaren was beginning to look like more than just a jaw-dropping widow maker. Like her father, there weren't many things in life that made Coy happier than tinkering with cars. A rebuild was just like any restoration, whether it was on a house or antiques, and she loved the painstaking process of removing the McLaren's broken pieces—and there were a lot.

She felt bad that Tegan had been cast off to her father mid-way through the disassembling process, but borrowing Greg's truck had been a no-brainer. Coy was able to load the junk parts on each time and take them to the scrap yard rather than hooking up her trailer and taking up more of Sawyer's driveway. She would have had something to say about it.

Coy looked up from where she was removing the driver's seat, pausing when she noticed Sawyer standing on the last step in the garage. Still sour over having to work the Sunday a week and a half earlier, Coy had been doing her best to avoid her helpless gaze lingering on Sawyer for too long. Still, she knew the woman enough to sense there was something seriously off. Uncertainty was coming off the older woman in waves, her face scrunched up in deep concentration as she made her way to Coy. She carried a Tupperware dish in one hand, a coffee thermos in the other, and wrapped utensils dangled from her fingertips.

Coy set the seat down beside the pallet with the parts she was keeping. She waited, wondering what Sawyer would do. Hell, she wondered if Sawyer knew. She seemed uncharacteristically lost. Finally, she turned to Coy, taking a deep breath as if to compose herself.

Coy reached up to remove her earbuds. "Sawyer? You alright?"

Sawyer blinked, staring down at Coy in a daze. She nodded slowly, holding out the ceramic Tupperware dish for her to take. "You probably ate already, but I was experimenting in the kitchen, so ..." was all she said.

Coy checked the wall clock, one eyebrow lifting. "It's early to be experimenting, but thank you. I'd never pass up one of your meals." Accepting the container from Sawyer, Coy casually grazed her fingertips along the back of her hand during the swap. Sawyer inhaled sharply, pulling back, and Coy had to catch the dish before it fell. "Sorry," she mumbled.

Sawyer turned on her heel to leave and then, as an afterthought, she set the thermos down on the bench beside Coy. "Coffee, cream and sugar. Just how you like it."

Sawyer had paid attention to what was written on her takeout cups? Her stomach bottomed out seconds before butterflies took flight low in her belly. Coy cleared her throat, aware of her sweaty palms yet wishing she could reach for Sawyer. She wanted more than anything to touch her again. "I appreciate it. And the food. You're gifted, Sawyer. I-in the kitchen, I mean. How long have you been a chef?"

Her back straightened, and when Coy was sure she wouldn't get a response, Sawyer surprised her. "Twenty-three years."

"Twenty-three?" Coy's eyes widened as she looked Sawyer up and down more closely. "What did you do, drop out of school?"

Sawyer turned to frown at Coy. "Exactly how old do you think I am?"

Coy shrugged, her gaze roaming over Sawyer's face, pausing on the partially disguised left side. There was a scar or something there that she tried to hide behind her hair and foundation, but if anything, it only made Sawyer more attractive in Coy's eyes. In certain light, the salt and pepper strands of her black hair didn't blend in as easily, but again, it only added to her character. Sawyer's smoky eyes were flawlessly proportioned with her high cheekbones, angular jaw, perfect, pert nose, and lips that were made for hour-long make-out sessions.

"This is precisely why older women don't talk about their age," Sawyer snapped, breaking Coy out of her embarrassingly intense examination. She gave Sawyer a bashful grin, feeling the heat rising to her cheeks.

"Sorry. For a minute, your beauty made me lose my train of thought."

Sawyer scoffed. "Is everything a joke to you?" Her piercing glare made Coy shrink back slightly. Confusion and hurt blanketed her anger, and in a momentary lapse of that iron-clad facade, Sawyer's emotions were so raw Coy wished she could turn back time and rephrase her words. "What are you, McCoy, twenty-five? *Esti*, I could be your mother, for God's sake. I had you sign the contract so we could avoid these deceptions."

Any time Coy had seen her in the past few weeks, Sawyer carried herself with such confidence and grace. She'd never given Coy the impression she was anything but. Was it hard to believe Coy would find her attractive?

She swallowed hard. "Look, I'm sorry, okay? I-I flirt when I'm nervous, but I wouldn't bullshit you. *Wait*, please."

Coy's heart was pounding as she jumped from the workbench, catching Sawyer's hand as she turned to leave. Her palm was soft in Coy's, and for a millisecond, Coy didn't do anything but marvel over how easily their fingers linked together. *Like she was made for me.*

She glanced up at Sawyer, disappointed when her hand wrenched free from Coy's once more. "I'm twenty-seven," she admitted, shoving her hands in her pockets so she wouldn't accidentally reach for Sawyer again. Their eyes met and held. "And age is just a number. You are ... Sawyer, you're the most beautiful woman I've ever seen."

Coy expected her revelation to bring relief to Sawyer, but she was mistaken. The older woman just scowled and left the garage. Once again, Coy wondered what the hell she'd said wrong.

Coy wiped the sweat off her brow, bending to pick up the last of her tools from the concrete floor. She felt good about the progress she'd made so far. Finding the time and ordering parts was going to be a bigger challenge than the actual rebuild. She packed her screwdrivers and ratchet set off to the side of the McLaren and out of the way. Next, she carried her reciprocating saw and charger out to the truck, tucking them on the floor of the backseat. After, McCoy made sure the ratchet straps were secured in the bed. She wasn't concerned about the junk parts getting wet, but it would be bad news to have a piece of the fender fly off while she was on the bridge.

She returned to the garage slowly, taking in the McLaren and appreciating the supercar for what it was. Even stripped down to the main frame and tub, its design was a masterpiece. At an impressive acceleration speed of zero to sixty in two point nine seconds, it could easily be a deathtrap for an inexperienced driver. Or a cocky one. Coy wondered which was the case for Sawyer's husband.

Shaking her head, she headed over to the workbench to retrieve the Tupperware dish Sawyer had thoughtfully handed her earlier. She'd made a chicken stew but had added dumplings to the broth. It was an unexpected, delicious treat for her morning. It'd been a long time since Coy had eaten any that didn't come deep-fried. She was resting the dish on the step leading into the house when thanking Sawyer came to mind. She hadn't been very receptive to Coy entering her house on earlier occasions, but the guilt over their conversation was nagging at her. She'd said something to set Sawyer off. It seemed like she couldn't get anything right around her. Coy was either making a fool of herself or inadvertently insulting Sawyer.

Pulling her lip between her teeth in thought, Coy climbed the three steps to the door. What was the worst thing to happen? Sawyer snarling and telling Coy off happened almost on the daily. It was like she had all these preconceived ideas about who Coy was as a person, and nothing she said or did could change her mind.

She rapped her knuckles on the door, and as she waited, she examined her hands, hoping they were clean enough. She'd tried wearing gloves before, but they ripped so easily, and it was hard handling small nuts and bolts with them on.

Knocking a second time, Coy waited, silently counting to ten before trying the doorknob. It was a big house, so it was entirely possible Sawyer couldn't hear the knocking. It turned easily, proof that Sawyer hadn't been in her right mind when they'd last spoken because Coy had watched her lock it time and time again. *Maybe this isn't a good idea.*

She pushed the door open. "Hey, Sawyer? It's only me. Whoa," Coy said as she got her first look inside Sawyer's massive home. Even in the long hallway, the ceilings must have been ten feet high. She scrambled to get her steel-toed boots off, setting them by the garage door before continuing further into the house. The hallway opened into the kind of kitchen even Gordon Ramsay would love. It was beautifully designed with large south-facing windows to capture most of the sun and a fancy stovetop with two built-in ovens. A medium-sized shelving system filled with herbs sat off to one side.

"Sawyer, just wanted to say thanks," Coy called again, setting the Tupperware dish inside the sink. She didn't want to break one of Sawyer's hard-pressed rules by snooping. She was about to leave the way she came in when she heard the faint sound of a piano. Coy tiptoed into what appeared to be the living room, straining to hear it again.

The soft melody began once more, and when Sawyer came into view, all of McCoy's breath left her in a *whoosh*. She was perched on a piano stool, hunched over the keys, the long, elegant fingers of one hand gliding effortlessly back and forth. Sawyer was dressed more casually than Coy had ever seen her, wearing just a lavender silk bathrobe. The gently crimped waves of her long hair draped over one side of her chest, exposing her toned shoulder where the robe had slipped off.

"When did you know you were gay?"

It took a moment to register that Sawyer had not only heard Coy enter the living room but that she was speaking. The softness in her voice had Coy's knees wobbling, and she quickly grabbed the back of a nearby sofa. Clearing her throat, it took her a few tries before she could get her reply out. "I, um, prefer the term queer," she admitted, her gaze on Sawyer's back. She still hadn't turned, but Coy got the feeling it was easier for her to talk this way.

"Is one term more acceptable than the other?"

Sawyer sounded genuinely curious. It was strange listening to her without her usual bite after each sentence. Coy rolled her shoulders, watching Sawyer's hand on the piano keys and wishing she would play more. It was hard to concentrate when she was around Sawyer. "I guess gay is an umbrella term, but more in reference to those who identify as men. I use lesbian and queer interchangeably. Everyone is different. My sister is pansexual, but most of the time, it's easier for her to say queer. Especially to people like my nana."

"I see."

"Mm-hmm." What a strange conversation to have with her crush. A part of Coy appreciated it, though. Sawyer opening up a little could only mean she was beginning to trust Coy, right?

Sawyer began playing again, a soft ballad echoing in the silent room. The notes were rusty, as if it'd been years since she'd done so. But not to Coy, who stood there absolutely mesmerized by Sawyer's fingers fondly stroking each key.

A disappointed sigh left her when the music stopped. Then, "Are you going to make me ask twice?"

"Twice?" Coy echoed, racking her brain for snippets of their conversation because she'd be damned if she was the cause of it ending. The answer dawned on her, and she perked up. "You asked when I knew. And my answer is always. My sister was into all things girly, and I liked to follow my dad around everywhere. I know that alone doesn't scream queer, but I felt different than the other girls. It took Sloane a lot longer to figure out her sexuality. Why do you ask? Are you ... are you unsure? I'm sorry if I ever said something to—"

"No. I've always known, too," Sawyer interrupted before turning back to the piano. She played, continuing to speak over the music. "That I was different. Not like other girls in my church. It wasn't until I was old enough to understand the scriptures that it changed for me. That I learned homosexuality was a sin."

Hearing the outdated, derogatory term was like a bitch slap to the face. Defensive replies were at the tip of Coy's tongue until she realized Sawyer hadn't meant it the way it sounded. She was talking about herself and how that twisted mentality affected her upbringing.

Coy crossed the room in long strides, uncaring anymore if she dirtied the furniture. Sawyer was sitting more to one end of the piano bench, so Coy straddled the opposite side, finally getting a look at Sawyer. Coy's fingers tingled to reach for her, to swipe away the hair falling in her eye, to kiss away her doubt. "Sawyer, no matter how you identify, know that you're incredible. It's not a sin to live your truth. My nana has a whole spiel when it comes to inaccurate religious beliefs, but I won't get into that. She's as old school as they come, and she was the first one to know I was queer. Whatever you were taught, whatever bullshit politicians are still coming up with, they're lies."

"Such a Gen Z thing to say." Sawyer's voice was bitter. Her hands left the keys, and she slowly shifted on the bench. A slight gasp left Coy as she got her first unfiltered look at the scar tissue on Sawyer's cheek. The full lighting in the living room left nothing to the imagination. Without makeup on, her eyes seemed paler, the fine lines above her top lip more noticeable, but it was the scar Coy's eyes kept flickering to.

Sawyer looked away. "Not so beautiful now, am I?"

"You're joking, right?" Coy sucked her teeth, having a battle of wills as she debated how to explain how responsive her body always was to Sawyer, scar or no scar. Launching herself at Sawyer seemed inappropriate for the mood, and besides, she had given Coy zero confirmation the attraction was mutual.

Despite her back and forth, Coy's hand still found its way to Sawyer's face. Instead of tugging her in for a kiss, she held Sawyer's gaze, very slowly tracing the contours of the scar. Her fingers slipped over the leathery texture, dipping into the uneven ridges until finally landing on her parted lips. Coy's thumb hovered there, in limbo, waiting for permission to do what she had wanted since the night they first met. Sawyer's eyes drifted closed, and Coy's gaze dropped to her chest, watching the quick rise and fall of her breasts beneath the robe. Coy's tongue darted out to lick her lips as she leaned in closer.

She was inches away from kissing Sawyer when the spell broke. Sawyer's eyes flew open, and she shoved Coy with such force Coy's ass connected with the living room floor. "Get out." Sawyer's snap was back, and oddly enough, her accent was thicker when she was superbly pissed off. Her death glare had Coy wishing she could sink into the luxurious floorboards. "Get out, and don't ever use your ... your womanizing skills on me again!"

Coy clambered to her feet, her heart stuck halfway up her throat. When she bolted from the house moments later, confused tears blurred her vision. She ran to her father's truck and jumped in. Her hands trembled as she shoved the keys into the ignition. She didn't know why, but she felt dirty. Like Sawyer had mistaken their almost kiss for something truly nefarious. Is that how she saw Coy? She wasn't a villain; Sawyer had had more than enough time to back away or say no.

God, her heart hurt. She couldn't recall the last time she'd cried over a girl.

Coy shifted into gear, wiping runaway tears from her cheeks with the back of her hand as she left Sawyer's. She was halfway home when she couldn't deny the strange rawness seeping into her gut. Her thoughts on Sawyer, Coy's stomach churned until her throat was raw, too. Ugh.

Was she falling for Sawyer?

Chapter 15

Sawyer

"Haven't you been paying attention to anything?" Sawyer barked at Shane at work the following day. She grabbed his wrist before he cut his fingers off. "You're slicing onions, not playing the fucking cello! Fold your fingers in and hold the knife the way I showed you."

"Sorry, Chef."

Sawyer scowled, wondering if she'd made a mistake promoting him. If he hadn't learned how to use a knife properly yet, then perhaps he was dumber than she'd first thought. There was no place for idiots in her kitchen. It was hazardous, and they were time-consuming to teach.

"I love this job, Chef. I'll do better, I promise," Shane added, and she noticed him anxiously watching her. He had to have learned something if he could read her body language so well.

"See that you do, Shane. Practice at home if you have to. I don't want to see that" —she imitated him swinging the knife all over the place— "in my kitchen again. Understood?"

"Perfectly, Chef."

"Good."

Aware the kitchen had fallen silent, Sawyer turned to glare at the rest of her staff. "What? Does anyone have a problem with the way I run the back house?"

Usually, she at least pulled someone off the line before reaming them first, but if she'd waited much longer, Shane would have cut his fingers off.

"No, Chef. You're the boss," Leon replied, lifting his gaze from the salmon he was cleaning to meet her eyes.

Sawyer nodded in satisfaction. She turned to her rotisseur chef. "Micah? Any problem?"

"No, Chef," Micah stated softly, unable to look at Sawyer.

Her gaze landed on Barb, who had stopped stirring the stew to frown at Sawyer. Before either of them could speak, Kelly called out Sawyer's name from the kitchen's entrance. "Our 2 p.m. interviewee is here."

That brought on a new scowl for Sawyer, and she whipped around to face Kelly. "Cancel it or interview them by yourself."

"Chef, we're short-staffed and can't afford to cancel interviews."

"Then you sit in on the interview, Barb," Sawyer said. She headed in the direction of her office. "I'm not in the mood for the guaranteed headache that will follow." She needed another coffee. And maybe a new personality. She felt like she'd been slowly unraveling since Sunday evening. The heart-to-heart with Cindy and Lori brought back painful memories and parts of herself she'd set aside for so long. She was out of sorts—the morning prior was proof of that. Her throat and chest had been raw since McCoy had all but run from her house. Her stomach was still in knots, sour like she'd sucked on a dish full of lemons. The worst part was Sawyer couldn't even look at McCoy when she'd shown up to work that morning. *I still can't believe I shoved her so hard.*

There was a knock on her door, and Barb ducked her head in. It didn't take a genius to see how upset her sous-chef was. "Chef, can I speak with you?"

"You know you can call me Sawyer, Barb."

Barb nodded. "It's not my job to give interviews, Sawyer. I'm not a head chef, nor do I want to be. I have enough on my plate managing the kitchen staff when you're not here."

Sawyer stiffened, her mind and body rapidly switching back to attack mode. Her voice was gravelly as she bit out hoarsely, "Then quit, Barb. Fucking quit. If you can't handle the pressure, it's high time I find someone who can." With that, Sawyer pushed past her, leaving Barb to stand in her office alone.

Her cell phone was vibrating by the time she was heading back to her office an hour later. The two back-to-back interviews had been a complete waste of her time. She was beginning to doubt Kelly's ability to find capable young people who wanted to work.

Sawyer snatched her phone out of her pants pocket just as she was entering her office. Bree's face lit up her screen, inviting Sawyer to accept the video call. For a nano-second, she considered not answering it, but that just made her feel worse. She took a deep breath, closing her office door with a lot more grace than earlier. She collapsed into her swivel chair, scrubbing a hand over her face. "Hi, love," she forced out once her daughter was live on-screen. The seriousness in Bree's eyes had Sawyer sitting up in her chair. "Everything okay?"

"Did you really try to fire Barb?"

Sawyer tensed. *Seriously, Barb, you phoned my daughter?* To Bree, she tried for a smile, but even by force, it wasn't happening today. "Bree, honey, I think Barb might have stretched the truth a bit."

"She said you told her to quit *twice* so that you can find someone else more capable."

A strained laugh slipped from Sawyer. She squinted into the phone, wondering how she could dodge this. Things must have been dire if her staff were calling her daughter. Sawyer's heated discussion with Barb felt like days ago. "Surely she didn't take me seriously."

Had Barb quit? Sawyer hadn't heard anything while in the interviews, and she'd been too busy rushing to her office to bother doing a head count of her kitchen staff.

"She didn't, but she was worried you were serious. She's concerned about you, *Maman.*" Bree blew a raspberry, the few strands of mocha brown hair in her face flying out of the way in the process. Her big brown eyes that were so similar to her father's narrowed. "I think I should come home for the summer."

"Come home? Haven't you already started your summer job?" For reasons unknown, McCoy's face was the first to come to Sawyer's mind. She didn't want the mechanic to be working on the McLaren if her daughter was visiting. Not after they'd come so close to—

"I did, but I miss you. It might be good for you too. I could help at the restaurant in the evenings and give you a break."

"Bree, I ..." Sawyer trailed off, hating how hopeful her daughter looked. She didn't need anyone to come save her. The stress test was coming up tomorrow, but whatever the results were, she'd be fine. She was fine on her own, figuring life out post-Olivier. Her wounds were scarring over, some more concealed than others, but scarring all the same. She grimaced, lowering her gaze from Bree's. "I think you should stay in California. A weekend visit before your semester begins is one thing, but giving up your summer for me isn't what I want."

"*Maman*, I wouldn't be—"

"It's my decision. Please respect it."

Bree's face fell. She nodded. "Okay."

They spoke for a while longer, but Sawyer didn't feel any better by the time they hung up. She'd been hateful to everyone for the better part of two days, the reminiscence of McCoy's thumb on her lip an endless torture from which she had no reprieve. The sensation of that strong body so close to hers made Sawyer quake with a need so ferocious it genuinely terrified her. She'd lost control then, and even though she'd managed to kick McCoy out, Sawyer still felt a staggering loss of power. She'd been taking her anger out on everyone but McCoy, too humiliated by her breakdown to admit it.

"Fuck that," she stated loudly in the small office. Sawyer slapped her hands down onto her desk, pushing off them to get to her feet. Reaching for the buttons on her chef coat, she quickly changed into her day clothes. She'd never left work so close to the supper rush, and yet, nothing seemed more important to her in the moment than rectifying what happened with McCoy on her piano bench.

Sawyer didn't waste time once she pulled into the packed parking lot of Miller's Mechanics & Restoration. On the drive over to Richmond, she'd done a stellar job building her frustration up toward the aggravating mechanic. McCoy had no right to put moves on Sawyer. She'd been vulnerable, and McCoy had cashed in on the chance to get close to her. She was arrogant and crueler than even Sawyer if she was willing to swoop in for her own benefit when it was obvious sex was the last thing on Sawyer's mind. Somewhere along the way, McCoy had taken some of her power; Sawyer was there to get it back. It was time someone put the playgirl in her place.

"Hey, ma'am, you can't go in there!" the younger blond man shouted after her as she marched through the door adjoining the car bay and reception area. Sawyer ignored him and kept going, dodging the heavyset man named Chip as she made her way to where she'd seen McCoy the first time here.

"Gotcha," Sawyer muttered through clenched teeth, zeroing in on her target. McCoy was wearing her coveralls and trademark neck bandana, likely to cover up all the hickeys she received each night.

Sawyer's gut twisted more with the thought. Her steps faltered, one high heel wobbling on the oil-stained concrete. McCoy was standing underneath a sedan, her muscular arms stretched above her head as she worked on tightening a part. Sawyer's breaths were shallow as she rounded on her, stepping right under the vehicle as well.

McCoy's lush green eyes darted over in surprise. "Sawyer, what—"

"Stop," Sawyer interrupted, and her chest heaved as she grabbed a fistful of Coy's bandana to yank her closer. "Just ... just *stop* talking."

Somehow, just by looking at McCoy, all of Sawyer's anger vanished. Before she knew it, she'd dipped her lips down and latched onto McCoy's. The kiss surprised them both, but McCoy recovered first, melting into Sawyer's mouth. There was a soft moan, and then the tool McCoy had been using clattered to the concrete floor seconds before strong arms wrapped around Sawyer's waist.

Sawyer couldn't breathe as McCoy's mouth devoured hers, wholly unprepared for the onslaught of dizzying arousal flooding her senses. McCoy's unique scent of oil and cologne was engulfing, melting every last defense she'd reinforced on the drive over. It was terrifying. Exhilarating.

And over far too soon.

"Sawyer," McCoy rasped, gently pulling out of Sawyer's grasp and snapping her back to awareness.

Sawyer blinked, dazed. Her legs felt like jello, not at all like she was going to march back out of the garage like she'd anticipated. She had planned to bring McCoy down a peg, not kiss her until they were both gasping for air. But when she'd reached McCoy, all Sawyer saw was the kindness and affection she'd come to expect and love. She *loved* how McCoy looked at her.

"I shouldn't have kissed you back, I'm sorry." Remorse and misery overshadowed the usual flare of mischief in McCoy's eyes, and she dropped her gaze from Sawyer's. "I-I decided yesterday after you kicked me to the curb. I don't wanna do this with you."

"Do what?" Sawyer's cheeks grew warm. Her heart was crashing against the walls of her chest for a reason unbeknownst to her.

McCoy bent to pick up the wrench she'd dropped. She still wouldn't look at Sawyer as she replied, "Countless women have tried kissing me over the years, and I swear I've never made one feel like I felt yesterday. All you had to say was no, Sawyer."

"I am ... You took me by surprise. I—" Sawyer clamped her mouth shut, not knowing what she was trying to say anymore and realizing anything right now would be voiced in frustration. McCoy was right, though. Deep down, the truth had been gnawing at her like a rotten tooth festering for too long. The way Sawyer had reacted the morning before had been out of character and, truthfully, downright humiliating on her part. Belittling McCoy in that way was akin to what Olivier used to do to her all the time. Since when had she become that person?

Mon Dieu. It was how she'd been treating everyone lately. *What is wrong with me?* Sawyer placed a hand over her stomach, the nausea returning with a vengeance now. A tingling sensation was causing an ache in her arm and chest, but she shrugged it off and wiped at the perspiration dotting her brow. "I am ..." she began again, only to freeze once more. Her mind blanketed in a mist of brain fog, and she shook her head. Her throat was thick with emotion as she croaked, "I have to go."

"Sawyer ..." McCoy started to say, but she was already speed-walking out of the shop and into the fresh air. Perspiration soaked through Sawyer's thin camisole and into her blouse by the time she made it back to her SUV. The pressing heaviness in her chest squeezed now, and her breaths were shallow as she fumbled with her car keys.

"C'mon, focus." She gritted her teeth, reaching a trembling hand up to wipe the sweat from her eyes. Her whole damn body felt off, but she refused to go home. That Michelin star she and her staff were working so hard for wouldn't earn itself. How would her team feel if she took the evening off after her episode earlier? Her near meltdown Sunday was having lasting effects.

Sawyer's car keys slipped from her hand, and she clumsily went to pick them up. Dizziness washed through her, and she stumbled headfirst into the Rover.

"Sawyer!"

McCoy's strong arms caught Sawyer seconds before she face-planted in the parking lot, lifting her in the air like some damsel in distress. Sawyer sagged against McCoy for about two seconds before she remembered herself.

"Put me down. I'm fine."

She wasn't sure that was true, but she'd be damned if she let McCoy see her weak like this. Sawyer wasn't weak.

"You're not fine. How long has this been going on?" McCoy asked gently, lowering them both to the ground. She didn't let go until Sawyer was safely leaning against the Rover's front wheel well. Sawyer stared at the mechanic through blurry, unfocused eyes, aware of McCoy's calloused hand pushing strands of her damp hair off her cheek. "It'll be okay, Sawyer."

"It's my friend. She collapsed but is conscious." Sawyer's gaze widened a little, and she watched McCoy speak calmly into her cell phone as she unlocked the Rover. "Yes, Miller's Mechanics. 4580 No. 3 Road, Richmond."

McCoy's voice faded in and out as Sawyer struggled to remain upright. She was so tired, and her entire left side felt numb, but her eyes blinked open once McCoy was crouched in front of her moments later. She was rifling through Sawyer's purse. "Yes, um, Sawyer Marie Lavoie. L-a-v- ..."

Sawyer took slow, even breaths, concentrating on her soothing voice.

Chapter 16

McCoy

"Sawyer, here, take these." Coy gently pressed the two low-dose aspirin against Sawyer's lips.

Sawyer's eyes flickered open, and her hand left where it'd been clenching her chest to shakily grasp the Yeti water bottle on the ground. Coy saw this and shook her head. "Chew them. The ambulance will be here soon, but those should help if you're having a heart attack."

She scanned Sawyer's body slowly, noting the restrictive blouse and slacks she wore. "Your clothes are too tight. Can I?" Coy asked, her gaze not leaving Sawyer's as she gestured to Sawyer's blazer. Upon Sawyer's slight nod, Coy reached for the blazer's buttons, hoping Sawyer couldn't see the tremble in her fingers.

She's a victim, a patient. Just like the ones you've helped on the trails.

But try as she might, Coy couldn't get the image of Sawyer falling out of her head. Had she not been so thrown by their kiss, she might have known earlier that something was off with Sawyer. Coy had noticed Sawyer a few times holding her stomach or rubbing her neck, but Coy had chalked it up to the strangeness of the situation. If Coy hadn't had regrets of pushing Sawyer away and decided at the last minute to run after her, who knows how long Sawyer would have been alone, possibly dying?

Tears burned her eyes, blurring the last button on the blazer so Coy had no choice but to blink. She swallowed, wiping her damp cheeks with the heel of her hands and darting a quick look Sawyer's way. Her eyes had drifted closed once more. "I'm just gonna undo the first few buttons on your blouse," she explained, reaching for the material. Sawyer's normally tanned skin had taken on an unusual pallor, and as Coy revealed Sawyer's collarbones and chest under the blouse, the ragged, uneven rise and falls of Sawyer's breath were unmistakable.

"Call Desmarais. Tell Barb ... I'll be late," Sawyer mumbled, opening her eyes long enough to meet Coy's concerned gaze. They closed again seconds before she slumped over, unconscious.

"Shit. *Shit*, Sawyer," Coy exclaimed, slipping her hands around Sawyer's waist and carefully guiding her the rest of the way to the ground. Falling to her knees, she placed two fingers against Sawyer's neck in search of a pulse. Nothing. Coy's eyes darted to Sawyer's chest, noticing the lack of movement, and immediately ripped the remaining buttons open on Sawyer's blouse. She could feel her own breath coming out short and choppy as she reached for the small scissors in her First Aid kit. Making quick work cutting off Sawyer's bra, Coy ignored the few bystanders now hovering close by and began CPR.

One, two, three, four ...

The distant sound of sirens sometime later was music to Coy's ears, and she had to force herself not to sag in relief. *Not yet*, she thought through clenched teeth, not daring to let up too soon on the rigorous chest compressions. She had to keep Sawyer's blood circulating until ... until ...

A hand landed on Coy's shoulder, and she flinched in surprise, looking up bleary-eyed to find a paramedic. "Thanks, we've got her from here. Great job."

Coy blinked and reluctantly let Sawyer go, aware of the tears dripping off her chin to dampen her coveralls. She answered the paramedics' rapid-fire questions as they hooked up an AED to Sawyer's chest, but her voice sounded far off, like she was stuck inside a dream or the situation was happening to someone else, not her.

"Clear!"

"Okay, we've got a pulse!"

Greg appeared beside her at some point, wrapping his arms around Coy. "You did good, kiddo. Probably saved her life. I'm proud of you."

Why don't you go wait for news at the hospital? Cancel your plans with Naz.

Coy closed her eyes as she sat at the foot of her bed hours later, her father's parting words haunting her "guys' night" like some kind of twisted, anti-lust omen. When she was putting back shots with Naz at the strip club, she thought the tequila would eventually drown out her old man's voice. She'd foolishly hoped that once she'd seen Jasmine's newest dance routine up on the stage, she'd forget she'd left a piece of her heart with Sawyer hours before.

As it turned out, tequila and the promise of uncomplicated sex no longer made Coy forget. In fact, the guilt of going on with her life when she had no clue how Sawyer fared caused crater-sized hollows in her gut. While they'd been at the strip club, she'd taken off twice to the washroom to call Sawyer, only to reach her voicemail. When that didn't work, she called the hospital, but no one would give her any information. They either didn't know of an update or wouldn't share it, and the lack of news drove Coy insane.

Now, hours later, Jasmine stepped between Coy's thighs, her sultry smile a promise of all the kinky things she had planned for the three of them. "You're so strong," she crooned, skimming her palms up Coy's arms. Coy was still wearing her sports bra, but Jasmine let out a grunt of satisfaction as her nails scored her back and shoulders. She licked Coy's closed mouth, kissing a path to her ear where she whispered, "I love it when you pick me up to straddle you."

"Yeah?" Coy murmured, willing her body to respond. A flicker of butterflies, moisture at her core, *something. Am I broken? 'Cause Jasmine always does the trick.* As Jasmine teased Coy's mouth until she opened, she reconsidered. She wasn't broken. She was human, a half-decent one at that. One who'd witnessed their crush have a heart attack. It made sense that sex wouldn't magically erase the last hour of her workday when Sawyer had stormed in only to be rushed to the hospital.

"I think maybe she's hinting something," Naz whispered, stepping behind Jasmine. Deft, tattooed fingers slipped into Jasmine's jeans, circling her waistline before landing on the enclosure. "Fuck, you're gorgeous." Naz's voice was sweet, like honey, and the way Jasmine responded to the tattooist as Naz laid wet kisses along her bare shoulders was all the reason Coy needed.

"I, um ..." Coy swallowed past the lump choking her, needing to get out of there pronto. She lifted Jasmine easily, but instead of placing her on her lap, Coy smoothly laid her down on the bed. "I'm so sorry, but I ... I can't do this tonight. You two have fun, though." A ghost of a smile reached Coy's lips, and she reached out to cup Jasmine's cheek before slowly climbing off the bed. Then she gave Naz a little push toward the bed.

"You're not joining us?"

"Nah, I'm ... I need to go check on something." Coy shook her head, not feeling the scene at all. How was her father always right? All she could think about was Sawyer, and how Jasmine didn't smell or feel quite like her. It was stupid to think she could forget about a woman like that through meaningless sex. Her gaze landed on the far wall, and she noisily cleared her throat. "Use my room, though. Have fun." Grabbing her earbuds and phone off the nightstand, Coy left them to it. As soon as she was in the hallway, she sagged against the wall, suddenly weak in the knees. "Fuck," she whispered, scrubbing a hand over her face. She peered bleary eyed at her phone, still mostly drunk, and the early morning digits on her screen made her realize just how much time she'd wasted. She couldn't exactly rush to the hospital at two thirty in the morning.

Coy padded barefoot to Sloane's bedroom, knocking softly before inching the door ajar. A gust of cold air from the fan hit her bare skin, and she shivered, creeping across the carpet for the hoodie draped over the armchair. It fit perfectly, and Coy silently thanked her sister for wearing her hoodies a size too big.

"Who's that?" Sloane's muffled voice broke the repetitive whirring of the ceiling fan.

"Me. Can I sleep in here tonight?" Coy asked, already pulling back the bedcovers.

"Mm-hmm. Date not good?" Rolling over, Sloane's sleepy visage came face-to-face with Coy's. Her sister grimaced. "You stink like cigars."

Coy chuckled, tucking the covers in around them. "You know a guys' night isn't complete without them."

"Says Naz."

"Says Naz," Coy agreed, burrowing under the warmth of the duvet. The preferred temperature in their bedrooms was not something they had in common. Sloane slept like she was in the arctic, regardless of the season. Coy liked to think she fell more in the "normal" spectrum; she used a fan when it was hot and a heater when it was cold. Life didn't need to be complicated.

"So, what's up? You never turn down Jasmine."

Coy sighed, shifting onto her back. She watched the shadows on the ceiling from a nearby streetlamp before admitting, "Sawyer has, like, taken over my damn mind or something. I can't concentrate on anything else."

"J.D. told me what happened at the shop. Were you scared?"

Coy nodded. "For her. I was terrified. Sawyer is always so strong-willed, you know? She's fierce, and cold, and when she collapsed, I ..." She stopped, her throat thickening as she struggled with the words.

Fresh tears stung her eyes, taking Coy back to that afternoon and how scared Sawyer had looked. She shrugged, helpless. There were no words, none that would make sense to Sloane. Coy's sister wouldn't understand why she was hung up on Sawyer of all people.

"I bet you're feeling pretty guilty right about now. You've never caused a heart attack after kissing a girl before." Coy frowned, and Sloane rushed to add, "Not that it was your fault. Purely coincidental, I'm sure."

Coy would be lying if she said she *hadn't* thought of that. Truthfully, Sawyer going into cardiac arrest moments after their kiss had plagued Coy's thoughts all night. She couldn't help but wonder what would have happened if Coy had not pushed Sawyer away? Had Coy's rejection tipped Sawyer's stress levels over the edge?

"Shit, sorry, Coy. Lame joke."

"Sawyer kissed *me*," Coy affirmed, sounding downright indignant, but seriously, since when had Sloane become so callous in her thoughts? "But yeah, you fucking suck right now. The single life must be making you bitter." With a huff, she rolled over in the bed, facing away from Sloane.

Within five minutes, her twin had fallen back to sleep, but slumber refused to come to Coy. She was upset, confused, and could hear Jasmine's muffled mewls coming from down the hall. After an hour, she slipped out of bed again and grabbed her keys. Walking to the hospital would be more favorable than enduring another damn second in the apartment.

CHAPTER 17

Sawyer

SHE CLENCHED AND UNCLENCHED her jaw, scowling as she watched the nurse strap the blood pressure cuff to her arm. "If it's high, you might consider the fact I was woken up every hour on the hour through the night."

"*Maman*," Bree chided from her seat beside Sawyer's bed.

"What? It's true. I haven't felt this sleep-deprived since you were in diapers." Her usual insomnia was a hell of a lot better than what she was enduring now.

The nurse only chuckled, not at all fazed by Sawyer's hostility. She'd just begun her shift, so there was still plenty of time to get under her skin. "I'm Diane, by the way. It'll be me and Marissa popping in to check on you today."

"Thanks for the heads up. I suppose all my sleeping will have to wait until I'm home again."

"Okay, stay still. Try not to talk for a minute, and I'll be out of your hair in no time." Diane raised an eyebrow, shooting Sawyer a pointed look as she adjusted the cuff. Sawyer glanced away, knowing she was extra miserable but unable to stop hating everyone. She'd been in a foul mood since she'd woken in the intensive care unit two days ago. She was exhausted and sore all over. Her chest was so bruised, it looked like someone had taken a bat to her. Bree informed her McCoy had administered CPR, but the last thing Sawyer remembered before waking in the hospital was the comforting warmth as McCoy held her in her muscular arms.

McCoy, who had not visited in the entire time Sawyer had been laid up. Not that Sawyer had expected or even wanted her to. They'd both established the kiss had been a mistake and if anyone could respect standing by a decision, it was Sawyer. McCoy's decisiveness was impressive, responsible.

Then why is the radio silence so goddamn deafening?

Except for two missed calls when Sawyer had first landed in the hospital, she'd heard nothing else from McCoy. At the very least, didn't the fact that she'd *saved* Sawyer's life deserve a text?

Yes, from you, not her. Stop deflecting. One word is all it would take. Thanks. *How hard could it be?*

"She was just doing her job, *Maman*. You didn't have to be rude," Bree said the moment they were alone again. She was twisting her long brown strands atop her head in a loose bun, a bemused expression on her face as she stared at her mother.

"I know," sighed Sawyer, her head falling back onto her pillow. Exhaustion was hitting her already, and she'd only just had breakfast. Her body was bone-tired, like she could sleep for a week straight. If only the nurses would quit coming into her room. "I need to get back to work."

Bree's hand landed on the arm not attached to an IV, and she gave Sawyer a light squeeze. "Work is the last thing you need. The restaurant will be there when you're all healed up. Cindy's running the kitchen like she's worked there for years. And I know you don't like it, but I'm helping too. Seriously, you could have the whole summer off if you wanted to."

"Absolutely not," Sawyer breathed, unable to believe Cindy had quit her job to help her out. Especially since Sawyer had been so miserable lately. Why would Cindy subject herself daily to Sawyer's bitchiness? "I'm still upset that you're here when I told you not to worry about me."

"You had a heart attack. Would you have even told me if Barb hadn't?"

Sawyer closed her eyes. "I just want you to be happy, *mon amour*. I know ... coming back here brings up bad memories."

"I don't want to get into it and bring on more stress, but I will say this much: you're wrong, *Maman*. All my bad memories died a year ago. We're free now, and I love coming home to visit you."

Sawyer took a deep breath, willing herself to remain calm in front of Bree. She'd known there was no love lost between her daughter and husband, but to hear Bree speak so frankly was alarming.

There was a knock on the door, and even as Sawyer thought of ways she could ignore the interruption, Bree was exclaiming, "Holy flowers. *Maman*, are you seeing this?"

Opening her eyes again, the first thing Sawyer noticed was the enormous bouquet coming into her private room. The daffodils were effectively blocking her view of the person carrying them, and it wasn't until the figure set the beautiful display down on the dinner table that she saw who it was.

"Hi, sorry I'm late. They, uh, wouldn't let me in when you were in intensive care," McCoy greeted her, looking self-conscious as she darted a glance in Bree's direction.

Surprised and secretly pleased, Sawyer sputtered, "Hi, McCoy."

McCoy visibly swallowed, her lips looking as tempting as they had the day she'd kissed them. "Hi. How are you?"

"Did you say McCoy?" Bree interrupted, standing up as well now. A hand flew to her throat as she stared incredulously at McCoy. "You're the one who saved my mom."

"It was ... I did CPR. Oh!" McCoy exclaimed, awkwardly accepting Bree's hug. A faint blush covered her cheeks as she met Sawyer's gaze. "I'm just glad I was there."

"Me too. God, you have no idea." Bree wiped away a fleeting tear, laughing as she pulled back from McCoy and really looked at her for the first time. Then Bree glanced at Sawyer. "Isn't McCoy the one working on *Papa's* car? Cindy told me."

"She is, yes," Sawyer replied, her gaze fixed on McCoy's. She cleared her throat. "Bree, can you give us a moment?"

Bree's eyebrows shot up, but she nodded. "I'll just grab a coffee."

Once they were alone, Sawyer studied McCoy silently for long enough that she eventually had the younger woman squirming where she stood. She was dressed impeccably in non-work clothes, wearing a pair of torn, punk-style black skinny jeans, Converse sneakers, and a blue and black checkered flannel long-sleeve shirt. For once, her chestnut hair was loose, reaching mid-point to her ear and sloping to one side over the disconnected undercut. She took Sawyer's breath away.

"May I?" McCoy asked, breaking the silence. She pointed to the chair Bree had occupied before taking a seat. Seconds later, the chair legs scraped as McCoy pulled closer to Sawyer's bedside.

"You know CPR," Sawyer said when nothing else came to mind.

McCoy glanced around the private room, absently rubbing the back of her neck. Sawyer recognized it as one of her nervous habits. "Yeah. I, um ... I've volunteered for years with the mountain bike association as one of their First Aid responders."

"So, you mountain bike?" That could explain Sawyer's fascination with McCoy's biceps, right? Mountain biking sounded like it took a lot of upper body strength.

"I do. My sister and cousin do, too. The young blond-haired guy at the shop is my cousin, J.D."

Sawyer recalled seeing someone with light hair the other day when she breezed through the waiting room, but she didn't comment on it. Instead, she said, "Thank you for the flowers, but why are you here, McCoy? If ... you're wondering about work, then it'll be another few days before I'm home."

"What?" She seemed shocked Sawyer would suggest as much, and she wagged her head back and forth in denial, her expressive green gaze wide.

"No, I ... I came to see *you*. I'm so sorry, Sawyer. I-I can't help but feel like I had something to do with what happened."

Sawyer frowned. "So you're here in ... what? A friendly capacity?"

McCoy looked confused, but she nodded slowly. "Sure, yes. If that's what you want."

"It's not. I have enough friends." Cindy and Lori were often more friends than she had time for. She certainly didn't want McCoy to fall into that category only to later torture Sawyer with tales of her sex life.

The tip of McCoy's tongue darted out to wet her lips, but Sawyer forced herself not to lower her gaze at the action. *Send her on her way.* "Okay, well, I'm here in any capacity you want me to be."

Sawyer swallowed, her throat suddenly parched. Images of kissing McCoy and more teased the edges of her mind. The memory of those solid shoulders beneath her grip increased the temperature in the room by several degrees. Sawyer's cheeks were hot as she muttered, "My employees don't bring me flowers and certainly not the largest bouquet money can buy. It tends to blur lines."

There was no mistaking the disappointment that flashed in McCoy's eyes, but Sawyer held her ground. Not blurring the boundaries between boss and employee any more than they had already was for the best.

"Right. Again, I'm sorry." McCoy's lips tightened, and she started to stand.

"Wait, I don't mean—" Sawyer let out a breath, grimacing when the exhalation hurt her ribs. *I just want to look at you a bit more.* The thought was there, the tremulous feelings she now got when McCoy was nearby, but of course she couldn't voice them. It'd be more than inappropriate. It would show another shard of vulnerability Sawyer couldn't afford to offer up. "Please don't leave just yet."

"Okay." McCoy flashed her a tentative smile before settling into the chair again. She had a vibe about her that Sawyer didn't think she'd ever tire from. Today, she was the perfect balance between rugged and soft, and her exposed throat was like a homing beacon for Sawyer. Like a mouth-watering morsel Sawyer was dying to taste. And those dimples when she smiled ...

"Tell me more about your sister. Is she older? Younger?"

"Random, but okay." McCoy let out a soft chuckle, resting her elbows on Sawyer's mattress. She hooked her fingers together, her thumb rings tugging at Sawyer's attention for some ungodly reason. "We're twins but I'm technically ten minutes older."

"Identical?" Sawyer managed, proud she was able to keep her tone neutral. Again, she swallowed. God there really were two McCoys walking around Vancouver. She could just imagine the path of broken hearts left in their wake.

"Yep. Well, I mean, we don't look exactly alike anymore. Sloane is a lot more femme. She even wears heels sometimes—can you believe that? Definitely not like me."

McCoy was rambling, but somehow in the last few months, her nerves around Sawyer had become more charming instead of annoying. When had that happened? A feminine version of McCoy flaunting around in a dress and heels stuck in Sawyer's head, and a sleepy laugh popped out. She didn't know who was more surprised. McCoy, if her million-dollar wide grin was any indication. Her dimples were entirely too distracting, and the way she was looking at Sawyer had her wishing they'd kiss already. Just put Sawyer out of her misery.

"Unique names you both have."

McCoy glanced away, giving Sawyer a clear view of her tantalizing throat bobbing up and down as she swallowed. "My mom insisted they name us after we were born, but ... she died giving birth." McCoy gazed at Sawyer, a sad smile appearing. Sawyer's heart twisted. "My dad named us—me, after his favorite motorcycle driver, and Sloane was my mom's maiden name."

"Oh. Well, he did a good job," Sawyer managed, an unfamiliar feeling bubbling up in her throat. *Send her on her way.* She needed to backtrack.

Their conversation was getting too friendly, too far out of Sawyer's comfort zone.

Thankfully, Bree chose that moment to return. Sawyer sighed, grateful when the conversation shifted to Bree and McCoy soon after, and she finally dozed off.

Chapter 18

McCoy

Coy zipped down through the narrow trail affectionately named Fred, her complete focus on the wooden ramp approaching lightning fast. She bucked her knees for impact, moving her body with her bike as she went. There were a lot of roots and rocks to go over on Fred, and it happened so quickly, there wasn't a window big enough for mistakes. Fred wasn't the most challenging trail she'd ridden, but this section of Diamondhead in Squamish was certainly one of her favorites in B.C.

She could hear Sloane behind her, singing Fletcher's latest song at the top of her breathless lungs. They were missing J.D. today, but it was always nice to get some time in with just Sloane. Between Coy's work and Sloane's, as well as her sister training for the upcoming bike race, their time together had been sparse the past month or so.

They finished Fred and biked their way into Tinder, a shorter trail leading out of the woods. It connected Fred to Your Mom, which was another fun trail for Coy to enjoy. Your Mom took her and Sloane back into the woods, and Coy came close to elbowing one of the trees so close to the trail's path. She gritted her teeth, bending her knees and angling her body as her bike took a few sharp curves before coming to another wooden ramp.

"Having fun yet?" Sloane called out once they'd reached the beginning of Alice Lake trail.

"Hell yeah!" Coy shouted back with a grin. She led the way onward to Alice Lake's Treasure Trail, one of the more grueling trails they would face today. When they were younger, it had taken a long time for Sloane to even go down the steep descents. "Remember, just stick your ass back off the saddle," she added, guiding her bike down the first boulder. From there, it was a blur of forest beauty and tight maneuvers. With its treacherous wooden ramps and slopes steep enough to make you feel like you would tip the bike over, Treasure Trail wasn't for the faint of heart.

"Dude," Sloane exclaimed, high-fiving Coy as soon as they'd gotten off of Treasure Trail. "You flew off that last ledge like a pro. Seriously, I had to brake just before because the granite is fucking gnarly, but not you."

Coy smiled, glancing up at the GoPro camera attached to Sloane's helmet. "Were you recording?"

"Of course. We'll need it for this week's post."

They started biking toward Boney Elbows, enjoying the break, especially after that last trail. "Did you have a chance to look over the last footage at the shop yet?"

Sloane nodded. "Yesterday. It needs a bit of editing. I can work on it tomorrow."

"Cool, thanks."

Coy didn't know what she'd do without Sloane. There certainly wouldn't be a *Sloane & McCoy* social media presence with such a huge following. It worked out well for them because Sloane hated being in front of the camera, and Coy wasn't skilled with the behind-the-scenes stuff. Their followers went bonkers the rare times Sloane accompanied Coy in a video, like she was a guest celebrity. Their videos always went viral then, which was odd. Usually, they were just fooling around, being silly, perhaps mixing cocktails or trying to make a recipe from one of their favorite cookbooks. Sometimes, Coy liked to throw together strange concoctions that their viewers would suggest she try, and then she'd rate how edible it was after.

Coy checked her watch. It was almost noon. "Break at our usual spot?"

Sloane playfully arched a brow. "You know I'm all about routine."

By the time they were parked off the side of the In n Out Burger trail, enjoying Squamish's best scenic views, Coy's asthma was acting up. Biking at such high elevations always triggered it, but she was calm as she dug out her puffer and shook it. "So," she started, taking a deep inhale before continuing with a sly grin, "you ready for the big race? Will your nemesis be racing this year?"

Sloane rolled her eyes. "Hopefully not. Hopefully, she had an accident and had to drop out."

"Harsh."

"A broken leg or something. Nothing serious." Sloane shrugged, taking a swig of her water. "I'm not the villain in this story, trust me. She's crazy. Remember when she sideswiped me two years ago racing around that steep bend during the Okanagan race?"

"You told the organizers she tried to kill you," Coy laughed, uncapping her bottle and dumping some of the water over her head. Then she opened her mouth, letting the cool liquid gush down her throat.

"Because it was true. I'm glad I'm teaming up with J.D. this year. He can watch my back."

"I'm sorry I can't race with you." Her asthma simply wouldn't allow it. Racing all day for a week straight had always been too much for Coy, but she'd gotten over the disappointment years ago. The smaller races the association put on throughout the summer and fall were good enough for her.

"It's okay. Maybe you'll have time to cheer me on one of the nights. Come have a beer with us?"

"That'd be nice, but the island is kind of far for a day trip." Coy leaned back on her elbows, gazing at the stretch of mountains beyond them. It was a beautiful Saturday, the air clear and mild after days of rain. She hadn't had the pleasure of traveling around the world, but she honestly didn't think anywhere else held a candle to B.C. Coy always felt at peace when she was outdoors. It was a nice distraction from her Sawyer confusion.

"You're quiet."

Coy tilted her head in Sloane's direction, her brow raised in confusion. "Am I? Guess I've got a lot on my mind."

Sloane tore open a bag of trail mix, taking a handful before offering the bag to Coy. "Does it have anything to do with the pretty woman home from the hospital? You're going there tonight, right?"

"I am," she began, helping herself to the trail mix. She examined the handful, picking out all the cashews and eating them first. She could feel Sloane watching her but didn't particularly want to rehash whatever was or wasn't happening between her and the chef. "She got home yesterday. Her daughter's staying with her, I think, for the summer." Meeting Bree at the hospital had been a surprise. Not necessarily a bad one—Coy just hadn't expected her to be so grown. Which was ridiculous, considering she lived away from home. Of course she'd be an adult. *But she's seven years younger than you, dude.* Could that be why Sawyer was so hesitant to admit she liked Coy?

"Oof, that's gonna be a buzzkill." Sloane laughed, snatching the trail mix. "How are you gonna work your magic and walk away after with a kid in the house? You don't even like kids."

"If you're gonna keep up with those smart-ass remarks, then I'll stop telling you shit," Coy warned, scrubbing a hand over her face. She didn't bother to correct her sister about Bree's age. "I know you don't believe me, but there's nothing going on between us." Just a kiss neither of them would talk about last week when Coy visited. The kiss Coy couldn't stop thinking about, no matter how hard she tried. Thinking back on it, Coy was pretty sure the kiss hadn't been thought out. When she'd noticed Sawyer standing under the car she was working on, she thought for sure the woman was about to tear Coy a new one. And then, *bam*!

The sexiest lips in the whole world assaulted her mouth in a state of sheer recklessness.

"But you want there to be. So what's your plan? You even switched your schedule around again." Sloane rolled her eyes, but one edge of her mouth curled up. "No doubt so you can ogle her in the evening now that she'll be home."

"Stuff it. That's not why at all." Coy rolled her eyes. "It's 'cause she'll be waking up later now, and rebuilds can get loud. And, to answer your question, for once, I don't have a plan."

As she was packing up her things at Sawyer's late that evening, Coy noticed a beautiful curvy woman leaving the house, car keys in hand as she walked down the short pathway. Her gaze landed on Coy, still inside the truck bed, a grin spreading across her face. "You're the one who hit on Sawyer at the warehouse, right?"

Coy pinched her brows together, studying the other woman. She looked vaguely familiar, but before Coy could say anything, the woman was patting Coy's back. "Yup. I'd remember that handsome face anywhere. I'm Lori, doll, Sawyer's friend."

Coy opened her mouth and then closed it, not quite knowing what to say. She turned back to her task, lifting the subframe for the McLaren gently out of the truck before a reply came. "So she does have friends." *It's just me she doesn't want to get to know. Figures.* The first woman to catch her eye longer than just a night, and she had absolutely no inclination to get to know Coy.

Lori laughed. "Sawyer said she didn't? My wife met her during their time in the culinary, and they've been friends since. Chef Lavoie isn't the easiest woman to befriend, but I'd hazard a guess that you've already figured that out about her."

Coy nodded, realizing she hadn't properly introduced herself, so she held out her hand. "I'm McCoy, by the way, Sawyer's mechanic. Of the *non*-friend variety."

Lori must have picked up on Coy's sarcasm because she laughed again, shaking her waiting hand. "Oof. Is it sad that I can almost picture how that conversation would have gone down?"

"It ended before it really got started," Coy admitted, her tone wistful. She slipped her hand away, lifting the subframe and carrying it into the garage. When she returned, Lori was leaning against her Prius, watching her.

"She likes you, you know," Lori offered, jingling her car keys. "It's just hard for Sawyer to let people in, especially ones she could potentially love."

Potentially what now? Coy's lips parted, her heart skipping a beat at the implication. Butterflies erupted in her stomach like they'd shot from a cannonball, and the pit of her stomach dipped. Thinking Sawyer's feelings may have been mutual was a helluva lot different than hearing the admittance come from someone's mouth.

"H-how is she tonight?"

Coy cringed at her breathless stammer, swiveling away from Lori's perceptive gaze. She set her air compressor in the bed of the truck and closed the tailgate.

"Oh, you know," Lori drawled out. "If a grizzly and a cobra had babies, Sawyer would be the result. She's more ornery than usual, and her glares are so frigid they could bring big burly men to their knees, but I read that irritability and depression are common after a heart attack."

Coy nodded; she'd read that too. And knowing Sawyer, her depression would likely come out as anger anyway. "I'm gonna pop in to say hi."

"Thought you might, doll. She's resting in the living room." Lori made her way around to the driver's door. "Oh, there's an extra hotplate in the fridge if you're hungry. Cindy and I are trying to keep the boss out of the kitchen as long as possible, so we whipped up a few freezer meals."

"Good idea. And thanks."

Lori sent her a little wave over her shoulder as she climbed into the Prius, calling out, "It was great to finally meet you, McCoy."

"You too," Coy replied, then reprimanded herself because she hadn't even known Lori existed ten minutes ago. She watched the older woman reverse out of Sawyer's driveway before heading into the house through the garage. Like she'd done the last time she'd ventured into Sawyer's private space, she rang the doorbell and knocked as she let herself in. Unlike the last time, the salivating scent of lasagna wafted down the hall from the kitchen, instantly the cause of Coy's stomach rumbling. She'd had a protein shake after her bike ride, but that had been hours ago.

Choosing not to go about calling Sawyer's name in case she'd fallen asleep, Coy removed her boots and placed them on the mat before heading deeper into the house. As the lavish kitchen came into view, she didn't feel as though she was snooping through the house like she had the first time. Besides the almost kiss on the piano bench, Sawyer hadn't given any indication that Coy was imposing that night.

She pulled the dinner plate from the fridge and popped it in the microwave. While it was reheating, Coy washed her hands in the sink, paying close attention to the grease wedged under her blunt fingernails. She smirked, remembering the disgusted look on Sawyer's face the first time she'd brought Coy supper and her dirty fingers had touched the plate. Sawyer had looked like she'd have an aneurysm.

"Oh my ... *hell*, this looks unreal." Coy's eyes widened as she extracted the plate from the microwave. The steaming pasta sauce was oozing off the lasagna noodles, and bits of cheese had pushed out of the middle. Coy licked her lips, opening the fridge again in hopes there would be Parmesan to sprinkle on top. She spotted a small, round container of the freshly shredded stuff and gleefully crowed, "I knew it. It's gotta be an essential staple for a chef." Setting her plate down on the island long enough to add the cheese, Coy realized she still didn't have a fork. She bit her lip, now feeling like she was snooping as she quietly went on the hunt for one. Thankfully, the utensils were in the second drawer she'd pulled out.

Digging into the lasagna, Coy shoved a forkful into her mouth as she made her way to the living room. It didn't feel right to eat alone in the kitchen when Sawyer might not know she was even in the house, so Coy figured she'd take her chances this way. When she reached the living room, she noticed Sawyer lying on her side on the leather sofa, a cooking show playing at a low decibel on the flat screen. Sawyer didn't seem to be paying much attention to it as she scrolled through her phone. The fleece blanket she'd been using had fallen onto the hardwood floor.

A warmth spread through Coy's chest as she stood there for a moment, watching, marveling over Sawyer's understated beauty. She didn't even have to try, and she still looked delicious. Her long black hair was thrown up in a messy bun as if she secured it back haphazardly to get it away from her face. The look made her seem younger, and her complexion was a lot better than it had been the week before. Her skin was richer and more inviting. It had taken Coy days to get the image out of her head of Sawyer sprawled out on the ground, white as a sheet, so looking at her now was ideal therapy. She was dressed in a well-worn, baggy Bon Jovi T-shirt and plaid, drawstring pajama pants, and hell, looking so cozy that Coy had a strong urge to be the big spoon. Or the little one, it really didn't matter. Whatever Sawyer wanted, Coy was quickly realizing she would give it to her. As far as Coy's original game of chase was going, winning Sawyer over was the longest marathon she'd ever been on. The stakes were high, and it came with possible heartbreak, but damned if she didn't yearn for the challenge.

Coy saw a cute cat curled up on the back of the sofa that she hadn't seen before, but when she opened her mouth to say hello, it took one look at her and darted out of the room.

Coy frowned. *WTF. Cats love me.*

"Are you coming in to make yourself more at home in my house, or do you plan to just stand there all night and stare?" Sawyer glanced her way, one perfectly shaped eyebrow raised.

"Um ... hi," Coy said, blushing under Sawyer's scrutiny. Averting her gaze, she came into the room more, taking a look at the empty chair beside the couch.

Sawyer gestured to the floor beside her place on the couch. "Sit here. I don't want my furniture soiled from the grease stains on your clothes."

Coy bowed her head, her pulse kicking up a notch as she shuffled her way to Sawyer's side. Lowering herself to the floor, she bit back a moan as the seam of her jeans caused friction against her throbbing sex. She was almost always turned on when she was near Sawyer, so hearing the chef's soft command had arousal pooling in her boxers. She disguised her reaction by shoveling another forkful of cooling lasagna into her mouth, asking as she chewed, "What's the kitty's name?"

"So you haven't limited your affections to just dogs, then?" Sawyer replied dryly. Then, almost as an afterthought, added, "Her name is Patches. Bree named her."

"Fitting. I like it."

"Duly noted."

Coy bit her lip. Lori had been right. Sawyer *was* in a mood. "How are you feeling?"

"Why does everyone keep asking me that? I'm fine, better than fine, even. I had a moderate heart attack and survived." Agitation bubbled up in her words, and Coy grimaced in understanding.

"I'm sorry; it must get tiresome answering that question. But you know Sawyer, it's okay if you're not. Fine, I mean. What you went through was scary."

Sawyer's fingers wrapped around Coy's short braid, and she gave it a gentle tug. Coy's breath caught in her throat, and it was a good thing her mouth was void of food, or she would have choked. "I don't want to talk about how I almost died, McCoy. Surely you didn't help yourself to my house to dwell on that. What did you come in here for?"

Coy shifted around so she could see Sawyer more clearly, getting momentarily distracted by the sight of her bare feet and painted toenails. Coy swallowed, her fingers itching to touch them. "To see you. I missed you this week." She froze, wincing at her admission. *Dude. Why??*

Her pulse shot through the roof as Sawyer's hand closed around the back of her neck, her nails gently scraping across Coy's flesh. "You missed the McLaren." When Coy didn't bother to argue, Sawyer continued, "Now you're here to distract me."

Coy's eyes fluttered closed, and she drew her bottom lip between her teeth as she took a deep breath. This wasn't real. Sawyer was toying with her, likely hoping that teasing Coy would be a cruel punchline after a gruesome week. "I-I don't mean to be. We can just watch TV together."

Sawyer was silent for a minute, but eventually, Coy caught her picking up the remote out of the corner of her eye. The cooking show began playing again, and Coy let out a soft sigh, leaning back a little against the couch until she felt Sawyer's warmth permeating from behind. Then, "Finish eating, McCoy."

Coy broke out in a grin, and she scooped up another forkful. She was dying to look at Sawyer but didn't want to ruin whatever was happening right now. They were sitting closer than they ever had before, and for someone who claimed she didn't need any more friends, Sawyer was doing a terrible job at kicking Coy to the curb.

As she chewed, a thought occurred to Coy. Perhaps all Sawyer had meant was she wasn't interested in being *just* friends. Her eyes widened with the revelation, and she almost dropped the dinner plate. Sawyer didn't make a smart remark over her clumsiness, and Coy carefully placed the plate on the coffee table. She turned toward Sawyer but found her fast asleep on the couch. One hand still held the remote. Coy sighed, although she couldn't be upset over her bad timing. Sawyer needed all the sleep she could get as she recovered. Truthfully, Coy was pleasantly surprised Sawyer felt safe enough in her presence to drift off in the first place. It spoke volumes to how far their relationship had come.

It was past nine already, and as much as Coy didn't want to leave, it felt wrong to hang out without Sawyer. They weren't that close. *Yet*. And she wanted to be someone Sawyer could trust.

With another sigh, she reluctantly got up, reaching for the remote and shutting the TV off. Next, she took Sawyer's cell from where it peaked out under the pillow and set both on the coffee table. She retrieved the blanket from the floor, and her heart was a mess as she carefully draped it over Sawyer.

"Good night," she whispered, bending to give Sawyer a soft kiss on her forehead. The scent of her skin was incredible, and Coy couldn't help but breathe her in as she slowly pulled away. Fuck she was beautiful, with soft snores pushing out past her parted lips. Coy swallowed, backing away to pick up her plate again. She gave Sawyer one last lingering look before dimming the lights and leaving the room.

Chapter 19

Sawyer

Never in her life had Sawyer felt such extreme exhaustion. She was tired *all* the time. Going up a flight of stairs to her bedroom wore her out so much that she had to take a breather before going ahead with whatever had brought her up there to begin with. Yesterday, she slept past her alarm. She couldn't recall the last time she'd done that, if ever. In fact, it was Bree who had turned off the alarm in the end, gently shaking Sawyer awake to ensure she was still alive.

There was a knock on Sawyer's bedroom door before Bree stuck her head in. "Oh, you're up, perfect. Need help getting dressed?"

Sawyer shot her an annoyed look, turning back to her task. She grabbed the gray joggers off the bed and carefully lifted one of her legs. She refused to answer that question. She had a heart attack; she wasn't dead. Bree had already taken over every aspect of Sawyer's life, and now she wanted to help her dress? *Over my dead body.*

"Good, you chose something comfortable. Remember, the doctor said we need to start slow, going for short walks—"

"I, not we," Sawyer corrected, slightly out of breath now as she stood to haul her joggers up over her hips. She picked up the sweater also on her mattress, sliding her arms and head in before turning to Bree. "I love you, sweetie, but please stop trying to micromanage me. You have better things to do with your life."

"That's crazy talk," Bree replied, wrapping an arm around Sawyer's waist as they left the room. She was shorter than Sawyer, just barely reaching her shoulders, but as Bree insisted on holding on to her as they made their way down the stairs, Sawyer was the one who felt small and helpless.

"Bree, this is ..." Sawyer's voice trailed off as they reached the dining room. She never used the dining room anymore. It was too formal and reminded her of years of toxic family dinners. Two place settings were set up, both with bowls of hot porridge topped with fresh berries and a carafe with, she assumed, coffee.

"I know you weren't hungry for breakfast yesterday, but I'd like you to try and eat a little this morning," Bree explained, giving Sawyer a gentle squeeze before letting go. She walked over to the plate setting at the head of the table and pulled back the chair, gesturing for her mother to sit.

"I can seat myself," Sawyer bit out, embarrassed she was being treated like an invalid. Once she'd taken her old place at the table, she added, "I eat at the island."

Bree froze as she was about to sit down. Her eyebrows shot up. "Is that new? Sorry, I don't mind moving us to the kitchen."

"It's fine. Just so you're aware for next time, since you seem hell-bent on catering to me." Sawyer was aware of how irritated and unappreciative she sounded, but she honestly couldn't help it. She'd been doing everything for herself for far too long to suddenly stop. She picked up her spoon, eyeing the too-healthy breakfast with a grimace. She'd raised Bree on crepes, pancakes, or bacon and eggs unless they were in a rush, but even then, she'd made certain to have homemade cinnamon rolls or pastries up for grabs along with their usual staple of yogurt and fruit. Olivier had demanded it.

"I'm not trying to take over, *Maman*, I promise," Bree said, looking down at her food. She bit her lip before glancing back up to Sawyer with glistening brown eyes. "I just want to be here for you. I know you're angry that I'm here, but can you blame me? I almost lost you."

Sawyer's throat burned as she watched her daughter trying not to cry. She swallowed down the ache, reaching out with a tentative hand for Bree's shoulder. She placed it there, feeling awkward and inadequate when it came to offering comfort. "I don't blame you. I'm sorry I'm not a better patient." The apology was forced, but it was the best Sawyer could do. She knew Bree was just trying to help, that she loved Sawyer, same as Cindy and Lori. Even Barb and the rest of her staff had stepped up in the last week, doing everything in their power to keep Desmarais running smoothly while she was out. Cindy had taken to her role as executive chef like a moth to a flame, but Sawyer had expected nothing less. Her friend had been born to run a kitchen, and in a way, Sawyer was pleased to be able to offer her the opportunity to try her hand. She patted Bree's shoulder, trying for a smile. "Now, how about we dig in?"

Bree returned her smile, though she reached up to brush a fleeting tear off her cheek. She barked a laugh. "It may be cold now. Let me know, and I can nuke it."

"I'm sure it's perfect, love." Sawyer helped herself to the small container of milk, pouring a splash over the berries in the bowl before setting it back down. "Would you mind grabbing the maple syrup out of the fridge?"

Bree shook her head, tapping a dish she hadn't noticed with her spoon. "This is stevia, *Maman*. It has zero sugar and no aftertaste like the old sugar substitutes."

Sawyer frowned. "I know what stevia is, Bree, but why is it in my house?"

"I placed a grocery order yesterday while you were napping. Picked up a bunch of heart healthy options for you, too. Those pamphlets you were given mentioned limiting sugar as much as possible."

Sawyer closed her eyes, praying for patience. She took a deep breath, or as deep as her body would agree to these days and exhaled slowly. "Maple syrup has a high nutritional value."

Bree nodded. "I'm not disagreeing, but you can't just fall back into the same lifestyle you had pre-heart attack." She pointed to a dish of pills sitting behind Sawyer's coffee mug. "I ordered vitamins as well, supplements to help with whatever you're not getting anymore in your food. Your heart pill is in there, too."

"Fine. It's fine." Sawyer shrugged off the unease clouding her person and scooped out a sprinkle of the sweetener. She would not get upset at Bree, who was only trying to help. She stirred her porridge, sucking her teeth as the hot cereal didn't even change color from the sweetener. What other consequences to her over-working and not watching her diet were in store for Sawyer? She was a French-Canadian chef for fuck's sake—sweet and savory was practically her middle name. "How's Scott?" she asked, eager to get her mind on anything else.

"I don't know," Bree admitted with a shrug, spooning a bite of porridge into her mouth. She chewed and swallowed before adding, "We broke up."

"Broke up? Why? I hope it wasn't because you dropped everything for me." Sawyer swallowed her own bite.

"No, nothing like that." Bree was looking at her as she uncapped the carafe, her brows pinched together slightly, deep in thought. She poured steaming coffee into both their mugs. "It just wasn't working out. He wanted me to drop everything and be available whenever he was, and honestly, his narcissistic tendencies started feeling too much like Papa's."

"*Calisse,* Bree. *Je suis tellement désolée.*"

Bree set the carafe down, and Sawyer reached across to clasp her daughter's hand in hers. She should have known Bree wasn't happy. Why hadn't she *known*?

Bree flashed her a brief smile. "Thanks, *Maman*. I'm not worried or upset or whatever. I'm just not settling." She shrugged again, turning back to her breakfast.

"You're strong, love." Sawyer forced out a smile. *Stronger than I was so long ago* was what a part of her wished she would say, but that would be opening the conversation up to a place Sawyer didn't wish to go.

She ate more porridge, though she wasn't a bit hungry. When Bree's attention shifted to her phone, and she thought it safe to do so, Sawyer pushed away her bowl and picked her coffee up instead. As soon as the mug touched her lip, she smelled delicious hints of cardamom and cinnamon. She smiled, pleased that at least Bree hadn't altered her favorite recipe.

As she drank, she observed her daughter, who was grinning at a video on TikTok. She felt herself soften, her damaged heart warming at the lightness that was Bree. Even though she hadn't had the best childhood at times, she still managed to always be smiling. Her beautiful, sweet girl. *No, woman,* Sawyer silently corrected. Scott may have turned out to be an idiot, but one day, her grown up little girl would fall in love. Sawyer hoped more than anything that whoever she ended up with treated her like a queen. Not settling was an excellent start.

"How did everything go last night?"

Bree glanced up from her phone. "At the restaurant? Great, actually. Slammed until eight and then steady right up until closing. Cindy was so cringe with how the dishes looked going out, so you don't have to worry there."

"I'm not worried." She definitely was. She'd thought of little else in the last three months than working toward another Michelin star, and now, it seemed like her goal was damned near impossible. Besides, how would she keep the star she had if Bree and her friends, not to mention her doctor, were all but begging her to stay home? "Can you grab my phone from upstairs? I forgot it on my nightstand."

Sawyer hated to ask, but she'd learned her limits yesterday when she'd done the exact same thing. She'd carried herself back up the stairs to retrieve her phone only to need another lie down. Seriously, she was considering moving her bedroom downstairs for the next few weeks. Dr.

Cooper had said the fatigue should wear off by then, but rather than wallow in the exhaustion, he advised walking every day.

"Sure thing," Bree chirped, pushing back her chair and disappearing from the room. Seconds later, Sawyer heard her bounding up the stairs, and she chuckled a little. Her daughter was one of a kind and probably one out of a few her age that would jump to her mother's command. That was one thing Sawyer had been thankful for. Even as a teenager, Bree had never been difficult.

"Some interesting texts you're getting from your mechanic," Bree stated, a huge grin on her face as she came into the dining room again. She had her head down, focused on Sawyer's phone. "'Can you check?'" she read aloud, giggling. "'It might've slipped under the sofa. P.S I hope I didn't dirty anything.'"

"God, give me that," Sawyer exclaimed, mortified. Her cheeks flushed, and she snatched her phone from Bree's grasp.

"What is she talking about?" Bree stifled more laughter and fell into her chair again.

"*Tabarnak.*" Sawyer unlocked her phone, briefly wondering if there would ever be a time McCoy Miller wasn't raising her blood pressure. Memories of her the night before had teased Sawyer even in her dreams. She still couldn't believe she'd pulled McCoy's hair. She didn't know what had come over her, but she'd *liked* it. And by McCoy's sharp inhale, she didn't think she was the only one. There was something about McCoy that made Sawyer want to take control of every situation, more than normal. McCoy had her craving dominance. In her dream the night before, she'd been tying McCoy to her headboard. She'd woken sweaty and more aroused than she'd ever been.

Sawyer scanned the message, breathing a sigh of relief at the relatively innocent question McCoy had asked. She cleared her throat, still flustered, but glanced at her daughter. "Can you check around the sofa and coffee table for a small black key? It's for a bike lock. McCoy thinks it might have fallen out of her pants pocket."

"So, she was in our living room, huh? She's totally hot, by the way."

Sawyer scowled, not enjoying the bitter taste in her mouth at the thought of her daughter being attracted to McCoy. "Since when do you check out women?"

"Not for me, for *you*. She's totally into you." When Sawyer's eyes only narrowed more, Bree made a tsking sound, reaching over to pat her knee. Her eyes were full of acceptance as she softly added, "It's not too late to be who you were meant to be, *Maman*."

Sawyer was speechless, shell-shocked even. She sank back in her chair, her hand flying to her mouth in surprise. "H-how?" she stammered. She'd never felt safe enough to talk about her sexuality while Bree was growing up, so how could she have—

"Three things," Bree admitted sheepishly, reaching up to wipe a tear off Sawyer's cheek. She hadn't even known she was crying. "I heard you and Papa arguing once or twice about it. And ... when I was in grade seven, you used to, um ..." She paused, chuckling. "I'd see you freshen up anytime Hannah was on her way over. Her mom would always drop her off, and you'd invite her in for coffee even though you'd be late for work. After two years of that, they moved away, and you seemed so sad."

"Melissa," Sawyer murmured absently, surprised at how observant her daughter had been at thirteen. Melissa, she was certain, had been at least curious about women. After all these years, Sawyer still remembered how often Melissa would touch her hand over coffee. She cleared her throat. "And the third?"

"Kelly hired a new server when I was in high school. What was her name? Amanda?"

Sawyer smiled, fondly remembering the petite blond. "Ami."

"That's it. Well," Bree said with a laugh, "I was old enough to notice how flustered you would get whenever she came into the kitchen. What happened to her, anyway?"

"Your father fired her." Bree hadn't been the only one to notice Sawyer's attraction to Ami, but she was past being bitter over all the ways her husband would throw his control around.

"What a jerk," Bree spat, startling Sawyer. She was rarely ever angry. "Well, he's gone, and we can really start living now."

Sawyer's eyes drifted closed at her words, letting herself imagine how that might look. The idea of opening up to a possible partner was debilitating.

Before she knew it, Bree's arms were circling her, holding Sawyer in a comforting hug. "I love you, and it seems to me that a strong, tattooed, *pierced* masc lesbian has caught your eye as well. What are you going to do about it?"

Sawyer huffed a laugh, opening her eyes to see Bree peering down at her phone where a new message from McCoy awaited. "She's only seven years older than you. And, dare I say, less mature."

"But *hot, Maman,*" Bree replied, throwing her head back to laugh at Sawyer's obvious embarrassment. She tapped her mom on the nose. "I'm not saying marry her. You haven't dated in years. But you have to admit, she'd be a good place to start."

CHAPTER 20

McCoy

"YOU KNOW THIS IS completely out of our way, right?"

Coy flicked on the blinker to go left, turning Tegan into Sawyer's neighborhood. "Yes, but I have to make a quick pit stop."

"Well, you missed the turnoff to Abi and Tess's place." Sloane jerked her thumb over her shoulder.

"Not there." Coy chewed her lip, lowering her voice as she drove. "I, um, forgot something at Sawyer's."

"You're kidding, right? Aren't you going there tomorrow after work?"

"Yeah, but ..." Coy tossed her sister a sheepish look. "I locked up both our bikes yesterday with my key, and you're planning to go for a ride with J.D. tomorrow. It dropped out of my pants last night."

"Seriously?" Sloane looked at Coy like she didn't believe her whatsoever. She shook her head incredulously. "You even find ways to see that woman on your day off."

"'That woman' has a name, Sloane. Don't be an ass." Pulling into Sawyer's driveway, Coy parked before glancing at her twin again. "I like her, okay?"

Instead of feeling an ounce of empathy toward her sister's situation, Sloane only snorted. "Sure, Coy. You like a lot of women—and don't think I didn't see your texts from Frankie. What are you gonna do about *that* woman, huh? How do you plan to manage them both? Are you gonna tell Sawyer about your arrangement with my boss? Or about anyone else? Maybe how you sometimes hook up with Ash?"

"No, no, none of that." Coy held her hand up in a 'slow down' gesture, frowning at Sloane's sour expression. "I just want Sawyer. I haven't talked to Frankie yet, but I will."

Sloane let out a disbelieving laugh, which was quite a feat considering her face was still twisted up like she'd sucked on a lemon. "Sorry, but I don't believe you."

"Don't believe ... Excuse me, what?"

"Coy, no offense, but you can't go without sex for a week, and you're, what? Gonna give it all up and pine away for Sawyer until she decides she might want to kiss you again?" Sloane blew a raspberry. "Fuck, you're all over the place. Just yesterday, you told me nothing was going on between you. Not to mention how allergic you are to the idea of monogamy."

Coy *had* said that, it was true, but something about last night felt different. The way Sawyer had touched her hair, or how comfortable the vibe in the living room had been. There was *something* between them, and despite Coy's initial upset after the whole piano bench incident, choosing not to pursue Sawyer when there was an inkling of hope wasn't an option. Her heart was already halfway in.

"Look ..." Coy glanced away from Sloane to stare out past the windshield to the house. She cleared her throat, took a deep breath, and said as calmly as she could manage, "Just because I've never been monogamous before doesn't mean I can't be."

"Bullshit. Do you even know what you're like at the pub? I've seen you chatting it up with someone and getting distracted when another with a finer ass walks by."

"This time, it's different. C'mon, Sloane." Coy let out a tense laugh. "Give me some credit, yeah? What's it gonna take to prove it to you?"

As soon as the words were out, she wished she could reel them back in again. She could practically see the cogs turning in her sister's mind, and her stomach sank a little at the devilish glint in Sloane's eyes.

"Let's bet on it. You give everyone else up but Sawyer, sticking with only her, for ... what, one month? Think you can handle that, playgirl?"

Coy's upper lip curled in distaste, but she held her hand out for Sloane to shake. "Better make it at least three, which is the length of most of your relationships."

"Fuck you, Coy. At least I haven't fucked half the city," Sloane shot back. She held her hand out as well. "It's a deal. If you lose, you owe me fifty bucks and are on dish duty for a month."

"And if I win, you owe me the same, but I also want you to start putting more faith in me. Deal?"

"Deal." They shook on it, Sloane's palm noticeably clammy. As Coy climbed out of Tegan, she wondered what her sister had to be nervous about. It wasn't as if her character was up for debate.

Sloane and her fucking bets, Coy thought as she faced Sawyer's home. The Rover also sat in the driveway, although it was probably Sawyer's daughter using it since the heart attack. Instead of going through the garage like she always did, Coy went right up to the front entrance and rang the doorbell. A moment later, Bree answered the door, a dusting of flour on her face and wearing an apron.

"McCoy. So nice to see you again. No flowers today?" Bree beamed, pulling Coy inside the house. She shut the door behind them.

"Just Coy is fine." Coy held her hand out for Bree to take. "And no, unfortunately. The last bunch didn't seem to go over well with your mom."

Rather than shake Coy's hand, Bree pulled her in for a hug. Her reply was so soft Coy strained to hear. "*Maman* isn't used to getting flowers, but that doesn't mean she wouldn't like them on occasion. I thought it was sweet."

"Yeah?" Coy didn't bother to hide her surprise. Surely Bree didn't think the flowers were platonic?

"Yeah. You seem like a good person, and … my mom needs someone like that in her life. Someone who can see past her indifference and treat her like a queen. All my father did was hurt her."

Coy swallowed, her belly tensing at those words. If he'd been such an ass, why was Sawyer having her rebuild the McLaren? And why did Bree's statement hit so hard? It was as if she was giving Coy permission to date her mother without actually giving permission. Right? And why was her heart suddenly racing?

"McCoy, must you flirt with every woman you come in contact with?" Sawyer's icy voice flitted across the entrance, and Coy jumped away from Bree like she'd been burned.

"I-I wasn't, I—"

"I gave Coy a hug, *Maman*, that's all." Bree shot Coy an apologetic smile.

"Coy, huh?" Sawyer pushed herself off the wall she'd been leaning against. She looked casually pretty today, and Coy's gaze dipped down to witness the way the sweatpants hugged Sawyer's thighs. She didn't think there was an outfit Sawyer wouldn't slay. It was too bad she didn't smile nearly as much as her daughter did. "Why am I calling you McCoy if you prefer Coy?"

"Um," Coy stammered, blurting out, "H-Honestly, I just love how you say my name."

Her eyes widened. *Where* was her filter? Her brain repeatedly failed her around Sawyer, but this was getting ridiculous. How many times could she embarrass herself before Sawyer laughed her off her property? And in front of her daughter, no less.

Coy groaned, covering her face with her hands and acutely aware of Bree's giggle. "Can I just … Please just give me what I came for, and I'll go. I'm sorry. Fuck, I don't know what's wrong with me."

"Can you stay for lunch? I'm making soup and sandwiches," Bree offered with a smile so wide it became abundantly clear she was playing matchmaker.

The knowledge unnerved Coy, and before she could think of a response, Sawyer cut in smoothly, "Bree, *qu'est-ce que tu fais*? I'm sure McCoy has plans already."

Coy's eyes flared with Sawyer's rough voice rapidly speaking French. A nervous, breathless laugh escaped her, and she jerked her thumb in Sawyer's direction, her gaze on Bree. "Whatever she said. Besides, Sloane's outside waiting, and she is definitely the less patient twin."

"You have a twin? Can we meet her?" If it was possible, Bree appeared even more excited. She glanced at her mom, "*Je t'aide, qu'est-ce que tu penses?*"

"Err ..." Bree's French didn't hit the same way Sawyer's did, and for that, Coy was grateful. It was just as effortless, but thankfully Coy's heady reaction seemed to be for only one woman.

"You're both welcome to stay if you like. I've made chicken and egg salad sandwiches and a homemade butternut squash soup."

Coy acknowledged Bree with a soft thank you, caught between wanting to stay and having a strong desire to bolt. Having Bree and Sawyer together gave off a domestic vibe Coy wasn't sure she was ready for. What if Sloane was right? Coy had never even been in a real relationship; how could she begin to qualify for a place in Sawyer's life? Still, she found herself watching Sawyer, waiting for permission, and knowing she'd lap up any and all time she had with the gorgeous older woman.

Sawyer stared at her so intently that Coy averted her gaze to Sawyer's slippers instead. After ten long Mississippis—and yes, Coy counted them—Sawyer finally relented. "If you and Sloane agree, I suppose it would make sense to stay for lunch. Bree made enough for a neighborhood."

Coy let out the breath, a gush of relief flooding through her. She pulled her cell phone out and quickly sent Sloane a text, telling her to come in.

Sloane: I knew this would happen ffs. Nana is expecting us.

"She'll be right in," Coy told them, lifting her head from her phone to see Sawyer already making her way to the kitchen.

"Don't mind *Maman*. She's tired. She'll probably lie down after lunch," Bree whispered before opening the front door to admit a flushed-faced Sloane. Yep, she was not happy with Coy. "Wow, you're like a prettier version of Coy." Bree laughed and grasped the pink tips in Sloane's hair, not at all concerned that she was virtually a stranger.

Coy let out an uneasy chuckle. "Sloane, this is Bree, Sawyer's daughter."

"Daughter?" Shock registered on Sloane's face, and then her mouth slowly curved into an impish grin as her gaze raked over Bree. "Wow, I had no idea."

Coy gave her a light swat on the arm and slipped off her Converse. "They invited us for lunch."

"But Nana—"

"We'll head over after and still be there for a visit and supper."

"Coy—"

Coy sent her a pleading look, practically dragging her down the hall after Bree. Sloane scowled but didn't complain further. She did, however, lean over and whisper, "You forgot to mention your lady had a stunning *adult* daughter. How about some warning next time?"

"How about you listen more than talk next time?" Coy shot back, her whisper louder than Sloane's had been, and both Sawyer and Bree were watching them as they entered the kitchen.

"It must have been difficult telling you two apart in school, huh? Or did you always dress so differently?" Bree asked, looking back and forth between them.

Coy glanced at Sloane, catching her eye, and then they both broke into identical grins. "Let's just say it came in handy a few times during exams," Sloane returned, then threw her head back to laugh.

"You didn't?" Now Bree was joining in the laughter, acting so comfortable around her and Sloane, it was like they'd known each other forever. "Twin switching actually works?"

"It did until Coy forgot whose exam she was writing and aced all the math equations."

Coy felt the low blush begin to heat her cheeks, and she darted her gaze to Sawyer, who was watching her with an indiscernible look in her smokey gaze. Coy gulped, heat flaring low in her belly, and just like that, she was wishing they were alone again. As much as she enjoyed getting to know Bree more, nothing made her happier these days than the few precious moments she spent trying to disarm Sawyer's defenses.

"Sloane, I'm Sawyer," Sawyer announced, her knowing glance on Coy a second longer before she held her hand out for Sloane to shake. Her greeting could have been friendlier, but Coy was counting the entire visit a win in her books.

"So you're the one living rent free in Coy's head these days. Nice to finally meet you," Sloane said, as if she hadn't just bet against Coy's future with the older woman. Coy ground her molars, watching as Sloane jutted her hand out to receive Sawyer's greeting.

"Sloane," she protested.

"McCoy has been working hard on rebuilding my late husband's car." Sawyer's response was cool, her face devoid of emotion as she tried her best to derail Sloane's idea. "I believe the supercar is what's stealing all her focus, I'm afraid."

"Uh-huh." Sloane didn't sound at all convinced but thankfully let it go. They took seats around the island, and as Bree whipped up two more sandwiches, she filled the silence with more questions directed at Sloane. There was an ease between them that shouldn't have surprised Coy, but it did. Sloane had a way with people; perhaps it was one of the reasons she was a bartender. She could literally strike up a conversation with anyone. Normally, it came easy enough for Coy as well, but sitting so close to

Sawyer had her on high alert, and she struggled with finding something to say.

Sensing her unease, Sawyer finally cleared her throat and asked, "How is the car coming along? Are you finding all the parts easily enough?"

The question lacked its usual bite, and Coy took a moment to savor that husky voice. She was close enough that their thighs were almost touching, close enough she could smell the faint floral fragrance of Sawyer's shampoo and the sugar rub lotion she'd spread over her skin. Lightheadedness engulfed her as she inhaled, and she forced herself to meet Sawyer's gaze. "Most of the parts are coming from Europe, so sometimes, it's a waiting game. But it's going well. Out with the old and in with the new, as they say." She barked a laugh, aware of her pulse rushing to her ears now. Damn, what she'd give not to humiliate herself around Sawyer.

Her foot was bouncing erratically on the floor like a junkie anxious for a fix, her stomach twisting and bottoming out from the nerves. She couldn't grasp why she responded to Sawyer the way she did, and it was frustrating that the feelings hadn't subsided in the last month.

"I don't know much about cars, but it looks like you're doing a great job." Sawyer's gaze dropped to Coy's leg.

"Lunch is served," Bree said, a sly smirk on her face as she placed a plate of soup and sandwich in front of first Coy, and then Sawyer. "*Bon appétit.*"

"Thanks, love," Sawyer replied, and Coy watched as she sent her daughter a grateful smile. A genuine smile, and it was so captivating it stole Coy's breath. Sawyer was a completely different woman around Bree. Softer, more nurturing. Even her eyes had warmed up watching her daughter work in the kitchen, the pride evident on her face. Honestly, Coy couldn't decide which side of Sawyer was more intoxicating. Every snippet into Sawyer's private life felt like the greatest gift imaginable, and Coy was hungry for more time with her.

Sawyer's hand landed on her thigh, bringing Coy's bouncing to an abrupt halt. In a whoosh, all the air left her lungs, the heat from that hand searing the skin underneath her cargos. She was frozen, too cowardly to lift her gaze from her plate in case her face gave her away. It wasn't until Sawyer gently squeezed that she stammered out a thank you for Bree.

"I-it looks delish. When, um ..." Coy swallowed, her gaze flickering to the lean hand still touching her. *Fuck, even her hands are sexy.* "When we were your age, we lived off KD, so I'm impressed. Homemade soup?"

"I grew up in the kitchen. *Maman* taught me everything I know."

Coy shifted her gaze in time to see Bree and Sawyer sharing a fond look across the island. A slight pang settled in her chest as she witnessed the obvious love between them. She'd wondered her whole life what it would have been like to have her mom by her side. Her father had done his best filling the role of both parents, but she'd always felt the absence in the house.

"You're fortunate to have each other," Sloane spoke, her gaze on Coy as she bit into her chicken sandwich.

"We are." Coy felt Sawyer stiffen a little, and then she was retracting her hand from Coy's thigh. The loss was immediate, but Coy shrugged the feeling off. "Where does your nana live?"

The subject change was welcome, and Coy rushed in with a reply. "About an hour's drive, in the country. She's lived alone since we lost our grandpa a few years ago."

"I'm sorry to hear that." Sawyer spooned some of her soup in, swallowing before asking, almost as an afterthought, "Are you close with her?"

That brought a smile to Coy's lips, but Sloane answered before she had a chance. "Yeah, Nana is a force to be reckoned with. She's kind of like our mom in some ways, and she legit has a soft spot for Coy. We're headed over to help her navigate the new stairlift Coy bought her."

"Wow, I can't imagine those are cheap. Is that why you agreed to work for my mom?" Bree canted her head to the side as she observed Coy. It made her nervous all over again.

For what seemed like the tenth time that hour, heat crept up Coy's throat to splotch her cheeks. She ducked her head to her barely touched food. "One of the reasons," she admitted, pleased with the casual tone in her voice. "Ever since Nana broke her hip last fall, it's been harder to get around. So I've been doing what I can to make it easier."

"Yeah, she refuses to move into community care," Sloane said with a roll of her eyes, but Coy knew how much they both loved their nana.

"Change is scary, right, *Maman*?"

Sawyer gave a slow nod, her gaze full of something Coy couldn't begin to decipher, but damn if she wouldn't gladly take the rest of the day and night to try. "I don't know if I'd use the word scary," she said, staring directly at Coy as she spoke. It felt like she could literally get lost in those deep pools. Her foot bounce resumed, and once again, Sawyer reached out to stop the distracting motion. "Change is hard because it takes a while before you know if it was worth it or not. The unknown is what's terrifying."

Chapter 21

McCoy

Sawyer hadn't been exaggerating—the unknown *was* terrifying. It had Coy tossing and turning for the next two nights. On Tuesday, she crawled out of bed at a quarter to five in the morning, finally giving up on any sort of rest. Her limbs were dead weights, and she staggered from the bathroom to the kitchen like she'd binged watched *The Walking Dead* for a week straight.

Sloane was still passed out in her bedroom, having worked the night before, so Coy tried her best to be quiet as she rummaged around the kitchen for the new pack of coffee filters. She couldn't stop rubbing her eyes as she spooned the coffee into the maker, and when she reached for the jug of milk for her cereal, it slipped out of her hands and dropped on her foot.

Coy inhaled sharply, muttering curse words as she hopped around on one foot until the throbbing pain passed. Today was going to be a shit show—she just knew it. It was like she was blessed with knowing the future. To make matters worse, she hobbled to where her bowl of Fruit Loops sat beside the coffee maker to witness the hot liquid percolating all over the counter. "Why? Just why?" she hissed, throwing her hands in the air and glaring at her ceiling like she was asking some higher power.

How was she supposed to go through with tonight when she couldn't even brew a cup of fucking coffee? Frankie was going to chew her up and spit her out.

Groaning, Coy unplugged the maker and tossed a towel over the mess. She poured milk into her cereal and left the uncapped jug on the counter, wandering into the living room to claim the recliner that had been meant for her dad. It was comfortable, with overstuffed armrests and a cup holder on either side. She didn't know why her father hadn't wanted it; it was perfect for watching the game. Coy dug into her cereal, unlocking her phone and setting it on the armrest. She scrolled Instagram as she ate, softening as she saw the new posts Abi had put up of her and Tess. They really were a remarkable couple, and so in love, Coy bet a blind person would be able to feel their chemistry. Coy had spent most of her life determined she didn't want that. Now, she wasn't certain of anything but how being around Sawyer made her feel.

And Sloane can't even see it, see that this is different.

In the two days since their lunch, Coy had successfully chipped away a little more of Sawyer's armor. Even minuscule amounts were wins in Coy's eyes. They had texted periodically throughout the day yesterday, and then when she'd gone to Sawyer's house in the evening to work, Sawyer had come out to the garage. She'd brought with her the supper Bree had cooked, and then they'd just ... talked. About work on the McLaren, but also about personal stuff. Sawyer seemed to prefer learning about Coy rather than talking about herself, but Coy got the feeling she was lonely. Sawyer seemed different since she'd come home from the hospital. Not depressed exactly, but almost like she didn't know what to do with herself if she wasn't working.

A direct message from Abi popped up on her Instagram, and Coy was already grinning as she clicked into it.

Abi: Miss your face! Can't sleep?

Coy: Miss yours more, beautiful. And no. AND I ruined my coffee. FML.

Abi: That's the worst! One day I'll upgrade you to De'Longhi. It's an espresso machine, and like, sex in caffeine form.

Coy: LOL. Not sure what that says about Tess's skills, but I'll be sure to bring it up when I see you guys next.

Abi: Don't you dare. Tess is AMAZING in bed.

Coy: Haha. Srsly miss you Abs. You coming to the party this weekend?

It was hers and Sloane's annual summer celebration this weekend. They hosted at their apartment and invited way more people than was probably up to code, but so far, they'd only been shut down once by the police. Usually, the few neighbors in their building were understanding, and it wasn't like they partied every weekend.

Abi: You bet. I've even convinced Tess to come, so long as she doesn't back out at the last minute.

Coy smirked at that. Tess was so shy, it surprised Coy that the barber had the guts to pull off organizing her sister's pre-wedding, weeklong activities the year before. Not to mention sneaking around with Abi in the middle of it all.

Coy: Remind her how sexy you thought she was when she helped you over the bridge at the waterfall. Boost her confidence.

Abi: That *was* sexy. Shit, I think she's awake. I wanted to give her a special wake up call. Gotta run, playgirl xxo

Coy laughed, shaking her head but typed out her exit message as well before closing the app. Abi's happiness had been a long time coming. Glancing across the apartment at the mess on the kitchen counter, Coy groaned at the thought of having to clean it up. She'd no doubt need to brace herself for the day ahead.

When Coy stepped into the pub late that evening, her hands were already shaky as she headed straight to the bar. Sloane and another worker, Andy, were working, and as Coy approached, her twin's all-knowing gaze was already turning away to reach for the bottle of Jacks. "She's upstairs waiting. Still think you're gonna win the bet?"

"Damn straight I do." Coy nodded, believing it. She had to win, or else it meant she hadn't changed. And for once, she truly wanted that not to be true. More than ever, she wanted what so many of her friends had.

Sloane poured out two shots and slid one to Coy. "Well, I'm proud of you."

"If you were proud of me, you wouldn't have made that fucking bet," Coy muttered, raising the shot glass.

Sloane raised hers as well, arching one eyebrow as she clinked the glass against Coy's. "Being proud of you for trying isn't the same as accepting that you'll probably never change, Coy."

"To me it is, but that's okay. I'll prove it to you." Coy tossed the shot back the same time as Sloane, and the liquor burned going down. She absently rolled the rim of the shot glass between her thumb and forefinger before setting it down on the counter. Taking a breath and then another, as if the extra oxygen and puffing of her chest would give her the courage she needed, Coy added, "See you soon, Sloane."

Sloane fist-bumped her without hesitation, then left to take care of another patron. Coy turned toward the back stairs that led to Frankie's apartment above the bar. As she made her way up, the significance of what she was doing wasn't lost on Coy. She was about to cut off her only tie into the BDSM lifestyle. Not even Naz was into the more involved kink, and Naz was usually game for anything. Coy had always been too insecure to attend the kink parties in the city by herself, and then she'd lucked out finding Frankie.

Coy reached the door to Frankie's apartment and, not for the first time that night, she hesitated. What if she never felt the fulfillment she got as a sub again? What if chasing Sawyer turned out to be pointless, and Coy was busily rearranging her life for nothing?

What if Sloane is right and I come crawling back to Frankie a week, a month from now?

"Come in."

Frankie's command was equally alluring and anxiety inducing, a magnetic field pulling Coy into a dangerous vortex. Even after all these years. Heat coiled in her belly as she pushed the door open, stepping silently into Frankie's two-bedroom apartment. Coy spotted the older woman instantly, seated in the middle of the room on one of her dining room chairs. She was dressed in her trademark business attire, her halfway unbuttoned blouse flashing a swell of creamy breasts Coy's way. Red heels completed her look, and in her hands was a black bondage rope.

"Lock the door."

"Yes, Mistress." Coy's body went on autopilot, eagerly soaking in the instructions.

"Now strip, my pet."

Coy's mind went blank, and she froze, caught between *needing* to strip and her earlier desire to have a proper non-submission or sex-related conversation with her Domme.

"Don't make me tell you twice, pet. Today we'll start out here and finish in the playroom."

Kicking out of her Nikes, Coy scrambled to remove her shirt. Frankie looked on in anticipation, her mocha brown gaze hooded as she studied Coy. She looked beautiful and sexy and dangerous—all the things Coy had come to crave. She didn't know what was wrong with her, why she couldn't stand her ground, but before she knew it, she was down to her boxers and sports bra.

"Stop," Frankie ordered when Coy dipped her fingers into the waistband of her boxers. "Leave them on. Now I want you to crawl to me."

Coy's pussy clenched in absolute need, and for the life of her, she couldn't remember what she'd planned to do tonight. She sank to her knees, a soft sigh leaving her as she crawled on all fours to Frankie. She caught the heat in her mistress's eyes as she gleefully watched Coy crawl across the floor. "Good, pet," she crooned, bending to cup Coy's cheek in her palm. Frankie's nails scraped along Coy's jaw, and she gasped, desire shooting to her core. Frankie's hand circled Coy's throat possessively, and when she held Coy still and roughly claimed her lips, Sawyer's storm cloud gray eyes and sensual mouth flashed behind Coy's eyes. It was almost like warning bells going off in her head.

Frankie stood, and with her hand still wrapped around Coy's throat, she guided her to her feet as well. Frankie shifted their positions so that Coy was now in front of the chair. "Sit, pet," she directed, her hand sliding to Coy's chest and giving her a light push. Coy fell into the chair, her chest heaving as thoughts of Sawyer swirled round and round.

"Safe word—tell me it." Frankie's voice was low, throaty by design, but it wasn't having the same effect on Coy as five minutes ago.

"I, uh ... Frankie, I—"

"Tell me your safe word, McCoy," Frankie repeated, reaching for Coy's arms, the rope dangling in her opposite hand. She had about one minute before Frankie had her bound to the chair. Which was hot as fuck, but ...

"Peaches," she blurted.

"Good, pet. Now we can begin."

"N-no I mean, peaches, Frankie. I-I can't do this. I'm sorry." Coy pulled her hands away from Frankie's firm grip, twisting around in the chair to face the older woman.

Frankie was squinting at her, clearly confused. The rope fell to the floor, and she swiped her long brunette hair away from her face. "What's wrong? What do you need? Where are you tonight? Not with me."

"I'm sorry," Coy whispered, bowing her head. Tears pricked her eyes, and she wasn't at all surprised when Frankie's hand fisted her jaw seconds later, tugging her face toward her once more.

A rueful smile appeared. "Who is she?"

Coy closed her eyes as the tears fell. She and Frankie weren't even in love, and it was still killing Coy to do this. "Her name is Sawyer."

"I see. Fuck." Frankie released Coy immediately, backing up several paces.

"I'm sorry," she repeated, softer now. She glanced around for her clothes, not waiting for Frankie's permission to redress. She was numb as she pulled her jeans back on.

Frankie was facing away from Coy, one of her hands resting on the chair for support. A pregnant pause filled the air, before she said quietly, "You're free to go, Coy."

"I'm sorry, Frankie. I-if it wasn't for her—"

"Don't apologize. You ... owe me nothing. If anyone is in the wrong, it's me. I-If only I could ..." Her voice trailed off.

"Frankie?" Coy took a hesitant step forward.

"Was I not a good Domme to you?"

"What?" Coy's jaw went slack. She took another step, and then another, until all she'd need to do was reach out and she'd touch Frankie. Coy jabbed her hands into her pockets. "You were a great Domme. That was never the problem." Frankie had never failed in that regard. It was everything else she struggled with. Coy didn't want to be just a part-time play toy anymore. She wasn't sure at what moment things had changed for her, but she needed to invest more than just her body into a relationship. "I'll miss being your sub, Frankie." The words were out before she could stop them, but that didn't make them any less true. Coy's throat bobbed up and down as she swallowed hard. She cut her eyes toward the door, her shirt and shoes in her arms.

She was almost over the threshold when she heard Frankie rasp, "Not as much as I will, pet."

CHAPTER 22

Sawyer

"McCoy?" Sawyer's foot landed on the last step, and she waited for the younger woman to notice she'd entered the garage. In all the time she'd known McCoy, she'd never seen the woman with such a forlorn look about her.

It took a moment for Sawyer's presence to register, but McCoy finally wiped a grease-stained arm frantically over her eyes, trying to disguise the fact she'd been crying. A low blush began on her cheeks as she jumped out of the newly installed driver's seat of the McLaren. "S-Sawyer, I didn't see you there."

"I can see that," Sawyer said slowly, descending the final step to the concrete floor. There was a twinge in her chest she hadn't felt around McCoy before. Not a flutter, as she'd felt that as much as she tried not to. It felt almost like an ache, like the sadness emanating from McCoy was affecting her somehow. She had the strangest urge to close the distance between them and wrap her arms around the younger woman, to soothe any troubles McCoy might have once and for all.

Ridiculous. You need to pull yourself together.

Sawyer cleared her throat, searching for McCoy's gaze under the glare of the garage's fluorescent lights. She could be civil without turning to mush around her. Sawyer had never been the type to get heart eyes over someone, and she liked it that way. She'd lost enough of her control to risk losing that as well. "What happened to crack that notoriously optimistic personality you're so adept in shielding yourself with?" she joked, but since she couldn't quite lighten the edge to her voice or relax the muscles in her face, the question came out just slightly softer than her usual bite.

Whatever *was* bothering McCoy had to be significant, and a gut-clenching thought flashed in Sawyer's mind. "Is it ... Surely, your nana is ..."

"Nana's fine," McCoy mumbled, and Sawyer watched as she yanked fingers through her loose hair, clearly forgetting about the grease marring her hands. She didn't recall a time when McCoy hadn't braided or wrapped it in a bandana before work, so that alone hinted at her current state.

The younger woman grimaced, her gaze still landing somewhere over Sawyer's shoulder, and for once, Sawyer wished they could strike up an easy conversation. Since they'd met, McCoy had been a terrible flirt, consistently making her attraction known. Things had been different between them since the heart attack, at least for Sawyer. It was difficult to put a finger on, but it was almost like she and McCoy had ... trauma bonded? It was ridiculous to think about, but why else were Sawyer's defenses on the verge of crumbling whenever they were together now? McCoy had saved her life, helping to restart her heart and essentially witnessing Sawyer at her most vulnerable—surely that should ease some of McCoy's trepidation around her?

Sawyer watched as she fidgeted with the screwdriver in her hands before shrugging. "I don't ... I can't talk about it. Not yet. I'm sorry," McCoy finished in a whisper, and for a fleeting second, her pained meadow green gaze clashed with Sawyer's own storm gray.

Sawyer silently assessed her, closing the gap further so they were almost in touching distance. "How about a drive?" she asked, surprising them both. She gestured to McCoy's vehicle, which wasn't the truck she'd been borrowing from her father lately. "I'm a caged animal in here,

McCoy. Besides, haven't you been dying for an excuse to show off your Jeep?"

At the mention of her beloved steel pet on wheels, McCoy brightened a notch. "I'd be honored to introduce you to Tegan." She hurried to set her tool down and head to the wash basin against the back wall, calling over her shoulder as she scrubbed, "But are you okay to go out now?"

"I didn't have open heart surgery," Sawyer tutted, folding her arms across her chest. It'd been two weeks since the heart attack, and in that time, she'd been forced out of her restaurant and practically force-fed a bland diet. She was going stir-crazy in her too-big house while Bree and Cindy took over her entire career. Her doctor's appointment wasn't for another three days, but Sawyer doubted Dr. Cooper would mind if she went on a short drive.

"So long as you're sure," McCoy replied, and then in a voice so soft Sawyer had to strain to hear, she finished with, "because I couldn't bear it if you got hurt again."

Sawyer softened at those words, not believing for one second that she was meant to hear them. McCoy's personality was a continual, pleasing surprise to Sawyer. At first glance, she came off as a huge player with a singular focus: racking up the number of partners she slept with. Sawyer now knew how multi-faceted the younger woman was. How family-oriented and kind she was, how hardworking or silly she could be. In fact, if they hadn't initially met with McCoy trying to take her home, Sawyer knew she wouldn't have pegged the playgirl label to her so harshly.

McCoy opened the passenger side of the Jeep before taking one of Sawyer's hands. "It's higher up than what you're used to," she explained, pointing to the footrail.

"Thank you," Sawyer murmured, and as McCoy placed her other hand lightly on her hip to help her into the seat, that unfamiliar fluttering began once more somewhere low in her diaphragm. It made her stomach tingle and her pulse pound. She cleared her throat, her smile unsure. "And who said chivalry was a thing of the past?"

"You shouldn't strain yourself too soon." McCoy's voice was gruffer than usual. Her warm breath fanned Sawyer's cheek, and they locked eyes as McCoy reached for the seatbelt, strapping it carefully across Sawyer's chest. The act was completely unnecessary, meant solely for bringing their bodies closer, and a part of Sawyer—the teensy, needy part that hadn't felt desire for another person in years—relished the rarity of McCoy's boldness.

"So, this is Tegan," Sawyer said once they were driving away from her neighborhood. McCoy looked fetching behind the wheel, one strong arm extended and two of her fingers hooked into the oval opening in the steering wheel. Her other hand rested casually on the gearshift, although Sawyer had noticed how it hovered over her thigh before settling away from her. Something about Sawyer's demeanor must have shied McCoy away from touching her, but she couldn't put her finger on what. *Is she still trying not to "do this with me" as she so eloquently put it at the mechanic shop?* Sawyer thought she had been more than friendly since her heart attack.

"Yep. Isn't she a beauty?" McCoy lovingly stroked Tegan's dashboard and slipped a wry grin Sawyer's way. "She's the first vehicle I ever completely rebuilt. Took me two years and a lot of trial and error. My pops oversaw it all, but I'd wanted it to be something I completed myself, you know?"

"To prove you could?" Sawyer guessed, shifting in her seat to glance into the backseats. It was a beautiful, strong vehicle. She'd noticed that the moment McCoy had driven up alongside her in the rain to aid in her busted tire. It was obviously well-maintained, and if Sawyer had to guess, Tegan's monthly bills were double what she spent on Patches's diabetic medication.

"Exactly." McCoy nodded enthusiastically, looking at Sawyer like she was the only one who truly understood her. "I bet you had to do that often since owning Desmarais. Bree told me your restaurant earned its first Michelin star. Was that to prove yourself?"

An eyebrow shot up in disbelief. "You talk to Bree about me?"

McCoy looked properly chastised at the question, which plagued Sawyer with further questions. *Just how often did the two of them talk?*

"Er, yeah. I mean, we did a bit while you were in the hospital. You'd fallen asleep, so we chatted before I went home."

"Oh. Alright, then," Sawyer finally said, warming to the idea of Bree and McCoy becoming friends. She cleared her throat. "I only came into true management of Desmarais once Olivier passed," she amended, surprising herself that she didn't mind talking about it. "My name was on the deed, but I always knew my place was in the back, running the kitchen."

"Your place?" McCoy echoed, her lips thinning in disapproval. "Sawyer, no offense but that sounds—"

"Controlling?" Sawyer cut in with a shrug. "That was my husband in a nutshell. He didn't think I was business savvy enough to handle the restaurant by myself, so he managed the front, and I the back. It worked for us."

"Really?"

Sawyer couldn't blame McCoy for the doubt in her voice. *Had* it worked for them? Not for several years, she conceded. Olivier had used the management of the restaurant as a way to spy on Sawyer and criticize every single move she made. He'd had no qualms whatsoever with telling people that owning a business was a man's job. In the eyes of men like her father and Olivier, women were meant to be seen and rarely heard.

"Did you love him?"

The question was innocent enough, but the answer was ... not so much. How could Sawyer explain how her feelings for Olivier went well beyond hatred? That there were nights she lay awake, listening to the loud snores coming from her husband after a rough grunt between the sheets where only he got off, when she considered suffocating him with her pillow? After years of abuse, there was a darkness inside of her. A twisted vulnerability she'd disguised with a chilly demeanor out of the need to further protect herself.

I'm the result of staying and surviving a failed, misogynistic marriage.

"No," she admitted, deciding McCoy had earned at least a partial truth. She looked out the window, noting the Jeep turning toward the water. "Not for a second."

"Once you're healed, I'd love to take you off-roading sometime. If you'd like that," McCoy told her later before taking a drink of her smoothie. After driving through Kitsilano and pointing out where her friend Abi lived, she'd guided them across the bridge and into downtown Vancouver. It had been so long since Sawyer had taken time out of her busy day to visit there that she found she could no longer cope with the hustle of the city as well as she used to. Wedged between cars during late afternoon rush hour was a lot different than the supper rush in the kitchen, and it wasn't until they were heading toward Richmond that she breathed fully again.

Now they were parallel parked in front of McCoy's apartment building, a simple six-unit structure that had likely been a boarding house several years ago, sipping fruit smoothies. The trip across the city had been nice with McCoy, and even when silence permeated the Jeep, it was comfortable and easy. Either McCoy had the longest game imaginable, or she was content to let their relationship develop organically. Sawyer hoped it was the latter because regardless of how attractive she found McCoy, she was in no way ready for sex with a woman.

"I guess I should get you home now, huh? You're probably wiped from all the driving." McCoy examined her, an unfettered yearning beneath her gentle expression.

Sawyer gnawed the inside of her cheek, ignoring the flutter of desire from the way this woman looked at her. She drew in a breath, McCoy's addictive cologne and the smell of engine oil filling her. The scent was both comforting and arousing. The thought of going home to her large house, alone, or how the loneliness seemed to saturate every room unnerved her in ways it hadn't before.

"No," she reasoned after a moment. "We didn't drive all the way here to merely park at the curb." She sipped her own smoothie, peering out the window to the darkened apartment on the top floor before glancing back at McCoy. "At least show me your apartment."

"My ... apartment?" McCoy gaped.

"Mm-hmm," Sawyer replied, amusement widening the slyness of her grin. The need to touch McCoy hit her, not for the first time today, and she crooked one finger under the younger woman's chin, gently closing it. "Perhaps I'll even cook you a meal."

Chapter 23

McCoy

Coy couldn't believe Sawyer was standing on her doorstep, patiently waiting as she fumbled to unlock the entrance to her apartment. Hell, she hadn't even known patience was a virtue Sawyer held. Frankly, Sawyer had been anything but in the months since they'd met. Yet here she was, close enough behind Coy she could feel Sawyer's breasts graze her shoulder blades once or twice, quietly waiting.

Coy sucked her teeth. "S-sorry," she said unnecessarily, hastily twisting the knob and pushing the door inward. She gestured for Sawyer to go on ahead of her.

Sawyer's smile was as beautiful as it was rare, and when she directed it at Coy, it felt like the ground could come up and greet her any moment. Her heart rate jacked up, and she swallowed down her nerves, trying and failing to return that wide, earnest smile.

Who *was* this woman, and what happened to the old Sawyer?

"Nice place you have," Sawyer commented, glancing around at the minimal furnishings throughout the apartment. Her gaze landed on the two mountain bikes secured to the far wall behind the sofa. One eyebrow arched up. "Does Sloane live here, too?"

"She does, though she's at work tonight. Late shift at the pub," Coy explained, setting her keys on the table in the entranceway. She wiped her clammy hands on her dirty jeans, only then realizing the state she was in.

Jesus, had she really dropped everything she'd been working on to steal away for the afternoon with Sawyer? She'd been a mess since calling it off with Frankie. She couldn't understand, not really. It wasn't like she *loved* Frankie, not like she could love Sawyer if given the chance. Still, Frankie had a hold on Coy.

"Why don't you grab a shower, and I'll whip something up for supper?" Sawyer suggested, reaching out to skim her fingers lightly down Coy's arm.

Coy's mind went blank at the feel of those soft fingers against her hot skin. Goosebumps broke out, and she shivered, raising her eyes to Sawyer's. With flats on, Sawyer was only about an inch or so taller than Coy. If she crooked her mouth up, just a little, their mouths would meet.

"You could come in with me." Coy wagged her eyebrows, because of course she did. For some fucked up reason, she'd turned into a chronic moment killer when it came to Sawyer.

Grimacing, she took a small step back, opening her mouth to apologize when Sawyer surprised her with a finger against her lips.

"I might be willing to entertain this little idea you have of the two of us," she quietly stated, her gaze lingering on her finger skimming across Coy's mouth, before focusing on her eyes, "but make no mistake, McCoy. Things will progress at my pace or not at all."

Unable to stop, Coy puckered her lips and kissed Sawyer's finger, a grin breaking forth at the subtle intake of breath. "I'll go whatever speed you want."

She hurried with her shower as much as she could with grease rubbed into her chestnut locks. She had to wash with the shampoo three times, but eventually, it was all gone, and she was scrubbing her body down. When Coy, finally dressed in clean clothing, took a seat at the small kitchen table, Sawyer was plating two omelets with a side of toast.

"Wow. I didn't know we had ingredients to make all that. Thank you, Sawyer," Coy watched as Sawyer returned to the counter and poured them each a mug of coffee. She wore loose fitting slacks today, but Coy enjoyed the snug way they fit over her gorgeous backside. She couldn't recall ever seeing a woman with a finer ass, and that was saying something.

"You're welcome. And yes, some items in your fridge were questionable. A dated container of black beans and spoiled mushrooms, cauliflower ... I tossed them all."

Sawyer placed a mug in front of Coy before taking a seat across from her. Dark circles formed below Sawyer's magnetic eyes, dulling the shade some in the last half an hour, Coy noticed. A thin sheen of perspiration had collected along her temple as well. Profound guilt made Coy's chest tighten at the sight. *What was I thinking, running Sawyer all over the city when she was still healing?*

"I should be serving you, not the other way around." The statement came out husky, but Coy didn't have the wherewithal to apologize, especially not when it was the truth. A woman like Sawyer needed to be worshiped, cherished. Coy watched as Sawyer took her first bite. "You look tired."

Sawyer gave her a shrewd stare as she chewed, replying only after she'd swallowed. "For someone with your assumed sexual experience, you should know that's rude to say, McCoy."

Coy bowed her head, unable to hide her blush at the gentle rebuke. "I'm out of practice," she self-consciously admitted, "and, well, you have a way of putting me on edge."

"Out of practice?" Sawyer's face was a mask of disbelief. "You're sending selfies to me several times a week from the pub. Surely, there are girls your age to flirt with."

Coy blanched. "Girls? Sawyer, I haven't looked at anyone else for months. I tried to. I-I had a guys' night planned with my friend Naz the day of your heart attack. We brought Jasmine back here, but ... all I could think about was you."

"You had a ... threesome?" Sawyer's eyes narrowed, and when she turned back to her plate, she stabbed her fork into the egg dish forcefully.

"That's what I'm trying to tell you," Coy insisted. "I couldn't. The idea of being with anyone but you had me literally sick, Sawyer. I don't know what's happening o-or why I feel like this." *I'm scared*, she almost said, but it was too soon to admit just how deep she was in when it came to Sawyer.

They continued to eat in silence, Sawyer not helping to ease Coy's doubts by adding anything to the conversation. Coy wondered what she was thinking or *feeling* for that matter. Did she feel this twisty mess of strangled emotion deep inside, too?

"Supper was delicious, but you didn't have to cook. Not that you're not a great chef because you are, I just don't expect anyone to slave over a stove for me," Coy rushed to say, standing to clear away their dishes. "People probably always expect that of you, right?"

"I learned a long time not to bend to someone else's will," Sawyer replied, an edge to her words that hadn't been there before. "No one can make me do something I don't want, McCoy."

"Yeah, I guess not." Coy turned to see Sawyer taking a precarious seat on the worn-out leather sofa in the living room. She fidgeted with the lone thumb ring she had on, unsure if she should join Sawyer or sit in the recliner. What were they doing? What were they? Friends, maybe more than friends right now?

She stepped closer to Sawyer, observing how stiffly she was perched. Her long fingers absently rubbed the back of her neck, her eyelids periodically fluttering open and shut. An idea formed, and Coy headed to the bathroom for an unopened bottle of massage oil. She wasn't confident Sawyer would be receptive to any intimacy just yet, and she certainly didn't want to kill the off chance by flashing a bottle she'd used on a past lover.

"What's that?" Sawyer asked when McCoy returned, eyeing the bottle in suspicion.

Coy sat beside her, turning her body. She faced Sawyer head-on and held the massage oil out. “Your shoulders and neck are tense. I thought I could rub them for you.”

Sawyer brushed Coy’s words off with a scoff, shifting her gaze away to the flat screen on the wall. “Why? It’s not as if it will lead to sex.”

Coy bit back a sigh. *Why* was Sawyer so damn defensive? “I wasn’t trying for that, but it’s nice to know you think I couldn’t possibly care about anything else.” She sank further into the sofa, reaching over to place the bottle of oil on the end table.

“Why would you offer a massage if you aren’t wanting sex as a reward?”

Coy’s forehead wrinkled in confusion, and she stared at Sawyer. “Why wouldn’t I? I give Sloane a massage all the time. Her shoulders hurt from carrying around trays of food and drink all night. It’s just ...” She paused with a shrug. “It’s something you do for someone you care for.”

Sawyer’s eyes narrowed, her gaze on Coy for a long moment. “And you think you ... care for me?”

The doubt in her voice broke something in Coy, like the thought of anyone genuinely caring for or longing for Sawyer was inconceivable. It left McCoy with more questions than she had answers, namely the unspoken subject of Sawyer’s husband. Had Olivier never given his wife a massage after being on her feet for fourteen hours? What kind of moron wouldn’t jump at the opportunity to spoil this woman?

Coy’s smile was sheepish, and she couldn’t quite meet Sawyer’s gaze. “Sawyer ... I don’t think I’ve liked anyone the way I like you.” Never had a statement been truer. What made Sawyer different from any other person Coy crossed paths with? She’d had umpteen lovers over the years, and not one had grabbed ahold of her the way Sawyer was doing.

Right now, Coy’s fingers were trembling where they squeezed the sofa cushions. She was itching to touch Sawyer—on her hand, her arm, her face. It didn’t matter, so long as they were skin on skin and giving Coy that physical connection she so craved.

Coy's gaze shot up as Sawyer slowly got to her feet. Wait, she wasn't leaving, was she? Had Coy said the wrong thing? Her stomach twisted at the thought of their evening being cut off so abruptly. "Sawyer?"

But then Sawyer's lithe fingers were pushing Coy backwards on the sofa, the stormy gray of her eyes locked on Coy as one long leg at a time straddled Coy's thighs. Her hands fell to Sawyer's hips, a hot need shooting between Coy's thighs, and she had to hold in her groan of pleasure. "Oh? Oh, please, yes. Please, please, yes."

"Always with the sweet words, McCoy," Sawyer whispered, her gaze roaming over Coy's features. She was leaning in close, close enough that Coy shivered as her warm breath fanned her cheek. Their lips were almost touching when Sawyer added, "Do you ever get tired of it?"

"No," Coy breathed, reaching one hand up to palm Sawyer's jaw. She tugged her closer, their mouths grazing before parting once more. "Not if it gets me you."

Sawyer pulled away before Coy could chance another kiss. Her palms landed on Coy's shoulders again and held her in place. Her mouth twitched, like she was trying not to smile. "My pace, darling. Remember?"

"Darling?" Coy's eyebrows shot upwards, laughter spewing out. "My, my, Sawyer, already with the—"

Sawyer's index finger landed on Coy's mouth, and then two things happened. She forgot what she was about to say, and Sawyer's lips claimed hers with abandon.

CHAPTER 24

Sawyer

THE TASTE OF McCOY was better than she remembered.

Their lips glided sensuously together like they had all the time in the world. Sawyer breathed her in, McCoy's fresh shower scent teasing, reminding her of the earlier offer to share.

Not yet.

Still, the unspoken promise that she would one day see McCoy unclothed had Sawyer moaning against the younger woman's mouth. Desire coiled through her and she squeezed her thighs tighter around McCoy, relishing her whimper as she did so. She slid her hand along McCoy's throat as she deepened their kiss, slipping her tongue inside the same time her hand applied a teensy amount of pressure.

McCoy's hips jolted underneath her, strong hands sliding up Sawyer's thighs to circle her waist. Tingles erupted along Sawyer's spine as she felt the calloused fingertips on the bare skin under her shirt, and her back arched instinctually into McCoy, bringing her stiffening nipples flush against McCoy's face.

"Sawyer," McCoy groaned, her eyes fluttering open to peer up at Sawyer as she nuzzled her breasts. Her lush green gaze was strong enough to hypnotize a weaker woman, but Sawyer resisted.

"Enough for now," she told McCoy, balking at the rough tenor of her voice. She was breathless from exertion, embarrassingly so. She reached behind her to capture McCoy's hands that had wandered under her shirt, pulling them out to rest in her lap. McCoy looked dazed, like she'd just woken up from a dream. Sawyer bit back a smile, leaning in to kiss her gently on the lips. "Now, didn't you promise a massage?"

For the first time in perhaps ever, Sawyer woke feeling well rested. It had been so long that it took a moment to realize there weren't dried tear stains on her cheeks and her body wasn't stiff from all her usual tossing and turning. Her bedroom was still mostly dark, which struck her odd since she always left the bathroom light on and its door ajar. She blinked, sprawling out more on the bed and giving herself a long stretch. She felt ... *good*. Too good for this early in the morning.

She caught sight of the window above the bed and stilled, momentarily confused. She didn't have a window above her bed. Next observation was the classic car table lamp on the nightstand, but it wasn't until realizing she was in someone else's long T-shirt that memories of last night returned. The kiss, how incredible McCoy kissed, McCoy's hands ...

"God, her hands," Sawyer whispered, her eyes drifting closed as her hands slid languorously up her torso to stroke her bare throat. She bit her lip. McCoy's deft hands kneading her sore muscles had been exactly what Sawyer hadn't known she was missing. "I must have fallen asleep during." Her gaze landed on the empty space beside her, and she sighed, her shoulders relaxing at the unrumpled pillow. McCoy hadn't slept beside her.

Sawyer slipped from the bed, tugging off the nightshirt in exchange for her bra and blouse she'd left on a nearby chair. Her cheeks burned at what she'd done. She shouldn't crave McCoy's touch like this. Hadn't she learned her lesson with Olivier about expecting *anything* from anyone?

Regardless that she hadn't loved him, she'd stood with him at the altar of her parents' church and vowed to be faithful and take care of one another. Yet Olivier had hurt her again and again.

Sawyer had sworn no one else would ever get the chance to do so again, so why was she standing in McCoy's bedroom?

Calisse! Sawyer's stomach rolled with sudden anticipation. *Bree has no clue where I am.*

Had her daughter been up all night worrying? Panic surged through Sawyer, and she looked around wildly for her cell phone to no avail. Wait. It was out in the living room. Right, the room Sawyer had *first* started losing her mind.

"It was all a damn mistake," Sawyer grumbled, yanking on the bedroom door handle. She padded her way down the hallway toward the kitchen and living room. Pictures formed a row down the center of the walls, but Sawyer didn't pause long enough to appreciate them. She found McCoy at the stove, stirring a pot and wearing nothing but a black pair of Calvin Klein boxers and black sports bra. A T-shirt was draped over her shoulder. Sawyer came to an abrupt stop, eyeing the obvious strength in McCoy's arms, shoulders and legs. It wasn't a body one spent hours sculpting at the gym. Rather, the broadness of McCoy's shoulders and back, and the muscled calves were testaments of what she loved best: working on cars and mountain biking. Sawyer swallowed thickly, her gaze flitting all over McCoy before it landed on the coffee pot resting on the countertop. Squaring her shoulders, she said, "Why didn't you wake me?"

McCoy turned away from the stove, an easy smile already gracing those wondrous lips. Sawyer tensed in wait for McCoy's usual sickly-sweet innuendos, but they never came. "I was about to, but you beat me to it. Figured I could take you home before work."

"I meant last night." Sawyer's patience zapped. "Patches was left without supper, and I didn't let Bree know I'd be out." Heading for her phone in the living room, she snatched it up and audibly groaned when her efforts to connect with her daughter were met with a dead battery.

McCoy's arms circled her waist a moment later, her hands rubbing up and down Sawyer's arms in a comforting gesture. It felt good to have McCoy's breasts pressed into her back. Wonderful, really. Despite her best efforts, Sawyer felt herself relaxing against the younger woman. "I updated Bree last night after you fell asleep. She said she'd feed Patches when she got home."

"You should have woken me." Sawyer pulled out of McCoy's arms to frown down at her. "Have I somehow given you the impression I need someone to make decisions for me?"

A tic began in McCoy's proud jaw, and a part of Sawyer was dying to bend down and kiss the spot. She held her ground, needing to get the boundaries between them clear before any type of relationship could continue. "Well? Have I?"

"Actually, yes," McCoy stated, staring down her nose at Sawyer with a spark of annoyance flaring in those mesmerizing eyes. "Ignoring your health and not getting enough sleep seems to be your M.O. which, if you've forgotten, is why you're recovering from a heart attack in the first place. If someone doesn't start making good decisions for you from time to time, then who the fuck will?"

"Not you. You won't become my keeper, McCoy." Sawyer's jaw hurt from clenching so hard, and her words came out rough through her gritted teeth. Emotion swelled in her throat, and rather than continue this conversation and find herself more upset, she headed for the apartment door.

"I don't want to be your keeper, Sawyer. Girlfriend would be nice, though."

Sawyer heard the longing in her voice, but she refused to succumb anymore. She slipped her feet into her flats and arms into her blazer before grabbing her purse, holding her head high with a final acknowledgment in McCoy's direction. "I'm too old for a girlfriend. Now, can you call a rideshare for me since my phone is dead?"

"A rideshare?" McCoy echoed, staring blankly at Sawyer. She jerked her thumb toward the stove. "I made porridge for breakfast, I thought we could eat and ..." Her voice trailed off, and she sighed, her head hung in defeat. "Never mind. Let me dress and I'll drive you."

"An Uber will be fine, McCoy."

"Are you sure? Not gonna lie, this feels weird, you leaving the morning after like this." McCoy gestured between them, her confusion paramount. "It's not like we had sex."

And thank God for that.

Sawyer didn't think her heart was ready for sex with McCoy. Taking a deep breath, she let it out slowly and tried to get a hold on the kaleidoscope of emotions building inside her. The need to remain here with McCoy was strong, almost as fierce as the need to flee for the sanctuary of her home. She could cuddle Patches alone in her room and not worry about how weak-willed she was, how old she felt, how jaded. How much baggage was too much? How much of this back and forth with McCoy could she take before she spilled all her secrets?

"Enjoy your day," Sawyer told her, spying Sloane watching them from the hallway before turning back to McCoy. She bowed her head, opening the apartment door and leaving before she changed her mind.

Leaving was safer. At least for now.

Chapter 25

McCoy

She used to live for the chase. Before she'd met Sawyer, having beautiful people fall for her charms had been half the thrill for Coy. But now, watching as multiple half-naked women traipsed around her apartment, trying to get her attention, was an eye-opener for Coy. She felt like bait trapped in a cesspool with horny queer predators. Everywhere she turned another person she'd slept with popped up, either to drunkenly tell her off or to try for a repeat. It was exhausting, and truly had Coy questioning her life choices of the last ten plus years.

"Hey, baby." Mallory, who Coy had spent the night with several months ago, slipped her hand in Coy's, tugging her to a stop. "Any chance you're unattached tonight?"

Smiling politely, Coy carefully disengaged their fingers. She glanced around the apartment, half expecting Sloane to be lurking around the corner. Something was off tonight. "Erm, actually, no, I'm not. Unattached, that is." Coy gave her a nervous chuckle, already backing away. "Sorry Mal, but damn, it was nice to see you. Thanks for coming to the party."

It was the worst kind of torture for someone like Coy, withholding sex during their annual pride celebrations, but she was willing to do anything it took for a chance with Sawyer. They were going at her pace, after all.

"Quick, in here!"

Hands grabbed at Coy's shirt, yanking her backwards toward the bathroom. When she was certain her time on earth was up, Abi's face came into view, enclosing them into the small space. She locked the bathroom door. "What …" Coy's voice trailed off when she noticed Tess camping out on the closed toilet seat. She gave Coy an awkward wave.

"Hey."

The party was loud, way louder than it should have been in an apartment building, so Tess's greeting was muffled to Coy's ears. She lifted her hand for a hesitant wave, observing the beer in theirs. There was a better part of a six-pack sitting on the bathroom counter.

"Jasmine's in your bed, naked," Abi loudly explained, giving Coy a friendly push. She looked drunk already. "You're welcome."

Coy supposed she owed Abi one, considering that's exactly where she was headed a moment ago. She groaned, realizing what was happening. "Sloane pulled out all the stops."

"She's the one who offered you up as some sort of queer sacrificial virgin?" Abi's mouth fell open, and she glanced back at Tess.

"Yeah," Coy answered slowly, watching Abi's exaggerated shock in suspicion. Something wasn't right. "We made a bet, so she'll use every opportunity she can to win." *Not one of her better attributes, I assure you,* she added silently. She hadn't been overly impressed with her sister when Sloane gleefully explained what she'd done early that evening. Setting Coy up to fail was a lot different than being a silent spectator. It had to cross some kind of twin code or something. But getting their friends involved was going above and beyond. That was entering traitor territory. "Let me guess, you're in on it?"

Abi at least had the gall to look guilty. She giggled, slapping Coy's arm like the whole thing was a joke. "I bet you would succeed. That's good, right?"

How was any of this good? Coy was an utter mess over Sawyer, and her friends—her own family—were placing bets on her future misery or happiness? How fucked up was that? She swallowed down the bile building in her throat, forcing out, "How much, Abi?"

"Two hundred bucks?"

Beer spewed from Tess's mouth. "Say what?"

Abi shrugged, a drunken, uneasy chuckle emanating from her. "It's not just me. There's a pool going."

"Un-fucking-believable," Coy gritted out. Her cheeks flamed within the bathroom's suffocating enclosure. There was a tickling sensation happening in her throat and nose. She didn't know if she was about to scream or cry, but she was *definitely* feeling some kind of way.

"Coy ..."

"I ... My emotions aren't fucking ... lotto tickets to be scratched and won or thrown away," Coy burst out. *Oh no, no please not the waterworks.* But sure enough, blasted tears blurred her vision as she glared at her best friend. "Sawyer makes me want things. Different things, to *be* different. I-I feel it, Abi. I told you that. I *confided* in you." It could have been anyone else and Coy would have shrugged it off. But Abi? Why her and why this bet? Abi rarely bid on any of Sloane's stupid bets.

"Coy, I bet in your favor," Abi insisted. "Why is that bad? I know you're crazy about Sawyer."

Coy held her hand up. "Forget it. Have a good night." *Or not*, the pissed off demon camping out on her shoulder snickered silently.

Coy left, slamming the bathroom door behind her. She needed to get out of the apartment before she and Sloane had a throwdown. Coy marched to her bedroom, so busy wiping away frustrated tears that she almost toppled right into Ash. "Hey, Coy, you okay?"

Coy nodded, cutting her eyes to the floor on her way past. "All's good, Ash. It's great to see you," she called to them.

Jasmine was indeed in Coy's bed, but it didn't look as if she was hard up for company. "Don't mind me," Coy grumbled, not bothering to glance long enough to find out who had their face between Jasmine's thighs.

"Wanna join us?"

"Nope."

Coy grabbed her wallet and keys, and then she was gone again. Their downstairs neighbor was in the entranceway of the apartment when Coy approached to leave. She enjoyed witnessing the pretty ginger telling her sister off as she slipped past the open doorway.

Coy found herself keeping Tegan company, still in the apartment's parking lot. Her phone was hooked into the car charging port, and she was restlessly unlocking her screen to where she had Sawyer's SMS pulled up. Things between them had been going at a snail's pace since the night Sawyer had fallen asleep at Coy's apartment. Twenty-four days ago, but who was counting? Definitely not Coy, no sir.

It didn't help that Sawyer had returned to work two weeks ago, or the week before that J.D. took five days off to compete with Sloane in the bike rally so Coy had to clock in longer hours. Coy and Sawyer's schedule often didn't line up, so they'd resorted to text messages and late-night video calls. Sawyer's messages still left a lot to be desired, but Coy appreciated the effort. Truthfully, she'd grown quite fond of Sawyer's no-nonsense personality.

Coy: How are you? Miss you.

Coy almost dropped the phone when a reply came back almost instantly.

Sassy Sawyer: I've already met drunk, cheesy pickup line McCoy. Stop while you're ahead.

Coy simpered, all too aware of the butterflies doing a happy dance in her stomach.

Coy: You'll be happy to know I only had two beers tonight. Not in the mood, I guess.

Sawyer must have been busy at work, because five minutes passed before she replied.

Sassy Sawyer: If you're not in the mood to drink, what are you in the mood for?

Coy's heart skipped a beat. *You,* she wanted to reply. *Always you, Sawyer.*

Sawyer would forever be an enigma. Coy would just be feeling like perhaps she'd figured the older woman out and then Sawyer tossed a random question out like this one.

Coy: I feel like that's a trick question. Is that a trick question, Sawyer?

Sassy Sawyer: Well, how else will I keep you on your toes, darling?

Coy swooned. There was no other word for it. Right there in the driver's seat of Tegan, she swooned like the lovesick fool she was. Never in her life, or in the lives of all the fictional lesbians she'd read about, had a pet name achieved that.

Coy: I'm in the mood for calories. Currently sitting in Tegan, wondering if I want a burger or Chinese food.

Sassy Sawyer: The meat pie at Desmarais is quite nice late at night.

Coy's stomach flip-flopped as she read the message. She grinned from ear to ear.

Coy: Was that a hint, or ...?

But the reply never came. Coy was left in limbo, undecided if showing up this late at the restaurant would be welcome. She started the engine anyway and drove toward the west side and Sawyer. Because what was life without taking a risk now and again?

When she pulled into the parking lot of Desmarais only a handful of vehicles remained. The restaurant was closed, but the staff would still be cleaning and getting ready for the following day. She sidled Tegan between an older model hatchback and a newer looking sedan, turning off the ignition and climbing out.

An unopened box of shortening currently held the back door of the restaurant ajar and Coy read that as a good sign. The door wouldn't be left open if no one was expecting her, right? Ugh. Coy peered down at her clammy palms, wiping them on her skinny jeans before pulling the door open wider. Compared to the stillness in the parking lot, crossing the threshold into the kitchen was like stepping into the twilight zone. Staff were everywhere, some with platters of dishes, others carrying produce or containers with what appeared to be leftovers. And it was loud, which was surprising. Coy had imagined Sawyer keeping her kitchen as quiet and tightly in line as possible, but no. Music blared from a tabletop speaker, and there was dancing. Well, at least some heavy hip swaying, Coy mused, watching as a familiar face bobbed her head as she made her way over.

"Coy, you came," Bree greeted with a wide smile, leaning into Coy for a quick hug. She still had her chef coat on but had traded the hat for a bandana to secure her hair.

"Your mom told you?" Coy asked slowly. Inviting her here was a new move for Sawyer and Coy didn't know what to expect. Her eyes widened as another thought came. Was Sawyer even out of the closet? She stood still as Bree gave her outfit a head-to-toe appraisal, settling on the black suspenders over her black dress shirt.

"Very handsome. *Maman* won't know what to do with you."

"What? Why do you say it like that? Like she doesn't know I'm coming?" Coy's stomach sank as she realized what had happened. Her gaze darted behind Bree, widening slightly as she spotted Sawyer coming toward them all business like. Sweat broke out on her forehead.

What's with the constant interference into my love life?

"McCoy. What are you doing here?" Sawyer asked, barely concealed surprise coloring the question. Tension radiated from her rigid shoulders as she stood entirely too far apart for Coy's liking.

"And that's my cue to leave," Bree announced, turning to pat her mother on the shoulder. "Later, Coy."

"Yeah, see you," Coy murmured, not taking her eyes off Sawyer. Even bone-weary tired she was a sight Coy could never tire from. Nerves took hold of her, and suddenly she didn't know what to do with her hands or facial expressions and began glitching like some character in a video game. Her lips went up and down between a smile and a frown and her arms did something similar until finally a jittery cackle flew out of her mouth.

"McCoy?" Sawyer prodded, folding her arms and sighing. She glanced over her shoulder, noticing they had an audience, and said in a raised, clipped voice, "Back to work!"

"Sooo," Coy said, dragging the word out. She took a deep breath, waiting for Sawyer to face her again before exhaling. "Funny thing about that. I thought I was texting you? But I wasn't?"

"I don't understand. You texted me once, and I replied." Sawyer studied her, puzzlement clear in those lovely storm-cloud gray eyes. Her gaze traveled over Coy's outfit, the same as Bree's had, but this time Coy's body lit on fire with the attention.

"Y-yeah." Another oddly inappropriate chuckle escaped. Coy swallowed, lifting a hand to swipe the perspiration building across her forehead.

God, it's like an inferno in here.

"I think Bree got a hold of your phone, pretending to be you. Um ... something about meat pie?" Coy scratched her head, feeling sheepish. "You know I'm always hungry. So I came."

"Bree!" Sawyer looked completely nonplussed over the situation.

Her daughter returned carrying a plate of food, winking at Coy as she handed it to her. "*Oui, Maman?*"

"Explain."

Bree shrugged. "Coy's message was up on your phone, and I saw it. She wasn't up for partying and missed you, and since you miss her too but will never say, I figured why not speed this along?"

"I don't ..." Sawyer started before slamming her mouth shut. Her cheeks pinkened, and then it was her turn to breathe deeply. "*Arrête de jouer à Cupidon, mon amour.* Please."

"I'll stop playing cupid if you start letting people in," Bree said, reaching up to kiss Sawyer's cheek. "*Je t'aime aussi, Maman.*"

"Oh, no, don't worry about that," Coy said around a mouthful of savory meat pie. Sawyer and Bree both looked expectantly at her, so she swallowed before continuing. "I've been getting in there, trust me. Small increments, but I've been told I'm irresistible, so." She beamed. "One day, I'll have your mom falling at my feet."

Bree laughed, and Sawyer's eyebrow shot up. "Somehow I highly doubt that," came her crisp reply. Taking Coy by the arm, she added, "Come with me. Bree, I'll speak to you later."

Coy followed Sawyer's fast clip across the kitchen, noting several heads turning their way. So many curious gazes, all likely wondering what Sawyer was doing with her.

"So it appears you aren't drunk," Sawyer stated, leading them into her office. She closed and locked the door. Coy's eyebrows raised, but she said nothing, only tracked Sawyer's fingers to where she pointed to the vacant chair across the desk from her own. "Sit down. If you're eating, I'd rather not see it all over the floor."

Coy did as instructed, but quickly said, "I don't need to eat. I'd rather talk with you."

"You can't do both?" Sawyer went to her phone sitting on the desk, picking it up and unlocking it. Staring at it for a few seconds, she then muttered, "Unbelievable. You were fooled by this?" Sawyer held the device out for Coy to see, their previous text thread open.

Coy blushed. "Wishful thinking, I guess."

"I guess so." Sawyer set the phone down and came around to lean against her desk, her long legs inches from where Coy sat. "So tell me what pulled you away from the party. Besides your wish to see me, of course."

Coy ducked her head, not having any desire to reveal the bet her and Sloane made. She focused on her food, which was quickly cooling, and took another three bites before Sawyer gently gripped her plate and set it on the desk. And then she did the most surprising thing of all. She took Coy's hands in hers, tugged Coy out of the chair, and gave her a hug.

Chapter 26

Sawyer

"What's wrong?" Sawyer asked, wrapping her arms around McCoy's shoulders. *Now I'm a hugger?* But she couldn't stop the sudden fierce need to protect McCoy.

"Sloane and her stupid bets," McCoy muttered, her expression dour. She wouldn't meet Sawyer's eyes. "She thinks ... er, never mind."

Over the last month, Sawyer had become well-versed in the stories of bets McCoy and her twin would often make. It was childish and often outrageous as they mostly revolved around McCoy and her ... private life. Sawyer stroked McCoy's hair, not hating how her head felt nestled into her shoulder. It'd been a week since they'd been in each other's bubble. Sawyer found herself longing for McCoy throughout her workday. Checking her phone more than she ever had before. Taking longer to get ready in the morning and touching up her makeup mid-shift even though she seldom saw McCoy unless it was an arranged late-night video call. Yet here she was now, so close that Sawyer could hear McCoy's subtle intakes of breath as if she was inhaling Sawyer's scent and committing it to memory.

"Sloane thinks that I'll get bored of this, of you. She bet that I couldn't stay with one person, and then ..." McCoy's shoulders tensed. Sawyer smoothed her hands over the tightly wound muscles, thinking of Sloane's suspicions as well now.

"And then what?" She couldn't help but ask when McCoy didn't continue. She'd be remiss if she didn't consider McCoy cheating on her a possibility. After all, it's what Olivier did most of their marriage. Perhaps it was one of the reasons she was so reluctant to take things further. The age-old apprehension that once McCoy got what she wanted from Sawyer, she'd stray, and then Sawyer would have no choice but to cut her loose. Gone were the days she remained silent in the background, watching it happen.

"She invited a lot of my old hookups to the party, hoping, I guess, that I'd be interested. What's worse is that ... there's a pool going, Sawyer." McCoy looked up at her then, and Sawyer's breath hitched at the tortured expression in her gaze.

"A betting pool?" Sawyer's mood darkened as she thought of McCoy's sister always placing bets. Yet she was always winning them, too. McCoy had laughed once that Sloane won five bets to every one of McCoy's wins. Would she win this too? Was Sawyer wasting her time? Surely Sloane didn't know McCoy more than McCoy knew herself.

Unease settled over Sawyer, and she tried to shake the feeling off. So what if McCoy had more casual flings than Sawyer could count on two hands? Hell, more than she could likely count on all her fingers and toes. Did it matter since McCoy had come to her tonight and not someone else?

Of course she would. She's trying to win a bet, after all.

McCoy must have sensed Sawyer's hesitation because she pulled out of her embrace, tugging at the collar of her dress shirt as she paced the office. "Yeah, I mean, why wouldn't they?" A sarcastic laugh came forth, and Sawyer watched with muted interest as the younger woman slowly unraveled. "I've never had a girlfriend. The only sort of relationship I've ever had with someone was Frankie, and she wouldn't let me touch her. Hell," McCoy expressed with another self-deprecating laugh. "I've never even taken someone on a real date before."

"Dates are overrated. So much pretense when the expected end result is always the same. Sex." Sawyer crossed her arms. "Why bother at all?"

"But that's not how it's supposed to be." McCoy closed the distance between them once more, taking Sawyer's hands between her own. "My pops used to tell us all kinds of stories about mom and him; how they met, how they went on dates and slowly fell in love. Dating should be about the romance, too."

"Really."

"Yeah, I mean, I think so." McCoy gave a vehement nod as if she desperately wanted to believe what she was saying. She lifted one of Sawyer's hands to hold it palm down against her cheek, briefly closing her eyes at the contact. "If you would let me date you, actually date you, I'd romance the shit out of you."

"For your bet," Sawyer decided, though her heart sped up a little at the idea. It'd been years since she dated, longer since she'd been anywhere with someone she was genuinely attracted to.

"No, for me," McCoy shook her head. "For *you*. To prove I can and will treat you better than he ever did. I'll open up to you more than I have anyone else."

"You're already an open book," Sawyer reasoned, but she had to fight back a smile.

McCoy laughed, a real one this time. She turned her face into Sawyer's palm, kissing it softly. "Fair enough. But you're not. Maybe ... maybe dating me would change that."

Sawyer stiffened, and unfortunately, McCoy felt her innate need to fight or flight. Her face fell, and she backed wordlessly away, but damnit, what did McCoy expect? That she'd spoil Sawyer with a handful of dates and she would then spill her guts? She hadn't learned to master her life's baggage over the years for nothing. But that wasn't what McCoy was saying, was it? She wasn't asking Sawyer to delve into sordid tales of her marriage or the trauma of her childhood that she'd stuffed so deep into the recesses of her mind that it only threatened her when she was asleep.

No, realistically, all she hoped for from Sawyer were the more basic lighter facts. Tidbits of information into her personality that wouldn't risk ruining dinner over.

The air in the office became saturated, thick and heavy with things left unsaid. Emotions ran high, and Sawyer struggled to catch her breath. She cleared her throat, not knowing what to say.

"It's late," McCoy said after several awkward moments in silence. She seemed lost, sad even, and when she turned to leave, Sawyer reached out, like she would hold her back, but then froze. She didn't beg or plead, and isn't that what she'd be doing now if she caved to McCoy's whims? Or worse, if she apologized for being so aloof?

"Good night, Sawyer."

McCoy's rough tenor was a knife to Sawyer's already frail heart. She cringed, worrying her bottom lip, and watched as McCoy unlocked the office door.

"Wait," Sawyer blurted as the door opened. McCoy paused but didn't turn around. Sawyer closed her eyes, unable to believe she was giving this notion a second thought. "I'm a busy person, McCoy. If you want a date, prove to me my time will be worth it."

CHAPTER 27

McCoy

"IT'S BEEN TWO DAYS. You can't avoid me forever," Sloane said, both hands on hips as she hovered beside the sofa in their apartment.

As painful as it was, Coy had discovered it was, in fact, possible to ignore her twin. All she had to do was resist eye contact and not fall for Sloane's petulant need for attention, and this revenge could last at least a week.

"Naz, you hear something?" Coy asked, pulling her gaze from the video game they were playing on the TV to look at her friend.

Naz huffed a laugh, scratching her nose and looking everywhere but at the irate woman glowering at them. "Just the pathetic cries of defeat from whoever we're playing," she replied with a smirk. Sure enough, there was a bout of cursing in their headset coming from a fellow gamer.

Gotta love the bro code that keeps Naz from taking her side.

Thankfully, tiffs between Coy and Sloane were rare because she earnestly adored her sister. Just not when she crossed lines she had no business crossing. In her peripheral vision, Coy saw her sister pick up a throw pillow and biff it at her. With a shocked laugh, Coy maneuvered out of the way on the sofa and caught it, all without taking her eyes off the screen. Her avatar died, though, but they would have regardless because seconds later, Sloane was in front of her and Naz, blocking the TV.

"Aww, c'mon," Naz cried, throwing her hands, controller and all, up in a *what the fuck* motion.

"Coy. Fucking look at me, please!" Sloane's voice was elevated, bordering on shrill, like she was fighting back tears. No doubt part of her sick little game.

Coy wouldn't be so easily persuaded. She had plans that didn't involve mollycoddling someone who'd wronged her. Besides, part one of her plan to romance Sawyer had begun, and she needed her full attention on the reply that she was certain would come. Eventually. Coy had arranged for the bouquet to be delivered to Desmarais right before the supper rush, so it made sense Sawyer might take hours to acknowledge them.

"I did you a favor by inviting your old marks to the party," Sloane insisted. "You saw you weren't missing anything, right?"

"*Don't* call them that." Coy tossed her game controller aside and pushed off the sofa, facing off with Sloane with a scowl. Her hands shook, and she crossed her arms so Sloane couldn't see how upset she was. "You're out of line, Sloane. Are you so bored with your own life that you've got to fuck with mine? Out of everyone, I thought you would understand. I thought—" Coy's mouth snapped shut. She blinked, shock filling her as she felt the first burn of tears threatening. She swallowed, forcing her legs to turn away from Sloane and leave the room. The hell she would cry with an audience.

Deep breaths. Deep breaths. Bitch, do not cry—

Coy had felt more emotional than usual the last few days. Come to think of it, the dreadful visit she received monthly should be any day now. What was worse was the fact she and Sloane had always synced their periods.

"Maybe that's why she's in her fucking villain era," Coy grumbled, escaping into her bedroom. She didn't slam the door, even though there was a strong urge to do so. Rather, she clicked it shut quietly and flopped down on her bed.

The bedroom door swung open hard, bouncing off the stopper fastened to the baseboard, and in walked a tearful, flushed-faced Sloane. "I just want you to talk to me," she exclaimed, reaching up with two jerky hands to wipe her damp cheeks. "What did I do wrong?"

Coy sighed, absently reaching up to pinch the bridge of her nose, which just happened to be a move Sloane hated. Sure enough, an aggravated noise left her sister. "Which time?" Coy countered, checking her phone for messages. Nothing yet. Another sigh, but thankfully the urge to cry was over with. "You call them marks like they're pegs on a board. Like I'm some kind of sexual deviant. Go fuck off already, Sloane. I'm done with this conversation."

"I didn't mean ..." Sloane spluttered.

"Ash, Jasmine, Molly, Laura, every one of them have names. I might have wanted things kept casual, but I never called them marks," Coy rebuked, appalled at the idea.

"But it was the game."

"It was never a game to me." Guilt hit Coy immediately. Hadn't it been just that? A constant bet between them about whether or not McCoy could earn someone's number?

God, why did I do that? Why did Sloane?

Horrified, Coy sat slack-jawed, unable to do anything but stare at her phone's blurry lock screen. She blinked, allowing big, fat tears to cascade down her cheeks. No message from Sawyer. Was Coy deserving of a date with the history she had? Sawyer would be ashamed if she knew. Coy rubbed the ache growing in her chest, saying softly, "I'm done betting, Sloane. Sawyer isn't a prize, and this bet makes it seem like my feelings aren't genuine. And for the record, even if things don't work out with her, I've realized slow and steady is more my speed these days, anyway."

"That's sweet and all, but you can't forfeit the bet," Sloane expressed wide-eyed.

"What? Of course I can."

A nervous giggle left her sister, and she wrung her fingers together as she continued, "I've got to front a grand if I lose, so you know, no quitting for you, playgirl."

Coy's eyes bugged out, but Sloane's latest bet wasn't her problem. She climbed off the bed, choking out, "What the fuck, Sloane? You just completely disregarded my feelings. Why are you doing this to me?" What would make anyone do this? Sloane used to be her closest confidant, her ride or die, yet the person standing before Coy was unrecognizable.

Coy rounded on Sloane, her heart hammering against her chest as she pushed her sister out of the bedroom. "Our bets used to be fun, just between you and me. Now the stakes are high and you're, like, a totally different person lately. It's not even fun anymore, and honestly, I miss the old Sloane."

This time, Coy slammed the door, relishing the dramatic way it shut Sloane up and how the force shook the picture frames on her walls. She marched back to her bed but was too tense to sit. So she grabbed her phone and paced the length of the small bedroom. Deep inhales and long exhales focused her thoughts so that she could properly unlock the device. She felt lightheaded as she read Naz's text.

Naz: Sorry, Coy, I'm out. Txt when you're done so I know you're okay.

Great, just great. Sloane ruined her guys' nights on top of everything else lately. Jealous, petty bitch that she was. Her own love life was lacking, so she deemed it her life mission to sabotage Coy's?

"Fuck off with that. I am *done* with her level of crazy," Coy grumbled, wiping away another tear. A deep ache settled between her breastbone as she once again searched for a reply from Sawyer. How long did it take to type "Received, thank you" to someone?

Coy paced some more, deep in thought. What if Sawyer hated the flowers? At the time, it'd been a toss-up between a bouquet and a pot of basil, but Coy figured Sawyer probably had more than her fair share of herbs. Sawyer didn't seem the flower type either.

"Maybe I should show up again," Coy said, then balked at how cringe she was being. And as she continued to pace, the truth dawned on her. She was acting like her sister whenever Sloane got hung up on someone new. "Well, shit."

Coy was officially doomed.

Chapter 28

Sawyer

It was no surprise to see the first bouquet of flowers arrive. Or the second. Or even the third. Three days, three bouquets was, however endearing, a bit excessive, but Sawyer allowed it. Unfortunately, the old saying, "Good things come in threes," must have skipped McCoy's generation.

"I've never seen so many flowers in all the time I've known you," Barb observed as she came into Sawyer's office on the fourth day. She set the latest arrangement of red roses and lilies on the desk, pausing to fuss over a wayward lily before tossing Sawyer a sly smile. "Something you wanna tell me?"

"No," Sawyer deadpanned, though the traitorous blush creeping up her throat was a dead giveaway that *something* was going on. She leaned forward, breathing in the pleasant fragrance before carefully pulling the attached card out. Tucking it into her desk, she said, "Thank you, Barb. You can tell Mikey to display them out front with the others."

"Sure thing, boss. These obviously romantic flowers are just what the dining room is missing." Barb smirked, picking the bouquet up again. Once at the door, she paused to add, "It's slow tonight. You should get out of here early. Go home and rest."

"Rest. Right." Sawyer thought she *had* been resting. She'd been enjoying the rare silence inside her office while there was a lull in the dinner rush. Though, she was tired, and there was a full crew on tonight. If she took Bree with her, they could watch a movie before heading to bed.

The moment Barb left, Sawyer retrieved the card from her drawer, unable to stop the small smile as she read McCoy's words.

Sawyer,

A little bird told me customers are loving the flowers in the dining room, so I figured, one more should even it all out. She also told me you've got these cards stashed inside your desk for safe keeping. I love that. I love how you're a secret romantic. You're a good and beautiful person, and I can't wait to see you tomorrow morning. Enjoy the rest of your night.

XOXO

McCoy

"Of course, Bree told her." Sawyer's soft laughter rang out harmoniously throughout the office. A burst of affection swelled in her chest, and she reread the card, still smiling. Then she pulled out the first three, rereading them as well. McCoy wasn't overly sappy or flakey with her writing, which Sawyer respected. She also valued the time and dedication it must have taken McCoy to leave a personalized card with the flowers in the first place. No one had bothered to before.

... You're a good and beautiful person ...

... For our first date, I'd love to take you to my favorite spot to eat. ~~Frankie's got the best nachos around.~~ Scratch that. Forgot you need to eat healthier. How about grilled chicken and salad?

... How do you feel about cooking as part of a date sometime? I'd love to learn from you.

P.S. Last night I dreamt about our first kiss, but this time you had me on the ground in the shop. Like you'd ever get your blouse that dirty! ...

... You're a great mom. I love the way you look at Bree. Anyone in your life is lucky to be there. Remember that ...

"McCoy, what are you doing to me?" Sawyer whispered, tracing the words with her fingertips and so caught up in her feelings, she didn't hear the door open. She flinched in her chair as Bree appeared beside the desk.

"I think she's hoping you'll fall in love with her," her daughter said, watching as Sawyer hastily stuffed the cards back in their respective places.

"That's ridiculous." Sawyer locked up her desk, scoffing. Then she stood and started unbuttoning her chef's coat. Bree was already changed and ready to leave for the night.

"Is it? Anyone can see how she looks at you, *Maman*."

"She's young. Too young for anything long-term with me," Sawyer said as she pulled on her jacket. Even a month post-heart attack, fatigue bored down on her. She was grateful for all the caring people in her life, like Barb, who told her to go home. And now that Cindy and Bree were on payroll, there was no excuse not to sometimes. So she shouldered her bag and led the way out of her office.

"She's twenty-eight next month and co-owner of Miller's Mechanics & Restoration," Bree argued behind Sawyer. "She and Sloane are a huge success on social media, so much that they have a YouTube sponsor. She helps take care of her nana. What more do you want? She looks at you like you're the sun, the moon, the stars, *and* a buffet table of her favorite foods."

"Bree," Sawyer chided, choking back laughter.

"I'm just saying," Bree chortled, wrapping an arm around Sawyer's waist as they headed outside to the Rover. She leaned up and kissed Sawyer's bad cheek as if making a point. "Age gap or not, you and Coy look amazing together. And she makes you smile. For that alone, I'd keep her if I were you."

Sawyer made a noncommittal sound, choosing to sit on the passenger side for the trip home. She was tired, and driving was another thing she needed extra focus on. They rode in comfortable silence for two blocks, and then Sawyer took her phone out of her purse and texted McCoy.

Sawyer: Thank you, McCoy. I'll see you in the morning.

Sawyer came downstairs, steam from her shower still clinging to her skin. The silk bathrobe she wore teased her nipples with every sway of her hips. Her breasts were heavy with a desperate, ferocious need. Begging to be touched, but not just anyone would do.

McCoy Miller.

Ugh. No. It could never be her. She couldn't trust McCoy not to break her, and she'd already been broken and had to repair herself a thousand times over.

McCoy.

"Stop," Sawyer scolded her helpless inner thoughts as she entered the kitchen. They had no voice *here*, in the real world.

"Stop what?" McCoy asked, and Sawyer practically jumped out of her skin. McCoy was leaning against the sink, watching Sawyer with lazy intent in her eyes.

"*Calisse*, McCoy. Are you trying to scare me to death?"

McCoy pushed off the sink, closing the gap between them quickly. She reached for Sawyer, skimming a hand down her arm and, in the process, grazing her stiffened nipple. "Never. I want you too much for that."

Sawyer sucked in a breath, glancing down at where her bathrobe had come apart. Just wide enough to tease the woman before her. She swallowed past the dryness in her throat. "How dare you show up after putting your moves on me."

"What? You mean on the piano bench? Sawyer ..." McCoy dragged her bottom lip between her teeth, assessing Sawyer. Mischief danced in her eyes, and then she leaned upward to whisper in Sawyer's ear. "You would know when I was putting on my moves. It would start with whispering sweet nothings in your ear, like this." McCoy's nose nuzzled against her skin. "You're gorgeous. I wanna taste you."

Sawyer began trembling, all the want and need she'd had to stuff down over the years exploding to the surface with one hushed declaration.

"Can I taste you, Sawyer?"

"Oh, God," she whined. Arousal soaked her thighs, and she clamped them closed.

McCoy kissed her ear, whispering, "Is that a yes, Chef Lavoie?"

"Yes."

"In that case," McCoy scooped Sawyer into her arms and carried her to the kitchen island, her throaty laughter doing wicked things to Sawyer. The granite countertop pressed into her ass as McCoy set her down on the surface.

Sawyer glanced around the kitchen. "Here?"

"Mm-hmm," McCoy fixed her gaze on the tie in Sawyer's robe. She reached for the rope, tugging it open until Sawyer's front was completely exposed to her. "Fuck, you're sexy."

Instinct had Sawyer moving to cover herself, but McCoy grabbed her wrists, pinning them behind her on the counter. She kissed Sawyer deeply. "Let me look at you, please."

"Yes."

When did her voice become so breathy? She squirmed, her body flushing all over as McCoy kissed a path down her torso to her sex. There, she didn't waste time, instead grabbing Sawyer's hips and pulling her closer to the edge of the counter. Then she got on her knees and used her fingers to spread Sawyer open.

"Sexy," McCoy gushed just before she buried her lips in Sawyer's pussy.

"Oh, yes," Sawyer cried.

"You taste like *tourtière.* So delicious," McCoy said, her mouth glistening as she stared up at Sawyer.

Tourtière? Sawyer's eyes widened. She tasted like meat pie? "What?"

"*Maman*, good morning. I made breakfast," Bree sang out from somewhere behind them.

Sawyer froze, scrambling away from McCoy. She lost her balance and fell off the island.

"*Maman*. Are you okay?"

Sawyer blinked, rubbing her eyes to clear the blurriness from them. Bree came into view, concern written all over her face as she crouched beside her on the floor.

"Bree, what are you ... McCoy?" was all Sawyer managed. Her pulse seemed to be pounding everywhere at once. It took her a moment to get her bearings, but when she did, her hands flew to her robe only to discover she was wearing one of her T-shirts and bikini briefs. Her eyes darted to her surroundings, spotting the familiar esthetics of her bedroom. The relief she felt was paramount, and she sagged into the carpet momentarily, an uncharacteristic giggle escaping her.

"McCoy, huh? Did I wake you mid-dream?" Bree teased, helping Sawyer stand.

Oh, God, Sawyer realized. Bree woke her from a *sex* dream. A hot, albeit strange, kitchen sex dream with McCoy. Her blush started at the tips of her ears and didn't stop until her entire body was warm with it. How mortifying.

Bree noticed but thankfully didn't comment on it. Excitement had her bouncing from foot to foot, and before Sawyer could prod, Bree said, "There's no rush to come downstairs. I just wanted to let you know breakfast is in the oven keeping warm. I'll be in the garage with Coy. She's gonna teach me how to install the wiring in the McLaren."

"Ok-kay." Sawyer frowned, digesting this. Why did Bree need to know that? But her daughter was already racing out of the room, shutting the door behind her. "Well," she muttered, heading to her ensuite bathroom for a real shower. "What a way to wake up."

CHAPTER 29

Sawyer

SURE ENOUGH, SHE FOUND McCoy and Bree in the garage an hour later in deep conversation. Sawyer watched from the garage door window, one hand on the knob, one hand pressed against her chest to calm her racing heart. Bree was seated in the driver's seat of the McLaren, hands on the new steering wheel in the same spot her father had bled out.

Trepidation and ... and *rage* flooded Sawyer. The McLaren wasn't a *leisure* toy to play with. It was the last materialistic thread Sawyer had to her piece of shit husband. It was a job, nothing else, an asset bound in contract with McCoy, and that contract most certainly did *not* include her only living child.

Sawyer swung the door open, gripping it tightly as she raised her voice. "Bree. Get out of the car."

The music playing in the background was loud, but Bree and McCoy both paused to look at her. "Hey." McCoy lit up at the sight of Sawyer.

She entered the garage in her slippers, descending the steps as quickly as she dared. Her knees quaked as she marched toward them. "Bree," she repeated in a shaky voice. She stopped several feet away, not daring to get too close to the supercar, and pointed to her daughter through the windshield. "Bree, get out of the car. Right fucking now."

"*M-Maman*?" Bree's eyes were as big as saucers. Her face paled, and then she scrambled to get out of the car, almost stepping on a drill in the process.

"Here," McCoy said, holding Bree's hand to help her around the obstacle course of various tools and car parts. They stopped in front of Sawyer, McCoy looking unsure of what she'd done wrong and Bree looking as if Sawyer had physically struck her.

"Sawyer, the dangerous part of the process is over," McCoy said, glancing between them, "Bree wanted to—"

"Bree ..." Sawyer's voice wavered. She took a deep breath and tried again. "Go into the house, please."

Of all the times, Bree chose this time to balk at Sawyer's request. "Maman, I told you I was out here. What's the problem?"

Sawyer's lip curled before she snarled, "*Tu ne comprends pas,* Bree. *S'il te plaît écoute-moi. Entre dans la maison!*"

"Okay, okay," Bree relented, tossing McCoy an embarrassed glance before trudging inside.

"Bree is not to go near the McLaren again," Sawyer said once she and McCoy were alone. She was shaking, and she had the strangest urge to slap McCoy for allowing this, and yet, a part of her wanted to be held, comforted. She wrapped her arms around herself so she wouldn't accidentally reach for McCoy.

"Sawyer, what's wrong?" McCoy asked softly, reaching out to stroke her arm. "My pops and I took the engine out. The McLaren's not going anywhere."

"I know that," Sawyer said through gritted teeth. Grinding her molars down was the only thing keeping everything else at bay.

"Do you? Would you feel better if you got a closer look at it? Come, I can show you."

"No. I know what that car is, McCoy," Sawyer snapped, wrenching away from the younger woman's touch.

McCoy stepped closer until their bodies were almost pressing together and tucked a lock of Sawyer's hair behind her ear. "You don't have to be afraid of it."

"Afraid?" Sawyer echoed incredulously. "I'm not afraid."

"Then what is it? Talk to me. I didn't know Bree wasn't allowed near it. It's not in the contract."

Swallowing hard, Sawyer looked away from McCoy's concerned gaze, saying roughly, "Maybe it should be. Next time ..." She cleared her throat, glancing briefly back at McCoy. "Next time my daughter wants to try her hand at mechanics, teach her on a different vehicle. Okay?"

"Of course. Anything you want," McCoy murmured. She widened her stance, folding her arms across her chest but kept her imploring gaze on Sawyer.

Sawyer didn't know why, but her brain chose that moment to dredge up the dream she'd had. It was unsettling to want someone as much as she wanted McCoy. She'd been force-fed religious crap for so long that she thought she should feel disgusted at the thought of McCoy lifting her up onto her kitchen island and fucking her. But she didn't. In fact, there was only one issue with that whole fantasy. She'd given McCoy all the control.

And that just wouldn't do.

"I want the date you promised."

McCoy looked shocked for a second, and then she broke into the biggest grin Sawyer had ever seen, her dimples disappearing into her cheeks. Sawyer had to hold herself back from kissing her. *Not yet*, she thought.

McCoy, however, had no sense of self-preservation. She stood on her tiptoes, slid her hand around Sawyer's neck, and pulled her in for a gentle yet heated lip-lock. Sawyer expected gloating, or at the very least, her latest one-liner, but McCoy surprised her once again. "Thank you, Sawyer."

"Yes, well." Sawyer licked her lips, savoring McCoy's unique taste. She regretfully turned away, knowing she still needed to apologize to Bree. "Thank you for the flowers. And ... the other thing."

Though she didn't face McCoy as she headed out of the garage, she heard the smile in her voice.

"Trust me, it's no trouble at all."

CHAPTER 30

McCoy

SHE STARED AT HER reflection in the full-length mirror hanging on the back of her bedroom door. Utterly naked, save for her bracelets, rings, and lucky black boxers with its attached dildo. It'd been a long time since she'd gone anywhere packing, but then again, it'd been just as long since she'd tried taking anyone home for the night. Wearing one was always a huge confidence booster, and tonight, she needed all the confidence she could muster.

Coy reached for her sports bra next, followed by her favorite black buttoned short-sleeve dress shirt. She remembered the way Sawyer had looked at her that time she'd gone to dinner with Abi and was eager to see the same expression tonight. Next came her black cargo shorts and red suspenders. Honestly, it was probably the suspenders that had Sawyer doing a double-take. She looked her outfit over, readjusting the dildo until it looked more natural. Still, she hesitated.

"Maybe I shouldn't wear it."

Coy worried her bottom lip in thought. Sawyer had made it abundantly clear they were going at her pace, and if she felt Coy packing, then it might spoil their date. The last thing Coy wanted to do was pressure Sawyer and ruin things between them.

"Ugh, why is this so hard?" She sunk onto her bed, grabbing her phone and shooting Naz a text.

Coy: Rethinking this, dude.

Naz: The date or the gear?

Coy: WTF. The gear, obvs. Duh.

Naz: LOL. Am I a mind reader now? Fml.

Naz: Has she ever been with a woman? Might wanna ease into it, if not.

Coy actually had no idea. There was so much she needed to learn about Sawyer. Had Olivier been her only lover? If so, that had to suck.

Sighing, she thanked her friend for the assist before swapping the harness boxers for regular ones. Afterward, she fastened her red bowtie around her neck and her chained wallet to her shorts for the complete look.

Sloane was waiting for her in the hallway, appearing more haggard than Coy had ever seen her. She looked like she hadn't slept in the days since they'd last spoken. "Coy, hey."

"Sloane," Coy said carefully, keeping an eye on her sister as she headed to the entrance to put on her Nikes.

They had never gone this long without speaking. Not even in the tenth grade when Coy had broken Sloane's boyfriend's nose because he'd made her cry. She'd spent two days blaming Coy for their breakup—which, you know, good riddance to the bastard—and only forgave her when she saw the loser making out with another girl. Then Sloane got angry.

"You never even asked how my race went," Sloane said in a dull voice. "You're never home anymore. If it weren't for the shop videos you send, I wouldn't even know you were alive."

"Erm, that's a bit dramatic, don't you think?" Coy narrowed her gaze on her twin. "I'm sorry I've been so busy, and I could've sworn I asked about the race. That was weeks ago. I know J.D. was filling me in at work. You guys came in fifth, right?"

"Yes, and we would've come close to winning if that bitch didn't sabotage my bike. The tires were flat, Coy."

"J.D. mentioned that." Coy grimaced. "I'm sorry you lost, and if I wasn't literally on my way out, you could vent all you want. Raincheck?" *Even though you've yet to apologize for the bet.*

"Oh. I was hoping you'd give me a lift to work."

Coy sighed impatiently, glancing over Sloane's outfit. She was dressed in her usual work attire, regardless that she looked like she'd gone on a bender the night before. "What's wrong with Sara?"

"Oh, I left her at a friend's place and took an Uber home."

Well, at least she wasn't drinking and driving. Technically, Coy *could* give her a lift, considering it was the pub Coy had planned on taking Sawyer. But she wouldn't have time to drive to Vancouver's West End and make it back to Sawyer's before five. She winced, knowing what that meant. She could say no. She *should* say no, especially after the way Sloane had been acting lately. But when had she ever been able to deny her sister anything?

"Okay," she caved, grimacing at Sloane's unnecessary air fist pump. "But under one condition. We're picking Sawyer up first."

Sawyer pulled open the door just as Coy was revving up to knock, looking so stunning all Coy could do was stare. She wore a forest green, off-the-shoulder top, navy blue denims, and zippered ankle boots. Her hair was down as it usually was, but it looked as if it now had some curl to the strands.

Coy opened her mouth, ready to dish out her first compliment, when Sawyer said, "You're late. I knew I should have driven myself."

"I know, I'm sorry. A five-foot-four wrench got thrown into my plans at the last minute," Coy apologized, reining in her disappointment when Sawyer moved past her before she could attempt to at least kiss her cheek.

Guess this is strike one, dude. Should've just come packing, she thought, as her remaining confidence dwindled away. She took a deep breath, jogging to catch up to Sawyer. "So I know you don't love surprises, but Sloane is currently in my backseat. She needed a ride, and since we're going to the same place ..."

Sawyer stopped and turned, one finely arched eyebrow raised. "The five-foot-four wrench, I presume?"

Coy huffed a laugh, blushing under her watchful gaze. "The very same. Um, can we ... are we okay? Again, sorry I didn't call ahead, Sawyer, but I'm really looking forward to spending the evening with you."

Sawyer slipped her hand in Coy's, her eyes softening slightly. "Olivier had terrible excuses."

"Did he?"

"Yes. All the time." Sawyer squeezed her hand, not letting go as they started toward the Jeep again. "Helping family, I can understand. I would do anything for Bree."

Coy stopped by the passenger door, "Thanks, but you might regret saying that. Sloane's in a mood lately."

"So you've said. Is she still concerned over your devotion to me?"

Devotion. Devotion. Coy lingered on the word, playing it round and round in her head. She liked the idea of being devoted to Sawyer. Sure beat all those empty promises she'd made to herself over the years about half-baked plans to ride the solo train for life. She couldn't imagine being anywhere else right now.

"How about we give her something else to talk about?" Sawyer said, pulling Coy back to the present. She caught the mischievous glint in Sawyer's eyes seconds before she grabbed Coy by the suspenders and claimed her lips in a hot, boxer-melting kiss. Coy hummed with pleasure, savoring the taste and feel of Sawyer's tongue against hers, prodding, searching the recesses of her mouth. Coy's head spun, and her hands flung out to hold on to something, anything. She felt the curve of Sawyer's hips and clung to her.

Oh, Goddess, she could spend millennia kissing Sawyer.

A loud knock broke up their moment before Sloane called out, "Gonna be late for work, Coy."

Coy groaned, but Sawyer smiled against her lips, giving her one last peck. She wiped a smudge of lipstick off Coy's mouth, whispering, "I think it worked, wouldn't you say?"

Nodding, her head still buzzing from endorphins, Coy laughed. "I think so, yeah."

A stupid grin was stuck on her face as she helped Sawyer into Tegan, expertly ignoring Sloane's eye roll as she did so. She ran around to the driver's side, and as she got in, she sent a quick prayer to any entity who would listen that the rest of the night go smoothly.

Chapter 31

Sawyer

"How long have you been bartending, Sloane?" Sawyer asked politely as McCoy navigated Tegan across the city. McCoy smiled, gratitude that Sawyer was trying to make conversation shone clear as day on her face as she reached for her bottle of water. Sawyer wasn't used to purposely taking the bite out of her voice when speaking. Or striking up conversation with someone she had little choice but to know solely because Sloane was important to McCoy.

"Going on six years. Coy actually got me the job when she started fucking Frankie."

McCoy choked on her water, bits of it spraying over the steering wheel. "What the fuck, Sloane?" she wheezed out, glaring in the rearview mirror at her sister. Sloane only smirked.

"Frankie is the owner, correct?"

Jealousy was futile—and juvenile—on so many levels, but Sawyer couldn't deny the abrupt pang in her chest at the thought of McCoy caring for someone enough that they were still close today. When McCoy had brought Frankie up days before, she'd failed to mention they were still in contact.

"Coy didn't tell you that your date was where her ex lives and works?" Sloane punched Coy's arm good-naturedly. Either she was genuinely so dense that she didn't know she was upsetting McCoy, or she was purposely being cruel. Sawyer wanted to slap her. *Fuck her for trying to sabotage my first date in years.*

"Sloane, stop it. *Please.*" McCoy darted a panicked look at Sawyer. "I am so sorry. I-I didn't even think of that. I-I read that romancing someone should involve sharing your favorite place to eat. Somewhere you're comfortable, you know? But that's stupid, I guess, considering."

"I think it's sweet." Sloane shrugged, wedging herself between the two front seats so she was facing them better. She was close enough for an elbow to the face should the need arise.

"Sweet?" Sawyer echoed, narrowing her eyes on McCoy's lesser half. There was something off about Sloane; Sawyer had felt it the moment they'd crossed paths. She'd considered McCoy immature at first glance, but she didn't hold a candle to her sister in that regard. Sloane was selfish, and her actions screamed of envy. Had she always been that way, or was she jealous that McCoy wasn't as easily at her beck and call?

"Yeah, I mean, at least Coy is trying. She's kind of throwing you to the wolves from the get-go with Frankie, though." Sloane shrugged again and laughed. "Kudos for finally dating again! God, remember the last one you went on? When was that, like two days before prom or something?"

A horrified, almost sick expression turned McCoy's cheeks ashen. "Sloane," she gritted out, reaching back to try to swat her sister, but Sloane dodged her.

"What?" she chortled. "You've grown up. Surely you don't plan on leaving Sawyer alone in the booth to hook up with some rando like you did back then?"

Sawyer's whole body tensed. Her gaze slipped to the woman behind the wheel, taking in the hurt McCoy tried so hard to hide, but there were tells. The steady twitch in her jaw, as if she was grinding her molars into a fine dust. Or how her eyes closed to half mast, like if she opened them too wide, tears would funnel out. Two hands clutched the wheel when she only ever drove with one. One on the wheel and one on the gearshift or entwined with Sawyer's. Anyone who knew McCoy should have seen how upset she was, but Sloane continued her useless monologue like an actress starved for a role.

"Honestly, that was crazy, even for you." Sloane patted Sawyer's arm, unbothered when Sawyer recoiled from the unwelcome touch. "Coy ever tell you about that? She'd gone to meet her girlfriend at the restaurant and ended up chatting with another girl we knew in the parking lot. Fucked her right there in the car and forgot about the one waiting inside."

A low, anxious fire grew in Sawyer, starting from her toes and expanding, burning her up inside until she thought she'd die if it wasn't unleashed.

"She wasn't my girlfriend," McCoy whispered over the roaring in Sawyer's ears.

"It must be quite a change for you, Sloane, not having McCoy all to yourself," Sawyer said, keeping her voice neutral even though she wanted to throw the girl from the moving vehicle. She shifted in her seat so they could speak face-to-face. "Are you lonely? Is that it? Not getting the attention you're used to from the one who loves you the most?"

Sloane drew back in her seat, mouth agape and looking absolutely affronted. Sawyer could have laughed. "I-I ... That's not it at all. I—"

"Isn't it, though?" Sawyer's tone grew icier. From her peripheral vision, McCoy's leg bounced, much like it'd done at her house over lunch the day Bree invited the twins in. Sawyer placed a comforting hand on her thigh and continued, "It's why you're seeking all this unwarranted attention. You're afraid McCoy might fall in love and leave you behind. Instead of being happy for her, you've set out to humiliate her in front of me. Why? You're being an *esti de cave*, Sloane, a fucking idiot, to risk your relationship with your sister."

"Excuse me?" Sloane flushed, the rouge shade doing little for the bags set under her eyes. She spluttered, "Coy, are you gonna let her talk to me like that?"

"It doesn't feel too good, does it?" Sawyer arched an eyebrow, her hand still on McCoy. She rubbed slow circles over her thigh. "My husband was a master manipulator. So, your antics? Nothing but child's play."

"You sure know how to pick them, Coy," Sloane snapped, shoving the back door open the moment McCoy found parking. She grabbed her purse off the seat and shook it at her sister. "Maybe next time you can find a woman who isn't a complete psycho?"

The door slammed, and then Sloane was hurrying up the sidewalk, quickly disappearing in the mass of pedestrians milling outside the collective restaurants.

How could twins be so identical and yet polar opposites? Sawyer looked at McCoy and saw new, frightening possibilities. A potential lover who could also be a friend. She was kind, funny, smart and handsome.

Sloane was ... none of those things.

An uncomfortable, suffocatingly queasy feeling filled her chest and throat. "Are you okay?" she quietly asked. Any louder and she was sure her voice would break. "I will not apologize for what I said to your sister because it would be a lie."

McCoy stared out the windshield, both hands gripping the steering wheel like Tegan was her lifeline. A tear slipped down her cheek. "All I wanted was to take you on a date. T-to prove to you ..."

Sawyer brushed the tear away, tracing McCoy's damp cheek with her thumb. "Is that no longer the case?"

"No, I still want to." McCoy sniffled, turning to look at Sawyer. "But the pub is Frankie's. I didn't have a plan B."

"Is she going to kick us out?"

"Well, no."

"Okay, then let's go in." Sawyer sighed before admitting, "Part of dealing with your past is not to avoid it but to learn from it."

McCoy huffed a laugh, stating dryly, "Honestly, I'd rather get a second date with you."

Sawyer's thumb drifted over McCoy's bottom lip, tugging on it seductively with the tip of her nail. "Don't wander off with someone else, and we should be fine, darling."

"So what do you think?" McCoy gestured to the nachos on the table between them. "Pretty good, right?"

Sawyer raised another bite to her lips, crunching down on the chip coated in toppings and a generous helping of *pico de gallo*. She chewed slowly, thoroughly enjoying McCoy's wide, eager eyes. It was as if she was a judge on her very own cooking show. She was so glad she'd insisted they share a tray of nachos rather than order the grilled chicken and salad McCoy had first suggested.

"Typical pub fare," she deduced after swallowing. At McCoy's crestfallen expression, Sawyer held back a smile, adding, "But absolutely delicious, as you claimed."

"Right?" McCoy grinned, scooping up nachos as well. She seemed lighter than she'd been after the Sloane incident, like she was ready to push past whatever *that* was and enjoy Sawyer's company. It would have been more convincing if she stopped looking toward the bar for her sister. "You sure you can eat this, though? I was talking to Bree and—"

"It's fine," Sawyer interrupted. "I've given up more than enough since the heart attack. I just won't overindulge, alright?"

"Okay." McCoy didn't look convinced.

"I appreciate your concern, darling. Truly." Sawyer reached across the table to pat her hand.

McCoy gave her a tentative smile before eyeing the tray of nachos again. Something else was on her mind, something that had been lingering since they'd walked into the pub. Sawyer wished she'd just spit it out already. Was it about Sloane? Sawyer admitted she could have used more tact with the younger woman, but hearing Sloane drudge up McCoy's past in such a negative light had goaded her to no end. Of course, nothing about how McCoy had treated either of those girls in high school was attractive in Sawyer's eyes, but how could she judge her for teenage foolishness? McCoy wasn't that person now.

"What you said about Olivier." McCoy's index finger swiped over the condensation on her glass of ale. She licked her lips. "I had no idea."

"Yes, well, Olivier was a lot of things," Sawyer admitted, instinctively tensing up. "A class A narcissist being one of them."

McCoy glanced at her then, those lovely green eyes brimming with empathy. "I'm sorry. That must have been awful for you and Bree."

"Mm-hmm." Sawyer cleared her throat. "But let's not ruin the evening by talking about that. Tell me about you. What else did you research for this date you've somehow convinced me to go on?"

McCoy nodded, clearly accepting Sawyer's desire to change the subject—just as Sawyer knew she would. "Um ... first date questions? But some of them were awful. I'd never ask you what your retirement plans are. Hell, I'd count myself lucky if I can get that second date I've been dreaming about."

Sawyer cracked a smile, McCoy's playfulness growing on her. "I genuinely don't know the answer to that. Ask me again in five years. If you're lucky."

McCoy laughed, taking another drink of beer. Sawyer studied her, surveying the outfit she'd chosen for the evening. She'd hardly been able to take her eyes off McCoy, loving how the short sleeves of her dress shirt showed off the definition in her arms. Or how the suspenders made her small breasts pop and the black eyeliner stand out. Or how that bowtie, even though it was brick red, made the green in her eyes sparkle like emeralds.

Oh, she recalled McCoy's outfit well.

"You look good, darling. I especially like the bowtie."

McCoy preened under Sawyer's attention, a blush blossoming over her cheeks. She toyed with her thumb ring. "Thank you. So do you. You look incredible. I-I can't stop staring at your collarbones." McCoy froze, her hand clamping over her mouth. A tense chuckle slipped out. "I can't believe I just said that."

"You have a thing for the clavicle, then?" Sawyer almost laughed, glad she'd chosen this top and not the blouse. It had been Bree who suggested it, saying Sawyer's collarbones were one of her best features.

"I have a thing for you," McCoy said simply, like it was the easiest thing she'd voiced all day. Sawyer wished she could be so free with her words, but in the past, each one had come with a price. It would take more than a few meals and conversation for her to trust McCoy with anything relating to her heart.

"So I've heard," she teased just as a beautiful femme approached their booth. Sawyer pulled her shoulders back, eyeing the newcomer and somehow knowing this was Frankie. She had long brown hair with hints of red and blond throughout, a strong, prominent nose, pretty eyes the shade of nutmeg, and curves for days. Sawyer was immediately envious of her full figure. She'd always felt a bit lacking in the chest and hip department.

The strangest urge to protect McCoy hit her, and Sawyer reached across the table to lace their fingers together. *God, I feel like I'm claiming her.* Probably because that's exactly what she was doing. Ugh. If Cindy could see her now, she'd be laughing her ass off.

"Hello, you must be Sawyer," the woman said, setting down the beer she'd been holding in front of McCoy. She glanced between Sawyer and McCoy, noting the way Sawyer's fingers gripped McCoy's, before giving Sawyer a small smile. She held out her hand. "I'm Frankie O'Rourke. It's good to meet you."

"You as well," Sawyer said slowly, not missing the way Frankie and McCoy watched each other.

"I was watching you two from the bar," Frankie continued, only having eyes for McCoy now. Sawyer's gaze narrowed when the other woman stroked McCoy's loose strands of hair. "And I understand now. I'm happy for you, pet."

"Frankie," McCoy croaked, wrenching her hand from Sawyer's. She jumped to her feet and threw her arms around Frankie, shocking her and Sawyer both, it seemed, as the other woman stumbled back a step before returning the hug. They held one another for far longer than Sawyer was comfortable with, and the embrace left her with more questions than she had answers. Who was Frankie? Her connection with McCoy seemed deeper than a mere ex-lover.

Sawyer was about to clear her throat—*loudly*—when the two women slowly separated. Both looked misty-eyed, but the biggest surprise of all was hearing McCoy whisper, "Thank you, Mistress."

Followed by Frankie's rough reply, "It's just Frankie now, McCoy."

"It's just Frankie now, McCoy."

Even hours later, after another appetizer and two games of pool, the precise way Frankie had said McCoy's name clung to Sawyer like a fleece blanket in the dead heat of summer. It chafed her to know she wasn't the only one using McCoy's full name.

They were pulling into Sawyer's driveway hours later when she couldn't hold back another minute. "Who was Frankie to you?"

The sensor light on the garage came on as McCoy parked and turned off the ignition. She was quiet for so long that Sawyer's hackles rose. "McCoy, the question wasn't difficult."

"Are you familiar with kink or BDSM?"

The response threw Sawyer off guard, and she faltered momentarily. "I ... Yes. Some. Just from what Cindy has shared in conversation."

McCoy watched her, indecision in her gaze. She reached up and unfastened her bowtie, whispering, "Frankie is a Dominant. She was … *my* Dominant."

Sawyer's eyebrows shot up, and McCoy rushed on. "I'm what they call a switch. I never wanted to submit to anyone full time. Frankie has … relationship hangups and no wish to be a submissive. So we just … worked, I guess. Part-time lovers with intense bedroom scenes."

"I see." She didn't, not really. McCoy's explanation left a lot to be desired. Sawyer would need to do some research at some point. Incognito so Bree couldn't stumble upon anything newsworthy. She understood one thing, though. "So, you like being tied up? Gagged? Spanked?" A shiver ran down her spine. "Do you expect the same of me? To be a switch? Because you can zap the fantasy of spanking me right now."

"Not at all, actually," McCoy admitted with a faint blush. "Maybe I'm a poor switch. I've never done anything more with a lover than the occasional handcuffs and toys. But …" Her blush deepened, and she avoided Sawyer's gaze. "As a sub, sometimes I crave all of those things you mentioned and more."

"Is that right?" Hadn't Sawyer dreamt weeks ago about tying McCoy up? She'd endured basic missionary sex for her entire marriage, and where had that gotten her? What would sex with McCoy be like?

Passionate. Intense. Sexy.

Ugh. She wanted to find out. She wanted nothing more than to throw caution to the wind with McCoy. Sawyer wanted, no, *needed*, to see what she'd been missing for the last twenty-seven years. The life, the *sex* she could have had if only she hadn't been caught kissing Beth Li in the eleventh grade.

Beside her, McCoy chuckled. She was eyeing her rearview mirror. "Bree's home."

Sawyer looked out her window in time to see her daughter pull up in the Rover. Bree noticed them and waved. Sawyer returned the gesture, pushing past her disappointment over the night ending early. *Perhaps it's for the best,* she thought. It hadn't been as if she was seriously thinking about sex after she'd explicitly told McCoy it was off the table on the first date. Had she?

Throwing caution to the wind was great in theory. She could pretend she was younger or more experienced with attractive, unmarred skin. In reality, McCoy could finally get her wish of falling into bed together, only to discover Sawyer was as mediocre as Olivier had claimed.

She turned back to the woman in question, swallowing the lump now in her throat. "I guess this is where we say goodnight."

"Are you kidding?" McCoy asked, incredulous. She unbuckled quickly and hopped out of Tegan, racing around the Jeep to Sawyer's side. Before opening Sawyer's door, she gave Bree a quick hug. Watching them together did strange, mushy things to Sawyer's already heightened emotions. McCoy smiled up at her, oblivious to the swell of ... of *feeling* lodged in her chest. Her sinuses burned in warning that she may very well cry if she didn't soon get control.

McCoy held out her hand. "What kind of gentlewoman would I be if I didn't at least walk you to your door?"

Sawyer took a deep breath. She didn't trust herself to speak yet, so she silently placed her hand in McCoy's and climbed out. Bree had already disappeared inside the house, no doubt giving them a moment alone. Sawyer almost wished she hadn't. At least then Bree could be the buffer Sawyer needed to duck away before McCoy could see, well, *her*. The real her.

"I had a great time tonight, Sawyer," McCoy said, lacing their fingers together. She raised them to her mouth, kissing the back of Sawyer's hand, and whispered, "Thank you for taking a chance on me."

"Mm-hmm." McCoy was too much. Too sweet. Too doting. Too earnest in her intentions. Sawyer swallowed. Swallowed again, croaking out, "Of course."

"Hey, are you okay?"

McCoy's palm grazed Sawyer's cheek, the side with the scar, and she wrenched free of the contact. "I-I have to go," she said roughly, ignoring the flash of hurt in McCoy's eyes as she took off into the house.

Chapter 32

McCoy

What was that about?

Coy stared at the front door Sawyer had disappeared through moments ago, dread creeping over her. They'd had a good time, hadn't they? Sawyer had acted like she'd been enjoying herself, and she hadn't completely freaked out when Coy brought up her love of kink. What changed? Had she come on too strong?

"Hell," Coy brought her hands up to rest on her head. It wasn't like she was going to walk Sawyer to her door and expect a nightcap. Sure, she was sexually frustrated, but nothing she couldn't take care of at home once they'd said their good nights.

"I did everything right."

Something else must have caused Sawyer's hasty departure. Coy had to know. It didn't feel right to just leave regardless of whether she'd see Sawyer in the morning. She had to know the older woman was alright.

Bree met Coy at the door, smiling sadly. She pulled Coy into her arms. "I'd hoped all that pacing outside would lead you in here."

"She ran into the house. Away from me," Coy said, hating how confused she sounded. Would there ever come a time when she wasn't constantly stumbling blindfolded in Sawyer's presence? What would it take for Sawyer to let her walls down enough to let Coy in? Snippets of detail here and there wasn't anything to go on, and Sawyer hated talking about herself.

"I know. *Maman* told me she needed to be alone. But I bet she wouldn't turn you away if you tried," Bree suggested, her brown eyes alight now with possibility.

Coy chuckled dryly. She pulled away from Bree, slipping off her Nikes. "She might skewer me to the door instead."

Bree giggled. "Somehow, I doubt that. Her bedroom is the first one to the right."

"Thanks, Bree." Coy shot her an appreciative smile before making her way to the second floor. She found Sawyer sitting on her bed, holding the cards Coy had given her and stripped down to just her bra and bikini-style underwear. Pajamas were tossed on the made bed, and Sawyer's earlier clothes had been strewn across the bedroom floor on the way to an opened, walk-in closet. They were still discovering each other, but Coy knew for a fact Sawyer disliked messes.

"Hi," Coy murmured, clicking the door shut silently behind her.

"I told Bree I wanted to be alone," Sawyer said, her voice low and husky.

Coy couldn't help but stare for a moment, marveling over Sawyer's slender frame and inviting warm skin. The collar bones that had nearly driven Coy with lust earlier were just a starting point to her wandering gaze. She swallowed, dragging her gaze from Sawyer's breasts. "Don't blame her. I needed to see if you were alright. After, with me." Coy moved to the bed, wringing her hands together, watching as Sawyer clutched the cards closer to her chest. "Did I do something wrong?"

Sawyer shook her head, strands of black hair tumbling off her shoulders to frame her face. "No. McCoy, I don't ... I can't talk about ..." She cleared her throat, but the tears in her voice were unmistakable. "You were exceptional."

Coy's mouth quirked up. Reaching out, she tucked Sawyer's hair behind her ear. "Really? Second date exceptional?"

"Don't get ahead of yourself," Sawyer muttered. Her eyelashes were damp, and she wouldn't look at Coy.

"Sawyer," Coy said, her voice soft. Her hand went to Sawyer's other cheek, cupping her jaw and slowly turning the other woman's face toward her. Her makeup had been washed off, so Coy got the unfiltered version of Sawyer's beauty. Brushing the rest of Sawyer's hair aside, Coy closed the small gap between them and pressed a kiss to her lips. Then kissed the corner of her mouth and her jaw. Sawyer clutched her arm, her nails digging into the skin as she let McCoy's lips caress her scarred cheek.

"McCoy, please. It's ugly," Sawyer choked out, but she didn't push her away.

"It's beautiful," Coy corrected and nuzzled her nose against the scar's uneven ridges. She wet her lips, laying sweet kisses over Sawyer's cheek again. "Is the skin sensitive here?"

"Sometimes," came Sawyer's raw response. Then, "I've never let anyone besides Bree touch it."

"Not Olivier?"

"Especially not him." There was so much pain in those few words that Coy pulled back just as a tear slipped out. "Not that he would have. He said just looking at it made him sick."

Are you shitting me right now? Goddess, if Coy could only travel back in time, find Olivier, and kick his ass, she'd already be leaping through the portal.

"Not to speak ill of the dead, but I think I hate that guy." Coy kissed Sawyer's tears away. She shivered, so Coy reached behind them for the nightshirt Sawyer had waiting. "Here, let me help with this."

"I'm not some damsel, McCoy," Sawyer griped, shoving the cards she'd been reading into her nightstand. She went to grab the shirt, but McCoy placed her hand on hers.

"I know that. Believe me, I know that," she said, giving Sawyer a soft smile. "Let me do this for the same reason I gave you a massage and tried to cook you breakfast. You're important to me, Sawyer. Needing or wanting someone doesn't make you weak, sweetheart."

"I never said it did." The retort had lost some of its bite from before, and Coy's heart swelled as Sawyer allowed her to pull the shirt carefully over her head. Then she added under her breath, "It's just ridiculous. I can do this myself."

"But it's more romantic since I'm sitting so close. We were having a moment," Coy reasoned, her grin widening. She stood up, undoing her dress shirt and shorts, letting them fall to her feet. Then thought better of it, picking them back up as well as Sawyer's discarded clothes. She draped everything over the chair by Sawyer's walk-in closet.

"What do you think you're doing?"

Sawyer eyed Coy warily, who was wearing just her sports bra and boxers.

"I don't know if you've realized, but my love language is through touch," Coy murmured, crawling into bed with Sawyer. "And I really, really, just wanna hold you tonight. Or you hold me, Sawyer. I don't care. But your vibe is off, and the last thing I wanna do is go home and doubt if you're feeling anything like what I'm feeling."

"And you think touching me will help absolve you of that?" Sawyer looked skeptical, but she didn't shoot Coy's idea down. That was good. Sawyer might not realize it, but Coy was pretty sure physical touch was her love language as well. She just didn't know how to ask for it.

"I do, and don't worry," Coy said and felt herself relax when Sawyer got under the covers as well. "We're still going at your pace. You're the boss. Tonight is all about the snuggle."

"You're impossible." Sawyer rolled her eyes, but Coy thought she saw a slight smile as she turned off the lamp. "I'm too old to snuggle."

"Never," Coy said, reaching through the semi-darkness to pull Sawyer closer. She tucked Sawyer as close as possible, back to chest, and Sawyer's ass pressed snugly against Coy's hot core. Burying her face in the crook of Sawyer's neck, she inhaled her deeply. Her stomach flip-flopped, and she whispered, "Just like you're not too old to be my girlfriend."

Sawyer was quiet for the longest time. Her body was still tense, so Coy knew she hadn't fallen asleep. Her obvious reluctance to speak or sleep had Coy doubting her plan. She'd basically told Sawyer she was sleeping over, but surely Sawyer would have kicked her out if she didn't secretly wish for that as well?

Coy was dozing off when Sawyer whispered, "I've only been with Olivier."

Her eyes snapped open. It took a moment for Sawyer's words to register, but then Coy mumbled, "Oh. Well, that's okay. We'll learn together what the other likes." Her arms tightened around Sawyer. "I swear I'll never pressure you. Your pace, remember?"

Sawyer held Coy's arm draped across her midsection, giving it a light squeeze. "My pace."

Chapter 33

Sawyer

Sawyer woke with a scream caught in her throat. She flew up in bed, scrambling to get the covers off. Her heart raced. It was hard to breathe, and tears streamed down her cheeks. Yanking her nightgown up, her movements were jerky as she frantically patted down her bare, flat stomach.

A sob broke free. "Oh, Brian," Sawyer whispered brokenly. "Oh, *mon bel amour*."

He's gone, long ago. Just a nightmare.

Sawyer laid back down and held a hand to her chest, waiting for her erratic pulse to slow. Tears seeped out, mixing with the drying sweat against her hairline. Her back felt damp as well, the nightgown clinging to her skin. No matter how much time passed, how many nightmares plagued Sawyer's subconscious, or how many tears she shed, the agony of losing Brian somehow felt infinite.

Sniffling, she slipped from the bed, careful not to jar the sleeping woman next to her. *McCoy*. Fragments of the night before returned as Sawyer padded the few feet to her bathroom. Warmth settled over the abysmal ache in her chest, and as she peeled off her nightgown and bra and stepped into the shower, the pleasant memory of McCoy showing up was full front in her mind. McCoy had anticipated what Sawyer needed before she even knew. How was that possible? It was like she understood Sawyer in a way no one had before. McCoy had known Sawyer was upset last night, but instead of prying and possibly pushing her away, she had made up a ridiculous excuse of needing comfort. The gentle manipulation was obvious, but rather than the crap Olivier would often pull, McCoy's antics had been out of the goodness of her heart. And Sawyer had welcomed it.

After her shower, Sawyer dried off in front of the vanity mirror, taking a good long look at her face and paying close attention to the dips and leathery ridges of her bad side. Not once in the last fifteen years had she seen the melted skin and considered it beautiful. But McCoy had. In fact, she'd spent so much time kissing the scar that Sawyer could almost believe she meant it.

McCoy was still sound asleep when Sawyer returned, positioned halfway on her stomach with her arm draped across the space Sawyer had vacated. The sliver of light from the bathroom cast a faint glow around McCoy's youthful features. Sawyer didn't think anyone had ever been so attractive to her, but it went well beyond her handsome face and muscular, tattooed arms. McCoy was a rarity in the world. She was protective, yet instinctually subservient, and Sawyer gravitated toward her. For the first time in Sawyer's life, she wanted someone to see all her scars—on the inside and the outside. She wanted to confide in McCoy, tell her things not even Bree knew. She wanted someone she could trust to share her burden, and she theirs.

"McCoy," Sawyer whispered, bending to scatter kisses across her face. Her lips found McCoy's bare shoulder, and nipped the skin. She was wide awake now, a sense of urgency in her movements as she gently shook McCoy. Her hand slid down McCoy's back to cup her ass through her boxers. That did the trick.

"Whaa—? I'm-I'm up, yes," McCoy mumbled, fluttering her long lashes open and peering up at Sawyer. A sleepy grin appeared. "Why, hello."

"Are you serious about your intentions with me? I don't play games, McCoy."

McCoy blinked, the sleep fading slowly in her eyes. "As serious as a heart attack." Then she cringed, muttering, "Sorry. Terrible, terrible joke."

Sawyer opened her mouth, ready to spill the nightmare she'd had, but froze. She didn't want to share more sorrow in the last few hours they'd have before work became priority once again. She wanted to feel closer to McCoy, yes, but not through shared pain, not now.

"Kiss me," she instructed softly. She needed McCoy's lips on her like she needed her next breath. She laid down beside McCoy again, facing her, and reached for her hand. Their eyes met in the dim light, and Sawyer slowly brought McCoy's hand to her towel, whispering, "Now. Kiss me everywhere, darling." *Make me feel beautiful.* "I want you." *I need you.* God, did she ever. The realization terrified Sawyer, and yet, there was a fluttery sensation mounting in her belly as she gazed at McCoy's lips.

"Whatever you want, Sawyer," McCoy breathed, eyes heavy with lust. She shifted so that she was on top rather than beside Sawyer, the chin-length strands of her top-knot tickling Sawyer as she lowered her head for a kiss. "You've got a chokehold on me, sweetheart, and I'm not even mad," McCoy dropped light kisses along her jawline to her ear. Then she scraped her teeth over Sawyer's earlobe before sucking it into her mouth.

Sawyer's back arched off the bed, and she clung to McCoy, a faint moan escaping her. She angled her head, exposing her neck to McCoy, desperate for more. The younger woman didn't disappoint.

"Oh god." Tingles erupted inside her with the stroke of McCoy's tongue along her neck and shoulder. Goosebumps broke out over her arms, and her nipples tightened. McCoy alternated between using her tongue and teeth to drop open-mouth kisses and love bites along

Sawyer's skin, and as her mouth worked, her hands were busy rubbing a sensuous path up and down Sawyer's arms.

"You have the softest skin," McCoy marveled, her heated gaze catching Sawyer's. Her hands slipped into Sawyer's, and she placed soft kisses over her knuckles, her fingertips. She sucked Sawyer's index finger into her mouth, and Sawyer's breath hitched in her throat.

"McCoy," she started, going to pull away, but McCoy held her still.

"Shh, it's okay," McCoy said softly, flashing an impish grin before stroking the length of her tongue up Sawyer's middle finger. Sawyer's pulse kicked up as she watched, transfixed on what McCoy was doing. Her whole body felt flushed and warm all over like she was having a hot flash. "I'm going to kiss, and lick, and suck, and nibble every inch of you. How does that sound?"

Sawyer's mouth went dry. "You play a switch very well."

"Mmm." Another finger disappeared inside McCoy's mouth. Sawyer's breath left her body, her pelvis arching up to grind against McCoy's thigh. McCoy withdrew again, letting go of Sawyer's finger with a *pop*. She closed the small gap between them, her lips brushing Sawyer's as she whispered, "But being a switch isn't a game. It's who I am."

"Yes." Sawyer could see that now, and her eyes closed as McCoy swiped her tongue across her lips before kissing her deeply. Sawyer sighed, untangling her hands from McCoy's to wrap around her strong body. Her fingers roamed the contours of McCoy's back, and with each touch, McCoy's muscles twitched. Her body was so different than Olivier's had been. McCoy was strong, yet her skin was so soft, and although her form was stockier than most women Sawyer knew, there was no mistaking the feminine curves of her hips or, as Sawyer stroked her foot up McCoy's calf, her soft, hairless legs.

McCoy reached for the opening on Sawyer's towel, her mouth leaving Sawyer's and kissing a wet path down her throat as she pulled the material back, inch by agonizing inch. A hand passed down Sawyer's naked torso, and Sawyer squirmed, her nipples stiffening into two hard peaks at the brief contact.

"What are you doing?" she croaked as McCoy sat back on her haunches to watch her. Sawyer flushed under the younger woman's smoldering gaze. She was too exposed like this. Even in the semi-darkness, McCoy could see the rest of her scars if she looked close enough. She opened her mouth, a demand for the lights to be off at the tip of her tongue.

"You're so fucking beautiful, Sawyer," McCoy gushed, reaching for her now. She slid her hands up Sawyer's legs, past her throbbing center, over her small mommy pooch, that no matter how much she ran, Sawyer still couldn't fully rid herself of, to cup her breasts. McCoy's thumbs circled her nipples before tugging on them. Sawyer gasped. "You drive me crazy. I'm so wet for you right now, and we're just getting started."

"You're wet?" Sawyer couldn't help the disbelief in her tone. How could McCoy be so turned on already? Sawyer had barely touched her.

"Mm-hmm. Kissing you, tasting your skin has me all worked up," McCoy admitted. She moved down Sawyer's body once more, starting on her feet with open mouth kisses. Everywhere she touched, she left a wet path in her wake. Sawyer's body thrummed from the attention, the care, and the patience McCoy was putting into pleasing her. She expertly avoided kissing too close to Sawyer's inner thighs, instead using her teeth and tongue in sensitive areas Sawyer hadn't known existed. Who knew the back of her knee or the inside of her wrist could make her squirm and moan?

"McCoy," Sawyer whimpered as McCoy rolled her onto her stomach. Seconds later, the heat of her body was pressing into Sawyer's ass, and her lips dragging over Sawyer's back, the nape of her neck. Her hands slid under Sawyer to massage her breasts as she traced the shell of Sawyer's ear with her tongue once more. Sawyer's pulse sped up, and she groaned into the pillow. Her whole body vibrated, aching in need, and each time McCoy scraped her teeth along her skin, Sawyer's clit spasmed in response. "McCoy."

"I love my name on your lips," McCoy spoke softly into her ear. "I'll love it even more when you scream it for me."

"*Calisse*," Sawyer uttered, pushing her ass up into McCoy's hands. A breathy cry escaped her when McCoy's wet kisses landed on her lower back. Then over her bare ass cheeks. Her tongue inched closer to Sawyer's most intimate spot, and she tensed. Surely, McCoy wasn't—

"I could taste you like this," came McCoy's honey-smooth voice. Sawyer yelped when teeth nipped her flesh. "But I want our first time to be with me facing you, watching how you respond to me."

Sawyer's ears pounded in time with her clit. She was still trying to think of a response when McCoy flipped her over again, pressed her knee into Sawyer's dripping sex, and sucked her nipple into her mouth.

"Fuck." Sawyer's head flew back, her back arching until it was almost completely off the bed. The slick feel of McCoy's tongue as it swirled around her hot nipple had Sawyer feverish. She moaned, sinking her fingers into McCoy's hair and holding her in place. "I want ... God, I need ... McCoy," she panted, lifting her legs to lock her ankles around McCoy's ass. She was going to combust if McCoy didn't—

"That's it, sweetheart, take some of the pressure off," McCoy encouraged, switching to Sawyer's other breast as Sawyer gyrated against her thigh. McCoy raked her teeth over the swollen bud, licking and flicking with her tongue. She groaned softly, her lush green eyes staring up at Sawyer. "Your perfect pussy feels so good on me right now."

Perfect pussy? Sawyer's cheeks burned, but she was too far gone to care about McCoy's dirty talk. She was desperate for relief.

"You're so wet," McCoy continued, massaging Sawyer's breasts. She kissed her way down Sawyer's body, pausing briefly to pay special attention to Sawyer's cesarean scar.

"Please," she begged, pushing McCoy's head down further.

"So beautiful," McCoy whispered, running her tongue along Sawyer's inner thigh. She reached for a pillow, tucking it under Sawyer's ass. Then she spread Sawyer's thighs apart and settled between her legs, blowing air on her sensitive lips. Sawyer stifled another cry. "So ready for my kiss."

She expected a tentative swipe of McCoy's tongue or maybe rough fingers trying to find her clit, and she gasped as McCoy devoured her.

"Relax, sweetheart, I've got you," McCoy said, holding Sawyer in place. She winked, her face already glistening from Sawyer's arousal.

"McC-oh!" Sawyer's legs shook as McCoy's tongue stroked the length of her pussy, then swirled and flicked the bundle of nerves begging for release. Sawyer clutched the bedsheets, her ragged breaths mounting with each inhale. Her body was on fire. She couldn't catch her breath. McCoy sucked her clit into her mouth, and pinpricks of light danced in Sawyer's vision. Her chest squeezed like it was a tension ball, and a flare of panic hit her. It was too much. Too much.

My heart's going to burst!

"Stop," she sobbed, throwing her arm over her eyes to shield herself from McCoy. "I-I can't—" Another sob, and the moment McCoy withdrew, Sawyer twisted her legs free.

"Sawyer? What's wrong?"

Sawyer shook her head, unable to speak past her tears. She was weeping for no reason, and yet her heart felt like it was splitting in two. McCoy's hand landed on her arm, and she flinched like it had burned her.

"It's okay. Just breathe, sweetheart. I'm sorry. You're okay."

Arms wrapped around her, and then McCoy was cradling Sawyer to her chest. She trembled, caught between needing McCoy and needing to push her away. Sex had never caused fear before, but then, she'd never had sex like she did with McCoy. Like all her nerve endings were exposed and raw, like her clit was so overstimulated she'd combust where she lay. She'd never come close to feeling like that.

"That's it. Slow your breathing. Can I get you anything?"

Sawyer shook her head, relaxing into McCoy's chest. She felt McCoy's comforting touch drawing circles over her back, and after a long stretch of silence, her eyelids grew heavy. She sniffled, allowing sleep to take her, so she wasn't certain she heard McCoy's muffled declaration correctly.

"I've gone and fallen in love with you, haven't I? Well, shit."

Chapter 34

McCoy

Later that morning, Coy found herself rummaging through Sawyer's kitchen as she tried to locate a lighter for the propane stove. The beginnings of her nana's special porridge recipe rested in a pot beside the stove. "Oh, lighter. Come out, come out wherever you are," Coy sang under her breath, opening another cupboard. She had a headache, and she still needed coffee. In Sawyer's big, fancy kitchen with all the gadgets in the world, there wasn't a percolator in sight.

A giggle sounded behind her, and then a sleepy voice said, "It's a gas stove, so ... just turn the knob."

Coy turned to see Bree mid-yawn, clad in an oversized hoodie and baggy drawstring pajama pants. Patches wasn't too far behind, butting her head against the back of Bree's leg. "Ah, thanks, you're a lifesaver."

"No prob. Whatcha making?" Bree yawned again, padding her way to the way-too-modern-for-Coy espresso machine. "Want an Americano or latte or something?"

"Uh ..." Coy racked her sleep-addled brain, trying to remember what she'd had at Abi's all those weeks ago. Scratching her head when nothing came to mind, she shrugged. "Whatever you can make that's not too sweet, thanks."

"Sure."

Coy got the stove going the first try, and immediately felt like a fool for not thinking to do that first. Lack of sleep had her barely functioning without caffeine. "I'm making my nana's famous porridge recipe. Me and Sloane practically grew up on this stuff. Figured you and your mom might like it."

"Well, thank you. I know I'll appreciate it. Who can say for sure about *Maman*? So far, she's choked down any porridge I've given her."

Coy smiled, accepting the wooden spoon Bree handed her. "Yeah, I think she'd prefer a cinnamon roll. She doesn't really like change, does she?"

The delicious aroma of coffee filled the kitchen as Bree fiddled with the machine. She tossed a smirk in Coy's direction. "Says the one who spent the night in *Maman's* bed."

Coy blushed, turning back to the porridge. She made sure the burner setting was on high before going on a hunt for the eggs. Patches met her at the fridge, rubbing her head against Coy's bare leg and meowing. Coy was more of a dog person, but she had to admit the calico was a cutie.

"C'mere girl, let's get some breakfast into you," Bree said, scooping Patches up. She kissed her head, strolling over to the walk-in pantry for the calico's food. "You're right, though," Bree added, glancing up at Coy as she opened a can. "*Maman* doesn't like change and hates surprises. But you're a bit of both, and by the looks of things, she's adjusting."

Coy considered that. Had Sawyer been adjusting by allowing Coy to touch her? When she'd woken with Sawyer still in her arms, it had taken everything in Coy not to stay put. Nothing had ever felt more right than a naked Sawyer draped over her, fast asleep.

But what happened at the end?

Coy had her suspicions. During scenes with Frankie, Coy would sometimes get so overstimulated that she became a sobbing mess. When that happened, she begged Frankie to let her come. She knew a lot about the raw emotions that came with it, too, but she and Sawyer hadn't been doing a scene. Hell, if their intimacy had to be categorized, Coy would say it was pretty damn passionate. She'd never wanted to make love to anyone before, and yet, taking her time with Sawyer came naturally. It'd been perfect until Sawyer panicked.

I've only been with Olivier, Sawyer had mentioned.

If Coy's suspicions were correct, then the loathsome late husband had never taken the time to properly please his wife. *But what about masturbation?* Had Sawyer never made herself come before?

"So," Bree said, bringing Coy's attention back to their conversation. She set a coffee down beside Coy. "Is this where I'm supposed to ask what your intentions are with *Maman*?"

Coy smiled, not looking at Bree as she lowered the burner setting and cracked eggs into the pot of porridge. "You could, yeah." She stirred in the eggs before setting the spoon down. "Do you have frozen fruit I can add in?"

"Yep." Bree climbed off the stool and went to the freezer, retrieving a bag of mixed fruit moments later. When she sidled up beside Coy, she examined her closely, studying her eyes.

Coy's cheeks heated under Bree's intensity. "Is that your way of asking?" An awkward laugh escaped her, and she broke the weird eye contact to pull the porridge off the burner.

"I don't need to, but I *will* thank you." Bree wrapped an arm around Coy's shoulders, kissing her cheek. "When do you plan on telling her?"

"Oh, I um," Coy cleared her throat. Her heart was in her throat as she slipped past Bree for a bowl. Was she referring to Coy's feelings for Sawyer? Was she that obvious? She took the fruit, emptying some in the bowl before placing it in the microwave. Fresh fruit in her nana's porridge just wasn't the same as frozen. "Where can I find chocolate chips?"

"You're deflecting, but it's okay. I just, I really like you, Coy." Bree handed her the bag of chocolate chips, and for the first time, Coy noticed the shyness in her. She looked like a young, shorter version of Sawyer standing beside Coy, but with Olivier's eyes and hair. "I don't want you to up and disappear after your job is done."

"Never," Coy promised, her throat swelling with emotion. She pulled Bree into a hug, murmuring, "You're incredible. No matter what, I'll always just be a call away if you or your mom need anything. Besides, I still need to get you out on the trail with me and Sloane."

"And J.D.?" Bree blurted and flushed adorably.

"Oh, I see how it is," Coy teased, ruffling Bree's hair affectionately. "You've been creeping his Insta, haven't you?"

"He's single."

"Mm-hmm. So does that mean you'll be sticking around, then?" Coy asked, leaning against the counter and opening the bag of chocolate chips. She shook a few out in her palm, watching Bree pull bowls out of the cupboard.

"Maybe. It's nice being close to *Maman* again. I'd missed her, missed my friends, you know?"

"Yeah, that'd be hard," Coy agreed, wiping her hands off. Bree helped her plate the porridge, laughing when Coy insisted the chocolate chips had to go on the bottom of the bowls. Then the porridge with a dollop of butter, the fruit, shredded coconut, and finally, a sprinkle of brown sugar.

"This isn't fair," Bree complained, hip-checking Coy as she grabbed her bowl to take to the table. "Of course, *Maman* will love your porridge. It's not bland and super-duper healthy like mine was."

"It's totally healthy ... ish." Coy grinned, sitting down with Bree as well. "Be healthier with dark chocolate, I suppose, but not nearly as good."

"Definitely." Bree took a bite of the porridge, and her eyes widened in surprise. "This is actually really good, Coy."

"You doubted my nana?" Coy feigned disbelief. Patches jumped on the table with them, and Bree shooed her away.

Sawyer entered the kitchen, already showered and dressed in business attire. Coy's mood sank a little as she took in her lover, noting the aloof mask was back on display.

Even after we—

"Good morning, Bree. McCoy." Sawyer glanced between Coy and Bree and cleared her throat. "I assumed you'd left already."

"Ahh, no," Coy replied slowly, her gaze trained on Sawyer as she went to the espresso machine. She hardly recognized this woman from the one she'd made love to just hours earlier. "I made breakfast. And it's Sunday, so no work if I can help it. I'll head over to my pop's in a little bit to watch the game, though." She glanced at Bree, who was watching their exchange intently. "Do you like baseball?"

"I don't know enough about it to say one way or another," Bree admitted, frowning in her mother's direction. She quickly finished her breakfast and carried her bowl to the sink. "Good morning, *Maman*," she murmured, rubbing Sawyer's back. "Are you okay? *Peu importe ce qui se passe, tu as besoin de lui en parler. Je vais vous donner du temps seul.*"

One of Coy's eyebrows shot up at Bree's obvious attempt to speak privately to Sawyer. What better way to do it if Coy didn't understand a lick of French?

Gonna have to change that. Duolingo, here I come.

"What was that about?" she asked when Bree left the kitchen.

"Nothing." Sawyer still didn't look at her. She was pouring frothy milk into her mug, a stiffness to her shoulders that Coy would have spotted a mile away. She sighed, standing with her empty bowl and mug and dropping them into the sink just as Bree had done.

"Is this about last night?" Needing to busy herself, Coy grabbed the sprayer attachment and began rinsing off the dishes.

"Last night was a mistake."

"*What*?" Okay, that was the last thing Coy expected her to say. She retracted the hose and shut off the water, turning to face Sawyer. "You don't mean that."

"Don't I?" Sawyer challenged, her stormy gaze flashing in warning.

"I don't think so, no," Coy stated softly. She stepped closer and touched Sawyer's arm, sliding her fingers down to lace in the other woman's. Her heart caught in her throat. "I think something happened last night, and now, you're pulling away. Please Sawyer, don't ... don't diminish what we have by calling it a mistake."

Sawyer pursed her lips. "Your generation is entirely too sentimental." She headed toward the kitchen's exit, bypassing the untouched bowl of porridge as if Coy making food for her meant nothing. And that just wouldn't do.

"Go ahead, be stubborn, sweetheart," Coy called out, racing after her. She caught Sawyer with one foot on the stairs and reached for her again. Their eyes met, and behind Sawyer's stony facade, Coy could see the fear plain as day. "Lash out instead of talking to me. Go ahead, I can take it, but please, eat. I know it's not "Michelin star" worthy, but I took the time, and you need to take care of yourself. Hell, I'll even get out of your hair, so you don't need to glare and chew."

Coy backed away from Sawyer, breathing hard as they stared at one another. It felt like she'd just done a five-hundred-yard sprint after being sedentary for too long. Her legs were rubbery, and she took two steps before stopping. With more courage than she thought possible, Coy closed the gap between them again and pulled Sawyer down for a kiss. "Last night was *not* a mistake." She brushed her thumb over Sawyer's bottom lip, then forced her legs to move, not daring to look back as she left the house.

CHAPTER 35

Sawyer

FOR A LONG TIME, she stared at the closed door, half expecting McCoy to walk back in. And for just as long, she stared at that door, half expecting her feet to move on their own and run after her. Neither happened. Sawyer folded her arms across her midsection, pressing her lips together in a tight grimace.

"You can come out now."

Bree appeared before her moments later from the direction of the living room with a sheepish look on her young face. Together, they returned to the kitchen, Sawyer sitting down at the island while Bree nuked her untouched breakfast.

"How'd you know I was listening in?" Bree set the bowl of porridge down in front of Sawyer, followed by a spoon and milk.

"You weren't as sneaky as you thought growing up, and you're still just as curious." Sawyer gave her a wan smile, picking up her spoon. "Thank you, darling."

"*Maman*, Coy loves you," Bree said, hands on her hips now. She blew out a frustrated breath, a wayward strand of brown hair blowing off her face in the process. It was such a familiar gesture to Sawyer that she almost smiled.

Sawyer stirred the porridge, quietly replying, "McCoy has never been in a relationship before. She's never had to work very hard for someone's attention. It might seem like she loves me, but I doubt—"

"I can't believe you're gaslighting her right now. You, of all people." Bree shook her head and snorted, looking nonplussed. "How utterly audacious of you. Papa would be proud."

Sawyer sucked in a breath, Bree's words acting like a knife to her already tremulous gut. Her spoon clattered to the counter. "*Esti*. Why would you say that? *Mon amour*, you have no idea. None whatsoever."

"I know Papa was mean to you. He may not have hit you, not that I saw, but loveless words and abandonment go a long way," Bree tearfully proclaimed. She clasped her hand over Sawyer's arm, prying Sawyer's blurry gaze from the countertop to her daughter's. "I know that when Papa was drunk, he'd blame you for Brian's death."

"Bree Sophia." Sawyer gasped, her hand flying up to cover her mouth.

A massive ball lodged itself in her throat. It was a struggle to make anything out behind the well of tears, so Sawyer turned her face away from Bree and let them fall. Dizziness overcame her, and for a second, she thought she might be sick. Burying her face in her shaking hands, faint images of a stillborn Brian fluttered through her memory like wings on a moth. Colorless and disappearing from her reach far too fast.

Muffled sobs filled the kitchen. Sawyer wasn't sure if it was her or Bree, perhaps both. Arms wrapped around her, holding her for all she was worth, and then Bree's voice was hoarse against Sawyer's ear.

"Je suis désolée, Maman. Tellement désolée."

"You don't know ..." Sawyer whispered brokenly.

"I know it wasn't your fault."

But it was. Just like Olivier loved to remind her. It *was* her fault. If only she had taken better care ... if she had rested more ... fought with Olivier less ...

"I shouldn't have brought that up," Bree sniffled. "I was wrong to do so. I just wanted you to see that Coy is nothing like Papa. Let her in,

Maman. Let her love you. Let her help heal some of the broken inside you."

"Bree ..."

Bree pulled away, and fresh tears pooled in Sawyer's eyes as her daughter cupped her cheek with one hand. She placed the other palm up over Sawyer's heart. "You're a force to be reckoned with. Everyone knows that. But only I know what's really in here, hidden from the world. Not even Cindy and Lori know all of you because you hold them at arm's length. *Tu n'es pas fatigué, Maman*?"

Sawyer swallowed, blinking past more tears. She nodded. "*Tellement, mon amour.*" Tired was an understatement. Life was exhausting ... but mostly, she was tired of running from it. *I don't know how to stop.*

"You can start by showing up on Coy's doorstep and apologizing," Bree surprised Sawyer by saying. She hadn't realized she'd spoken those thoughts aloud.

"Let's say you're right, and Coy doesn't actually love you." Bree shot Sawyer a speculative look. "Maybe it's lust. How will it grow into anything more if you don't give her a chance?"

"Hmm," Sawyer hummed, noncommittal. She wiped her eyes, picking up her spoon again. Bree made more coffee as she ate. The porridge was cold but delicious. *I'll have to let McCoy know.*

"For the record, I think you're wrong."

"Hmm. Maybe." Was it possible to genuinely fall in love with someone over the course of a few months?

Sawyer needed to find out.

Three hours later, Sawyer realized she didn't remember McCoy's address. She didn't know Greg Miller's address either, or even if McCoy was truly there. It was Sunday, so the shop was closed, but would McCoy go there if she was upset to tinker on a car? It bothered Sawyer that she didn't know. She prided herself in learning every nuance there was to someone, especially since she'd permitted McCoy to discover such an intimate piece of her.

I slept with a woman, Sawyer marveled for the umpteenth time. She slowed her Range Rover down for a red light. Was she being rash again, hunting McCoy down throughout the city? It would be simple to just call the younger woman or send a text, but each time Sawyer tried, nothing came out. To put everything she felt into words seemed as daunting as it was proving impossible.

"I had sex with McCoy," Sawyer said into the silence of the Rover. It was difficult to bask in the pure enjoyment of the act when she was so humiliated over not climaxing. Was sex supposed to feel so out of control? Sawyer thrived on discipline. Every single moment with Olivier had been on his terms, but one thing he could never command had been her lack of response to him. With McCoy, Sawyer had become lost in wanton desire for the first time, and it had been terrifying.

"Turn right onto Davie Street," directed the SUV's GPS. "Your destination will be on the right."

"Okay," Sawyer breathed. Moments later, she parked a few doors down from O'Rourke's Pub. "God, what am I doing?" If anyone knew the address to McCoy's place, she figured they'd be here. Perhaps Sloane was working, or Frankie. So much had happened that it was hard to believe Sawyer's date night with McCoy had been just last night.

The pub was busy with their noontime rush when Sawyer entered, so she asked the first server she spotted if Sloane was working. "What about Frankie? Is she in?" Sawyer asked when she learned Sloane was off today as well. *Is it a Miller tradition to keep Sundays work-free?* If so, it was no wonder McCoy got annoyed that time Sawyer insisted she come in.

The server pointed down the short hallway off the side of the bar, "In her office, the last door on the left."

"Thank you," Sawyer replied, before heading in that direction. The office door was closed when she arrived, and Sawyer squared her shoulders, taking a deep, encouraging breath before knocking.

"Come in," came Frankie's low, almost sultry, voice.

Tabarnak, Sawyer thought with a shiver. If Frankie's voice gave *her* goosebumps, then she could just imagine what it'd done to McCoy in the past. *Ugh, don't think about that.*

"Sawyer, what a surprise," Frankie said when Sawyer opened the door. She stood from her desk, gesturing to Sawyer. "Please, come in."

"Sorry to show up unannounced," Sawyer began, taking in the attractive, pin-stripe white suit Frankie had on. If memory served, she'd been wearing a different suit the night before. "I was hoping you could give me McCoy's address. I want to surprise her and can't remember the exact street in Richmond."

"She's not home. Shut the door. Let's have a chat."

Sawyer blew out a breath, and as she shut the office door, she said, "I don't have time—"

"McCoy is upstairs. In my apartment."

"—for a chat," Sawyer finished slowly. Frankie's statement sunk in, and she narrowed her gaze on the other woman. "What did you say?"

"No need for jealousy." Frankie waved the idea off with a flick of her wrist. She sat back down, gesturing to Sawyer to do the same, and then crossed one thigh over the other. Her confidence as she controlled a room was breathtaking to watch. "I've known McCoy a long time, Sawyer. Though some might say it was just about sex, they wouldn't have a fucking clue what it's like in a Domme/sub dynamic."

Sawyer frowned further. "Why are you telling me this?"

"Because I'm who McCoy turns to when she's feeling vulnerable." Frankie shrugged, studying Sawyer from across the room. "I was her Domme, and I promised to protect her wellbeing."

"You aren't her Domme now," Sawyer said tightly.

Frankie smiled. *Smiled*, and Sawyer had the strongest urge to slap it off her face. "I can see why she's so entranced with you. Have you noticed yet that McCoy is a bit of a chameleon around others? Maybe not, since you're just discovering one another, but if you pay attention, you'll see she acts differently depending on who she's with. With her friend group, "The Fab Five" as they call it, McCoy is the funny one. With her friend Naz, she blends in to be part of "the guys" even though she hates smoking cigars. Sloane brings out the mother hen in her, and out there—" Frankie paused to point outside to her pub, "—she was the player. For years, I watched her flirt with others and lead them to the washroom or out the front door."

Why is she telling me this? Sawyer tensed. She knew McCoy wasn't like that, at least not with her. Was this Frankie's way of steering Sawyer away from her? She opened her mouth to put a stop to the conversation when Frankie held up a finger in a "just a minute" gesture.

"And then up there"—Frankie pointed to the ceiling—"behind closed doors, McCoy can just be. No pretense, no judgment, as vulnerable as she needs to be. I noticed something last night though, Sawyer. McCoy is all of those things with you. It's kind of incredible to witness. Her eyes never wander far from you. She makes you laugh, fusses over you. From what Sloane told me, you protected McCoy. So why is she moping on my sofa right now?"

"You love her."

Frankie hesitated and looked away. "Not in the way you think."

"How could you not? McCoy is ..." *Everything*, Sawyer almost said. She tugged her bottom lip between her teeth, holding the words in.

"McCoy never once gave up anything to be with me. Not like she's done with you," Frankie explained, her voice raspier now. "I kept waiting for the hookups to stop, and then maybe I would have ... but it never happened. Now I know why. McCoy was never meant to be mine, Sawyer."

"Yes, well." Sawyer cleared her throat, turning toward the door once more. She was over the threshold when she thought to add, "You might ask yourself, Frankie, what were you willing to give up to be with her? I've chosen. Maybe next time, with someone else, you will, too."

Chapter 36

McCoy

A KNOCK SOUNDED ON the apartment door just as Coy was putting back her second slice of deluxe deep-dish pizza. No one but Frankie and a few of her staff came up here, and Frankie had a key. "Just a minute," she called, uncurling from her position on Frankie's sectional. She tossed the blanket off her lap and begrudgingly set the pizza down, then decided against it. Picking the paper plate up again, she took a bite of the cheesy goodness as she opened the door. "S-Sawyer," Coy choked out around the mouthful of pizza.

"And you talk about me eating healthy," Sawyer said wryly, one eyebrow arched to the ceiling as she examined the deep dish. She was dressed in a pair of black slacks and a red blouse under her raincoat. Her damp black strands were in their usual downward comb-out, and some of her mascara had smudged, likely from the rain. Coy had been holed up in Frankie's; she hadn't realized it'd begun to rain.

"I'm so glad you're here. Why are you? At Frankie's." Ugh, she was back to rambling. Coy swiveled around, searching for a place to set the pizza down, and settled for the small corner entry table.

Sawyer's hand slipped into hers from behind, surprising Coy, and she melted into the physical contact. "I'd hoped we could talk. And I wanted to apologize for this morning."

"Talk?" Coy echoed dumbly. She blinked, glancing back at Sawyer and the door, still open. She twisted away, closing and locking it before gesturing to Frankie's apartment. "Here? We can go somewhere else. I was watching the game, but it's not the same by myself. I usually go to my pops for pizza and beer, but Sloane's off and I wasn't—"

Sawyer silenced Coy's prattle with a long kiss, teasing her with tongue before pulling away. Dazed, Coy glanced up at her, taking notice of her slight smile and satisfaction in her gray eyes. "Let's have pizza and beer and watch the game while Frankie is busy downstairs."

Coy frowned. "You can't eat that."

Sawyer placed her finger over Coy's lips, still swollen from their kiss. "But first, there are things I need to explain."

"Sawyer—"

"I'll explain, and you will listen, darling." Sawyer slipped off her low wedge heels and jacket, revealing the blouse underneath. Three of the buttons were undone, and Coy's attention zeroed in on the hint of Sawyer's cleavage. She couldn't believe she'd had her face buried between those breasts and—

"Let's sit, McCoy," Sawyer murmured, guiding Coy to the sofa. Once they were comfortable, and with a slice of pizza and beer each, it took a long time for Sawyer to start the conversation. Coy grew antsy waiting, and when her leg began to bounce, Sawyer set her food and drink aside and opened her arms. "Come here, darling."

Coy didn't think, merely acted, and scrambled into Sawyer's arms so that she was halfway sitting on the other woman's lap. Her head fit snugly under Sawyer's armpit against her heart. She sighed contentedly, butterflies in her stomach.

Sawyer laced their fingers together, kissing the top of Coy's head. Oh yeah, she had to be feeling all this. There was no way she wasn't.

"I'm sorry for last night," Sawyer said quietly. "About ... how I reacted, and ... for not climaxing."

Coy's eyes widened, and she would have pulled away, but Sawyer held her still. "Sawyer, that's okay—"

"Please, let me finish," Sawyer interrupted. Coy felt her swallow. "It wasn't just last night that I didn't climax. I've never ... not that way, not even by myself. I should have stopped it before it went too far."

Coy's brows knitted together. She traced Sawyer's exposed clavicle with her index finger, deep in thought. "Thank you for telling me. I understand how overwhelming it can be when you're ready to come. Frankie used to ... ah, never mind. The important thing is we're still going at your pace. I'm sorry if I got carried away last night."

"What would Frankie do?"

"Oh, um." Coy cleared her throat, thinking of her previous lover. "She liked edging; *we* liked it. She never did anything I didn't agree with."

"Edging?"

"Yeah, you know." Coy slid her hand lower to the open buttons on Sawyer's blouse. Her finger grazed the curve of one breast, and Sawyer caught her hand, holding it. "Bringing me close to orgasm over and over, but never granting it. Not until I was insane with need and begging her to let me come."

"*Calisse*, darling. That sounds like torture," Sawyer laughed softly.

Coy's ears perked up at Sawyer's favorite curse word. "What does that mean, '*calisse*?'"

"Fuck, but with more fervor than when I say *tabarnak*." Sawyer kneaded her fingers into Coy's scalp as she held her close and gave another breathy laugh. "Which also means fuck."

"You say that a lot, then." Coy smirked, raising her face to Sawyer's. The older woman smiled down at her, pressing a soft kiss to her lips.

"Perhaps."

Things were silent for several minutes. Coy turned the game back on, content on cuddling with the woman she was absolutely crazy about. But one thing nagged at her, and she had to say it before it was all she thought about that afternoon.

"Sweetheart, if you're willing, then there are ways to ease you into a clit orgasm." She glanced up at Sawyer again, watching for any hint of rejection. "I could teach you how to pleasure yourself. Toys are amazing to use, too. You just let me know when and if you're ready, okay?"

Sawyer pursed her lips. "I'm forty-three, McCoy. I'm too—"

"Don't you dare say old," Coy laughed, tickling her gently in the ribs.

Sawyer squeaked, falling back onto the sofa. Coy settled between her legs, kissing her again. Their eyes met, and Sawyer's smile slowly faded as she gazed up at Coy. Feeling daring, Coy rocked her hips against Sawyer's, not mistaking the slight hitch in her breathing.

"When you're ready, there's also this," Coy whispered against Sawyer's lips. "Good ol' fashioned tribbing and penetration."

Sawyer took a deep breath, letting it out slowly. "Good to know, darling."

"I wanna do it all with you, Sawyer. No one else." Coy stroked the back of her hand over Sawyer's scarred cheek, gazing at her with all the affection threatening to topple out.

Sawyer's eyes closed, but she leaned into Coy's touch. "You've never asked about them."

"No." Coy swallowed, thinking of the other scars she'd seen the night before. They were the same type of burns as her face, but the ones on her neck, breast, and ribs were fainter. It had been a shock to see during her exploration of Sawyer's body, but the old wounds only made her more beautiful in Coy's eyes. "You'll tell me when you're ready."

Sawyer tensed underneath Coy. Had she said the wrong thing? Maybe she shouldn't have touched the scar again, although Sawyer had warmed up to it last night when they were—

"It was a kitchen accident," Sawyer spoke softly, opening her eyes to peer up at Coy. Turmoil had a front-row seat in her gaze, but she gritted her teeth, looking strong as ever. "I was deep frying potato chips and dumped a bowl of them too wet into the pot. The oil was too hot and exploded. That's all I'll say about it for now."

"Okay." Coy nodded, but inside, her heart was breaking for Sawyer. What a horrible thing for someone to go through. "Well ..." She cleared her throat, flashing one of her disarming grins. "I don't know what you looked like before, but it couldn't possibly compete with how gorgeous you are now."

Sawyer rolled her eyes. And then she laughed. Which was exactly what Coy had been going for.

"So, I've been thinking," Coy said to Sawyer one night, two weeks later. They were cooking a late supper at Coy's apartment, to which Sawyer had dubbed her their sous-chef for the occasion. It wasn't a bad gig overall. So far, all Coy had to do was cut vegetables up and make a salad. Sawyer was just as efficient in the kitchen as Coy always suspected she was, and she got great satisfaction in watching her girlfriend expertly maneuver around the tiny space. Stuffed chicken breasts were baking in the oven, and there was a custard cooking for dessert on the stovetop.

"You're always thinking." Sawyer uncapped a bottle of lime sparkling water from the fridge, pouring half into two glasses. She held one out to Coy, a hint of a smile on her lips. "It's actually one of your more endearing qualities."

Coy's eyebrows shot skyward in surprise. Sawyer openly expressing what she was feeling was new, and honestly, Coy couldn't get enough of it. Her stomach swooped and dipped as nerves caught her in a chokehold, and she stammered, "Thanks, s-so like what if we went on a double date sometime, you know, with Lori and Cindy? I've only sort of met Lori once, but they seem important to you."

Sawyer eyed her long enough that Coy grew uncomfortable and looked away. Then she heard her sigh. "I don't think that's a good idea,

McCoy. Cindy is ... she'll make a big deal out of it all, and I want to enjoy what we have. Just you and I together, darling."

What does that mean?

Coy frowned at the cryptic response. Did Sawyer think her friends wouldn't like her? Was it the age gap she was worried about? Coy supposed that just because Lori had seemed fine with the idea of the relationship didn't mean Cindy was.

Fuck, was Sawyer *ashamed* of her?

The feel of Sawyer's hand slipping into hers did little to soothe Coy's mounting unease. Then Sawyer was pinning her against the counter so that their bodies were flush together. She held Coy's gaze, reaching up to place a surprisingly strong hand along her neck.

"Is it so awful that I don't want to share you?" Sawyer's whisper was harsh, unforgiving, yet as she stroked the column of Coy's throat, her eyes held a tinge of regret. "Cin is ... a handful at times, and you and I are still getting to know one another. Why jinx it?"

Coy heard what she was saying and tried not to let her hang-ups bother her. Sawyer was right, after all. Regardless that their first kiss was almost two months ago, they'd only been officially dating for two weeks. Unfortunately, it wasn't easy to put a timeline on her feelings or try to cram them into a box until Sawyer was ready to open them.

"It's fine." Coy forced a grin to her lips and pushed down the swell of disappointment. *I'm being ridiculous,* she thought. "We're going at your pace. I haven't forgotten."

"Thank you," Sawyer said, pressing a lingering kiss to Coy's lips. Her fingers scratched the base of Coy's hairline, managing to both entice and massage the tense muscles in Coy's neck. Her eyes fluttered closed, a breathy sigh escaping when Sawyer's lips found that little spot under her ear that drove her crazy. "Besides, ma *chérie*, haven't you enjoyed having me all to yourself?"

Oomph. Sawyer sure knew how to play hardball. They'd been practically inseparable since Sawyer had shown up at Frankie's. After work, they'd taken turns going to each other's house, cooking or ordering takeout, watching a movie, and making out. Every part of it had been perfect, even the occasional awkward run-ins with Sloane. Who Sawyer was still wary of—and she was quick to remind Coy of that during their meal.

"You let your sister dip into your account whenever she feels like it?"

Coy couldn't decipher the edge to her tone, but the disbelief and disapproval were obvious. "Well, no," she quickly amended, wishing she hadn't brought the subject up. It'd been more of a passing mention than anything, in between what she'd had for lunch that day and what she was currently working on at the shop. "I noticed money missing and asked her about it. Sloane said she took some for upgrades on some of our camera stuff."

"Did she provide receipts?"

Coy lowered her gaze, pushing around the chicken on her plate. "Well, no," she repeated. "I mean, I can ask for one, though."

"I no longer speak to my brothers, or my parents for that matter, but if I did, I still wouldn't let anyone have access to my bank account."

"You have brothers?" Coy couldn't hide her surprise. For some reason, she'd imagined Sawyer as an only child. She shook her head. "We've known each other for almost five months, and I'm just finding that out?" Of course she was. Just because Sawyer had softened some around her didn't mean she trusted Coy.

"You're missing the point," Sawyer said coolly, cutting into her chicken and taking a bite. She chewed, and Coy's gaze dipped to her sensuous mouth. When she swallowed and swept her tongue out to her bottom lip, a spark of lust ignited inside Coy.

"Point?"

"Yes, McCoy. You're too trusting. Too giving. You would probably give *me* access to your bank account if I asked."

"I would." Coy didn't need to think about it. She knew she would. Perhaps she was jumping the gun on their relationship, but she had surmised long ago that there wasn't anything she wouldn't do for Sawyer.

Sawyer only scoffed. "Then you'd be an *esti de cave*, darling, just like I was for so many years. Don't ever let anyone have so much power over you. Not your sister, not Frankie. And not me."

"With all due respect, sweetheart, I would rather trust too much than not at all." Coy bit her lip, thinking of the many vulnerable encounters she'd had with Frankie. Thinking of the little she did know of the lone wolf. "I trust Frankie with my life. I trust Sloane because she's family and has never given me reason not to." Coy got to her feet and went around the kitchen table to Sawyer. She knelt in front of the older woman, looking up at her with wide, earnest eyes and praying Sawyer believed what she was hearing. Coy whispered, "And I trust you, Sawyer, with every part of me. I refuse to think up scenarios where you break that trust. I am ... this is it for me, sweetheart. You hold all the power here."

Sawyer's eyes darkened. Her hands tightened on Coy's forearms. "What are you saying?"

Coy swallowed, but she refused to back down. "I-I think you know."

"So, what? You're willing to do anything I ask?" Sawyer's hand cupped the back of Coy's head, her nails scraping along her undercut. Her voice grew husky. "Even crawl across the floor like a cat? Or strip off all your clothes right here in the kitchen? What if I told you to walk naked into your bedroom, put on the strap on, and let me ride you until I come?"

A gush of air left Coy, and she bowed her head into Sawyer's lap. Giddiness and anticipation rode a tidal wave through her, and she shuddered. "Fuck yes." She was eternally grateful for the late nights they'd spent talking about sex toys over the last week, although the option of Sawyer riding her cock was the last thing—

"Then do it, darling. Strip for me."

Arousal pooled low in Coy's belly at the command. She had to hold back a groan when she jumped to her feet and brushed her crotch against

Sawyer's knee. With gazes locked together, Coy scrambled to undo the buttons on her dress-shirt, cursing the fact she didn't go casual tonight with a hoodie.

"Not like that." Sawyer shook her head, a hint of mischief behind her eyes. "Slower. With music. Dance for me."

Was she mocking Coy? Was this Sawyer's way of testing her devotion? Either way, Coy was game. She was no pro like Jasmine, but if her girlfriend wanted a striptease, that's what she would get.

"Yes, ma'am," she purred, pulling up Spotify on her phone.

"Don't call me ma'am," Sawyer replied, but her lips were curled in a half smile.

Coy pulled up her favorite sexy playlist, choosing not to dwell on the random lovers she'd taken to bed with it playing in the background, and began swaying her hips. Sawyer watched her dance, an amused—albeit disbelieving—expression on her face. Coy felt a bit too clumsy to pull off proper seduction, but she tried her best.

"Now unbutton your shirt."

Coy licked her lips, never taking her eyes off Sawyer as she undid her overshirt, still swaying her hips to the music. Her clit was already swollen and throbbing, and they'd just gotten started.

"That's it," Sawyer murmured, her gaze smoldering as she watched the dress shirt fall to the floor. The feel of Sawyer tracking Coy's every move had her body flushing with arousal. Being the center of Sawyer's focus, even briefly, was incredibly intoxicating. "Your arms are exquisite, darling. Now your tank top."

Reaching for the hem of her ribbed tank top, Coy pulled it slowly over her head, flexing her arms as she did so. A breathy sigh left Sawyer. "*Mon Dieu, Chérie. Si forte et si alléchante. Tu me captives.*"

Coy didn't want to break the trance to ask Sawyer to translate. She had her suspicions anyway, and the idea of her captivating Sawyer was a dopamine boost like no other.

"This is all for you," she said softly, reaching for her belt buckle.

"Not yet. Take off your bra next. I want to see you." Sawyer grabbed Coy's belt and tugged her closer. Coy grinned, unable to resist straddling one of Sawyer's thighs as she tugged her bra over her head. The material fell away, and then Coy put her arms around Sawyer's shoulders, *absolutely* loving the response Sawyer had to her breasts being so close.

"You can touch them."

Sawyer's cheeks pinkened, and she swallowed. "You'd like that, wouldn't you?" She tutted with a shake of her head. "I think not, darling. I believe you owe me your jeans next."

"Of course. Anything," Coy murmured, her pulse picking up as she slid off Sawyer. She danced a few feet away, turning so that her back faced Sawyer, and slowly shimmied out of her faded denims.

"Underwear too," Sawyer croaked, and it occurred to Coy then that Sawyer probably hadn't thought she'd actually do it. Strip down naked in the middle of her kitchen at nine thirty at night. If there was a chance Sloane would walk in, perhaps she wouldn't have, but Coy knew her sister worked late.

She smiled, slipping off her boxers and socks before turning to face Sawyer once more. The heat in her gaze as she soaked Coy in from head to toe was like a volcano burning Coy from the inside out. She was hot, perpetually aroused, and for once, she wished she could see herself through Sawyer's eyes. Was she pleasing to look at? Did she live up to Sawyer's expectations? And then another thought occurred to her. Was this how Sawyer felt when Coy had soaked her up like the sunshine after a rain?

"Touch yourself, *mon amour*," Sawyer instructed, unbuttoning a few buttons on her own shirt. She fanned the collar like the temperature in the room increased. "Show me how to pleasure myself."

It was interesting how Sawyer worded that particular sentence, but who was Coy to complain? She pulled a chair over, placing it directly in front of Sawyer and took a seat. "Well," she began, spreading her thighs and giving Sawyer an unobstructed view of her pussy, "you could start like this." Coy cupped her breasts, massaging their fullness before rolling her nipples between her thumb and forefinger. She tweaked the firm peaks, enjoying the delicious ripple down her spine. Then her hand moved lower, down her stomach toward her dripping pussy. She kept her eyes on Sawyer, watching the gleam in her gaze darken inch by inch, the way she squirmed in her seat as Coy slowly fucked herself into a frenzy. Her fingers dipped in and out of her pussy, pausing to tease her clit before sliding back in again.

"Fuck, Sawyer. The way you're looking at me ..." Coy's breath hitched, quickening her fingers. There was something so erotic about Sawyer sitting there fully clothed and watching her. Her gaze was hooded, completely transfixed on the scene before her, and it only helped to further excite Coy.

"Look what you do to me," she groaned, scraping her blunt nails up her thigh, over her abdomen, to squeeze her breast. Her thumb strummed steadily against her clit as she tugged her nipple, and soon, her back was arching off the chair and tidal waves of pleasure vibrated through her as her orgasm crested.

"*Calisse*, darling. Now I know what you meant before. Watching you turned me on more than ever," Sawyer said, watching with blatant interest as Coy pulled her glistening fingers out. The tip of her tongue darted out to moisten her lips, and she lowered her voice. "I want to taste you."

"Yeah?" Coy looked on in amazement, half expecting Sawyer to drop to her knees, and gasped when she grabbed Coy's wrist and closed her mouth over her fingers. *Sweet mother of—*

"Now," Sawyer said, running her tongue along Coy's fingers one last time, "go get ready for me."

Coy broke out in a grin and she jumped up. "Yes, my goddess."

As she was darting to her bedroom, she heard Sawyer's muffled laughter. "There will be none of that either."

Chapter 37

Sawyer

I can't believe that just happened. Tabarnak, *who am I right now*? Sawyer licked her lips. The remnants of McCoy's arousal coated her tongue, the unusual yet so familiar mix of sweet and salty musk seeping into her taste buds and dousing her pores. It was sinful. Unholy. Exquisite. A revelation.

Watching McCoy tease and tempt her confirmed the last of Sawyer's doubts. *I'm not attracted to cis men. I never have been.* But it went one step further than that for Sawyer. The attraction she'd felt for women in the past was nothing compared to what she felt for McCoy.

You hold all the power here.

That line had completely done her in. Crumpled her defenses and amplified her ego and need for control. Ugh, that *line* ... Sawyer bit her lip, shaking her head. There was no time for reflection. She'd promised to ride McCoy until she came. And come hell or high water, she planned to do exactly that. A dildo couldn't be that different from the real thing, right? And she wouldn't have to put it in her mouth ... unless that was something queer people did?

I'll have to ask Cin about that, too, Sawyer thought, crossing the apartment to McCoy's bedroom.

You hold all the power here.

Sawyer smiled. Why yes, yes she did.

McCoy was waiting for her when she entered the bedroom, her back propped up against the headboard, and her hands relaxed behind her head. Straps adorned her hips to hold the harness in place, and in the center, there was an average-sized, indigo-blue dildo standing proud over McCoy's sex.

Sawyer's mouth opened in wonder. That was not what she'd envisioned at all. Her stomach fluttered, and she couldn't stop staring at McCoy as she began to undress.

"I take it by the way you just tore those buttons that this is what you want, hmm?" McCoy murmured with a lazy smile.

The question felt rhetorical, considering Sawyer now ripped at her clothes like there was a gun to her head. Her bra went flying, she didn't care where, as she was already reaching for her thong. Goosebumps broke out over her flesh at the sound of McCoy's soft laughter. "I would have preferred the thong hit me in the face, but beggars can't be choosy."

"Sorry," Sawyer offered, snatching the underwear off the floor. A bubble of laughter spilt out, and as she closed the distance between them, she dangled the thong around her finger. McCoy tracked her every move, her green gaze alight with the smoldering fire she got when she was aroused. Knowing she was the cause of such passion was empowering. Sawyer felt sexy, comfortable in her own skin. All of her skin, even the fragments left gnarled after the accident.

"Is this better, *Chérie*?" she crooned, trailing her thong upward on McCoy's naked torso. It tickled her throat and chin, and Sawyer relished McCoy's soft gasp.

"So much, sweetheart." McCoy's eyes fluttered shut, and she buried her nose and lips against the damp material. "Fuck. I'd happily suffocate in your smell."

"Oh, *oui*?"

McCoy didn't appear at all turned off by the idea. Sawyer wanted to sigh in relief. Perhaps Cindy had been right all those years ago—Olivier was the problem, never her. Sawyer snatched the material away, her heart hammering as she climbed onto the large bed to straddle McCoy. It was the first time they were both completely skin-on-skin, and she took a moment to revel in the contact. McCoy didn't move to touch her, which both frustrated and turned her on more. She was so aroused she was certain McCoy could feel her slickness against her stomach.

"*Touche-moi, Chérie*. Put your hands on me," Sawyer instructed, flexing her thighs against McCoy. She palmed McCoy's breasts, moaning when McCoy reached up and cupped hers as well. They held eye contact, toying with the other's sensitive nipples and Sawyer grinding her sex into Coy. The hardness of the dildo rubbed into her back until she couldn't take it anymore.

"McCoy," Sawyer gritted, reaching behind to grasp the silicone in her hand.

"Lift up, sweetheart. Let me help." McCoy kissed her, teasing her tongue along Sawyer's lips. Sawyer responded, whimpering when their tongues met in the middle. As their mouths fused together, Sawyer raised up and, with McCoy's help, positioned herself until the tip of the dildo pressed against her core. McCoy was guiding her hips, clearly trying to slow her descent, but Sawyer was having none of that.

"*Calisse*," she ground out as she sank down on the dildo. The fullness was somewhat familiar, but the punch of arousal that hit her with having McCoy inside her was entirely new. Sawyer sucked in a breath and reached for the younger woman, her hands trembling ever so slightly. "You feel so good."

"So do you, believe me." Coy hands began exploring Sawyer's body once again. Sawyer slowly moved her pelvis, clutching Coy's shoulder with one hand. She circled McCoy's throat with the other, noting the small gasp of pleasure that escaped her lover.

"You like that," Sawyer said, tugging her bottom lip between her teeth when McCoy squeezed her ass.

"Yes."

McCoy squeaked when Sawyer's grip tightened a fraction. She bent her head down, closing her lips around Sawyer's nipple.

"Yes, ugh, just like that." Sawyer's head lolled back as McCoy swirled her tongue over her nipples, one and then the other, flicking the taut bud up and down before sucking it into her mouth. Sawyer's eyes slammed shut, and she rocked her pelvis, getting utterly lost in pleasure. "Just like that, *Chérie. Donne-leur un* French kiss."

"Fuck, I love it when you speak French," McCoy gushed, reining Sawyer's focus in again. As she toyed with Sawyer's breast, McCoy lifted her lust-filled gaze to hers. Her cheeks were rosy, and perspiration dotted her hairline.

Sawyer opened her mouth to reply, but it was getting harder to focus on anything but her mounting euphoria. There was a fullness building low in her belly, pressing in on her walls with each thrust. Still, it wasn't enough. Sinking her hand into McCoy's hair, she held her in place and licked the sweat off her temple. "McCoy, I ... *more.*"

McCoy kissed her hard, panting. "I gotchu, sweetheart." And then Sawyer felt McCoy's calf pressing against her ass as she crossed her ankle over her knee on the bed. The support tightened their position, causing more friction on her clit as she rode McCoy. She quickened the pace, groaning each time the dildo hit a certain pleasure spot. She gripped McCoy's hair as she continued to tease and suck Sawyer's nipples.

"Oh my God. Oh fuck, yes!" Sawyer cried out, throwing her head back in ecstasy as she orgasmed. Lights danced in her eyes. Her pulse was erratic, everywhere all at once. The sensation of McCoy's attention on her breasts became too much, and she pressed her palm to the other woman's forehead. "That's enough," she croaked, sliding off McCoy. Her cheeks flushed when she saw the mess she'd made. Had she peed?

"That was incredible," McCoy marveled, gazing at Sawyer in complete awe. "You're incredible. My new favorite thing is watching you come."

"Can you not crack jokes right now?" Sawyer snapped, still trying to catch her breath. She couldn't stop staring at the wetness coating

McCoy's thighs and the sheets. "That's never happened before. I didn't even feel the urge to ..." She couldn't bring herself to say it. Her voice was so thick with emotion that it hurt to talk.

McCoy followed her gaze, and after a long moment, her eyes widened in understanding. "Oh. No, no, sweetheart, that's not pee. That's... You squirted. Perfectly normal. See?"

Before Sawyer could process it, McCoy was whipping off the harness and closing her lips around the dildo, sucking it clean and looking like she'd done it several times before. A cross between a laugh and a sob left Sawyer. *Well, that answers one question.* She flopped backwards onto the mattress just as another sob escaped. The lights turned off, and then McCoy was behind her, pulling her into her arms. "I love the way you taste. You're so sexy, Sawyer, and I'm the luckiest queer in the world right now."

Sawyer closed her eyes as McCoy pressed light kisses along her shoulder and behind her ear. She sighed, relaxing into the younger woman's affections. Their limbs entwined felt intimate but inherently *right* at the same time. As the days went on, it became harder and harder to consider a future without McCoy in it. But wasn't that just the lust talking?

"Will you come to Tess and Abi's engagement party as my date?" McCoy asked softly, her hand drawing slow circles over Sawyer's hip. Another kiss to her shoulder.

"Depends. When is it?" The thought of meeting McCoy's friends gave her the same feeling she got when she'd taken Bree on that rollercoaster ride years ago. Her stomach lurched.

"I actually have no idea," McCoy laughed. "Tess hasn't popped the question yet. According to her sister Tauni, she was supposed to yesterday but chickened out. I just meant, whenever the time comes, will you? So long as it doesn't interfere with the restaurant."

Sawyer felt herself relaxing again; McCoy's consideration of others had to be one of her most attractive qualities. "I don't see why not, so long as our schedules align."

"Amazing. Thank you." McCoy rolled Sawyer over so that they were facing each other and gave her a long kiss. "They're gonna love you."

"Really," Sawyer deadpanned.

McCoy smiled wide enough to show off both dimples, and Sawyer's breath caught in her throat. The same dimples that made her blood thrash in frustration and annoyance months ago now made her pulse quicken and her heart melt into a gooey pile. Strange how that happened without her noticing.

"Well," McCoy whispered, lowering her lips to Sawyer's again. Their eyes met, and a shaky breath left McCoy. "Maybe not like how I love you. Or like how you love me."

Sawyer's mouth went dry. "How ... I never said—"

McCoy cupped Sawyer's face, her gaze never wavering. "I might not know a lot of French, but I do know "*mon amour*" means my love."

Merde. Who knew rambling in the heat of passion would come back to bite her in the ass?

CHAPTER 38

McCoy

"CRAZY TO THINK IT's almost all over," Coy called to her father from behind her safety mask. They were in her auto body shop, and the almost completely finished McLaren sat before them in all her glory. Over half of her had been rebuilt to one degree or another, from the new tub and engine to hammering out dents from exterior parts that could be reused. The windshield had been installed two weeks before, and after a lot of groveling, Coy had convinced Sawyer to let her tow the McLaren across the city to be repainted. So here she was, after a week of priming and sanding and then painting, they were finally on their final coat of paint.

Greg patted Coy on the back. "You did a great job on this one, kid."

"Thanks, Pops," Coy grinned, patting him on the back as well. They remained in the semi-embrace for several moments, staring at the McLaren in silence. Come that time tomorrow, the incredible supercar painted the exact shade of yellow it was before the accident, would be sitting, completed, in her parking lot. Despite Coy's suggestion of going with a new look, Sawyer wouldn't hear of it. And, which didn't come as a surprise, once Sawyer had her mind set on something, it was hard to sway her opinion. Instead, she'd rather push someone away or hold them at arm's length if she felt they were coming too close to swaying her on anything.

And fuck, did it hurt whoever was on the receiving end.

She might not admit it, but I know she loves me. She's just the most stubborn fucking woman in existence.

Two days had passed since she'd spent the night with Sawyer. It was becoming a regular occurrence for Sawyer to disappear and avoid Coy after each progression in their relationship. Processing, Bree called it when Coy had texted her that morning to pout. Sawyer needed time to process and to decompress. And Coy understood that. She genuinely did, but what was wrong with her wanting to be there to help Sawyer through it? Her friends had that. Hell, Abi was helping Tess through panic attacks and dousing her with self-love every time Coy turned around. And Taunya had lucked out in finding a guy who'd fallen in love with her while holding her hair back to puke, of all things. There was nothing Derek wouldn't do for Taunya.

Why was Coy so attracted to strong, independent, *withdrawn* women? Would Sawyer ever let her in emotionally, or would five years pass like they had with Frankie, only for it all to be a waste?

"Is the plan still to keep the McLaren here for the weekend and deliver it to Sawyer's house first of the week?" Greg asked, pouring more paint into the waiting canister.

"Yeah. I mean. it was." Coy frowned, thinking back on her unanswered texts. Sawyer had left her on read since yesterday. It was confusing and likely something Abi would find disrespectful if she knew, but Coy couldn't help thinking it was at least partially her fault.

Who was Brian?

It was what she'd asked Sawyer after pulling her from a nightmare two nights ago. She wished she had impulse control, she really did, because even she knew launching questions at her lover when Sawyer was vulnerable was the equivalent of driving down a speedway blindfolded.

But who was Brian? Coy was dying to know. He'd have to have been important enough that Sawyer was weeping in her sleep. A heavy, highly uncomfortable feeling had settled over Coy, and since then, the sensation had only deepened. A part of her didn't want to know, and yet, a part of her needed to.

"Let's get back at it. You coming for supper tonight? Miranda's making chicken alfredo," Greg said and rubbed his belly like he was already picturing the heaping plate.

"Nah, I can't. I'm meeting Sloane at the pub."

Greg fastened the hose attachment to his newly filled paint gun. "Things better between you?"

Coy shrugged, reaching up to wipe sweat off her brow. "Define better. Am I wanting to choke her every time I see her? Not currently. Are we like we used to be? Hell no."

"She's your sister, Coy. You know how Sloane is. She's always struggled being apart from you."

"Doesn't make what she did right."

"No, it doesn't. But go easy on her. Sloane's not like you, Coy. She won't come out and say she needs or misses you. She could be drowning, and no one would ever know."

Something about that didn't sit right with Coy. It was true, and damn if it didn't sound a little like Sawyer. What was wrong with simply talking things out instead of running in circles all the time?

At eight the following morning, Coy chose all red roses this time. In the attached card she wrote, "I love you because ..." and offered up five reasons why Sawyer had stolen her heart and soul. Poetic and mushy as shit, but apparently, love made her a little like both of those things.

"Thank you," she told the florist after paying. Leaving the shop, she grimaced up at the dark thunder clouds looming in the sky. The forecast was calling for rain all weekend around the province, which wasn't unusual for Vancouver weather, but it would affect her biking plans in

Squamish with Sloane. They were scheduled to do another vlog, but perhaps Frankie would let them do a bartending special instead. It'd been a while since their fans had seen the twins side by side.

Abi appeared beside her, slipping her hand in Coy's. "You know you could deliver them yourself."

Coy tsked, reaching across with her free hand to tap Abi on the nose. "That's not how you give someone space, Abs."

"Yeah, well, avoiding the person you're sleeping with isn't great either," she grumped, and the sour look on her face lasted until they'd reached the supercar parked at the curb. "I can't believe we're driving this."

"*I'm* driving this. You, Abs, are my passenger princess. Hey!" Coy laughed when Abi swatted her on the ass.

"Well, if I'm a princess, then open my door for me," Abi countered with a saucy toss of her hair over one shoulder. A grin appeared. "I can't figure out how to operate the damn thing."

"Sure thing, beautiful, but hold still real quick." Whipping out her cell, Coy swiped open the camera app and directed it toward Abi. Her bestie was standing next to the car with the hood of her raincoat already up to protect her hair. Coy took a picture, explaining, "I'm gonna send this to Sawyer. She hasn't seen the car finished yet."

"It's still super odd to spend all that money rebuilding it," Abi commented as Coy helped her inside the vehicle. As Coy slid into the driver's seat, her bestie looked at her with one finely groomed eyebrow arched. "You ever get the answers from her?"

"No, and I won't pry. Sawyer is ... like an onion, okay? I've gotta peel layers back one at a time. You don't just stab into the middle of an onion and expect it to still thrive. It'll wither quicker, and that's definitely not what I want to happen with our relationship."

Abi's answering smile was soft, contemplative. "That has to be the sweetest thing I've ever heard you say. When did you become such a relationship expert?"

"I'm not." Coy shrugged and flashed a grin. "I just know Sawyer."

Driving the McLaren—really driving it, not just up and down the block where her shop was—was a fantasy come to life for Coy. She probably shouldn't have passengers in it since she was technically working, but she had to show off the car at least once before Sawyer came to claim it. What she did with it then, Coy could only guess. For all she knew, Olivier had put it in his will that she sell it or gift it to Bree. But that didn't make sense either, considering Sawyer's explosion the day she'd seen her daughter in the car.

After dropping Abi off at the office, Coy continued on to Richmond, pleased as punch anytime someone gawked at her during a red light. So what if she'd dressed her best this morning, just so she looked like she could really own a beauty like the McLaren? She fully expected her pops to shake his head when he saw her, and the man did not disappoint.

"You're too much, Coy," Greg laughed when she pulled up beside him in the parking lot.

"Just enough, Pops, just enough," Coy joked and continued past the main shop to her shop in the back parking lot. She wanted to fix the alignment again and tighten the brakes before she delivered it to Sawyer, but there was still time. Today, she had to repair a sedan that had recently been in a fender bender and also help her dad in the main shop. Hopefully, her role as an auto body technician would eventually garner enough clientele that they could hire another mechanic.

Parking the McLaren off to the side of her shop, Coy pocketed the keys and returned to where Greg was waiting. They, along with Chip and J.D., worked steadily all morning. It wasn't until Coy checked her phone during her lunch break that she saw Bree's text message.

Bree: Maman got your flowers ... it's not a good day for that. I'm sorry.

Bree: I wish I could explain things, but it's not my place.

Bree: We were baking and she just grabbed her keys and left. Maybe she went to see him :(

"What's going on?" Coy muttered, taking another bite of sandwich as she pulled up Sawyer's contact info and pressed the call button. It rang and rang before finally going to voicemail. An odd churning sensation began low in Coy's stomach, and she quickly reread Bree's last message. Who was "him?" Had she meant Olivier's gravesite? And how could a bouquet of roses set Sawyer off?

J.D. burst into Greg's office, his gaze sliding past Coy's to her father's. "Ah, Uncle? You might wanna turn that on," he rushed out, pointing to the surveillance monitor in the corner of Greg's cramped office.

"It still works?" Coy wondered, stuffing another bite into her mouth. She needed to reach Sawyer and figure this mess out. How was it possible to vibe with someone so well one day and feel completely disconnected the next?

"There!" J.D. exclaimed, tapping the camera image that faced the back parking lot and Coy's shop. "Someone's out there fucking up the McLaren."

"What?" Coy dropped her sandwich on the office desk and jumped from her seat to take a closer look. "Holy fuck." The image was grainy, but she'd recognize the woman anywhere. She bolted for the door, shouting over her shoulder as she went, "Turn the camera off. And Pops, block off the lot so no one can get up there."

She only had one thought as she raced from the shop and into the pouring rain.

Sawyer.

Chapter 39

McCoy

She reached Sawyer just as the tire iron came down like a whip against the brand new windshield.

CRACK!

"Sawyer, what the hell?" Coy cried, swiping raindrops out of her vision and wincing when the tool connected once more. An audible moan escaped as she took in the damage to the windshield, side mirrors, and spoiler. A large kitchen chopping knife protruded from one of the rear tires, the others already left with jagged tears down their middle. So much work, wasted. All those hours she'd spent—

A flash of red splattering onto the already wet pavement caught her eye, and she grabbed Sawyer's arm. "Stop, you're bleeding."

"*Calisse*, McCoy. Let go of me." Sawyer's eyes flashed wildly, her gaze the stormiest gray Coy had seen yet. "I need this."

"Okay," Coy whispered, looking around them. Her pulse was so erratic she actually worried she'd pass out, but she forced her head to move in a tremulous nod. "Okay, sweetheart."

Sawyer didn't seem to hear her as she was already beating the shit out of the McLaren again. Coy had to do *something* to help, if not for the logical reasoning that Sawyer simply wasn't strong enough to do much more than dent the carbon fiber doors.

"Fuck," she took off toward her shop, pulling out her keys as she went. Once inside, she quickly retrieved her sledgehammer, hoisting it over her shoulder, and running back out to Sawyer. *I can't believe I'm about to do this,* she thought incredulously and swung the sledgehammer into the car door like a baseball bat.

"McCoy," Sawyer choked out. Droplets of rain and tears had streaked her makeup, creating thin black lines that ran down her cheeks and into her open mouth. A pain so deep, so profound that it should have been immobilizing crossed her features. Coy sucked in a breath, her own heart squeezing as she took in her girlfriend's desperate plea for help.

"I told you before," she forced out, blinking past the threatening tears. Raising the sledgehammer again, she added thickly, "I'll do anything you want. I'd do anything for you."

Sawyer's chest heaved as she stared at Coy for a second longer, no doubt weighing the truth of her words.

"I'm crazy about you, don't you know that?" Coy reached for her, but Sawyer wrenched away at the last second, a guttural scream tearing from her chest.

"Arrgh!"

The tire iron smashed out one headlight and then the next. Coy followed Sawyer, striking the heavy hammer down again and again, pulverizing doors and tire rims, anything she could safely damage. Sawyer's sobs increased, racking her shoulders until the tire iron slipped from her grasp and clattered to the ground. Still, she wasn't finished. Coy's eyes widened as Sawyer shakily pulled the knife out of the tire, stepping over broken glass from the window with her sensible kitchen shoes. Hell, as Coy gawked, it only dawned on her in that moment that Sawyer was still in her chef's uniform.

She was crying and speaking in rapid French as she pulled open the car door. It was the closest Coy had seen Sawyer get to the McLaren, and as she watched the woman she loved straddle the passenger seat and tear the inside to shreds, a magnitude of inexplicable emotion filled her to overflowing.

She understood everything now. Or at least why Sawyer had spent so much money on a car she'd had no intention of ever driving. It was her final "fuck you" to a man she had loathed.

Sawyer was taking back whatever control she felt she'd lost.

"It's done." There was an emptiness in her voice as she limped toward Coy. Her shoulders were rounded as if she was already withdrawing, and the moment she let go of the knife, her knees buckled.

Coy dropped the sledgehammer and grabbed Sawyer before she fell. "I've got you, sweetheart."

"I'm tired, McCoy." Tear-filled eyes bore into Coy. Sawyer swallowed hard. "I don't have the strength to ..." Her voice trailed off, and she glanced over Coy's shoulder to the battered car behind them.

"Want me to?"

Sawyer opened and then closed her mouth. She nodded once, still not meeting Coy's gaze.

The trained First Aid responder in her was dying to set Sawyer down somewhere dry to look at any wounds, but she knew Sawyer wouldn't stand for that. For one reason or another, it was imperative that she see this through.

Coy made certain she was stable on her feet before picking up the sledgehammer again. Taking a deep breath, she hoisted it over her shoulder once more and ignored the twinge of protest from her aching muscles. Her own discomfort was nothing if it helped lessen some of Sawyer's.

Now that she didn't have to worry about accidentally hitting Sawyer, she made quick work of totalling the supercar. Under the weight of the sledgehammer, the roof and trunk caved in, side panels fell off, and soon, even the engine was smoking from the abuse on the hood. The silent acceptance in Sawyer's eyes had Coy dropping the hammer for the final time. She was out of breath and sweaty, and her arms felt like deadweights as she crossed the distance to where Sawyer was huddled on the pavement. Coy didn't say anything, merely bent and scooped Sawyer up in her arms, cradling her soaked-through body as she led the way to her shop.

Sawyer wept quietly into her hands, her head leaning against Coy's shoulder as she walked them to her office. It was used as more of a changing room for Coy, but it had a small washroom with a stand-up shower for when Coy got extra dirty at work. It was something J.D. teased her endlessly over, but the simple luxury was coming in handy now.

"Sweetheart, I'm just gonna get you warm, okay?" Coy set Sawyer down gently in one of the office chairs. Sawyer remained silent, but now she stared at the family picture on Coy's desk. She had bits of glass in her hair, and her clothes were torn in places. Coy chewed the inside of her cheeks wondering what to do, before she grabbed the First Aid kit out of her bottom drawer. Pulling on a pair of latex gloves, Coy carefully picked out the glass, dropping it in the garbage can she'd pulled over. Then she walked the few feet to the bathroom to start the shower. Sawyer was still sitting in the same spot, her empty gaze locked on Coy's family photos.

"Hey," Coy murmured, squatting to face Sawyer. She held Sawyer's jaw between her fingers, searching for recognition in her eyes. "Let's get you out of this, okay?" she said of Sawyer's shirt, pinching the hem between her fingers. Sawyer blinked, acknowledging Coy like she was waking from a deep sleep. The nod of her head appeared labored. Coy slowly removed her clothes, then her own, before carrying Sawyer into the shower.

"I'm so in love with you, Sawyer," Coy whispered as she helped tilt Sawyer's damp locks under the hot water. "You're the strongest woman I know, and I'm proud to be yours."

"Oh, McCoy."

Despite the temperature in the shower, Sawyer began to shake. Fresh tears mixed with the water on her cheeks. "It's my son's birthday today."

Coy's heart thrashed against her chest at the confession, and Sawyer's nightmare the other night came to mind. "Brian."

Sawyer nodded, collapsing into Coy's embrace. She buried her face in the crook of Coy's neck, choking out, "*Mon bel amour, mon bébé,* B-Brian Edouard. He would have been sixteen."

So he died. Coy took an unsteady breath, trying her best to school her emotions. Sawyer needed her strength right now, not her damn golden retriever ability to weep on command. A million platitudes popped into her brain and exited just as fast. What could she say? What *was* there to say? No amount of sympathy could replace what Sawyer had lost.

"Fuck," she mumbled at last. "I am so very, very sorry for your loss, sweetheart." She held her tighter, molding their slick bodies together as Sawyer wept in her safe embrace.

Coy never wanted to let her go.

Chapter 40

Sawyer

It felt like the deadest of weights had been lifted from Sawyer.

"I held onto that rage for so long," she whispered, unable to meet McCoy's eyes. Even though she knew McCoy would never judge her, it was easier to open up without staring at another person. They were cuddling in Sawyer's bed, with Patches purring at the top of Sawyer's pillow. She licked her dry lips and swallowed, reaching up to finger the strings on McCoy's hoodie. "I'd buried it so deep, and yet, every time I looked in the mirror, I hated myself a little more. It was like a poison, slowly killing me from the inside out." Sawyer looked up at McCoy then, her throat constricting as she swallowed the large lump that had formed. "I hated him so much, McCoy."

"Then, can I ask—"

"Why didn't I leave him?" Sawyer finished. A rueful smile appeared. "I almost did, a few times, and was quickly reminded of how much power he had over my life. That I was nothing without him, and he would make sure I never got to see Bree. So I stayed."

"What a manipulative asshole." McCoy scowled.

"He was." Sawyer nodded, placing her palm over McCoy's forehead to smooth the wrinkles out. She bit her lip, admitting, "I never wanted to marry Olivier to begin with."

McCoy's soothing hand stilled on her hip. "You didn't?"

"No, but at nineteen, I was scared to death of going to hell if I gave in to my true desires." Sawyer closed her eyes, relaxing into McCoy's caress. Two hours later, and she didn't think the younger woman had stopped touching her. Walking in on her destroying the car had clearly affected McCoy, and since physical touch was her love language, Sawyer could only assume McCoy was soothing herself as much as she was Sawyer. "I spent—" Sawyer froze, unsure how much of her past she should delve into.

"Sweetheart, I think you need to tell it," McCoy reached up to brush her thumb over Sawyer's bottom lip. The callouses on her skin made Sawyer quiver. "It's on the tip of your tongue now. Let it all out. I swear I'll only love you harder after."

Sawyer swallowed. Then swallowed again, grimacing at the persistent ball of thorns in her throat. "There was this girl in my church. Beth Li. She was new to the area and didn't speak a lot of English or French. That didn't matter. We became fast friends, and then, something more. She was so pretty and kind, and her parents were so much nicer than mine. My father didn't like them, though. He was racist and homophobic and thought he was better than everyone else. One day ..." Sawyer took a deep breath, hating how old memories still stung or how young she felt when dredging them up. It was much easier to push everything down and utilize her ice queen facade.

She reached for Patches, who was purring near her ear, bringing her closer to her chest and burying her face in the cat's soft fur. "My oldest brother Sebastion caught us making out in our treehouse and ran to tell *Papa*. I never saw Beth again. The next morning, I was packed up and sent to my first conversion camp. When I came back, I wasn't permitted to leave the house for the first week. By the second week, Beth and her family had moved away. My father drove them out of town, McCoy."

"Fuck," McCoy breathed, her hands fussing over the adhesive bandage she'd placed over the cut on Sawyer's forearm. Tears shone brightly in her green gaze. "Conversion camp? Sweetheart, that must have been …"

"Fucking horrible," Sawyer finished for her, swallowing again, and she added hoarsely, "Between the camps and the therapy while my parents homeschooled me, my spirit died. I became who they shaped me to be. I wanted out from their clutches, so when I met Olivier and they approved, we started dating. By nineteen, I was married and in cooking school. I thought that at least Olivier seemed progressive, you know? He let me learn and become a chef, and that was more than what I could say about my spineless mother. In a way, he supported my dreams. He was Catholic as well. Our fathers were business partners, but he was nine years older, so I didn't know a lot about him growing up. I hadn't realized until years later that he'd learned of my time with Beth."

McCoy began tracing gentle patterns over Sawyer's shoulder. "Your father?"

Sawyer scowled. "*Oui*. And for years, Olivier used to bring it up when he thought I needed atonement."

"But things were going okay for a while, right? You were becoming a chef. You went to France."

"It was … manageable," Sawyer whispered, reaching out to cup McCoy's cheek. For a moment, she studied her, trying to put into words how she'd felt then compared to now. "The … the way you make me feel … the *desire* … it was never like that with him. I was just … numb, I guess. He wanted us to have kids right away. I wanted to wait. I got pregnant and miscarried four times before Bree was conceived. I thought it was because I wasn't ready." She peeled her gaze from Coy's as the familiar prick of tears formed. It was difficult to admit how she'd allowed so much to happen. She'd been a spectator in her own life.

McCoy leaned forward to kiss away a fleeting tear. "You were young. It wasn't your fault, sweetheart."

Sawyer shook her head. McCoy wasn't getting it. She didn't *know*. "When I got pregnant with Bree, I was cooking full-time in my dream restaurant in the heart of France. It was an awful pregnancy. I spent so much of my time throwing up that the head chef placed me on leave. Still, Olivier wasn't happy. We made the move to Vancouver when I was six months along. Bought our first house and the restaurant within months. But nothing was ever enough for him. Running his family's business wasn't enough, so he rushed to get the restaurant. Said he was doing me a favor putting my name on the deed but that his name would be the one remembered. *Desmarais*. I was twenty-three, nine months pregnant, and had gestational diabetes. When I went into labour, they found out Bree was breech, and I needed a last-minute cesarean."

"Fuck, Sawyer." The meadow green of McCoy's eyes were gleaming with her own tears.

"Bree is my miracle baby," Sawyer smiled sadly. Her heart squeezed, knowing she needed to share the rest. Bree had told her as much weeks ago. To let McCoy in.

Can she heal the broken inside me?

"Olivier wanted a boy," Sawyer swallowed, her eyes drifting closed as memories washed over her. All the fighting, the pleading ... "He wanted a son and spent a lot of time trying to make one. Every night, it didn't matter if Bree was hungry, crying in her bassinet. I-I was trying to breastfeed, so one time I just ..." She shook her head, unable to say it. Instead, with trembling hands, she made the action of placing a baby on her breast, closing her eyes in shame. "It shut her up long enough for him to finish."

McCoy was crying openly now. Sawyer could hear her sniffles, feel how her grip tightened fractionally, as if she were afraid Sawyer would slip away. "That bastard," she growled.

"It was harder to get pregnant after Bree, and when I did, I miscarried." The rawness in Sawyer's throat made it difficult to speak. "Olivier began cheating somewhere around that time. Getting pregnant with Brian was a happy accident for us both. Olivier had all but given up on me, convinced that my miscarriages were a penance for being gay."

"Sawyer ... honey, you know that's not true, right?"

Sawyer's damp eyes fluttered open as McCoy pressed a soft kiss to her lips. Their gazes met and held. She was bone tired. All she wanted was to feel her bare skin on McCoy's and fall asleep holding her.

Just get it over with. Finish it. Tell her everything.

"My blood pressure was consistently high with Brian. I was working too much and took care of Bree and everything at home. My doctor put me on meds at thirty-two weeks. One night ..." Sawyer paused, taking a moment to suck more air into her lungs. She let the tears slip down her cheeks. "Olivier and I were fighting, and this happened." She gestured to her face. McCoy brushed her tears away once more. "I was in so much pain, McCoy. Everywhere. I-I thought I would die, and Olivier, he-he ran. Just left me there screaming with Bree asleep upstairs. He didn't come see me at the hospital. Our neighbor had to take Bree."

Sawyer squeezed her eyes shut, trying desperately to separate herself from that horrible night. The words tumbled out. "That night, I woke with inexplicable pain and bleeding. I was out of it from the burns and didn't realize right away what was happening. By the time the nurses examined me, it was too late. I had what they called a placental abruption."

A sob broke out, and Sawyer clamped her hand over her mouth. Tears ran down her fingers. "My blood pressure spiked, probably from the burns. I ... He wasn't supposed to come yet. We had an appointment scheduled a few weeks later for a cesarean. *Mon dieu*, McCoy. I-I had to deliver him vaginally, d-deliver Brian, even though ... even though he was already ..."

Dead.

She couldn't say it. Nothing was coming out properly. Her facts were in pieces, too dark to linger for too long. Sawyer's head sunk into the pillow, and she wept, unable to hold back any longer. Was it enough? Had she opened herself up enough? It felt like there was a crater-sized hole where her heart should be.

Patches was gently moved from her embrace, and then McCoy was guiding Sawyer into her arms. Distant memories of cradling Brian before the nurses took him away lingered as Sawyer cried herself to sleep.

CHAPTER 41

McCoy

IF SHE COULD BRING a man back from the dead just to kill him all over again, she fucking would. Hell, she'd bring Olivier back and let Sawyer do the honors. Coy already knew she was meticulous from the way she'd held onto a wrecked car for a year just to watch it get rebuilt so that she could destroy it herself. Coy could only imagine what her girlfriend would do to Olivier if given the chance.

Deep breaths, she thought, holding Sawyer even closer in the bed. Patches had started pawing at the closed bedroom door a few minutes ago, but Coy couldn't bring herself to get up and let her out. *Not yet,* she thought, her throat choking up again. She pressed a kiss to Sawyer's forehead, swallowing down the swell of emotion. It broke her heart to know everything Sawyer had been through, how she'd pushed the majority of it down for so many years. It was no wonder she didn't let many people in. Coy doubted even Bree knew all the facts; she couldn't picture Sawyer telling her daughter that Olivier was a disgusting pig who couldn't understand the difference between consent and coercion. And learning about Brian ... tears blurred Coy's vision. It would have been hard enough to get past something like that with a supportive partner, but having someone like Olivier must have been so much worse.

Coy's cell vibrated on the nightstand, and she grabbed ahold of it before the noise woke Sawyer.

Bree: Please tell me *Maman* is with you. I'm downstairs. Came home to check because she never answered my calls and texts.

Coy cleared her throat, wiping away a tear that slipped out before replying.

Coy: Yeah. Sorry, forgot to message you back. She's asleep atm.

Bree: Can I come up?

Coy: Of course.

Although Sawyer was dressed in another of her sleep shirts and drawstring pajama pants, Coy pulled the covers over her a bit more to give her privacy. They'd both been chilled after the episode in the rain, so when Coy brought them back to the house, getting naked wasn't on the table.

There was a soft knock on the door, to which Patches let out a loud meow in response. Bree entered, allowing the annoyed cat the escape, and closed the door behind her. The younger woman took one look at Sawyer, draped halfway across Coy's chest, and smiled sadly. "Good," she whispered and padded across the room to them.

Coy was silent as Bree crawled into the bed beside her mother, cuddling close and resting a cheek on Sawyer's shoulder. She reached for Coy's hand. "I'm glad she has you."

Another tear slipped out. Coy swallowed hard. "And I'm glad she has *you*."

Bree really was Sawyer's miracle, the only good thing to come from a life of misfortune. What would have happened if the doctors hadn't caught her in time? Where would Sawyer be now?

Coy was glad she didn't have to find out.

She woke an hour later with several messages waiting on her phone. Sawyer was still fast asleep, and Bree had left. There was an IM from Bree, and a sleepy smile appeared when she saw the picture of her and Sawyer.

Bree must have taken it just before she snuck from the bedroom. Coy saved it to her phone and considered using it as her lock screen display but thought better about it. She wanted her first official picture with Sawyer to be a happy one. Swiping to her next message, Coy pulled up one from both Abi and her pops and, surprisingly, two from Sloane.

"Huh." They were all old. Had they just come in?

Abi: Did you butt dial me at work again? Put the phone away while you're knocking dents out.

That made Coy chuckle a little. If her friend only knew.

Pops: I towed the car to the scrapyard. Is Sawyer okay? Get back to me asap.

Coy quickly replied with her thanks and a vague update. Thankfully, Greg wasn't someone who asked a lot of questions, and he didn't this time. A minute later, a simple "Okie, love ya" was sent back.

Sloane: Are you okay?? I'm super anxious all of a sudden.

Sloane: Hello? I called your cell and the shop and no one is fucking answering.

Sloane: Fuck off with making me worry Coy. I'm not in the mood. Call me!

"Shit," Coy's chest grew tight as she fired off an apology to her sister. She'd never made her worry this long before. Ten minutes later, Sloane's reply was less than ideal.

Sloane: Whatev. At least J.D. knows how to pick up the phone. He's good at sending pictures too.

A spark of apprehension hit Coy. What did that mean?

Coy: Whatever he sent you, delete them. It's no one's business.

Sloane: You had me thinking you were dead earlier, because of her?? Told you she was crazy AF.

Coy's throat went dry at those words. How *dare* she? Sloane didn't know a damn thing about Sawyer. Her pulse began to pound in her ears, and her fingers shook as she punched out another text.

Coy: FUCK YOU SLOANE.

The moment the message was sent, Coy shut her phone off and set it back on the nightstand. She knew it'd only be a matter of time before Sloane hit her up with half a dozen more texts and phone calls. As much as she loved pissing Coy off, she hated Coy being upset with her even more. Not having the option to bicker or grovel would drive her nuts.

Good, she fucking deserves it. Some days, it was hard to believe they were identical twins. As years passed, Coy swore they became each other's opposites.

A groggy moan left Sawyer, and moments later, she nuzzled her nose between Coy's breasts. "Your heart is racing," she said quietly, peering up at Coy. Weariness and fatigue dulled her resplendent gaze. "What's wrong?"

Coy shook her head, bending to give her a sweet kiss. She sighed against Sawyer's lips, the tightness in her chest fading the more she relaxed. "How are you?" she asked, pushing thoughts of Sloane away for the time being.

"Better, thank you." Sawyer drew back, giving Coy an apologetic smile. "I'll be right back."

"Okay." Coy reluctantly let her go, aware she was in a weird mood, but at the same time, couldn't seem to help it. She wasn't a needy person by nature, but now that the initial shock of the afternoon had worn off, she felt vulnerable. Any other time, she'd be calling around to Frankie's right about now.

Sawyer returned from the bathroom, dressed down to just a silk robe. She held her hand out, "Come join me in the bath, darling."

Coy perked up at the use of her pet name. Sawyer only used it when she was feeling bold and in charge of her emotions. Scrambling off the bed, she slipped her hand into Sawyer's. Her gaze roamed languorously over Sawyer's backside as she was led into the luxurious bathroom. It was like something out of a fashion magazine, with a massive stand-up shower and jacuzzi soaker tub large enough for two or three people. The water was running, bubbles bubbling, and Sawyer had somehow made a bottle of white wine and two glasses appear out of thin air. Confused, Coy looked around the bathroom for a fridge.

"You were there for me today," Sawyer whispered, her silken hands skimming Coy's stomach underneath the sleeveless hoodie she wore. "I didn't know you were what I needed, but there you were."

"Always," Coy promised, lifting her arms when Sawyer pulled off the hoodie.

"It's my turn now to be what you need, darling."

"Sawyer, it's okay—"

"Shh." Sawyer placed her finger over Coy's parted lips. The skin around her eyes crinkled in thought. "I don't want you turning to Frankie anymore. I'm not sure if I'll ever be Domme material, but I can at least give you this."

"Oh, you're Domme material. Trust me," Coy gushed, puckering her lips to kiss Sawyer's finger.

"If that's the case, then this is how things will go," Sawyer said, reaching for Coy's sports bra next. She pulled it over Coy's head, dropping it to the floor beside them before starting on the button on Coy's jeans. Her mouth found Coy's shoulder, and her teeth grazed the skin as she pushed the jeans off her hips. "You're going to do whatever I ask."

Coy held her breath, glancing up at the ceiling. Did Sawyer truly want this, or was the pressure of payback at the forefront of her mind? The submissive in her wanted to follow through, no questions asked. Who was she to complain if Sawyer wanted to practice her dominance? They were both seeking comfort. Coy needed Sawyer's strength, and Sawyer needed to regain her control. She just happened to be playing into Coy's current emotional state. That was a good thing, right? That they could read each other so well?

It's not like we're doing a scene. Relax.

"What would you have me do?" Coy asked slowly as Sawyer helped her out of her boxers.

"Go pee since I know you must be bursting, and then get in the bath."

Coy bowed her head. "Of course. Thank you." She *was* bursting and quickly relieved herself before walking the few steps to the jacuzzi tub. As she sunk down into the hot water with all the bubbles, she hummed in appreciation. It wasn't too often that she bothered with a bath, especially one as nice as this. "You're spoiling me, sweetheart."

The steam against her aching muscles felt glorious, and she leaned against the tub wall, watching lazily as Sawyer slipped out of the bathrobe. She stood facing Coy in all her glory, her wondrously tanned skin and faint white scar lines. Her breasts were perfect handfuls Coy yearned to cup, and the flare of her hips and slight pudge around her navel was proof of the life she'd created. Sawyer was perfectly imperfect, and Coy couldn't imagine looking at anyone else, feeling this way about anyone else.

"I love you," she blurted, her pulse quickening as Sawyer dipped one long leg in the tub and then the other.

Sawyer arched a brow, flicking a few droplets of water Coy's way. "So you say, darling."

Coy held back her grin, unsurprised by Sawyer's deflection of her feelings. There would come a day when she would say them back, Coy was certain. But, if she was wrong, it didn't really matter. Sawyer showed her love through touch, which Coy understood on a profound level, and by spending quality time with Coy and doing things like what she was doing now. Directing Coy simply because she knew Coy needed direction.

"First, I'm going to wash you." Sawyer positioned herself behind Coy, and her breath hitched as the erotic sensation of Sawyer's hard nipples pressed into her back. A blindfold appeared in front of Coy, and then Sawyer's lips brushed her ear as she murmured, "While you wear this. Then I'm going to give you a shoulder massage, and afterwards, I'll take you back to bed and fuck you. How does that sound?"

Coy whimpered, bobbing her head up and down. "Fuck yes. Oh, yes, please." Goddess, she hadn't realized how much she needed Sawyer to take control.

The blindfold went over her eyes, shielding her vision almost completely. Sawyer fastened it before dropping her hands away again. It wasn't the first time she'd been blindfolded, so she wasn't so much apprehensive as she was excited. The anticipation of where fingers or kisses might land was such a turn-on for Coy that she was already wet with arousal.

"So patient," Sawyer commented, the huskiness in her voice startling Coy. There was the sound of a seal breaking on the bottle, followed by the low gurgle of wine being poured. Seconds later, a sweet, heady aroma filled the air around Coy, and she inhaled deeply. "Do you like that?"

Coy licked her lips, nodding.

"Use your words, darling."

Sawyer's natural ability to dominate was one of the sexiest things about her, and it lit Coy's body on fire. "Yes, Mist—" Fuck, they really needed to think of a unique pet name for this situation. "Sweetheart," she finished as heat crept up her cheeks.

"Good catch." The tip of the wine glass rested against Coy's lips, Sawyer's other hand at the nape of her neck. "Tilt your head back slowly, darling."

As Coy did as instructed, Sawyer continued, a hint of resignation now in her voice. "Frankie was your mistress, and I'm not her. Please don't make that slip up again."

"Of course. I'm sorry," Coy mumbled. She was hot, as if the temperature in the bathroom had gone up.

"Do you wish I was more like her?"

Coy shook her head so fast, her face knocked the wine glass. "No, sweetheart. You're *exactly* what I need. The only one I want."

"So you say."

There was a smile to her tone now, of that Coy was certain. She grinned, pleased she'd given an acceptable answer. She heard the soft *clink* of the wine glass as Sawyer set it down on the tile and then the splash of water. Coy gasped when Sawyer's hands landed on her thighs.

"Now comes the washing part," Sawyer murmured, and Coy yelped when she nipped her shoulder. Sawyer's low chuckle was possibly the most seductive thing Coy had ever heard. "Try to relax, darling."

Relax, of course. She could do that. Coy was a master relaxer when there was a beautiful and very naked woman behind her. Naked, with breasts and nipples made for tongues and teeth ...

"If you want to reach the part where I'm fucking you, I suggest you let me wash you first and quit trying to guide my hand to your pussy."

A groan slipped out, but Coy pulled her hand away. Hell, she hadn't even realized she'd tried taking control of the situation. That wasn't like her.

"That's more like it," Sawyer crooned as Coy leaned back against her torso. It was an incredibly intimate feeling, cradled in Sawyer's arms and nestled between her legs. As the washcloth slowly moved over her body, Coy's thoughts drifted to earlier that day, to the last two days without Sawyer. The confusion and misery of being rejected.

"I didn't like when you were avoiding me," she admitted in a low voice. The washcloth paused, and Coy rushed to add, "After that night when I told you I loved you. And after I woke you from that nightmare. I can respect your space without you needing to ghost me altogether."

It was silent in the bathroom for several heartbeats, and then the washcloth dipped into the water again. "You're right. I'm sorry, darling." Sawyer gave Coy's hand a light squeeze. "I'll do better next time."

"Thank you."

Sawyer continued washing her, announcing a few minutes later that they were done and to scoot ahead. Coy did as she was told, groaning in pleasure as Sawyer's hands kneaded her shoulders. By the time they left the tub, her muscles were looser, and she was deliciously content.

"Are you comfortable keeping the blindfold on?"

"Oh, yes, thank you." Coy nodded, a silly grin forming when Sawyer walked them naked back to her bed. The moment the backs of her legs touched the mattress, Sawyer's mouth was on hers. Coy moaned into her parted lips, her nipples hardening with the languid swipe of Sawyer's tongue.

Oh, goddess.

She was everywhere, the taste and smell of the wine mixed with Sawyer's scented soaps and body oil making Coy lightheaded. Her skin felt tight, and her clit ached with the kind of urgency only a great orgasm could satiate.

"You're mine," Sawyer husked, capturing Coy's bottom lip gently between her teeth. She tugged, and another burst of arousal coursed through Coy.

"Yes."

"You're mine to toy with, to use, correct?"

Sawyer's hand wrapped around Coy's throat, and she gasped. "Y-yes, sweetheart. I trust you."

"Good, darling." With her hand still partially blocking Coy's airway, Sawyer gave her a slight push so that she fell on the bed. "Get on the bed for me with your back touching the headboard. I want to see you."

Coy did as she was told, fumbling a little as she scooted further onto the mattress. She felt around for the pillows, nestling in between them before leaning against the headboard. The room was silent, save for the consistent pattering of raindrops hitting the large bay window. Coy strained to hear Sawyer, wondering where she was and what she was doing. Her tongue darted out to wet her dry lips.

The bed dipped, and Coy started at the husky voice close to her ear. Shivers raced down her spine. "I knew the bandanas you leave around my house would come in handy,"

Coy barely had time to register what she meant before Sawyer was pinning one of her wrists to the headboard. She sucked in a breath as Sawyer secured first one wrist and then the other with fabric.

"Is that too tight?"

Coy shook her head, squirming on the bed as another wave of arousal hit her. "No, I like it."

"Excellent."

Sawyer was so close, close enough to touch, to have her kiss Coy again, but when Coy turned her head and puckered her lips, soft laughter rang out.

"Eager, are we, darling? Test the restraints. See if you can reach me."

Coy pulled, but just hard enough to know she could get free if she wanted to, and let out a little whine. "Sawyer, I need you."

"Mm-hmm, I can see that."

Coy gasped as Sawyer's warm hands landed on her thighs. She spread them apart, scraping her nails along the sensitive skin.

"*Mon dieu, Chérie*. Is this all for me?" Sawyer husked, and Coy groaned as a long finger slid into her drenched pussy.

"Fuck," she hissed, bucking her hips, searching for more, but Sawyer was already retreating. "Yes. I need more, please."

Sawyer tsked, "Not so fast. You'll come at my pace, darling, or not at all. Would you like that? For me to tease and tease, only for you not to come in the end?"

"No," Coy choked, and an image of her horny and uncomfortable all night flashed through her mind. She squeezed her legs together in an attempt to stave off some of the building tension. Her clit throbbed in response.

"I have a better idea." Sawyer's finger appeared against Coy's closed mouth, demanding entrance. Coy opened, and she dipped her finger in. "But first, clean up this mess you made."

Oh, my fucking goddess. Coy's eyes rolled back in her head as she closed her lips over Sawyer's finger, sucking her juices off with a lustful fervor.

"*Calisse*, darling, your tongue feels like silk against my skin," Sawyer whispered, so close to Coy's ear that the warmth of her breath caused an uncontrollable shudder to pass through her. "Lie down flat on the bed. Can you do that, restrained as you are?"

"Yes." Coy felt the bed shift again as Sawyer stood up. She took a deep breath, savoring the lingering scents surrounding Sawyer, before shimmying down further on the mattress. The position change tightened the restraints, but it wasn't uncomfortable.

"Your biceps are delicious. Do you know how long I've wanted to see you tied up? At my mercy? I've dreamt of it."

Coy whimpered, thrusting her pelvis up, silently pleading for Sawyer to fuck her. Still, Sawyer wasn't having it. She was enjoying this, taking control, basking in Coy's attention. A person didn't restrain someone to their bed if a part of them didn't also get off on it.

The mattress dipped again. Coy held her breath, waiting, eager as all hell for Sawyer to take her in her mouth. She was pleasantly surprised, however, when Sawyer straddled Coy's torso instead. "I've been researching ways women pleasure each other," Sawyer murmured, scratching her nails down Coy's arms and making her shiver again. "Tell me, darling. Is the idea of me sitting on your face pleasing to you?"

"Fuck, yes," Coy ground out, sucking in a sharp breath when Sawyer tweaked her nipples. She panted. "Please, sweetheart, I'm desperate for you."

Another tweak to her nipples, and then Sawyer sucked one into her mouth. Coy gasped, every single one of her nerve endings coming alive under the blindfold. Everything was so much *more* when she couldn't rely on her sight and touch. She was practically vibrating by the time Sawyer's thighs slid under her restrained arms and her pussy brushed her parted lips. Coy's tongue darted out, her own sex clenching as she got her first taste of Sawyer that night. *Utter bliss.*

"That's it, darling." Sawyer was breathless as Coy licked and sucked, and then Sawyer's fingers were sinking into Coy's hair to unravel the tangled braid. "God, yes."

Coy grinned, gasping again when Sawyer pulled her hair. Sexual tension coursed through her, its buildup almost to its peak. She took a deep breath to calm herself, knowing she couldn't come just yet. Some of Sawyer's arousal trickled down her cheek, but Coy didn't slow. She alternated between thorough licks and gentle sucks on Sawyer's clit, twirling her tongue around the swollen bud like it was a tasty morsel she wanted to savor.

"M-McCoy, oh. It's coming. I-I can't—" Sawyer jerked slightly away, her breaths sounding ragged from where Coy lay underneath her.

"You can," Coy encouraged, turning her head to nuzzle Sawyer's leg. "You're in control here, not me, sweetheart. Just let your body relax and trust that I'll catch you."

"I do. I trust you, darling." Sawyer's voice still held a higher note, but seconds later, the addicting scent of her pussy was once again filling Coy's nostrils. Coy inhaled her deeply, craning her face up, searching for its source.

"Sawyer, *please*."

Coy audibly groaned when Sawyer's sopping lips met her waiting tongue again. *Yes, fuck me, yes*. To be used solely for Sawyer's pleasure; it was everything she wanted. The only thing she needed.

"Take me in your mouth again."

Sawyer's low command was like gasoline thrown on an already raging inferno, shooting spirals of pleasure straight to Coy's clit. She bucked in response, clamping her legs closed once more. Sweat broke out on her forehead, but she ignored it, instead concentrating on the way her tongue slow-danced around Sawyer's swollen bundle of nerves. Next, she gently sucked the delicious bud into her mouth. She repeated the action, swirling and sucking, with the occasional languid stroke of her tongue along the length of Sawyer's pussy.

"Ugh, *oui. J'ai besoin de toi.*" Sawyer's pitch escalated the closer she came to release, and so did her French. Her voice alone was enough to soon send Coy soaring over the edge, and she let out a garbled moan when Sawyer gripped her hair and rode her face. Sawyer's clit spasmed against Coy's tongue seconds before her thighs began to shake as she came. "*Mon dieu*, McCoy!"

Coy lapped up Sawyer's essence, unable to hold back her grin. Hearing Sawyer scream her name in the midst of an orgasm was officially her favorite sound ever.

CHAPTER 42

Sawyer

HER LEGS SHOOK AS she climbed off McCoy. Perspiration dotted her forehead and back, and she hadn't yet caught her breath. A part of her was still in shock. Never in her life had she achieved an orgasm like that, and in such a short amount of time.

"That was ..." She cleared her throat, her legs wobbly as she got off the bed. "Thank you," she said when it was apparent she was at a loss for any other words.

McCoy smiled, her cheeks flushed and sweaty as well. "Thank *you*. That was incredible."

Heat crept up Sawyer's cheeks, and she was instantly grateful McCoy couldn't witness how easily embarrassed she was. Leaving her restrained, Sawyer retrieved their wine from the bathroom, taking a generous sip before placing them on the nightstand. She studied McCoy, looking for signs of discomfort or fear, but saw nothing but desire and contentment. And a lightness Sawyer hadn't ever seen before. It was as if the gravity of the world ceased to exist, and McCoy was floating on a cloud of happiness.

Sawyer would be almost jealous of McCoy's ability to switch life off if she didn't also adore every possible thing about her.

She returned to the bed, relishing McCoy's small gasp when her fingers touched her hot skin. Her legs fell open shamelessly, drawing

Sawyer's attention to her tempting pussy with its tidy patch of hair on the top. Any time she'd dreamt of this moment, something had always woken her up before reaching this point. What if she was terrible at pleasing McCoy? Feigning confidence and tossing words like "fucking" around in conversation was one thing. Doing it, and doing it well, was wholly different.

"Sawyer? Don't overthink this, okay? You could probably breathe on me right now, and I'd come," McCoy murmured, although her voice sounded a bit shaky. "Just use your fingers."

"No." That just wouldn't do. Sawyer wanted to give McCoy everything, and that included going out of her comfort zone.

Calisse. *Enough with all the pretense.*

Taking a deep breath, Sawyer lowered herself between McCoy's thighs. She held her in place, darting her tongue out for a taste. McCoy cried out, her hips jerking off the bed.

"Wow, you weren't joking," Sawyer teased, surprised when a giggle slipped out. She pushed McCoy back down in the bed, adding, "Stay still, darling,"

"Trying," McCoy panted, writhing as Sawyer licked her again. Her thumb toyed with McCoy's clit as she worked her over with her tongue. The second Sawyer sunk her finger inside, McCoy cried out as she climaxed.

After, when Sawyer had removed the blindfold and restraints, they cuddled in bed, sharing slow kisses and soft caresses. Once again, Sawyer marveled at the way McCoy looked at her. Even after everything she'd told her that day, after witnessing such a destructive catharsis, McCoy still looked at her like she'd gone and fallen into a bowl of lucky charms. Like Sawyer could rob a casino and McCoy would be waiting outside to be her getaway driver.

How was it *real*?

Sawyer didn't deserve love like this. Did she? Perhaps not, but she wanted it. God, did she ever want it. She wanted McCoy like she'd never wanted any other. She *craved* McCoy, her touch, her wit, her charm. Sawyer wanted to wake each morning and fall asleep each night wrapped up in McCoy. She wanted to laugh and bicker and fight just to have that epic makeup sex.

More than anything, Sawyer wanted to be who McCoy *needed*, not just who she thought she wanted. McCoy needed to be dominated, at least part-time. It was who she was, and Sawyer would never ask her to change. But would McCoy be satisfied long-term with what Sawyer could offer? She was no Frankie.

"*You're exactly what I need. The only one I want.*"

McCoy's earlier declaration returned in Sawyer's mind, settling her. She sighed, caressing McCoy's cheek. Her heart fluttered at the obvious love staring back at her.

"*Tu es la femme de mes rêves,*" Sawyer whispered, leaning in to kiss McCoy softly.

"What does that mean?"

Biting her lip, Sawyer blushed a little. "It means, 'You are the woman of my dreams.'"

McCoy smiled wide enough to show off those damning dimples. Sawyer swore she was half in love with those alone. "You're getting to be a big softie."

"Yes, and don't you speak a word of it," Sawyer muttered. "I have a reputation, you know."

"Of course. I would never." McCoy let out an exaggerated gasp before kissing her deeply. When they broke apart, she said, "I love you, Sawyer."

Sawyer cleared her throat, glancing away. "Well ..." Coughing, feeling like she needed to pull the words from her toes, Sawyer swallowed, murmuring, "What you said before, about me ... for you." Clearing her throat again, Sawyer snatched the last of the wine up and drank it in one gulp. She heaved a sigh. "I can see why you might think so."

Silence, and then McCoy's palm was resting on her cheek, tugging Sawyer's gaze back. Laughter shone in her meadow green depths. "Really. Sawyer Lavoie. You are totally in love with me, aren't you? Told you I'd have you falling at my feet in no time."

A laugh escaped Sawyer, "Please. If anyone is falling at someone's feet, darling, it'll be you."

She gave McCoy a light shove, only to pull her back in again and place a kiss on her forehead.

Coy winked. "Promises, promises."

Returning to work after spending almost a full twenty-four hours with McCoy felt like what she imagined coming back from vacation felt like. She was overtired, irritable, and perhaps a tad sulky. Sawyer was woman enough to admit it. Being a respected chef and owning a popular restaurant was incredible—it always had been—but having sex for hours with McCoy, followed by McCoy bringing her breakfast in bed, was nice, too. *Real* nice.

A bag of potatoes landed with a light *thud* on the prep table near Sawyer, and Cindy's face came into view. "You're in a daze today."

"Am I?" Sawyer gave herself a mental shake, blowing air out past her lips. She picked up her rolling pin again. "Surely not. I was just thinking of, you know, um, next week's menu."

"Uh-huh," Cindy snickered, giving Sawyer a gentle shoulder check. "I'm happy for you, albeit a bit disappointed Lori and I have yet to officially meet McCoy."

"Coy," Sawyer corrected, although the shortened version of McCoy's name sounded strange on her lips. When Cindy looked at her blankly, she added, "She goes by Coy."

"But you call her—"

"Cin, listen to me when I'm telling you something. Please." A laugh slipped out, and Cindy's eyes widened in surprise. The chatter around the kitchen halted to a stop, and every one of her staff within earshot turned toward them, stunned expressions on their faces.

A blush so deep set Sawyer's cheeks aflame, and she scowled, "*Calisse.* I'm certain you all have better things to do than eavesdrop on my conversation. *Retourne au travail.*"

"Understood, Chef."

"Sorry, Chef."

Barb grinned from where she stood at the stove. "Did all those flowers accomplish that melodic sound?"

"Nah, Barb, I'd say it's all the orgasms she's been having," Cindy said, quick-witted as ever.

"*Vas te faire foutre,* both of you," Sawyer sniped, but she didn't have it in her to be genuinely upset. God, what was McCoy *doing* to her? She couldn't afford to go soft in this business. She'd been carving a name out for herself for too long to allow feelings to cloud her senses.

"Hey, *Maman,*" Bree spoke up behind Sawyer, reaching around to plant a kiss on her cheek. Sawyer relaxed into the kindness of her daughter's gaze. "Don't be too hard on them. Your not-so-mysterious lover is all anyone can talk about."

"Ugh, love," Sawyer groaned. "Not you too."

Bree laughed.

The next two hours of prep sped by, with Bree and Sawyer working together to make the *tourtières.* Cindy shadowed Shane as he created his first dish all on his own, and Sawyer found her attention straying to their station often. Cindy was competent in the kitchen, and from everything Sawyer had seen since she'd returned to work, she'd make a good head chef.

Wait, what? Why was she thinking of that? An interim head chef was one thing, but to come on in a full-time, permanent capacity?

What would that mean for Sawyer?

"This is really nice," Bree said, glancing up at her. She had a spattering of flour decorating her apron and jawline, and perspiration dotted her hairline from the kitchen's warmth.

"What is, love?"

Bree shrugged, a small smile teasing the corners of her mouth. "This. Working with you. Making *tourtières* and baking *pouding chômeur*, butter tarts, *tarte au sucre*, and everything else. It brings back good memories. I've always loved helping you in the kitchen."

Sawyer hesitated, really considering what Bree might have been saying in between the lines. She'd never asked her if restaurant work could be a serious aspiration. In high school, Bree had mentioned possible careers with a background in social science, and Sawyer had all but thrown her on the plane toward her bright future. Anything to get her away from her father's toxicity. She'd never wanted Bree to feel trapped in her life like Sawyer so often had.

"You're not returning to California, are you?"

Everything was so clear now. The school year had already begun. Bree could have left a month ago if she'd wanted. Sawyer was getting by then, and with Cindy's help, could have successfully managed the restaurant.

Slowly, Bree shook her head. "If it's alright with you, I'd love to just keep doing this. We work well together, no?"

"We do." A smile threatened to take over Sawyer's face. She stared in wonder at her daughter, the purest form of love filling her chest. Before she knew it, she was enveloping Bree in a bear hug and swaying back and forth in the middle of the kitchen. "*Sais-tu à quel point je t'aime, ma chérie*?"

"*Je t'aime, aussi, Maman. Tellement.*" Bree buried her face in Sawyer's chest. "You know, if Cindy took over all the stressful stuff, with Barb as her sous-chef, you and I could do this every day. You'd still be the boss, right?"

"Technically, no. The executive chef runs the kitchen, *mon amour*." That was the problem right now, wasn't it? Sawyer had dreams of earning another Michelin star, of really putting Desmarais on the map at an international level. If she wasn't putting every ounce of fiber into the job, could she rely on others to do it for her? It didn't sit right with Sawyer.

She patted Bree's head, pushing her away enough to study her face. The eagerness in Bree's eyes was unmistakable. She wanted this, probably had been dreaming of the day she could get Sawyer's attention without the restaurant always coming first. God, how many school events had she missed over the years because she was tied up on the hot-line?

"I almost lost you."

Bree's words from days after Sawyer's heart attack plagued her on the best of days. The reality of her mortality was disconcerting. If she died, Bree didn't even have siblings alive to help her through life. She'd be completely and utterly alone. And so here she was, giving Sawyer a way to let some of the unnecessary stress in her life fall away. And then there was McCoy. Her McCoy. Her lover and friend.

Sawyer knew McCoy would stand by and watch her clock in fourteen-hour days if she chose to, but at what cost? The fact was, she couldn't work as much as she had pre-heart attack. She physically wasn't capable. In admitting that, Sawyer could also admit that relinquishing her tight hold on the restaurant didn't seem as terrifying if she had Bree and McCoy in her life.

"Well, even if Cindy was the executive on paper, everyone knows you're still the boss, *Maman*." Bree grinned and gestured up and down at her. "After all, you've got all that boss energy Coy loves so much."

"Bree." Sawyer fought back a smile and flicked a light dusting of flour at her daughter. "Think Cindy could earn us another Michelin star?"

"Chef, sorry to interrupt," Mikey's voice sounded from behind them. He was rocking back and forth on the balls of his feet with a huge grin as he held out a bouquet.

Sawyer inwardly groaned. *Seriously, this again?*

"You've got another delivery from—"

"I know who it's from, Mikey," Sawyer cut in, stepping forward to snatch the note from the peg in the middle of the red roses. Straightening to her full height, she narrowed her gaze as, once again, every team member in her kitchen paused to take in the situation. "*Esti.* Back to work, people!"

As they all wheeled around again, including Cindy, satisfaction settled over Sawyer. She smiled coyly. Yeah, she was still in control.

Chapter 43

McCoy

Coy: How long does a femme take to get ready? This is insanity.

Coy sent the message to the Fab Five group chat before expelling a long breath outside Sawyer's bedroom door. Her girlfriend had been in there for an hour or more. Coy had snuck in to say hi once she'd arrived, and Sawyer had just been going in the shower. She'd kept Patches company downstairs until she felt like she needed to do *something*. That impulsivity had taken her out to the garage, where she found herself changing the oil on the Range Rover. Now she was pacing the hallway with an oil stain on one of her favorite shirts after scrubbing her hands and face clean in the downstairs bathroom before coming up.

Multiple messages came in at once.

Tauni: It takes however long it takes, babe.

Abi: Get used to it, playgirl.

Abi: Can't wait to officially meet Sassy Sawyer.

Coy groaned, quickly firing out a reminder *not* to mistakenly call Sawyer that.

Krystal: I've been asking that for yrs. Tauni takes so long once I thought she'd made her own dress.

Tauni: Bitch, please. You're just jelly you can't pair an outfit to save your life.

There was nothing from Sloane, even though Messenger confirmed she'd seen their conversation. Coy's shoulders drooped a little as she thought of her twin. They'd barely spoken two words since that day three weeks ago. Whether it was the fact that Coy had been staying at Sawyer's more often or that any time she even looked at Sloane, her sister would shoot daggers at her was anyone's guess. Coy didn't know how Sloane would grin and bear it around her when they went to Nana's with their father and Miranda next week. It was Christmas, and every year they went to her house and spent a few days there. Coy had been trying to convince Sawyer and Bree to come, but so far was met with resistance.

Sighing, she typed out another message.

Coy: I'm going in. Maybe she slipped or fell asleep.

Abi: Highly improbable. She's probably still deciding what to wear.

Tauni: You're already gonna be late, so don't become entranced if she's half dressed. Sex can wait.

Abi: Life is too short for all that. It's my party Tauni.

Abi: Tess and I agree that if available, sex should rarely be put on hold.

Coy shook her head and laughed at that. Abi was something else.

Krystal: HAHAHAHA TESS AGREED

Krystal: Didn't mean to scream that. All caps were on.

Abi: well as much as she can boneless and sweaty atm LOL

Coy threw her head back, roaring with laughter.

Sloane: So that's why you haven't shown yet. Gonna be late for your own engagement party. FML. I need to get laid.

Tauni: Saw Naz checking out your ass last weekend.

"Gross," Coy muttered, knocking lightly on Sawyer's bedroom before pushing it open, "Hello?" As she was pocketing her cell, she saw the latest DM.

Sloane: Hard pass, thanks.

Coy had to agree, if for nothing else then the fact that Sloane hated her right now and Naz was a close friend. If they hooked up, it'd throw a wedge between the three of them.

Hell, I sound like Tauni. Her friend had thought something similar when she walked in on Tess and Abi years ago.

"Sawyer, you okay?"

She found the woman in question sitting in front of the makeup vanity in the far corner of her bedroom. Wearing just a bra and underwear, Coy's chest tightened momentarily as she thought of her lover stressing over all the scars she felt she had to cover. She was about to offer reassurance of how stunning she was when she heard Sloane's voice coming from Sawyer's phone.

And then Sawyer *laughed.*

"Sweetheart?"

"McCoy."

Sawyer spun around to face her, her phone flying out of her hands and skittering across the floor. Guilt had her not quite looking Coy in the eye. Rather, she kept glancing at her phone like she'd been caught watching porn.

"Erm ... what, ah ... what're you doing? Is Sloane on the phone?"

"Sloane? No, why?"

Coy frowned, picking up Sawyer's cell and holding it out to her. "Oh, I just thought I heard her."

Still looking properly chastised, which was new for Sawyer, she closed her hand over the phone and somehow unlocked it in the process. An old YouTube video of Sloane and Coy racing down the trails began playing. By the look of it, the video was half over.

Sawyer snatched the phone away, a beautiful blush staining her bare throat and cheeks. Laughter racked Coy's shoulders, earning a scowl from the older woman.

"If you'll excuse me, I'll finish getting dressed."

"That's what you've been doing all this time?" Coy gaped, warmth filling her chest. "How long have you been watching *Sloane & McCoy*?"

"I blame Bree." Sawyer lifted her face in a haughty manner, tossing her phone on the bed and heading for the closet. "Long enough to watch all your cooking and drink videos. Tell me something: how long have you been flying off slopes at dizzying speeds?"

Coy grinned, giddy at the thought of Sawyer wasting an hour watching videos of her doing something she loved other than mechanic work. She closed the gap between them, wrapping her arms around Sawyer's waist. She pressed a lingering kiss between her shoulder blades, nuzzling her nose against Sawyer's soft, freshly showered skin. "You smell so good."

Sawyer turned in Coy's arms, her hands coming up to palm Coy's cheeks as she held her in place for a kiss. "It's dangerous."

"I take every precaution," Coy replied, relaxing into Sawyer's touch. A soft moan escaped when Sawyer bit her lip. "Sweetheart, I promise." She slid her hands to Sawyer's hips and lifted her easily, walking the two steps to the closet's threshold as Sawyer wrapped her legs around Coy's waist. "First Aid kit and rations on me always."

"You do know First Aid," Sawyer agreed, meeting Coy halfway for another desperate, passion-filled kiss. Her nails scraped Coy's fresh undercut as her fingers tangled in Coy's locks. When the kiss ended, Coy slowly slid her lust-filled gaze past Sawyer's swollen lips to see the worry and love darkening the depths of her storm-gray eyes. But there was also a burning attraction staring back at her.

"Watching you straddle that bike for the last hour ..." A breathy sigh left Sawyer's lips. "I want you to fuck me. Right here, with your strap on."

Coy's eyes widened a little, and she was at once glad she came packing tonight. As she pulled Sawyer in for another kiss, she had only one thought.

Well, shit. At least Abi gave the okay to be late.

"I may be allowing you to drive me around whenever we go out," Sawyer said much later as they strode inside O'Rourke's Pub. Patrons were gathered around the large flat screen on their right, cheering and drinking to the hockey game that was live-streaming. Sawyer narrowed her gaze on the group before clasping her hand around Coy's arm. She gave it a light squeeze, leaned in, and added in a louder voice, "For now. But someday soon, we'll take the Rover. I will drive."

"Ooo-kay."

The smell of burgers and steaks cooking on the grill wafted out from the kitchen, or maybe it was from a nearby table, but it had Coy's mouth watering. She tilted her head to examine Sawyer closer, struggling to understand what she was saying between the lines. There was a stubborn look about her, as if Coy driving was an issue she'd been thinking about for days. Did it upset her that much?

"Erm ... sorry," Coy said to the three people behind them, still waiting to get in. Gently, she guided Sawyer to one of the few empty tables, pulled out the heavy wooden chair, and gestured for her to sit. She squatted in front of Sawyer, which probably looked odd, but Coy didn't care. Something in her was screaming *this is the way,* and who was she to ignore it?

"McCoy, what are you doing? People are staring," Sawyer said through clenched teeth, her exquisite gaze scanning the crowded pub. Coy did the same, meeting raised eyebrows of several onlookers before glancing down at how she was positioned in front of Sawyer.

That's not what I'm going for.

It looked like she was consoling Sawyer, but that wasn't Coy's intention at all. She wanted to *submit*. She considered herself a switch in the bedroom, yes, but when it came to matters of the heart, Sawyer owned hers.

Coy dropped down to her knees on the dirty pub floor, not caring who witnessed. They wouldn't understand what was happening, how much significance the moment held. Only Frankie, if she was lurking somewhere nearby, would grasp the situation for what it was.

"Sweetheart, I'm nothing like *him*." Coy emphasized the last word, hoping to all hell Sawyer learned to completely trust in her. She stared up at the love of her life, feeling the second her heart began to race. She reveled in the feeling, hoping the crazy, heart-pounding joy she experienced for Sawyer never left in the years to come.

Studying Sawyer's non verbals, Coy noticed the thudding pulse in the same spot she'd spent so much time kissing earlier. Right below her jawline. The erratic pulse was the only proof of how affected Sawyer was. Well, that and the tightness of her lips as she pursed them.

"It doesn't matter to me who drives, Sawyer. If you want the control and the freedom, by all means, take it. I am *yours*. Whatever you want or need, okay? I will never try to control you. If you'd rather drive, I'll be the best passenger prince ever."

That evoked a tense smile from Sawyer. She reached out to skim her hand over the top of Coy's hair, then down the side of her face to cup her cheek. "Well," she said, finally, her smile widening ever so slightly, "sometimes I like when you drive. And when you hold the door open for me."

Coy smiled back. "Yeah?"

"Yes. Now get up." Sawyer glanced over Coy's shoulder and grimaced. "I believe your friends have spotted us."

Ugh, this'll be good. Coy climbed to her feet and inwardly cringed as Abi and Taunya rushed over.

"Just a minute." Sawyer stood as well. Coy felt her hand slip into hers, and then she was twisting Coy around to face her once more. Their eyes met, a flare of mischief in Sawyer's, and then she dipped down to capture Coy in a kiss.

"That's a power move if I ever saw one," Taunya rang out behind them—and none too quietly either. Coy felt Sawyer smile into their kiss before she deepened the contact and brushed her tongue along Coy's lips.

"It's hot," Abi said just as Sawyer pulled away, leaving Coy's lips swollen and her brain filled with a prelude of what would hopefully transpire later that night.

"Hello, Abi, it's nice to see you again. Congratulations on your engagement," Sawyer greeted them coolly, and Coy witnessed Abi's excitement as Sawyer held a hand out for her to take. "And you must be ... Taunya?"

"That's me. It's great to finally meet you, Sawyer. You must have some kind of superpower to hold this playgirl down." Taunya winked at Coy.

"Okay, har har," Coy mocked with a roll of her eyes. She had a feeling that wouldn't be the last teasing she'd hear tonight.

"C'mon. We're at our usual corner booth," Abi told them, her gaze flickering curiously to Coy before she and Taunya started back to their seats.

"'Playgirl?'" Sawyer echoed, narrowing her eyes in blatant distaste.

It felt like a rock plummeted into the pit of Coy's stomach at those words. Her cheeks grew hot, but not from embarrassment per se. From *shame*. She cleared her throat, admitting, "It's been a running joke slash nickname for years."

"I don't like that your friends call you that. Do they realize how that makes you sound?"

Coy faltered, not wanting to have this conversation here. The problem was, she *did* know. Now. Years ago, when she'd first been dubbed the city's playgirl, she thought it was something to be proud of. No one could lock her down. She was living for a good time, not a long time, and for the most part, she hadn't taken life too seriously. Somewhere along the way, though, that way of thinking slowly changed. Watching Abi fall for Tess, or Taunya with Derek, or maybe even how Sloane consistently tried and failed to meet someone who just ... *got* her.

When she'd met Sawyer, Coy hadn't truly realized how ready she was for a relationship. Ready to slow down. To discover something worth sacrificing everything else for. To understand she'd been lying to herself for far too long.

"Come, darling." Sawyer's hand slipped into hers, and together, they made their way across the pub to her friends. After introductions were made and drinks were ordered, Sawyer clinked her glass. Conversation around the table fell silent, and Coy eyed her girlfriend curiously. Sawyer wasn't a shy person, not like Tess, for example, but Coy had never seen her go out of her way to garner attention. Her palms ached to touch Sawyer. She didn't overthink it, just reached out and placed her hand on Sawyer's thigh in quiet comfort.

"First, I'd like to give thanks for including me in your celebration." Sawyer's smile seemed forced, if the tension around her eyes and the rigidness of her spine was any indication. "I look forward to getting to know you all, as I plan to stick around." She turned to stare directly at Sloane, who was seated as far away from McCoy as possible. "You lost the bet, my dear. Now get over it. And for everyone else at this table, there is no playgirl here. If you can't call McCoy by her name, then come up with a less demeaning nickname."

If it weren't for the noise outside of the group bubble, Coy was certain they'd be able to hear a pin drop. The utter silence, and the multitude of facial expressions, from shock to annoyance, staring back at her and Sawyer was overwhelming. Coy had to close her own gaping mouth.

What the fuck just happened?

That was the last thing she expected Sawyer to say, and her brain was still grappling to catch up. Hell, should they leave? What if Sawyer wasn't welcome now that she'd stuck up for Coy?

Then, a slow clap started. Coy's gaze flew up to see Taunya doing the honors. And *grinning*. The others joined in, causing Coy to sag in relief.

"Finally. I genuinely hated that nickname," Tess, of all people, admitted.

"Ditto." Krystal clinked her mug against Tess's.

"Damn, you've got a good woman, Coy," Taunya said, raising her beer up high. "Raise your drinks, ladies and queers. Let's do another toast—this time to the end of an era."

Whoops and hollers went up around the table. Coy shook her head and laughed, leaning in to plant a kiss on Sawyer's satisfied smirk. "Fuck, I love you."

"What about 'lovergirl'? Is that nickname off the table?" Abi called out, earning a chuckle from Sawyer this time.

"I think I'll come to love your friends," she said, loud enough that only Coy could hear. Sawyer brushed her thumb across Coy's bottom lip, a thousand emotions swirling beneath the grayness of her eyes. Coy rode that turbulent rollercoaster, soaking up everything Sawyer couldn't put into words. It was all consuming. Her heart started to race in the intoxicating stare-down, and Coy felt the breath whoosh through her lungs when Sawyer finally smiled. "Not how I love you, though, darling."

Epilogue

McCoy

Eight Months Later

"When you two mentioned baking together, you said nothing about me and Sloane being some kind of judge," Coy said, perched on one of the island stools beside her twin as Sawyer secured a blindfold over her eyes. Memories of the first time she'd done so brought a grin to Coy's lips, and she puckered them for a kiss.

Sawyer obliged, her mouth caressing Coy's before she uttered a quick, "Behave, darling, or you'll leave me no choice but to punish you later."

Coy's grin only widened. Hell, if the punishment was anything like what she'd endured the night before, she was so down. She quickly reached for Sawyer, circling her arms around her waist. "You're getting exceptional with those knots, ma'am."

"I'm gonna barf," Sloane grumbled, though she didn't move off the stool to sprint to the bathroom. Instead, she swatted Coy hard on the thigh.

"Oow." Coy jabbed her elbow in her sister's direction but met nothing but air. "You can't tell, but know that I'm glaring so hard at you right now."

"Hold still while I tie this," Bree instructed Sloane. Her melodic laughter rang through the kitchen. "You think you'll barf? At least your bedroom isn't a few doors down from theirs. No offense, *Maman*, but I think you and I have different ideas of what punishment means."

"Bree Sophia." There was a high, almost nasally pitch to Sawyer's voice that hadn't been there a moment ago. "Why didn't you say anything? McCoy's been living here for, like ... five months now!"

A contented sigh left Coy. And what a fantastic five months those had been. Waking up wrapped around Sawyer each morning was not something she'd ever take for granted. Their relationship grew stronger each day, and what Coy loved the most was how they helped one another grow. Sawyer wasn't clingy and still valued her alone time but also encouraged Coy to do the same. It made those moments they were together all the sweeter.

Not wanting to embarrass Sawyer further, Coy drummed her palms on the countertop. "Okay, ladies, back to the task at hand. My sniffer and stomach can't take it anymore."

The results of Sawyer and Bree's bake-off that morning had left a drool worthy aroma throughout most of the downstairs. Sloane had shown up prior to and set up her camera equipment. Her beef with Sawyer was a thing of the past—most of the time, anyway. Coy suspected it didn't help that her twin had a lowkey crush on Bree.

Coy shuddered just thinking about it.

"I figured since we're on camera anyway, why not make a true game of it and give your viewers something entertaining to watch?" Bree's voice sounded from across the kitchen somewhere. By the oven, perhaps. Coy had a terrible sense of direction once the blindfold went on.

"And you agreed, *mon amour*?" Coy asked, her arms still wrapped around Sawyer. She tilted her face back as if she could see her through the blindfold.

"Reluctantly." Sawyer let out a sigh that sounded suspiciously light considering her dry tone. Coy felt her bend at the hips, and seconds later, her lips were being kissed again. "I'm not the only one practicing a new skill, I see," Sawyer practically purred against her ear, and Coy just hoped Sloane hadn't overheard.

Her stomach did the little dip it always did when Sawyer got all flirty, and Coy inwardly groaned. Why now, when she wasn't able to toss Sawyer over her shoulder firewoman style and rush her up the stairs? Coy cleared her throat. "So, I take it you haven't told her about ... you know?"

"Not yet. I thought we'd all have dinner tonight and chat." The top of Coy's blindfold came down, and Sawyer's lovely face came into view. "I promise, darling."

Coy smiled, knowing Sawyer didn't make promises lightly. She yanked the blindfold back up and shooed Sawyer away. "Go. Win your bake-off. I'm starving."

"I can't even see you guys and still wanna barf," Sloane grumbled. "Who'd have thought my sister would become this giant ball of cheesy goo when she fell in love?"

"Make fun all you want, but one day, you'll understand."

"I've been in love before," Sloane sniffed, and Coy was so very glad her sister couldn't see the way she rolled her eyes at the comment. When Sloane truly fell in love, she'd be knocked back on her ass.

"Move, or the sauce will burn."

"Go around me!"

Sawyer and Bree were talking either at or to each other, Coy wasn't certain which, and pots and pans were clanging. A beeper or timer went off every ten seconds. The only thing they were missing from their bake-off was the rest of Sawyer's staff.

A hand touched Coy's arm, and then Sloane whispered, "So what's the big talk tonight about?"

There was no reason to keep it from Sloane since she'd know soon enough anyway. "Sawyer wants to put the house up for sale and buy one together. You know, something untouched by Olivier. She's worried—omhmp," Coy garbled as something semi-hot and chocolatey-sweet was stuffed whole into her mouth.

"*Calisse*. Do you know that even your whispers are loud?" Sawyer hissed. "We can hear you two."

"Shii ..." Coy paused to awkwardly chew and swallow whatever Sawyer had silenced her with and tore off the blindfold. She saw the tic pulse in Sawyer's jaw and darted her gaze to where Bree stood with a tray of butter tarts. "Damn, I'm sorry."

"Hey, don't be sorry." Bree's face lit up. She set the tray down and rushed over to throw her arms around Coy. "Ohmigod, you beautiful human. *Je t'aime*," she laughed, kissing Coy's cheek. When she pulled away, tears were in Bree's eyes. She reached for both Coy and Sawyer's hands, bringing them together. "Buying a house means you're it, Coy. *Maman* chose *you*, and I'm here for it. Don't worry about me for a second."

"Well, we kinda hoped you might wanna move in with us." Coy grinned awkwardly.

Sawyer cleared her throat, still looking a tad annoyed at Coy's slip but not like she was about to throttle her. *Oh, well, there's always later*. "It wouldn't be until after we're back from Europe, but we'd like it if things remained as they are now. Although, with a minor adjustment in the sleeping arrangements."

Bree actually giggled. "No way. I'm twenty-one, you guys. I am well and capable of finding a roommate and living in an apartment. I even have a bit of money saved. Maybe you can help me car shop, though?" She directed the question to Coy.

"Erm ..." Coy chewed her lip, spotted the fresh scowl Sawyer wore, and swung her gaze to the left where Sloane sat, blindfold still in place, with her hand up in the air. "We're not in class, Sloane."

Her sister flashed a smile. "Apologies. But just wanted to add my two cents in. I happen to be looking for a roommate."

"No." This time it was Coy's turn to scowl. The thought of Sloane and Bree, together ... She shuddered.

“Easy there, tiger.” Sloane removed the blindfold as well, and this time, held both hands up as she eyed Coy. “Remember who you’re talking to and who you used to be. A year ago, who would you trust around Bree more? Me or you?”

“Excuse me, this is getting out of hand. Bree is straight for one thing.” Sawyer arched an eyebrow at her daughter. “Right?”

“Um ...” Bree giggled again, then began backing away. “Are we gonna kick this contest off or what?”

“This conversation is far from over.” Sawyer grabbed the blindfold and refastened it over Coy’s head, this time without all the fuss. Then she left to retie Sloane’s. Coy heard her muttering in French to her twin, likely nothing nice since Sloane was as poor at comprehending the language as Coy. When she left them alone again, she heard Sloane chuckle.

“I’m just saying.”

Coy groaned.

“Who was the one having threesomes and all-nighters in our apartment? It wasn’t me, Coy.”

Sawyer

From the balcony overlooking the picturesque *Praia dos Ingleses* shoreline, Sawyer closed her eyes and inhaled the fresh salty taste of the sea air. Seagulls squawked overhead, no doubt in search of their breakfast. In the distance, waves crashed gently against the rocks. Early mornings in Porto, Portugal were an absolute blessing. The heat of the sun on her face was enough to temporarily distract her from her numerous body aches and pains. But oh, how she’d received every one of them had been worth it.

Her eyes opened, and Sawyer picked up the coffee she'd made from the hotel carafe. She took a sip and sighed in contentment. These days, she felt freer than she'd ever been, like the weight of the past had finally lifted off her shoulders. She didn't know if it was the vacation making her feel that way or the tattooed, soft-butch lesbian she was traveling with.

"I thought I smelled coffee."

Strong arms wrapped loosely around Sawyer's shoulders, and she peered up at her girlfriend's sleepy smile. "Mornin', beautiful."

"*Bonjour, mon amour*. Did you sleep well?" Sawyer murmured, raising her face to accept McCoy's kiss. She breathed her in, melting into the embrace and the sure way McCoy led their lip-lock. Sharing life with a switch had to be one of Sawyer's greatest joys. She appreciated that she didn't need to be "on" all the time and could bring out a softer side.

"Like a baby. I think the crashing waves lulled me to sleep. How about you?"

Sawyer watched as McCoy headed for the breakfast cart that had been delivered maybe thirty minutes before. She had pulled on a pair of loose-fitting boxers and a sleeveless hoodie, but Sawyer fondly recalled how captivating a naked McCoy had been on her knees for her the night before.

"I slept well, actually, thank you."

McCoy looked up from where she was stirring a pack of sugar into her coffee. "Yeah? No nightmares?"

Sawyer shook her head, one corner of her mouth lifting up, and held her hand out. "Come sit with me, darling."

"Have you been awake long?" McCoy wondered. She set the creamer in the bucket of ice again before returning to Sawyer's side, mug of coffee now in her hands.

"Only since five. You know I can't sleep in." Sawyer's smile grew when McCoy took a seat on the chaise lounge, nestling between Sawyer's open legs. She was a bit bulky for the position, but Sawyer loved having her close. Over the last several months, physical touch had become both their love language.

"Mm-hmm, I do know that." McCoy leaned in to kiss Sawyer again. She rested her forehead against hers. "It's benefited me in so many ways since we moved in together. There's nothing like waking up mid-fuck, with your fingers in my pus—"

"Must you always be so crass, darling?" Sawyer stifled a laugh. "Not to mention the lie. We both know waking up to breakfast cooking is right up there with things you love."

"Ugh, woman, you wound me." Looking contrite, McCoy pretended she was holding a knife and "stabbed" it into her heart, falling backwards on the chair and spilling some of her coffee in the process.

"McCoy," Sawyer protested when coffee slopped a little too close to her bare thigh. "You're as melodramatic as your sister some days, I swear."

"Cuter, though, I hope." Coy rested her chin on the back of her hand and batted her eyelashes in a very feminine pose.

"Cute, yes, but also ridiculous." Sawyer shook her head, smiling as she lifted her mug to her lips again.

They sat and drank in silence for several minutes before Sawyer said, "Let's have breakfast and then take a walk on the beach before the tour this afternoon. How does that sound?"

"Perfect, sweetheart. Anything you want, I'm game." McCoy got to her feet and held her hand out for Sawyer to take. She pulled Sawyer up gently, grinning into another kiss. Her lips found Sawyer's ear at the same time her hand slid over her backside. "Nice outfit, by the way. I wish I could pull that off."

Sawyer shivered, McCoy's heated whisper shooting ripples of desire through her. She glanced down at the satiny silk emerald green lingerie dress McCoy had bought for her forty-fourth birthday. The cheesy come-on was a familiar one, and for a moment, Sawyer reminisced over the first night she'd laid eyes on her love. Carefully, she placed her coffee mug on the trolley. Then she slid her hands over McCoy's back to her stomach, slipping them under her shirt to graze her hot skin.

"Why pull it off at all when you could take me like this, *ma chérie*?"

"Fuck," McCoy groaned, setting her coffee down as well. A surprised yelp escaped Sawyer when she scooped her up in her arms, followed by laughter, as McCoy marched them toward the bedroom. "How about I just eat you for breakfast?"

"Did you know Porto was the original capital of Portugal?" McCoy asked as they walked hand-in-hand along the beach. At 10 a.m., there were already fifty or more people lounging on the sand or in the water. Even after a week into their month-long vacation, it still felt strange at times that Sawyer wasn't rushing to work. That she was willingly lazing about with McCoy, sipping cocktails and having sex like there was no tomorrow. "That's how Portugal got its name. Lisbon became the capital at the end of the Portuguese Reconquista."

"Is that right?" Sawyer bit back her smile, as she knew very well McCoy had been actively studying random information during the planning stages of their trip. McCoy's desire to learn and prepare ahead had her friends and sister at their wit's end at times, but for Sawyer, it was such an endearing quality. One of McCoy's best quirks that she'd fallen in love with in the past year.

The tour guide this afternoon will no doubt get a run for their money.

"Ugh, sorry, I sound like a broken record. I'm just so excited, you know?" McCoy glanced up at her, her meadow green eyes brimming with joy and affection. "This gift you've given me is a trip of a lifetime. Seriously, Sawyer, have I told you lately how incredible you are?"

"Not bad as far as anniversary gifts go," Sawyer agreed, giving McCoy's hand a squeeze. Since they hadn't been able to agree on when they'd started dating, they'd chosen their first date as a marker. No matter how much time passed, McCoy still somehow made each date night feel as special as the first. "Happy anniversary, darling."

"Happy anniversary," McCoy husked, pressing a kiss next to Sawyer's ear. She whispered, "I wish I could fuck you right here on the beach."

Sawyer's answering laugh was low, husky, and as she buried her face in McCoy's hair, thoughts of her soft butch on all fours the night before teased the forefront of Sawyer's mind. "Ever the romantic, aren't you? Besides, let's not be shy, darling. We both know who has been fucking who lately."

And never in my life would I have thought I'd be thanking Frankie for that heart-to-heart.

She heard McCoy's breath hitch as if she was remembering the previous night as well. It turned out that once Sawyer worked up to wearing a strap-on, it was something they both enjoyed immensely.

They spent the rest of the morning walking the beach and sunbathing before heading back to the hotel for a shower. There, Sawyer checked in on Bree and Cindy at the restaurant while McCoy repacked their backpacks for the upcoming tour. She noticed that, once again, McCoy put all the heavier items and ice packs in her own bag and left Sawyer to carry the change of clothes and map. One of the reasons McCoy had been so adaptable at changing her dream trip from backpacking to traveling Europe on the last of Olivier's dime was because she hadn't wanted Sawyer to strain her heart more than it was.

"You're a good person, darling," Sawyer said softly, studying McCoy's bashful response to her compliment. Most days, it was hard to believe McCoy was hers. That she could come from the life she did and find someone like her in the world. McCoy was so good, so gentle and loving, funny and silly. Sawyer didn't regret a single moment since she'd asked McCoy to move in with her. Five months of waking and falling asleep together, sharing breakfast time and Sunday evening movies, and bubble baths and wine. Bree often joined them during movie nights or when

Sawyer was also invited for Sunday games at Greg and Miranda's house. It was all so wonderful. Hell, Sawyer and Bree had even come to know the twins' nana, who was absolutely precious. It made Sawyer glad that, if nothing else, the decision to rebuild the McLaren helped McCoy's nana financially.

"What are you thinking about?"

Sawyer smiled, leaning over to tuck her cell phone into the front pocket of her backpack. "Us, your family, and what a blessing this past year has been."

McCoy lifted her bag off the mattress and carried it to the door. "They're your family now too, sweetheart. Did you notice before we left, Bree called my dad Pops? Hell, I don't even think she knows my nana's name. So when are you going to embrace it?"

Sawyer considered McCoy's words. She didn't know the answer to that. Maybe when her house sold, after she and McCoy bought something that was just theirs, their life together would feel more tangible. Right now, Sawyer felt like if she pinched herself, it could all be ripped away and she'd be once again alone, with Bree living her best life in California. Now she had her baby back and the greatest love she could have ever hoped for.

"Maybe when you put a ring on my finger," Sawyer heard herself say. Her eyes grew large the same time McCoy's did, and she coughed, hastily adding, "I mean, that might work. Who can tell for certain."

"I didn't know you wanted to remarry. Every time I brought it up before, you changed the subject." Happiness and a jovial, bubbly expression that was so endearing to McCoy's personality sprung forth as she stared in disbelief.

Sawyer took a steadying breath, wishing she could kick herself. Admittedly, remarrying was a topic she hadn't often allowed too much thought on. It hadn't gone so well for her the first time, so why repeat more vows if they would be deserted not long after? But the more she thought about a marriage with McCoy, the more in love with the idea she became.

"I've changed my mind," Sawyer replied, laughing when McCoy did a backwards, happy dance away from her.

"Wait 'til Bree and the Fab Five hear about this. They're gonna flip!" McCoy crowed, and Sawyer cringed as she toppled over the leather ottoman still sticking out in the middle of the room. Straddling McCoy on it that morning had seemed like a good idea at the time.

"*Tabarnak*, McCoy, *qu'est-ce qui te prend?* You'd think I announced that we won the lottery."

Grinning from ear to ear, those kissable dimples on full display, McCoy danced her way back over and swept Sawyer up in a tight embrace, effectively lifting her off the bed. "Sweetheart, I won the lottery the night I met you. *Je t'aime,* Sawyer. Forever and ever and ever."

"Still with the cheesy pickup lines, I see." Sawyer rolled her eyes, but another laugh bubbled up from her chest. She kissed McCoy deeply, longing for another fifty years of those same pickup lines.

"Je t'aime aussi, ma chérie."

Thank you for reading *For The Record!* If you loved Coy and Sawyer's story, please consider leaving a rating and/or review. Even just a line or two can really help an indie author get their work out into the world!

Sign up for my newsletter to keep up to date on new releases and other updates. I send them out once a month, and, when not sharing news of my own books, often share what books I'm reading or my current DIY project.

Acknowledgements

I have so many people to thank for the creation of *For The Record*. I'm not sure I could have finished it without you, or at least it wouldn't have turned out nearly as good. *For The Record* is a character driven romance, and I couldn't have built anything without Coy and Sawyer. As far as fictional couples go, they are one of the best I've had the pleasure of getting to know.

I want to thank my beta team first and foremost.

Amber, Sarah, Debbie – you three have been with me since the beginning when I was only throwing ideas to the wind. Thank you for believing in the story and me as a writer and for patiently steering me back on track when too many ideas and directions ran amok!

Lindsay and Greylin, thank you for your medical expertise. The authenticity of the story is crucial, and you've given me peace of mind. And Lindsay, thank you so very much for falling in love with the story and the romance and giving me the encouragement I needed when I got stuck.

Lisa and Dianna, thank you for taking a special interest in Coy and Sawyer. If anyone loves them as much as I do it's you two and Amber!

Michelle, Shannon, Myra and Charlie, thank you so much for the added feedback. I appreciate your time and support!

A special shout out to Sabrina! If you're reading this, you'll never know just how much I appreciated your endless feedback. The Québécois language is an integral part of Sawyer and Bree, and you helped give them a voice. Thank you endlessly.

To my editors Charlie and Lisa – thank you for all the hours you put in to help polish *For The Record* and make it shine.

To my family. Thank you for always supporting my dreams. And Colten, yes, the mechanic book is finally out LOL. I love you guys.

Finally, to you, the reader. Thank you for picking up this book and taking a chance on an ice queen/playgirl trope. There were doubts by some that it couldn't be done well. I can only hope I achieved what I set out to do. More than anything, thank you for supporting my writing and the wonderful characters in the 'Love In Vancouver' universe.

Much love and peace,
Jen-Lea

Québécois Terms/Definition Glossary

Tabarnak - Fuck
Calisse - Stronger emphasis of 'Fuck'
Esti - Hell
Esti de cave - Fucking idiot
Vas te faire foutre - Fuck off

Chapter 5

"Je m'ennuie de toi."

"I miss you."

Chapter 11

"Comment ça va, mon amour?"

"How are you, my love?"

Chapter 20

"Bree, qu'est-ce que tu fais?"

"Bree, what are you doing?"

"Je t'aide, qu'est-ce que tu penses?"

"I'm helping you, what do you think?"

Chapter 29

"Tu ne comprends pas, Bree! S'il te plaît écoute-moi. Entré dans la maison!"

"You don't understand, Bree! Please listen to me. Go into the house."

Chapter 33

"Mon bel amour."

"My beautiful love."

Chapter 34

"Peu importe ce qui se passe, tu as besoin de lui en parler. Je vais vous donner du temps seule."

"Whatever is going on, you need to talk to her about it. I'll give you guys alone time."

Chapter 35

"Je suis désolée, Maman. Tellement désolée."

"I'm sorry, mom. So sorry."

"Tu n'es pas fatigué, Maman?"

"Aren't you tired, mom?"

"Tellement, mon amour."

"So much, my love."

Chapter 36

"Mon Dieu, chérie. Si forte et si alléchante. Tu me captives."

"My God, darling. So strong and tantalizing. You captivate me."

Chapter 37

"Oh, oui?"

"Oh, yes?"

"Touche-moi, chérie."

"Touch me, darling."

"Donne-leur un French kiss."

"Give them a French kiss."

Chapter 41

"Ugh, oui! J'ai besoin de toi."

"Ugh, yes! I need you."

Chapter 42

"Tu es la femme de mes rêves."

"You are the woman of my dreams."

"Retourne au travail!"

"Get back to work!"

"Sais-tu à quel point je t'aime, ma chérie?"

"Do you know how much I love you, my darling?"

"Je t'aime, aussi, Maman. Tellement."

"I love you too, Mom. So much."

Epilogue

"Tabarnak, McCoy, qu'est-ce qui te prend?"

"Fuck, McCoy, what is wrong with you?"

Nana's Porridge

Nana Miller's Porridge Recipe

Ingredients (Makes 2 servings)

1 1/3 cup water

2/3 cup quick oats

3 large eggs

1 cup frozen blueberries

1 cup frozen strawberries

1/4 cup unsweetened shredded coconut

1/4 cup milk chocolate chips

1 tsp of brown sugar

1/4 cup raisons

dollop of butter

pinch of salt

1. Combine oats and water in medium sized pot. Shake in a dash or two of salt, and turn burner to 'high'. Stir occasionally.

2. While oats are cooking, heat blueberries and strawberries in two separate bowls, usually 1-2 mins.

3. Once the oats reach a boiling, turn the burner down to about 2 or 3. Add eggs and stir well.

4. Add 2 Tablespoons of plain protein powder. Gently mix

into porridge, along with a dollop of butter. Turn burner off.

5. Pour porridge into bowls and add your favorite toppings.
6. Eat immediately, because cold porridge is gross.

About The Author

Hiya, nice to meet you!

One thing you should know about me is I'm a huge, socially awkward book nerd who needs to ship characters or I get bored. I'm a lover of all types of sapphic romance and have a weakness for dominating ice queens and slightly unhinged fictional women. Buuut I also have a sweet, romantic side and can swoon over small-town gals, so long as in whatever I'm reading the spice is medium to red-hot!

Interests that don't include reading, writing, or daydreaming about future WIPs include: plenty of coffee, mood-music listening on Spotify, binge-watching episodes of *Yellowstone,* and watching the latest Gal Gadot or Cate Blanchett film.

I live in Eastern Canada with my wife and kids but hold an unfathomable adoration for Vancouver.

Also By

Have you read book 1 in the 'Love In Vancouver' universe yet? Check out *For The 1000th Time* below:

BLURB:

Years ago, Abi left Vancouver heartbroken. Now she's back — older, wiser, and sexier. Tess won't know what hit her.

Abi Young is well acquainted with unrequited love and the void it leaves behind. While she had hoped moving to a different city would extinguish any residual feelings for her best friend's older sister, it turns out absence really does make the heart grow fonder.

As the maid of honor, all Tess Moore wants is to give her sister the wedding of her dreams. Even if it means stepping out of her comfort zone and organizing a pre-wedding bridal party adventure. To make matters worse, the woman whose heart she shattered years ago will be participating. A woman she's never been able to forget.

After what happened between them, two weeks in proximity to Tess should be hell for Abi. Instead, she deems it one last chance to show Tess the woman she's become.

Will Tess be able to relax her role as the responsible sister long enough to notice? Or will Abi forever be seen as the kid with a silly crush?

Get it here: https://books2read.com/forthe1000thtime

Coming Soon

For The Price (Frankie's story)
Featuring:
Soft Butch/Femme
BDSM
Age Gap
Found Family
One-sided Enemies to Lovers
Workplace Romance

Interested in Kris and Courtney's story? Check out my gritty F/M, F/F, contemporary romance series under Angel Jendrick!

Claim Me (Claiming Kristopher #1)
Forgive Me (Claiming Kristopher #2)
Love Me (Claiming Kristopher #3)
Cage Me (Claiming Kristopher #4)
Hate Me (Claiming Kristopher #5)

How about sapphic YA romance? You can check out my trad published YA romances here:

Secret Me
Line Drive To Love

Blurb for Secret Me:

Tage seems to have it all: she hangs out with the school's most popular clique and has a handsome boyfriend. She's also living a lie about her sexuality.

Wren, a nonbinary schoolmate, has been the victim of bullying by Tage's clique, which leaves Tage racked by guilt because she's always been drawn to Wren. When Tage picks up Wren during a snowstorm and they are forced to spend a night together, their true feelings emerge.

With Wren's support, Tage has to decide whether to come out to celebrate herself and her new relationship.

Blurb for Line Drive To Love:

Rory is a talented and dedicated softball player. The only distraction in her life is her father's decline due to ALS, but he remains her biggest supporter. But softball plans get a lot more interesting when main-lander Shanti comes to stay with her grandparents for the summer – and the two fall into a fast romance.

Between her pitching aspirations, her father's health, and trying to date Shanti, Rory's focus may be spread too thin. With pressure building on all fronts, will she choose the game or the girl? With support from Shanti and her softball team, Rory learns that sometimes you have to make tough decisions about what you care about most.